A LIFE RECLAIMED

SECRETS OF THE QUEENS · BOOK 3

OLIVIA RAE

A LIFE RECLAIMED
© Copyright 2022 by Denise Cychosz
All rights reserved.

Please Note

This is a work of fiction. Names, characters, places and incidents are either the product of the author's imagination or are used fictitiously, and any resemblance to any actual persons living or dead, business establishments, events or locales is entirely coincidental.

Published by HopeKnight Press

For information, please contact:
www.oliviaraebooks.com
www.facebook.com/oliviaraeauthor
www.twitter.com/oliviaraebooks
www.instagram.com/oliviaraebooks

ISBN: 978-1-7320457-9-8

BOOKS BY OLIVIA RAE

The Sword and the Cross Chronicles

SALVATION

REVELATION

REDEMPTION

RESURRECTION

ADORATION

DEVOTION

Secrets of the Queens

A LIFE RENEWED

A LIFE REDEEMED

A LIFE RECLAIMED

Golden Ridge Series

JOSHUA'S PRAYER

Contact Olivia at

Oliviarae.books@gmail.com

Want notice of upcoming books? Join my mailing list:

Oliviaraebooks.com

Facebook.com/oliviaraeauthor

For my dear friend, Cindy Tavidian

You have weathered many storms this year.
God loves you and so do I.

And to the glory of God.

PROLOGUE

September 1571
Warring Tower
Borderlands, Scotland

Anguishing cries tore down the cold, dark hallway, rending Thomas's heart in two. Ma Audrey's wails meant one thing—his father was dead. His illness had been so sudden. One day he was riding the marches and bellowing out orders to his moss-troopers, and the next he had fallen ill. No one knew what caused his affliction. He awoke on a sunny morning and fell flat on his drooping face.

From there, *Da's* health deteriorated with every passing day. Even with all her wise apothecary skills, Gran could not alleviate his pain or determine what had caused the illness. Her face etched with fresh suffering; she wiped her nose with the back of her hand. "There is nothing more I can do. 'Twill not be long before he meets his maker."

Gran's chilling words clutched and clawed at Thomas's heart as he made his way to the tower's small chapel nestled near the spiral staircase. He removed a weathered stone from the simple altar and dragged out a worn wooden box. Carefully, he raised the lid and looked at the few precious possessions he had collected when he was a young lad—a bit of cloth, an old knife, an old coin, and a stick tower. He lifted up the tower and held it to the dim chapel light. His mind sailed back to when he had made the object. It had been the year after his mother had died, when Ma Audrey had come from London to live with them. Of course, back then, he called her Mistress Audrey. They were good friends, and she had helped him build the sturdy tower. He smiled and gently placed the treasure back in the box.

"Being English herself," Gran had said back then, "Mistress Audrey was an angel sent from heaven for she softened Thomas's father's heart and restored his faith." Indeed, things did change after she arrived. She had become a mother to Thomas and his wee brother, Marcas. Mistress Audrey was the only mother his brother had ever known.

Thomas reached beneath his shirt and clasped the ring he wore around his neck. From far beyond, he could hear his real mother's voice, soft and delicate. She would hum and sing him to sleep and tell him stories of great knights and mighty sultans. His fingers brushed over the raised blue stone. He'd never forget his *ma*, Edlyn Armstrong. Never.

The memory of his birth mother did not ease the growing sorrow that roiled his stomach and captured his throat. His father was dead. He shook the box. A few pebbles rolled, exposing a red ribbon he had found in a stable stall long ago. Nothing inside the box revealed the meaning of his father's mysterious words.

"My son. I am sorry. I should have been honest. You have the right to know. Look in the box." The words plagued Thomas. There was naught here that would give a clue to their meaning.

The chapel door scraped opened, and Ma Audrey entered.

"Oh, I did not know you were here." She dabbed at her red-rimmed eyes with a soft cloth. "Your father . . ." She hiccupped a sob.

"Aye, I know." Thomas knew he should go and see the body, but he could not bring himself to view the gaunt skeleton his father had become. Thomas focused on his possessions, fearing his own misery would spill causing Ma Audrey more distress.

She knelt beside him and put her arm around his shoulders. "He loved you very much." Her tear-clogged voice threatened to open the water gates in his own eyes.

"I know," Thomas said softly, shaking the box. "He left me something, but I *cannae* seem to find it? Something he wanted me to know about."

Ma Audrey drew in a sharp breath and clutched Thomas's shoulder until it ached. "You won't find the answer here."

He swiveled his head and met her gaze. "What do you mean? *Da* said to look in the box."

"Your father was going to tell you when you were a little older. He meant to protect you. There is another secret box." She fell back and placed a hand against her forehead. "Please, we shall talk about this once he is buried."

Secret box. Thomas should have honored her wishes. This was a house of mourning, and he should conduct himself in a worthy manner being the new laird of Warring Tower, but a betraying, impatient serpent twisted through his gut and wanted answers.

With his grief blinding him, Thomas stood and clenched his fingers into tight fists. "I am eight and ten. I am old enough. Where can this mysterious box be found?"

"Nay, Thomas. This is not the time." Ma Audrey held out her hand for his assistance.

Instead of helping her up, he backed away, reading the fear in her eyes. "Where?" The question came out like an icy stick jabbing through his pain.

Her body sagged, and her eyes pooled with fresh tears. "I love you and do not want you to be hurt. Not at a time like this."

The evasive words did not calm him, more to the contrary. His spine pricked with foreboding. A tightness grew in his chest, and nothing but the truth would cure what ailed him. "I want to know now. Where is the box?"

Ma Audrey shook her head as tears leaked down her cheeks. "Can you not wait?"

Her gaze pleaded, but he stood stone stiff. A ragged cry tore from her throat, and Thomas almost relented.

She shook her head in defeat. "Your grandmother has it."

For a moment, her words took him aback. Why would *Da* trust Gran with such an important item and not his wife? Thomas tucked the question away and walked briskly to the door.

"Thomas. It will only add to your agony," Ma Audrey cried. "Please wait."

He did not break his stride as he took the spiral stairs two at a time. Without a knock, he stepped into his grandmother's chamber. She stood, staring into the hearth's dancing flames. Her long, white hair swept over her sagging shoulders and framed her teared-etched cheeks.

With a frail hand, she poked at the fire with a gnarled stick. "My son is dead. I loved him dearly."

Briefly, Thomas's fury ebbed, and he wanted to take her delicate body in his strong arms to comfort her. "Gran," his voice cracked. "So did I."

Her blue eyes, circled by dark purple skin, met his. "But you are not here to speak words of adoration for your father, are you? I heard what he said to you."

Thomas brushed a hand through his russet hair, trying to tamp down his impulsive desire. "I need to know what my *da* meant. I need to know now, and I *cannae* wait until . . . where is the box?"

"Of course you cannot. You are so much alike, and yet that is not possible, is it?"

Thomas did not understand her cryptic words, nor was he in the mood to figure them out. "Please, Gran. I'll not rest until I know."

"You'll not rest once you do." She shook her head, and with a heavy sigh, she shuffled over to a large, ornate chest.

Quickly, Thomas rushed to her side and assisted her in opening the lid.

She bent forward, tossing gowns, veils, and shifts onto the floor until she extracted a gold-gilded case. Thomas remembered the decorative box. His father had bought it on an English and Scottish Truce Day. At the time, Thomas believed it was a gift for Ma Audrey; obviously, he was wrong.

"What does it hold, Gran?" he asked quietly like an awestruck child.

"A few years back, after a raid on the English went terribly wrong and many moss-troopers lost their lives, your father feared his own life could be taken before telling you the truth."

"Why *didnae* he tell me then?" Thomas reached out for the case, but Gran was quicker and pulled the box to her chest.

"You were not ready, and methinks you still aren't. But you are laird now, and the truth cannot be kept from you forever." She closed her eyes as an old torment tore across her face. "A secret kept too long can choke the life out of those it was meant to protect. Know this, I will always protect and love you."

Why could no one in this family ever speak plainly? Just because Warring Tower looked like it harbored ghosts did not mean that all within had to speak in shadowy language. Thomas firmly stuck out his hand. "Gran, that is for me."

"Aye, so it is." She gently placed the case in his hand and wrapped her fingers around his. "Everyone here loves you. No matter what you learn, we are kin. Always."

Thomas jerked his hand away and eagerly flipped open the lid. Inside, he found a folded piece of parchment stamped with his father's waxed seal. With a snap, the seal broke. His fingers trembled as he hurried to open the letter. His heart hitched and raced as he took in his father's scribbled handwriting.

"Perhaps you would like to sit down before you read," his gran suggested, offering a chair.

"Nay," he said gruffly, turning his attention back to the letter. The words swam before his eyes as they began to take focus.

My dearest son, if you are reading this missive, then it means I am no longer alive. I meant to have this conversation with you when you were a man.

Thomas paused, and his body heated with a mite of anger. At what age did his father deem that to be? He was a man now. Shaking off the troubling thought, he continued to read.

I do not know how to put this delicately, so I will give you the truth and hope that you will understand my reasoning for not telling you when you were young. You were already born when I met your mother. At the time, I was heavily in debt. I had lost the ownership to Warring Tower. Your departed grandfather offered me a great sum of money to buy Warring Tower back if I married his daughter.

Gavin Armstrong was not his true father? Thomas worked his mind trying to remember how things were before his mother died. His parents fought often. They hardly spent any time together. Yet never had he thought Gavin of Warring wasn't his father. Dread seeped through Thomas as he forced himself to read on.

It was not until after her death that I learned she was not your mother either.

Thomas's breath stalled. His heart sank to his belly. Nay, that cannot be true. He went back and read the line over and over again. He could feel Gran's tight gaze on him, but he dared not look up, not until he read the entire letter.

It seems your grandfather was heavily in debt also. You were brought as a bairn to his household by a clergyman from the English Tudor court. All your grandfather's debts and mine were paid by Queen Mary Tudor. Your true mother died at the block in the place of Lady Jane Grey, who was queen of England for nine days. Your mother sacrificed herself to give you a better life.

Know this, what started out as an act of greed has turned into love and devotion. I look back on the day I married Edlyn as one of the best days in my life because that is when I became your da. With all my heart, I love and consider you my true kin and heir. All I ask is that you take care of your brother in return.

My love is with you forever.

Da

Tears built up behind Thomas's eyes even as rage built up in his soul. Everyone had lied to him. His real mother died for some English queen. No one here was his real kin. He had always believed the glens, rivers, hills, and the very air of

Scotland lived in his bones. He had been wrong. Not a drop of his blood had ties to this land.

He crushed the letter in his hand and fixed his gaze on Gran. Nay, not his gran, just some old woman who could not be truthful.

"Thomas, this changes nothing. I love you. We all love you. You will always be my grandson." He shifted away when she reached out to touch him.

"You are all liars!" His hand shook as he tossed the note into the hearth. The letter twisted and curled as hot embers licked and burned away his father's words. Nay, a foreigner's words.

Thomas stormed out of the room and strode to his chamber, kicking open the door. He'd go to London and seek out the truth. Perhaps find his real father. With clumsy fingers, he jammed a few articles of clothing into a sack and fixed his jack of plate over his shirt. The wind outside whistled as rain began to pummel the tower. Thomas grabbed his sword and dirk and secured them to his belt before heading for the staircase.

At the base of the stairs, he found the fortress of Ma Audrey and Gran, standing shoulder to shoulder. He paused, gritted his teeth, and pushed through them as if they were stalks of wheat blowing in the wind.

"You are not thinking right," Ma Audrey cried, running after him, grabbing the back of his jack. "Has not this family suffered enough this day? Your father is dead."

Thomas stopped. Like a slow rotating wheel, he turned and stared at the deceivers. "He is not my *da*. Both of you knew, and not one of you thought fit to tell me." He fought to keep his fury high as his throat constricted. "Not one of you."

He whirled away and blinked, trying to hold back his tears. He would not cry. He would not feel pity for those who held the truth from him. With quick steps, he raced out into the wet, sloppy courtyard. The wind caught his fiery hair, swirling it around his head like a red storm cloud. Behind him, he heard the sound of feet slapping in the mud. Their cries of remorse chased after him. Did they truly think they could stop him?

A jagged bolt of lightning split the sky, followed by a loud rumble of thunder. "Return to the tower," he ordered. "Ye will all catch your death out here." He glanced over his shoulder expecting to find Ma Audrey and Gran standing there. Instead, he found his brother, Marcas, dripping, soaking wet. His narrow shoulders shaking.

"Where ye goin', Thomas?"

Though the lad had seen twelve summers, he was reed-thin. If the wind kept coming, he could very well be tossed about like a pile of withered leaves. Easily, Thomas scooped Marcas up into his arms and carried him to the stable. Once inside, Thomas gently set the lad on his feet, brushing his wet blond locks out of his soft blue eyes.

"Ye should not be out in this." Thomas grabbed a cloth from one of the stalls and handed it to Marcas. "Here. Wipe your face. When the rain stops, return to the tower, Gran and Ma Audrey will be looking for your comfort."

Marcas accepted the cloth but held his gaze on Thomas. "But where are you goin', brother?"

Thomas let out a heavy sigh and washed a hand over his face. "I *cannae* stay here anymore."

"Why? *Da* is dead, and you are laird. You are the head of the family now." Such bold words from a lad who but a few months ago played with wooden swords and stole Cook's chickens wishing to save their miserable necks.

"Listen to me. I am not laird, you are. 'Tis your birthright."

Thomas looked away and readied his mount. "Gran and Ma Audrey can explain. Look after them. It is your right."

"I *dinnae* understand. You are the eldest. You are Warring Tower's laird." Marcas reached out and grabbed the horse's reins. "*Da* was teachin' and trainin' you to be laird. You *cannae* be runnin' away."

The worry in Marcas's eyes made Thomas pause. Being responsible for your family, moss-troopers, and tenants would frighten even the strongest of men let alone a spindly lad. Thomas placed a hand on Marcas's shoulder and gave it a squeeze. "I have no claim on this land, but you do. You will be a fine laird. If you be needing help, ask Rory Maxwell, he dotes on you like a *grandda*."

"But you are my brother. I *dinnae* want you to go."

Tears flooded down Marcas's cheeks and ripped opened Thomas's heart. He pulled Marcas into a tight embrace and then removed the necklace from his neck and handed Marcas Edlyn Armstrong's ring. "Here, this is yours. Forget not your real *Ma* and remember me. We will always be brothers." Thomas drank in the field and stream scent that was his younger sibling, tucking it into his memory.

Releasing his brother, Thomas took his horse out to the courtyard, knowing one glance back would bring him to his knees.

Once he mounted the beast, another flash of lightning filled the dark sky. The animal reared up and threatened to unseat Thomas. Swiftly, he gained control and headed for the gate. Before crossing the threshold, his betraying eyes glanced back. Heavy drops of rain pelted Marcas's face, covering his tears. He raised up a weak hand in farewell before dropping it to his side, running toward the gate.

"Brother, brother," Marcas shouted. *"Dinnae* leave me."

Thomas's gut wrenched, but he could not offer up one comforting word, not without breaking down himself. He yanked his mount around and took off down the rutted path as if all that was unholy waited for him out in the storm.

CHAPTER I

May 1581
London, England

"You have one week, Armstrong. If I do not have payment in seven days, I'll cut off the fingers on your right hand and feed them to my dog." Oliver Ludwell's foul breath wafted on the mild spring air and invaded Thomas's nostrils. A drop of white spittle rested on the corner of Oliver's crooked mouth while he held a sharp knife against Thomas's throat.

"A month. A ship from the Malabar Coast and the East Indies *willnae* be here for at least another month." Ludwell slammed Thomas's back against the wattle and daub wall for the third time. He looked down the dark, deserted alley. There would be no rescue from this farce. Thomas winced and braced himself for more havoc.

"You're a liar. Your ship came in last week, and you were seen at the cockfights that very night. Pissin' away what was mine." Oliver planted a fist into Thomas's stomach, sending him crumpling into the mud. "You hear me, a week." After a swift kick to Thomas's groin, Ludwell sauntered up the narrow street with two other burly oafs.

Their laughter seeped into Thomas's fogging brain as he

gasped and gulped for air. A fiery pit of pain radiated throughout his body. He rolled to his side and slowly rose to kneel on all fours. Oliver Ludwell meant it this time and so did at least five other merchants, goldsmiths, and haberdashers. Thomas owed hearty sums. There was nothing for it, he didn't have a farthing to his name. He would have to try to talk to the queen again. A foul taste entered his mouth as her last words rang in his ears.

"No more! I am done paying your debts. A man of eight and twenty should know how to conduct himself and be mindful of his finances. I cannot tell you how many reports I have received about you throwing the dice, wagering at cards, and betting on cockfights. I love you as a dear younger brother, but you must learn to curb your gambling." She waved a royal finger in his face and bellowed, "Not a mite of gold, silver, or copper more. You are an embarrassment to me and your family."

Thomas wanted to point out he had no family, and despite his Tudor looks, he did not have a drop of royal blood in him. His relationship with the queen had been forged when he was but a lad and she had secretly come to Scotland. He remembered the day he had asked her to become his nurse; she found such great humor in the thought that she demanded he be brought to court yearly.

And thus the rumors started that he was secretly the queen's son, and if not her son, then surely someone of royal parentage. Queen Elizabeth delighted in the swirling gossip, and when Thomas came to London to live permanently, the stories became even more fanciful, such as he was the bastard son of Henry VIII.

But truth be told, he was nothing more than a commoner whom the queen had helped. He traded in spices, silks, and textiles. Unfortunately, gambling was his curse, and his profits disappeared as fast as the goods came into port. Yet the game of chance could be his cure too. All he needed was one or two grand purses to make all of his debts go away.

With a heavy sigh, he rose to his feet and headed down the lane to The Barking Dog pub. His belly throbbed from its beating. A cool drink might settle the ache and clear his tender brow. There must be someone left in London he had not borrowed from who would loan him the coin to pay off Ludwell.

The odor of ale and ripe, unwashed sailors greeted Thomas when he pushed open the door to the tavern. With the harbor full of ships, there was not a single open table. Thomas called for a brew and maneuvered closer to the hearth, examining the patrons along the way. Most were poorly dressed and probably had empty pockets, but by a warm table near the hearth sat a man dressed in a fine black doublet with gold piping around his crisp white cuffs and collar. His breeches were of a fine silk, and on his finger, he wore a large pearl ring that had to have come from the East Indies. The man's clean, clipped beard and soft shiny hair did not match his black, ruthless eyes. This was Charles Sharpon. A man many tried to avoid.

Where Ludwell might take a digit or two for lack of repayment, Sharpon would gouge out your eyes or cut out your tongue, then throw you into debtors' prison for the rest of your life. Nonetheless, Thomas did not see a way out of his predicament. The queen had made it clear she would not help him, and without a loan from someone . . . Thomas looked down and flexed his fingers. The digits looked nice where they were. Taking a large swig from his tankard, he weaved his way over to Sharpon's table.

"Good evening, sir," Thomas offered before giving a small

bow. "I am wondering if you would share your table with me?"
Dark brows snaked upward as Sharpon's gaze traveled over
Thomas. With a slight tip of the head, he said, "I do not do
business with beggars."

The man meant to make Thomas squirm. He folded his
hands penitently before him. "Sir, I am no beggar. I am Thomas
Armstr—"

"I know who you are," Sharpon snapped.

Of course he did. No one sat across from this man unless he
was desperate.

"Your connection to the queen will not help you here.
Unless . . ." Sharpon's dark eyes narrowed into tight black
beads, and his thin skin stretched over his bony cheekbones.
With his foot, he pushed out a chair. "Sit, Armstrong."

Thomas sat and took another drink. Bargaining with the
devil's spawn always came with a high price. Scanning the room,
Thomas searched for someone to save him. But alas, there was
no one.

"How can I help you?" The corners of Sharpon's mouth
curled upward, showing his yellow teeth.

"I need a small loan, which I will pay back within a year's
time." Thomas's rapid heartbeat eased. His prospects would
definitely improve by then.

"I shall set the terms of our agreement. First, I need to know
how much and by when." Sharpon leaned over the table like an
eager lad reaching for a plate full of sweets.

Thomas pulled back; his throat dried. He reached for his
tankard once more and downed the rest of his ale. "Well—"

"Thomas," a distant voice called from the doorway. There
he saw a familiar face.

Sir Francis Walsingham, the queen's spymaster, came

15

striding toward the table. What a man of his character was doing in this tavern and seeking out Thomas was a mystery. For the few times they had met before, the spymaster had always dismissed Thomas as being insignificant and a silly amusement for Queen Elizabeth.

"I have been looking all over for you." He slapped Thomas on the back and pulled him to his feet. "I have something I need to discuss with you, and it cannot wait." Walsingham bowed to Sharpon who looked like he had just lost his mother to the plague. "I am so sorry, but I must steal your companion."

A flood of relief filled Thomas when Walsingham grabbed him under the arm and led him to the doorway. His presence meant the queen had relented and would show him mercy by paying some of his debts. At least, that is what he prayed was the reason for the interruption.

"What are you doing with the likes of him? The queen would have my hide if I let you get tangled up with Sharpon. He'd chop you into little pieces and feed you to his dog."

"Actually, that is what Master Ludwell threatened to do if I *didnae* pay my debt."

Walsingham pushed Thomas into a waiting carriage. "Aye, I saw, but he is all bluster, whereas Sharpon is all action."

"You saw the beating, and you *didnae* come to my aid?" A pulse of ache lingered in Thomas's bones.

"Outnumbered by ruffians." Walsingham shook his head. "I am no fool, boy."

Aye, the spymaster was no simpleton. *Unlike him.*

Thomas assessed his traveling companion as the carriage rumbled through the dark streets. The man blended into the blackness like a rat hides in a hole. To get on the wrong side of Walsingham could be fatal. Just ask any Catholics who had the pleasure to cross paths with the spymaster. "You've been watching me?"

"Do not be absurd." Walsingham sniffed. "I have better things to do than to watch some fool toss away his life on imprudent wagers." By his own admission, the spymaster let his lie slip.

"Well then, perhaps you will enlighten me. Why am I in your presence now?" Thomas stretched out his long legs and let his shoulders ease into the fine velvet seat.

Walsingham pinned Thomas with a hard gaze. "My dear man, the queen wants to know what goes on with all of her favorites. You have been watched since you stepped foot on English soil ten years ago. She does not want serious harm to befall you."

Thomas pondered the man's words. "If that were true, then why did you let Ludwell put a knife to my throat? Come to think of it, why *didnae* your men stop all the beatings I have had over the years?"

The skin around the older man's eyes crinkled. "It was our hope those beatings would knock some sense into your thick head, but alas, we were wrong."

"We?" Thomas leaned forward, ready to punch the smug smile from Walsingham's face.

"Aye. The queen and I. But if you do not believe me, you can ask her yourself. She wants to see you immediately." The chief agent sat back into the shadows of the carriage, hiding his reason.

Why would Queen Elizabeth wish to see him now if not to pay off all of his debts? The thought fizzled in his mind. Nay, something else had propelled her to call for him at such an hour. Foreboding sunk deep into Thomas's soul. He was certain whatever she wanted would not bring him good fortune. And may even send him back into a dark alley.

Benedict Carlton, one of Walsingham's henchmen, slunk out of the queen's chamber as Thomas stepped in. The man was one foot above a snake and ten feet below a man of character. Carlton would stop at nothing to win Walsingham's approval, be it killing anyone outright or using torture to obtain secrets. No doubt, the minion told Her Majesty who Thomas had been sitting with at The Barking Dog. When he entered, the queen lounged casually in a rich green gown and silver slippers, sipping a glass of wine. He had hoped to find her in a good mood; unfortunately, she eyed him as a fishmonger's wife would eye a straying husband.

Thomas bowed low, praying his humble entrance would soften her heart.

"I hear you are up to your old tricks." She rotated her wrist, swirling the rich wine in the goblet. "I should let the wolves take you. Only a pup deals with Sharpon."

The tension that gripped Thomas's shoulders eased. Had she called him here to discuss his finances? Then she had relented and wished to help him again.

"Take a seat, Thomas. I have no wish to crane my neck."

He dutifully took the gilded chair across from his queen and gave her a smile that had stopped many a maid's heart. "You look beautiful this eve."

"Do not coddle me with sweet words." The queen may be a maid, but she was a woman of middling years and had been courted often. "Your flattery will not change our discussion."

She slammed the goblet on a small table at her side, sending droplets of red liquid into the air. "All young men make mistakes with their lives. Usually when they reach your age, they have learned some sense. My word, I was running a country when I was younger than you."

Perhaps he had been mistaken and she would not help him out of his financial predicament. He cleared his throat and tried another tactic. "I *didnae* get as fair a price for the spices and cloth as I thought I would—"

"Do not lie to me." She fisted her hands on the arms of her chair. "You sold your goods for more than what they were worth."

Thomas inched to the edge of his seat and licked his lips, his mind racing ahead in search of another lie. "That is not so, my queen. When you would not help me, I let the lot go for a cheaper price so I could pay some of my creditors." He dropped his gaze to his shoes in fake penance. How he hated lying to her. Would there ever come a day when his lips would drip with truth?

"Look at me, Thomas," the queen clipped.

Slowly, he raised his gaze and winced inwardly at the fury in her eyes. His act had not calmed her temper.

"Whom did you sell your goods to?"

Her query gave him pause. Never had she cared about whom he dealt with in business. That she asked now was a puzzlement. "I sold most of the silks to Reginald Forman, and Hubert Montgomery bought the spices." Truly, she did not plan on stringing those two up as thieves for, in truth, they were good men of impeccable character. Thomas swallowed hard. Perhaps he should have come up with a better lie.

The queen took a deep breath, which seemed to calm her

spirit. "Do you know who they purchased the items for?"

He shrugged. "More than likely they will sell off the goods to various spice merchants and haberdashers. 'Tis not my affair."

She drummed the arms of her chair with her fingers. "Perhaps you should pay more attention to whom you do business with for those two men work for me. I instructed them to purchase your shabby goods for more than they were worth."

Thomas's back broke out in a hot sweat. The pair had given him a hefty sum, which would have covered most of his debts, but he was certain he could double his profits if he bet on John Redding's rooster. The cock had not lost a fight . . . until that day. "My queen, I—"

"Stop with the excuses. It is clear to me you will not change until your life changes." She stood and made her way to her chamber hearth. "So I am going to help you out."

The moisture on his back spread to above his eyes and above his lips. He rose and then knelt down before her. Deftly, he grabbed her hand and showered it with kisses. "I promise this time I will become a fine merchant. I'll not step near a card table or cockfight or any other gambling establishment."

She pulled her hand from his when he eyed the unusual red birthmark that graced the inside of her forearm. Few knew it was there as she covered it with long-sleeved gowns and soft leather gloves when she was out in public. There had been whispers that all Tudors possessed the mark, but rumors usually were nothing more than gossip to tantalize the courtiers.

"I have heard this all before." The queen straightened her spine and wiped her hand on her gown. "You misunderstand me. I have told you I am through paying your debts. Pampering you has taught you nothing."

Thomas rose to his feet. His gut squeezed when he saw the

tight glint in the queen's eyes. "What do you mean?"

She stepped around him, heading to her gold-gilded desk. She picked up a piece of weathered parchment. "When you came to London ten years ago, you were in search for your true father or relatives who could tell you something about your mother."

A hard rock of resentment rolled over his memories. Without the queen's permission, he poured himself a goblet of wine. "My mother was a whore who slept with many. No one cared about her except when it came time to take the place of a traitorous queen at the block."

Queen Elizabeth frowned when he downed the glass. "All you say is true. But you wallow in self-pity and use your unfortunate parentage as an excuse to make horrific choices in your life. Since you seem unwilling to change your ways, I will change them for you." She thrust the parchment to him. "I cannot resurrect the dead, but I can do something else that would give you solace and perhaps quell those vile demons within you."

Thomas filled his cup again. His whole life had been a lie, and nothing in that missive could change his past unless he could put a blade in the chest of the cowardly woman who ran away while his mother died. He held his ground close to the wine.

She huffed. "Very well, I shall tell you myself. One of my sister Mary's spies left England over twenty-six years ago with Lady Jane Grey, the woman your mother died for."

"Old tales. They have disappeared on an ever-changing wind." He drained his goblet again. His heart couldn't handle another dead end. He almost laughed at the irony of his words. He had no choice. Once he was done here, he would seek out

Sharpon and accept any terms he was willing to offer. The loan would buy him time to figure out his prospects.

"Are you listening to me?" the queen shouted. "Put down the wine."

Like a petulant child, he gripped the chalice and reached for the flagon to fill his goblet to the brim. Why should he listen to her? Even if she was his queen, she had thrown him to the wolves.

"I know where you can find Lady Jane Grey."

The flagon slid from his fingers and fell to the floor with a loud *thunk*. Burgundy liquid oozed out of the metal decanter and seeped into the queen's eastern rug. She raised a disapproving brow. Thomas dropped to his knees and tried to mop up the mess with the sleeve of his doublet. "'Tis true?"

The queen pursed her lips as she assessed the damage. "I know you have always had a desire to meet the woman. Though I fear for nefarious reasons."

Her words gave him pause. Indeed. Lady Jane was the woman his mother had died for. He wanted to know what she was like. Did she have a family? Had she used her life in a worthy manner that served those around her? Was she a good woman? Had his mother's sacrifice been worth it? And after she had answered all of his questions, he would kill her and take her away from those who might love her. Or perhaps he would let her live and kill her loved ones instead, then she would know the pain he had suffered these last ten years.

"You said you *didnae* know where she lived." Slowly, he rose to his feet. Had the queen lied to him all these years? His gut brewed and bubbled with anger. Of course, she had deceived him like everyone else in his life. She had lied to him.

Queen Elizabeth dropped her traitorous gaze to the

22

parchment. "I found out Lady Jane's whereabouts from a Portugal merchant ship captain. It seems Lady Jane and her husband are residing somewhere along the Malabar Coast. He's a pepper merchant." She held out the documents that supported her claim.

Thomas took them and lowered himself into a chair as if the missive weighed a thousand stones. According to the queen's captain, a man matching Lady Jane Grey's husband's description has a thriving business exporting pepper throughout the European nations via Portugal merchant ships. The parchment dangled between Thomas's fingers when he looked up. "If this is true, then why are she and her husband not working with English merchants?"

Putting her hands on her hips, Elizabeth examined the red stain on her carpet with a frown. "Think on it. Would you if you almost lost your head on the block? Would it not be wiser to deal indirectly with your home country if you had escaped as a deposed queen?"

"From what I remember, the tale goes this spy was sent to track Lady Jane down and kill her, but then fell in love with her."

"Yes, yes. I suppose she was an attractive woman." Queen Elizabeth tapped her foot near the carpet stain. "Then supposedly she saved my sister's life. 'Tis why Jane Grey is still alive today." The queen shook her head. "I should have your hide for ruining this rug. 'Twas a gift from the Duke of Anjou." She wrinkled her nose and shrugged. "'Twas a ghastly piece of handiwork. Perhaps I should be thanking you."

Thomas rolled up the parchment and stood. What good was the information if he would be rotting in debtor's prison? He shoved the missive into his doublet. "If you *dinnae* mind, I have a deal to close at The Barking Dog."

The queen sucked in her cheeks. "Nay, you do not." She stepped around the stain and returned to her desk, pulling out another letter. "This is a note of passage for you on the *Lady Fair*. The ship sails tomorrow morn for the Malabar Coast and the East Indies. You shall be on it."

A laugh of relief escaped his throat. For the first time in the last ten years, the fates had finally smiled upon him. With fast feet and eager hands, he snatched the note from Queen Elizabeth. "My thanks, Your Majesty. Your kindness is too great." He paused and decided to push for a little more. His eyelids drooped, and his hand fell like a limp cloth at his side. "I *cannae* take such a voyage. I have no finances to help aid me in finding Lady Jane."

She narrowed her eyes. "Do not play me a fool. You need nothing until you arrive in the Indies. There you can contact the Crown's own man, Richard Commings. He will employ you while you search for Lady Jane."

Thomas could not hide his disappointment. He had hoped the queen would give him a few coins. How much better it would be if he could leave London without the likes of Oliver Ludwell breathing down his neck.

"Go attend to your affairs. I have told Captain Daniel you will be staying on board this eve."

Thomas would do nothing of the sort . . . he wondered how much the passage was worth?

She lifted a brow as if she knew he had other plans. "Hopefully, that will keep you out of mischief. Or you may wind up without a hand. Literally."

"Perhaps I could go on the morro—"

"Do not gainsay me. You charmed me as a boy. I do not find

your charms fanciful as a man. You will get on that ship this eve."

For once, wisely, Thomas held his words, for arguing with the queen could be very bad for one's health. Far worse than a kick in the groin.

CHAPTER 2

Thomas trudged up the gangplank to the *Lady Fair.* The weathered English merchant ship was anything but fair. Her wooden masts were soggy and shredded from years of being battered in the salty air. The hull creaked and groaned as it banged against the pier as if it wanted to escape the stench of fish guts and human waste splattered on the deck. Thomas fought the urge to cover his nose, making his way to the captain's quarters. With a swift knock, he was bid entry.

A man of middling years wearing a faded, greasy military coat stood over an aged map. The scraggily wig on his head resembled one of the mops used to swab the deck. The captain barely glanced from his study when Thomas entered. Before his arrival, Thomas used the few hours he had to learn as much as he could about the *Lady Fair* and her captain. After all, the voyage would be long, and with no coin, he was at this man's mercy.

The queries had paid off. Besides being one of the few English ships that sailed to the Malabar Coast and back with little to no trouble, Thomas had discovered part of Captain Daniel's success was due to the fact that he dabbled in a little privateering. Now this was a man after Thomas's own heart.

"Ah, you must be Armstrong." The captain's cheeks puffed up into a brittle smile.

Thomas stepped forward and held out his hand. "I am indeed, sir."

After the greeting, Captain Daniel quickly rolled up his map, then poured two glasses of wine. "So then, I understand from Walsingham that you wish to view *piper nigrum* in its original state. Rarely does a London merchant journey to such a place, nor is his passage booked by such a notable gentleman."

Obviously, Captain Daniel thought Thomas was an agent of the famous spymaster. "I can assure you, sir, my interests in traveling to the Malabar Coast are of a private matter. Nor does my sailing on your ship have anything to do with the affairs of Sir Francis Walsingham."

The captain took a sip of his wine and then placed his cup on his desk. "Aye, I know." The sides of his mouth quirked upward. "I have made a few inquiries into your business practices myself."

A dryness seized Thomas's throat. Why else would a captain with a shady background agree to take on a passenger known to the queen's agent unless that passenger was a scoundrel like himself? Thomas downed his wine. "Well then, you know I must make this venture profitable."

A tight laugh left the captain's throat. "Do not we all, sir. Do not we all." The smile fled from the captain's face, and his brow wrinkled and puckered. He picked up the rolled map and tapped it against his palm. "I have some private business that must be concluded before we proceed south. Just a short stop. I have a small package that needs delivering."

How cleverly chosen were Captain Daniel's words. No doubt the man spoke of smuggled goods.

Thomas tried to cover his curiosity with a yawn. "If you *dinnae* mind, sir, I am quite exhausted this eve and wish to retire. I will take my leave once you have directed me to my quarters."

"Quarters?" Once again, the captain's eyes sparkled with intrigue. "My good man, there must be some misunderstanding. Walsingham has secured you a working passage on my vessel. You shall sleep with my men."

Thomas gulped in the fresh air topside wondering how he was going to survive a journey down the coast of Africa, around the Cape of Good Hope, to the Malabar Coast when he couldn't even manage a short journey from London to the English Channel without puking. His bed was nothing more than a mass of ropes swinging between worm-eaten posts, and his companions were more foul-smelling and primitive than any sailors he had ever met before. If he had not known for certain, he would have suspected his deck mates were skeletons exhumed from the local cemetery. Even more perplexing, his berth swung below Harthal, a man who had a hard time keeping anything in his stomach or his bowels.

Being assigned minimal tasks such as wiping the deck and securing the ropes, Thomas spent most of his time in the salty air with a chance to discover what contraband Captain Daniel might be dropping off on his mysterious stop. The *Lady Fair* carried bolts of cloth, bails of wool, and some tin. None of which would raise anyone's interests. Perhaps it was what he planned to pick up that was so valuable. But no. Captain Daniel had clearly stated he had a package that needed to be delivered.

Since there wasn't anything of note in the cargo hold, maybe what was of value was in the captain's quarters. But there again was the problem. Thomas had not been invited to visit or dine with the captain since they set sail. In fact, the man avoided Thomas as if he were infested with the crawlers, which might be the case in a few more days. According to the men, they would be at the mysterious rendezvous by nightfall. The ship seemed to veer north toward the Bristol Channel, which made no sense. Not being a man of the sea, Thomas lacked navigational skills and very well could be wrong.

No matter where they were, if he did not secure part of the valuable cargo before the rendezvous, he would have nothing to barter with once he got to the Malabar Coast. Disregarded as one of the crew, there would be no invitation coming from the captain. Therefore, Thomas had only one recourse, he had to find the right moment to sneak into the captain's quarters. There had to be a note or a clue about this treasured cargo. Something that could give Thomas good fortune.

Captain Daniel stood topside barking out orders, his gaze intent on the sea around them.

"There be a storm comin'. I can smell the rain, and I can feel it in me bones," Harthal proclaimed. "The captain knows it too."

Thomas watched as Captain Daniel paced back and forth along the stern deck, slapping a narrow wooden stick against his leg. The sailors raised the topsails and secured the rigging. Thomas could not understand Harthal's prediction or the captain's agitation for not a cloud floated in the bright blue sky. Gentle winds filled the sails, and by Thomas's way of thinking, 'twould be easy sailing all the day long. So why did both men act as if they would have a fight on their hands?

Sailors raced about. Thomas slunk against the rail and made his way to the captain's cabin. With all the frenzy, his absence wouldn't be noticed. He pulled the latch, and to his amazement, the door sprung open. His heart hammered in his chest as he slipped into the snug quarters. Not knowing how much time he had, Thomas quickly went to the captain's chest. This too opened easily, and if he had faith, he would have thought God was being gracious. But Thomas had given up on the Almighty ten years ago, and he had no intentions of believing in the Deity now.

Thomas's hands dug through jackets, breeches, and hose, finding nothing of value. He was about to give up when his fingers grazed an iron ring fixed to the bottom of the trunk. Pulling the ring, a thin drawer popped open, revealing a dazzling gold and jeweled cross that was at least half a hand long. It hung on a heavy gold-link chain. This had to have come from some papist church or monastery. Worth a king's fortune, if you had the right buyer. Clearly, Captain Daniel did . . . this eve. But such an object would be missed, which explained the captain's urgency. As tempting as it was, Thomas knew he could not take the cross . . . not if he wished to live.

With a heavy sigh, he closed the drawer and snuck out of the cabin, his spirits as battered as the hull of the ship. All hopes were lost. Once he arrived at the Malabar Coast, he would have to work like an indentured servant if he did not find some coin or profits on his journey. He could be an old man before he found Jane Grey. An option that left his mouth bitter, and his heart tore like the *Lady Fair's* mast.

As the day waned, the captain ordered the men to drop most

of the sails. The last glow of the golden sun dipped into the western sea. The ship slowed and glided closer to a deserted shoreline. Suddenly, as if the captain realized he was far too early for his rendezvous, he ordered the ship to reverse course. They floated farther out into the bay before dropping anchor. The mention of the evening meal drew most of the men to their quarters. Even Captain Daniel made his way to his cabin. Being one of the first to have his plate filled, Thomas snuck back up to the deck to enjoy his watery stew that smelled a lot like the murky water they used to clean the ship's decks. Even though his gut grumbled, he ate the slop.

Soft purples and pinks graced the sky as he sat down near the bow of the ship and began to shovel the soggy mess into his mouth. Perhaps he could find safe haven above for the night instead of trying to sleep below Harthal's soiled rump.

Thomas had just finished his meal when Captain Daniel emerged from his cabin followed by his first mate. The pair was quickly joined by three other sailors who began to raise some of the sails. Ducking low, Thomas slunk behind a large crate. The anchor was raised, and the ship crept closer to land. His gaze was so intent on the coastline that when the cannons fired and the balls splashed close to the *Lady Fair*, Thomas leapt from his hiding spot and caught a glimpse of the larger galleon heading their way. The sound and smell of cannon fire drew all hands to the deck.

"We're under attack, men," the captain bellowed. Another cannonball landed near their hull. The galleon crept ever closer. Thomas was certain the next ball would land middeck.

Sailors rapidly began hoisting all the sails. The captain and first mate barked out more orders. A smaller merchant ship without guns, the *Lady Fair* swiftly started sailing out to sea, placing distance between them and the galleon.

As their ship pulled farther away, many on board began to speculate who would want to destroy a ship that carried wool and cloth? The moonlight illuminated their faces. Some exchanged knowing glances. Harthal spat on the wooden deck. "That galleon carried no flag or colors. The ship came out of nowhere. Like it was the devil's own." He scratched his stubbled chin and gazed up at the night sky. "'Tis a bad omen. A storm is comin', you wait and see."

The stars twinkled overhead, and the full moon shone bright. Either the smelly old seaman was a seer or he had spent too many years having his head bashed against the ship's timber sides. Thomas scanned the heavens again. Perhaps he should engage Harthal in a wager. 'Twould be easy earned coin, but just as Thomas opened his mouth, the old sailor slinked away mumbling what sounded like a prayer.

This time the old seaman was right. Not more than an hour later, winds assaulted the masts. Bleak grey clouds swept across the sky, hiding the glowing moon. The water began to stir into a frenzied froth. Shouts rang out in all directions to lower their sails as the wind began to howl and raise the waves crossways over the deck. A gaunt man screamed as a wave knocked him into the sea. Sailors worked feverishly to clear the deck. Thomas joined his deck mates in trying to save the ship from sinking. His arms and back ached, and his mouth filled with brine as he tried to lighten the cargo so the *Lady Fair* could ride the tip of the surf.

More shrieks echoed on the wind while Harthal pointed at the mass of rocks before them. "Drop the anchor," the captain shouted, desperately hoping the futile act would prevent their doom. The iron anchor was nothing but a child's toy to the riotous sea. They bounced around, creeping closer to the rocks. Thomas had worried he wouldn't make it to the Malabar Coast. Now he feared he wouldn't make it out of the channel. He probably would die here. What a waste of a perfectly useless life. But on the chance that he did survive . . .

A demon greater than the fear of death crept into Thomas's soul. A greedy demon. The shiny gold cross consumed his mind and drove him to crawl to the captain's quarters. The ship rocked and spun, but he managed to find the cabin's door and pulled it open. He tumbled across the room until he slammed into the captain's trunk. Frantically, Thomas hoisted himself up and flipped open the chest. Digging to the bottom, he pulled the iron ring. The secret drawer gave way as the ship pitched left. The cross slid from its hiding place. Thomas scrambled on the wet floor until he had the jewel in his grasp. He tossed the chain around his neck and tucked the cross under his shirt before making his way to the door. If he was going to die, better to do it trying to save a holy relic just in case the Almighty truly existed. And if by some miracle Thomas lived, then he would be twenty times richer and could probably buy his own ship.

He exited the captain's quarters as a loud crack split the air. The mast hurtled toward the deck. *Kaboom!* Splinters of wood flew in all directions. The boards beneath Thomas's feet vanished as he fell into the watery abyss.

CHAPTER 3

Spring 1581
Wales

Anne shivered as she spied the cargo that had washed up on the shoreline. Did she dare sneak out of her sea cave and see what booty she could find, or would the noon sun give her away? She rubbed her hands over the long sleeves of her dress and took stock of her supplies. A slice of bread, a few berries, one measly fish, and a jug of fresh water. Not much if she meant to stay here a few weeks longer. Soon she would have to venture out to the small town near Cardiff Castle and risk exposure to find work. Or perhaps she could catch a few more fish and forgo the trip a little longer. The dampness of the carved rock abode nibbled at her bones making it impossible to stay in the dank forever. Sooner or later, she would have to take a chance, earn some coin, and find passage to the English coast. The more distance she put between herself and her stepfather, the better.

Her stomach rumbled as Roland Getting's words raced through her memory. "Ye are going to marry that man if ye like him or not. A widow of your age should consider herself fortunate that anyone even wants ye."

Anne blanched and curled her lips inward at the memory of his pronouncement. The thought of marrying Mabon Bunner squirmed her insides until she thought for sure she'd choke on her morning crust of bread. The sheep farmer had been through four wives already, and all of them had died in a peculiar way. 'Twas the town's polite way of saying he beat them all to death. Even though the man was aged, he still had the ability to wield a strong stick. She'd not allow herself to be a victim of his abuse.

Over a month ago, she escaped her stepfather's filthy tavern in Newport and headed south with only the clothes on her back, knowing full well they would search northward. Now she only hoped they had given up the search for she sadly needed some provisions. Anne looked around her bleak surroundings one more time, then took a deep breath and slipped out of the cave. Hiding behind brush and sea plants, she crept toward the beach. She peered up the coastline and inhaled her breath. Could it be? Had God heard her prayers for deliverance? The coastline was littered with crates, barrels, and netting.

How often had she prayed that God would find her a way to leave Wales and Newport without being caught by Roland or Bunner? The bountiful cargo lying in the late afternoon sun had to be the answer to her prayers. If she could find enough to sell, she could buy her passage on a merchant ship.

Anne looked about making sure no other scoundrels or thieves lurked about the beach. Certain the sands were clear, she raced down to the shoreline as fast as she could, hoping to get a few precious items before anyone else discovered the loot. Her mind spun with the possibilities—grain to eat, perhaps a chair or a pot, anything she could sell in the next town over. Glee shot through her when she spied a large barrel rolling on its side near the edge of the sea. Without pause, she ran across the sand, not minding the wet granules that seeped into her slippers. Pulling the soggy barrel to shore, she pried off the cover with her rough fingertips. Lo and behold, a mass of salted fish spilled onto the sand. She would eat like the queen of England this eve. Thanks be to God.

Looking quickly about, and satisfied she was alone, she began stacking the fish on top of the barrel lid. Any moment, people from Cardiff could appear or, far worse, her stepfather and Bunner. Those brutes would sneak up and drag her back to Newport. So far, the waves lapped the deserted land. She saw no one. When the lid could hold no more, she carefully walked toward her hidden home.

That's when she saw him.

Like a beached whale stuck in the sand, the sailor lay on his side. She glanced at the lid with the strategically stacked fish and then appraised the man, hoping desperately he was dead. Her skin heated, and her mind began to scold for such an un-Christian thought. *But the fish*, her stomach growled. Her mind shouted, *Christian charity*.

Even though his leg moved and he gave out a moan, starvation won the battle. She glanced at her fish once more as a plan formed in her mind. Racing away from the water, she dug a hole and dropped the fish inside. Then she wasted no time covering her treasure with sand and placed a small pile of rocks and seaweed on top for good measure. Neither man nor fowl would find these fish. Her breath caught in her throat when she spied a mass of gulls circling the open barrel, gorging on a banquet of seafood. *Her food!*

"Get away," she rasped. With her arms flailing, she rushed over to the barrel and scattered the winged looters. Anne pounded the lid back into place. If the angels were pleased with her cunning, perhaps she could come back for the rest of the fish later.

Once the task was completed, she hurried toward the waterlogged sailor and rolled him onto his back. His eyes and creased cheeks were ladened with moist sand. His sodden hair hung about his face like masses of seaweed. A large puffy wound split his forehead. She wrinkled her brow as her examination intensified. Other older, yellow bruises rested on his firm cheekbones. Obviously, this man was used to beatings. Something the two of them had in common.

When her husband had died, she had been forced to return to her stepfather's house. A drunk, Roland Getting would beat her and the rest of his six children senseless. She was nothing more than his slave, cleaning out hearths and scrubbing pots. Fetching and chopping firewood, kneading dough until her arms fell off. She was coerced into doing any disgusting task he saw fit or didn't want to do himself. Once he had a fine job as a cook at Tretower Court but lost it when his drinking made him bold. His lewd comments to the lady of the keep caused him and his family's swift departure. They all wound up in Newport running Roland's grimy inn, but that past was behind her.

Hopefully, this sailor's luck had changed for the better for his chest rose and fell steadily. The waves had not ripped the clothes from his body. There left only one problem. How was she supposed to help him and save all her fish as well? She eyed the barrel where the squawking gulls diligently worked on pecking at the lid. Nay, she would not let them have one more fish.

Anne glanced from side to side. The cove remained empty. Could she possibly help him and then return for her bounty later? The man groaned, coughed, sputtered, and spewed seawater. Then he reached for his eyes, rubbing the lids raw. She stilled his fingers with her own. "Leave them be or you will make them worse."

The man tossed and turned and swore something fierce. Anne looked to the fading heavens, wondering if the Almighty had already gone to bed. The sailor tried to sit up and then fell flat on his back. Her gaze roamed across the beach again. Still, no one came. Her mouth watered when she thought about the bountiful fish just a few steps away. The seaman moaned.

"Why could you not have sent me a basket, Lord? Then at least I could fill my stomach and help this man as well." A large sigh lifted her chest and swelled her head with the strangest idea. "Pardon me a moment," she said to the man before racing to the barrel while loosening her bodice.

She shooed away the protesting birds. Once again, she swiftly pried off the lid, and using greedy hands, she packed the top of her shift with fish. When there was no more room between her breasts, she closed the barrel. Stealthily, she crept back to the man who continued to rub his eyes and screamed out the most un-Christianlike words. Even Roland at his worst never used such language.

Cradling one hand under her bodice to hold her blessed fish, she knelt down. "Are you able to sit up?"

He peeked out of one of his red-rimmed eyes. "I'm thirsty," he moaned.

Indeed he must be, especially if he gulped down a lot of seawater. "I'll get you a drink soon, but right now, I need you to sit up. Can you try?" When he made an effort, she pulled on his arms. A few fish slipped out of her bodice. *There went one meal.*

She went to pick up the fish when he fell back down with a long groan. The fish would have to wait. Anne scanned the beach again, this time hoping someone would come to aid her. She had the urge to leave the sailor where he lay when a gull swooped in and took the fish that had fallen from her bodice. Another pack of gulls landed next to the fish barrel. How long would it take them to peck through the lid? Clearly God thought she had taken enough. But then, why would he show her such bounty and waste it on rotund birds?

The man popped open an eye again. "What's all that squawking?"

She tightened her jaw and then mumbled, "Just a bunch of gulls taking off with a month of food." Anne yanked on the man's arms again. "Come on now. Sit yourself up."

This time, with a laborious grunt, he managed to right himself with her help. Two more fish slipped from her shift to the sand beneath her feet. The greedy gull dove and snatched the fish. *And there goes more, which would have broken tomorrow's fast.*

He swiped his sleeve over his eyes, removing most of the sand. "Are we near Bristol?"

"I wish we were, but nay. You are on the other side of the channel in Wales." The squawk fight around the barrel became fierce. Would the gulls come after the fish in her bodice? She would find a large stick and smash them on the sides of their feathery heads if they attempted to peck her stash. One of the nasty creatures started creeping her way. "If I help you, can you manage to stand?" she asked the man.

"I-I *dinnae* know." He sat, staring out at the sea as if he had lost his future.

'Twas the first time she noticed his strong jawline, wide

shoulders, and a glint of gold around his neck. Most sailors she knew were lean and weathered from a rugged seaman's life. None wore a stitch of jewelry. His fingertips were smooth, his hands soft. A gentleman? Not English by his speech. Just then a gull swooped in and snatched one of her wayward fish, which sat between the man's legs.

"Ahh." He raised his arms to protect his face. "What was that?" he cried.

She pursed her lips and scrutinized the wound on his head again. Perhaps the knock on the noggin had loosened something inside. "A lecherous bird. Come on then, let's get you up on your feet. Otherwise, the gulls may go for other parts of you."

That got him moving. He rose on wobbly legs as she hefted one of his arms around her shoulders. Sand and sweat tickled her nose, and she gave out a sneeze. Another fish plopped to the ground. Immediately, a gull swooped in. *There went another feast. Remember charity, Lord.*

The man's eyes widened. "Are ye full of fish?" He wrinkled his nose. "You smell of it."

She thought to pull her arm away and let him fall onto his face, but instead, she gave him a playful sideways glance. "Nay, that's just your eyes playing tricks." The gulls began to circle overhead. "Come along now," she urged. "I have a quiet place where you can rest a bit."

He nodded and placed his weight on one shaky leg after another. They stumbled along until they reached the cave. With a groan, he dropped to her makeshift pallet. Anne let out a tired huff before examining her bodice. Two scrawny fish remained nestled inside. *Alas, they would have a morsel this eve.*

The day had not been a whole loss. After giving the man a healthy drink of fresh water, he slept. Satisfied he would be all right on his own, Anne swiftly returned to the deserted cove. *If any of those winged beasts stole my hidden stash, I'll smack them clear across the channel.*

To her amazement, her buried treasure remained untouched, but the gulls had managed to peck a sizable hole in the lid of the barrel. Even in the settling darkness, some of the gulls stood guard. So then, which pile of fish should she go after first, that which she buried or the barrel? Since one remained undisturbed, Anne decided to go for the larger amount. She picked up a large piece of driftwood and swatted the thieving monsters away from the barrel. This time she had brought her apron. With nimble fingers, she pried off the lid for the third time. She scooped out the fish and dumped them into her apron. Protectively, she folded up the sides of the cloth. Not a single meal would be lost to those pesky birds.

Anne made the trip to the cove and the barrel three more times before retrieving her buried treasure. But she wasn't completely heartless, she left the gulls the scraps. How great the Lord was to once again provide for her needs. However, she did wonder how long it would be before others learned about the wreck and started combing the beach. Knowing the salted fish would fill her and the stranger's belly for a while, she started searching for other goods that might have washed up on the shoreline.

She squealed with delight when she spotted a piece of sail and netting. Why, she could use one to give warmth and the other, if repaired, could be used to catch fish indefinitely. Excitement all but burst from her soul when she spotted a wooden bowl. Oh what joy!

But her enthusiasm receded when she heard voices traveling on the wind. That must be the constable and his men. With haste, she went back to her cave but stalled at the entry. Smoke poured out from within. May the Lord help her. Had her hiding place been discovered? Rushing inside, she found the man sitting up and roasting one of her fish on a stick over an open flame.

How dare he! She dropped the sail and the net, then with lightning feet, she rushed over and kicked the fire out. "What do you think you are doing? It won't be long before the authorities start exploring the beach in search of missing cargo and crew. Do you want to bring them to our door?"

The man scanned the cave. He glanced at her pallet, her stacked firewood, and other things she had acquired since the night she left Roland's inn—the cup from a shepherd when she helped him find his missing sheep, the mug and plate she earned by helping the elderly shepherd's wife with her mending working for a few days at another tavern. And of course, her best gift of all, an iron pot she earned for helping a farmer's wife birth her babe. "It looks like you *dinnae* want to be found?"

Heat rose up her back as her tongue grew thick. What could she say? Every reason that entered her mind was a lie, and that was the one thing she could not make herself do. Best to say nothing. Let him draw his own conclusions. They couldn't be worse than the truth.

A rich, solid laugh filled the air, and his whole face lit up like a bright candle in a dark night. "I have never met a thief that could not tell a lie."

She lifted her chin and pulled back her shoulders. "This is my home, and I am no thief or a liar. How dare you suggest such a thing."

His copper eyes twinkled as he chuckled once again. He held up a submissive hand. "I have nothing against thieves. Why, I have been known to have lifted a thing or two myself when in dire circumstances."

As if by divine providence, a piece of the gold chain hidden under his soiled shirt sparkled and glittered before the dying embers of the fire. Did he own that prize, or had he stolen it? Surely he had not. Slowly, his gaze traveled up her form, and Anne wanted to punch him hard in the gut. A scoundrel for sure. Well, two could dance to the same melody.

"Forgive me for my outburst," she purred ever so sweetly. "The only thing I have to hide from the authorities is my privacy, which I value dearly." She motioned to his forehead. "But you are hurt. You should have someone with more knowledge and skill than I see to your injury."

He touched the fresh wound on his forehead and then rubbed the fading bruise on his cheek. "Fear not, I have had much worse in the past. This slight bump will not harm me." He pretended to act as if he were deep in thought, tapping a finger on his sturdy chin, but she was not fooled. "But perhaps you are right. No sense in arousing the authorities when we have all here that we need in this cave . . . uh, home."

We? I think not. She cleared her throat and placed her hands back on her hips. "I will let you stay the night, for God says we should be gracious to strangers and help the sick and injured. But if you seem just as spry tomorrow as you are now, then I will beg you to leave." Anne swept a hand around the cave. "As you can see, I am but a simple woman of few circumstances."

The villain's cheeks lifted into a devilish smile as he rose to his feet. He reached underneath his shirt and pulled out the long chain.

May the Lord take her!

A large gold cross, the size of a man's hand, studded with rubies, sapphires, and emeralds dangled from his fingers. The copper in his eyes shone like two bright topazes. "Mistress, your circumstances are about to change."

CHAPTER 4

Thomas expected the lass to fall into his arms and thank him for the golden prize he had brought to her door, but that was not the case.

"So you are indeed a thief, and the lowest kind." She set her jaw and crossed her arms over her chest.

Her words had his mind in a muddle. How dare she criticize him. Her frayed appearance and her reddish-brown hair sprinkled with salty sand spoke of trials, and perhaps a shifty past as well. He offered her a way out of that cave, and she had the spunk to lift her nose. Just who was this wench? "Pray tell, what is the lowest kind?" he asked coolly.

"You stole from God's own church." She drummed her foot on the dirt floor. Thomas's brow puckered.

"But I am certain it came from a Catholic church, so actually, I am doing God's work by taking it." Her face darkened like the cavern around them. Perhaps the lady was a Catholic and sought out this place of refuge to practice her faith. If so, he had made a grave mistake. He worked his mind trying to find a way to take back his words.

Her foot stalled, and she dropped her hands back to her hips. "Does not matter what type of religion was practiced, 'tis the

45

idea that you would steal a symbol of Christ at all. Right now, you need to drop to your knees and beg God for forgiveness."

Drop to his knees? Surely she jest. But nay, not one speck of humor rested in her hard brown eyes. He cleared his throat. "Mistress, forgive me, I do not know your name." Changing the conversation might change her attitude. Women did so love to talk about themselves.

She hesitated; her hands fell to her sides before she stepped back as if he had pulled a weapon instead of inquiring about her name. "Anne . . . Anne Howell." She paused again before she continued. "I am a widow."

He knew she was not much younger than him, perhaps even his very age. Yet he never expected her to be a widow. A woman running from an intolerable husband, possibly. But a widow? That would be rare. Unless she killed the man. Thomas gulped. "I am sorry for your loss, madam."

She averted her eyes before skimming her hands over the long sleeves of her dull brown dress. A habit he was fast learning she kept. "Save your sorrow for those who need it. He has been dead for some time and was not that great of a loss."

Did he beat her? Or was he mean and insufferable? 'Twould explain her lack of feeling and the distance she stretched between them. A slim slice of anger seeped into his soul. Thomas could not abide an abuser. What this poor woman suffered. "Did he beat you often?"

"Beat me?" She laughed. "He rarely touched me. Nay, you misunderstand. He was old and smelled something fierce, but he was never cruel. A shepherd who worked the fields by day and swiftly fell asleep after a hearty meal and a cup of ale." She lifted her chin; her earthy eyes softened. "He died in his sleep."

"Did he not leave you a home and land?"

Her hands curled into fists, and her lips thinned. "Those went to his greedy brother and his shrew of a wife."

"Ah, so that is why you are living here." He scanned the damp, mossy cave.

"Not exactly." Immediately, she bit her lip as if she had said too much.

There was more to her story, and Thomas was more than ready to pry the truth from her. "So you went to live somewhere else first?" he asked casually, pretending to examine his half-cooked meal.

She looked away and marched over to retrieve one of the *Lady Fair's* sails and netting. "It matters not where I lived."

Oh, but it did. It was the one piece of information that could give him the upper hand. "I only aim to get to know my host a mite better. Methinks you are afraid of someone and that's why you are living here."

She whirled around and glowered. Like a straight arrow, he had struck the mark. "Sir, I believe you are purposely trying to meddle in matters that do not concern you. Private matters."

The woman was as sharp as Queen Elizabeth, keeping her secrets close and her lips guarded. He gingerly touched his wound on his forehead. "Ah, and what were we talking about before?"

She waved off. "I can see asking a thief to beg for forgiveness is a futile act. I do not know what you meant with your offer, but I want nothing from you and beg you to leave as soon as you are strong enough. Master . . ."

"Armstrong. Thomas Armstrong." He gave a slight, unsteady bow. "At your service."

She cocked a brow. "Indeed. Well, Master Armstrong, your service to me would be that you leave on the morrow."

He should say nothing and let that hermit of a woman to her cave. But truly, what woman would choose this situation when she could have far better? Besides, she knew the area and would be an excellent guide. She'd know who to avoid and who would give him aid. "I have forgotten, where exactly are we?" He tapped a finger to his lips, hoping she would think him confused and give him pity. "Somewhere in Wales?"

Her defenses dropped, and she nodded. "Aye, a little north of Cardiff and south of Newport."

Feeling a little woozy, yet full of glee at this information, Thomas sat, crossed his legs, and scratched his head. If he had the coin, he'd bet she fled Newport. Most fugitives would head north for there was much more country to hide in, but she wasn't dull in the head, so she probably believed going south would thwart her pursuer. Now she was stuck with nowhere to go but across the channel. "Though I am not the best of sailors, I believe Portishead lies on the other side of the channel."

A keen glow entered her eyes. Oh, she was intrigued.

He rubbed his chin, trying to hide his grin. "If I make it there, 'tis not far to Bristol."

She inched closer. If his words were a piece of sweet meat, she'd be drooling.

Thomas lay down and cupped his hands behind his head. "Aye, that is what I shall do." He closed his eyes. "All you need to do is point me in the right direction. I'll find my way from there." He heard her shuffle closer.

"Perhaps I have been too hasty," she said eagerly.

Though he dared not open an eye, he knew her face held pure want. Cave dwelling did not hold her fancy.

"You might need some assistance in finding passage across the channel," she said softly.

Thomas yawned, trying to hide yet another smile. He had her just where he wanted her to be—needing him as much as he needed her.

The man was nothing more than the devil's own, enticing her with sweet, honeyed words. No matter how hard she tried to hide the truth, he knew she wanted to travel by sea. How he knew she did not know. Could he be a divine angel sent by God to test her? She eyed him again.

Not likely. More like a demon sent to torment her for disobeying Roland. By his tongue he was a foreigner, not English or Welsh, not unusual for a sailor. She should ignore him this eve and on the morrow bid him good day.

Not enough time had passed. If she ventured back to Newport or anywhere close, Roland and Bunner would find her. By waiting one more month, he might have found someone else to marry, and the lust for coin might leave her stepfather's eyes.

Armstrong yawned again. "I am sure for the right price I'll find a helping soul." He rolled onto his side away from her. "No need to worry about me . . ."

His breathing became heavy, and Anne wanted to shake him. "Now he sleeps," she muttered to herself, "when I want to hear more of his plans."

He snorted and sputtered. "Hey? What did you say?"

She gritted her teeth and resisted the urge to poke him in the back. Not only was he a thief and a liar, but he was a sneak and a faker as well. "I said nothing."

He rolled over onto his back, and his handsome features

feigned innocence. "'Tis too bad that you *dinnae* want to leave this cave, for I am certain a comely lass like you could find steady work easily in Bristol."

"Comely! I should kick your backside out of here right now. What are you implying? I am a good Christian woman and would never use my . . . my . . . Oh, how dare you."

He shirked back and held up a protective hand. "Madam, that is not what I meant. I would never presume. I only meant getting an honest job is always easier with a pretty face."

"Only if it is a man who is doing the hiring." She flopped down next to him. "All men are the same. In the eve, they . . ." Her cheeks began to warm. "By day, they wish to work you as a slave."

Armstrong now lay on his side facing her, propping himself up on one elbow. "I thought you said your husband was a good man?"

"I'm not talking about my husband," she snapped.

The sneak smiled at her. "Pray tell, then, who were you talking about?"

Oh, he was a crafty one, dangling what she wanted the most in front of her and then trying to gain what he wanted instead. Anne rose to her feet, picked up her sail and netting, and walked to the other side of the cave. "Try to get some rest. When it is later, much later, and I am sure no one lurks about, I'll cook you some food. As far as traveling with you, we'll talk about that in the morning."

With a happy sigh, he rolled over onto his back and closed his eyes without another word. Anne wanted to throttle him because he had guessed what her answer would be.

The next morn, she packed up a few provisions, put on her long cape, and pulled up the hood to hide her face. Not once did the thief mention their conversation last night. Nor did he say much through their late evening meal. After they broke their fast that morn, he smiled and said, "I guess we should be going."

Going, indeed. Hot with anger, she could not speak. Instead, she set to packing up what they would need to get them to Newport and hopefully to a quick ship. He helped her bundle up most of the fish. He went with her to fill the water jugs at a nearby stream and carried them back to the cave without complaint. Oh, he could act like a fine gentleman all he wanted, but she knew his true nature, and she wasn't going to let the sly, silver-tongued sneak get the best of her.

They avoided the main roads and went across low hills and fields instead. Not once did he question her about her chosen route. No doubt, being a scoundrel, he had already figured she needed to be invisible as much as possible. They stopped at farms along the way selling extra fish for coin. Each time they met a stranger, Armstrong tried to pass her off as his wife. She knew he did it as a means to protect her, but when he uttered such lies, she wanted to scream the truth. The sneaking around and alternate route took them longer than expected. They finally arrived in Newport late in the eve a few days later. Anne sent up a prayer of thanks that the journey had been uneventful. However, the true danger was still ahead of them. They had to avoid her revolting stepfather and find quick passage out of the port.

Thomas wanted to head straight for the wharf. "I am sure we can find lodging there for the night."

Aye, they could at Roland Getting's establishment, The Whistling Maiden. There were other taverns and inns nearby, but none were as cheap or bawdy as her stepfather's place. Thomas Armstrong would be drawn to the place like a wasp to its hive.

"The area is nothing but a den of iniquity, I'll not stay anywhere near there." She folded her arms tight around her body and held his gaze with a stern eye.

He let out a deep sigh and shook his head. "I have never known a widow to be so prim."

"And just how many widows do you happen to know?" she snapped.

"Well, quite a few, now that you ask, and most are quite friendly and enjoy warming a man's—"

"Stop." She held up a hand. "Pray that God does not hear another of your vile words!"

He shrugged and smiled. The man enjoyed teasing her. "Then where shall we rest this eve? Keep in mind, we are out of fish, and we need to save as much coin as possible to make the journey."

She wanted to point out that he still had those jewels in that golden cross, but perhaps he was having second thoughts about using the holy relic for evil purposes. Whatever the reason, they needed not stay at The Whistling Maiden. Anne started walking away from the docks. "I know a better place, and we can stay for free."

"For free?" He was right on her heels.

Pulling the hood of her cape around her face, she finally had the upper hand. "I have a friend who would take us in." *And not tell Roland I'm in town.* "We'll get a good meal too."

He stopped, forcing her to stall her steps. "If you had friends here, I fail to see why you decided to live in a cave. Seems quite odd."

For a scoundrel, he was quite astute, but then perhaps that is how all villains were, after all, did they not prey on the weak and defenseless? "When I lived near these parts, I helped a family or two." In truth, it was the Widow Young who had helped Anne when Roland had been in one of his wild, drunken fits. The widow's cottage was on the edge of town where she made a living by mending and sewing for local merchants. Anne knocked on the door. Upon answering, Widow Young pulled Anne into her arms. "As I live and breathe, I never expected to see you again. Where have you been?"

Anne looked around, hoping the widow's loud cries would not alert anyone else. "Hiding, and we seek lodging for the eve."

"We?" The widow stared past Anne, then lifted an eyebrow upon seeing Thomas. "Oh, I see, we have a new man in our life now." The widow's merry eyes held no censure. She stepped back and bid them entry, her gaze full of queries.

"'Tis not what you think," Anne said as she rushed inside with the handsome Thomas right behind her.

"And what am I thinkin'?" asked the widow.

"That we are a couple," Anne corrected as she lowered her hood.

Thomas gave a gallant bow and then took the widow's hand and placed a delicate kiss on her fingers. "Your servant, madam."

"Well, if it ain't what I think, then perhaps it should be. This one is far better than what your father had in mind. This one is finer than what you had before. If I be a little younger myself, why, I would be fightin' you for him."

With a suave smile that showed his bright white teeth, Thomas lifted his brows. "I told you widows loved me."

Anne blushed and turned away. It did not matter if all the women in Wales would fall at this man's feet, she would not. Never. Ever.

Needless to say, Widow Young waited on him as if he were the King of England. He complimented her cooking, her clean cottage, her bright eyes, her delicate frame. If Anne heard one more word of praise, she would be sick. By the end of the night, Thomas had Widow Young's bed close to the hearth, while Anne and the widow shared a small pallet in the loft.

"The lad needs the room," Widow Young crowed as she fought Anne for the flimsy coverlet. Oh, he needed something all right, and it wasn't being stretched out on a warm bed.

Finally after tossing and turning, Anne curled up and fell asleep. As if in a dream, she heard soft footsteps move across the cottage floor, followed by a brisk whoosh of air and a faint click. Forcing her eyes open, Anne peered at the ghostly moon rays stretching across the wooden loft floor. Widow Young snored, then mumbled, then snored again. Nothing seemed amiss, and yet something niggled in Anne's mind.

She eased herself off the pallet and made her way to the edge of the loft. "Armstrong," she whispered.

No reply came.

"Armstrong," Anne said in a louder whisper.

Nothing. Of all nights, the man sleeps like the dead. Of course he does, wrapped in a warm coverlet, lying by a toasty fire.

"Thomas," she all but shouted.

The Widow Young snorted, but not a sound was made down below. With a huff, Anne descended the ladder. What greeted her left her as hot as the flames before her eyes. That thieving, lying, devil's spawn was nowhere in sight. How dare he leave her behind. She grabbed her cloak off the peg near the door, jammed her feet into her shoes, and took off into the night. He'd better run fast for when she found him, she was going to pummel him until he begged for mercy.

She hurried straight to the docks, no doubt the rogue was trying to bargain a passage on one of the ships. Figuring out which ship might not be an easy task, especially if Roland lurked about. Her heartbeat slowed, and her courage rose as she noticed how deserted the docks were in the early morn. Surely her stepfather would be sleeping off his drink.

With more confidence, she began calling in a sweet, soft voice over the edges of every boat. "Thomas, oh Thomas, dear husband, where are you?"

Some sailors made lewd comments to her query, while others informed her no such man sought passage on their ship. She had but three more ships to search when a rough hand circled her waist while her assailant's other hand covered her mouth.

"I was sleepin' soundly outside me inn when I heard this angel's voice calling on the wind." Roland dragged her away from the docks to the dark shadows cast by the daub and wattle buildings. "I said to meself, I know that voice. Could the good Lord finally answer me prayers?"

Anne squirmed and kicked wildly to no avail. Roland was a hard block of a man. Finally, his hand eased until she could work her jaw. She bit into his grimy hand. "Let me go. I'll not marry Bunner even if you beat me to death," she shouted.

Roland backhanded her. Anne fell to the ground; warm blood oozed from her mouth. "Hush up, girl. I'm not givin' you to that dirty shepherd. They be wantin' you back at Tretower, and they are willin' to pay handsomely for you."

Tretower? Who would want her there? From what she could remember, the lord and lady of the keep couldn't get rid of her fast enough. 'Twas how she wound up in the clutches of Roland Getting.

He pulled her to her feet by her hair. "Stop your squirmin'. We got a long way to go."

Anne swung her arms and caught nothing but air. He dug his fingers deeper into her locks.

"Still as feisty as ever." Roland laughed. Like a hammer striking an anvil, Roland slammed a fist into her gut.

She gasped and doubled over; pain shot from her stomach in every direction. *Dear God, make him stop.* No one would intervene once the violent fever possessed Roland's body. Out of the corner of her eye, she saw Roland raise his hand again. She closed her lids, waiting for the heavy blow.

Thunk!

Her hair loosened, and the pull of Roland's rage vanished. A sound like a bundle of wool being unloaded onto the dock interrupted the morning calm.

Anne took a peek. There standing above Roland's body was Thomas holding a plank of wood. He tossed the board aside and held out his hand. "Widow Howell, I believe you owe me an explanation."

CHAPTER 5

Thomas had never called her Widow Howell. Widows were old and wrinkly and walked around in dowdy black clothing all day. Not always old, many were widowed young like herself, but still, the name hurt. Anne looked down at her drab brown gown with its long, prim sleeves that hid her dark defect on her inner arm. She cringed. Broken and marred, but at least her dress was not black.

Anne grabbed his elbow. "We must leave now."

Roland groaned, his legs moving against the dirt where he lay. "Anne . . .," he mumbled.

"Do you know this scoundrel?" Thomas pointed to her stepfather.

She tossed her hands in the air. "You may stay if you wish, but I am leaving."

Thankfully, Thomas did not wait for a further explanation. "Let's go, then." They stumbled down the street to another inn, which was just as rowdy and filthy as Roland's place.

The inn smelled of stale drink and urine. "I can hardly believe there could be a tavern worse than The Whistling Maiden," Anne remarked.

With a nod to the innkeeper, Thomas led her to a small

room above the common area. He slammed the door shut and motioned to a rickety chair near an equally shaky table. "Sit." Happy he saved her but still upset, she did not immediately comply.

He folded his arms over his chest and frowned. "You can stand if you like, but I was thinking you might be a little faint from your ordeal."

True, her legs were quite unsteady. She sat and then cast her gaze about the room. "So this is where you took off to. Widow Young will be quite upset that you snubbed her hospitality."

An impish grin settled on his lips, and he sat down on the bed across from her. "I *didnae* forgo her hospitality, I just had enough of it."

How dare he act so cavalier. Anne gritted her teeth, trying to hold back a whipping of words. Her throat bubbled and brewed as she formed a rebuke. Finally, her speech spewed forth. She slammed her hand on the table, shaking the frail structure. "How could you. In good faith, I brought you to Newport." She slowly rose and jabbed a finger in his face. "And you were just going to leave me at Widow Young's to fend for myself while you scurried onto one of these ships like the rat you are."

Silence. He answered her accusation with silence. Indeed a rat.

"You have nothing to say?" she snapped.

"Nay, I think you summed it up perfectly."

Many a time in her life she had been angry, but she had always remembered to keep her head. When Roland would punch and toss her around like a bag of wheat, she would hold up her hands in defense. When her aged husband snored until the rafters rattled, she took deep, calming breaths until the racket subsided. When teased as a young child at Tretower Court for being some noble's by-blow, she proudly lifted her chin. But now, standing in front of this smug, simpering slug, all she could think about was stomping her feet on his shapely, muscular body.

Anne threw up her hands. "You are a scoundrel, a rogue, a liar, a cheat, and a thief. May the Lord pluck your flesh until every sin you have ever committed leaves you bruised and bloody."

Thomas wiggled a finger in front of her. "Uh-oh, be careful. God does not look kindly on a Christian that is prone to swear."

"I did not swear." She folded her arms tight under her breasts, taming her wild rage. "I-I was just . . ."

"Yes?"

She glared at him.

He fluttered his russet lashes.

She released her arms and curled in her fingers examining her nails, debating if they were long enough to scratch his eyes out.

He gave a deep, attractive smile.

She rose and paced the room, tamping down the need to wallop him.

He casually crossed his calf over his other leg.

She swore if she would growl, he would whistle.

Finally, gaining some self-control, she sat back down. "You are a terrible person."

"Among other things." His lips twitched. "But I did save you."

So he had. As much as she wanted to kick him hard in the shin, he had come to her rescue. "You have a long way to go before your soul is redeemed." She sniffed and looked away.

"I think that is a point we both can agree on, but it is not my salvation that we need to discuss. Let us begin with the villain who aimed to harm you. Who is he?"

A lie pricked her mind, and she blushed at the thought. Without a doubt, Thomas Armstrong was a bad influence on her. She should get up right now and leave. But Roland lurked in the streets, and she desperately wanted to get to English shores without notice. This blackguard was her only hope.

Anne calmly placed her hands in her lap. "He is my stepfather."

"What does he want with you?" Armstrong leaned forward, his gaze intent. He would not leave her be until he had the full story.

"I moved back to his place once my husband died. He married again not long after that. I had become a nuisance to my new stepmother, though I do not know why. I was the one doing all the cooking and cleaning and watching of my stepbrothers and sisters." Anne paused, hoping that would be enough for Thomas to digest.

It wasn't. A tenderness entered his eyes, and his features eased like a priest listening to a confession. "Go on."

Those two little words let loose her tongue, and her anger withered. "I was supposed to marry a man by the name of Mabon Bunner who planned to give Roland, my stepfather, a good deal of coin." Anne shook her head. "I couldn't marry him. He had already beaten four wives to death."

"And you *didnae* want to be number five," Thomas said quietly. He curled one hand into a fist and ground it against his other hand. "Do not fear, I will not give you to him either even if there is coin involved. Beating a man is one thing, but beating a woman is unthinkable."

Anne laughed. "Maybe not where you grew up, but 'tis fairly common around here."

Thomas rose and made his way to the door.

She flashed to her feet. "Where are you going? I'll not have you leave me behind again."

He rubbed the back of his neck and then took off the jeweled cross, handing it to her. "Here. Being a scoundrel, a rogue, a liar, a cheat, and a thief, I wouldn't dare leave such a gem behind."

The cross was heavier than she thought, and the jewels were the finest she had ever seen at Tretower Court. Seven jewels graced the gold cross. Four rubies ran the length, four sapphires the width, and in the middle was a huge emerald. This jewel belonged to God for certain. Or perhaps to a royal or noble. Did Thomas realize the trouble this jeweled object could bring?

Perhaps he did. Was he like Roland with no moral compass to guide his way? Roland's words whispered in her mind, *They be wanting you back. They are willing to pay handsomely for you.* Why? They didn't want her long ago when her mysterious father died, so why now?

"Is something wrong?"

Anne looked up. Thomas's gaze was full of concern. "Nay. Just remembering something."

"Oh?" His eyes were keen once again.

She had no want for telling him more than she had. After all, he was a villain, and he might very well drag her to Tretower Court if he could gain a large profit. Better he thought he saved her from an unsuited marriage.

Anne shook her head. "'Tis not important." Her words seemed to satisfy him for the moment, but she knew he would return to the conversation at a later time.

"I'm going to secure us passage on a ship for Portishead. Get some rest. Tomorrow will be a long day. Take good care of my possession. We wouldn't want it to get lost."

He quit the room, leaving Anne holding the precious cross, pondering his cryptic words. Did he trust her? Or did he go to strike a bargain that would gain him more than a ship's passage? It seemed they both had secrets that neither of them were willing to share.

After a few inquiries in the tavern, Thomas stepped into the misty air and made his way to the docks. There he found the ship he was looking for, *The Prince's Prize*, owned by a Welsh privateer who claimed to be a Moor prince. The outlandish lie was what attracted Thomas to that ship in the first place, and the fact that it was the only ship that sailed first to Portishead before venturing down the coast of Africa.

Indeed, he had planned to leave Anne at Widow Young's place. It seemed a perfect arrangement that two widows should live together even if one was young and quite appealing and the other old and a little crusty around the edges. He had a clear conscience on the matter. All that changed when he heard Anne bellowing along the docks like a hussy. He didn't need a scholar's intelligence to know it was only a matter of time before sweet Anne would get herself into trouble. And he had been right. His gut twisted when he found her struggling with the lecherous lout.

That being said, he never expected the lout would be her abusive stepfather. Leaving her behind was no longer a choice, but he certainly wasn't taking her to the Malabar Coast either.

Finding a ship that served both of their purposes was a stroke of luck, though Anne would think it to be an answer to a prayer. Thomas jiggled his coin bag. They had just enough money from selling the fish to get her a passage to England and him to India. *The Prince's Prize* was notably a finer ship than the leaky, and now destroyed, *Lady Fair*. The masts looked sturdy, and the deck was smooth. A hint of ginger and mace cut through the sea air. The cleanliness of the vessel had him looking forward to the trip.

"What ye want?" A sailor dressed in soiled breeches whose breath reeked of spoiled conger blocked Thomas's entry. It seemed every ship had a smelly man like Harthal, who had slept above him on the *Lady Fair.*

"I have come to seek passage for my wife and myself. Is there room?" Thomas opened his coat slightly, exposing the top half of the coin bag.

The sailor worked his jaw and almost spat on the deck but then changed his mind and spat over the rail instead. A woman's laughter floated from within the ship. "The captain be a little busy right now, can ye come back later?"

If the captain was entertaining a lady, he might be in his cups as well. If that be the case, then Thomas might even secure a better price for passage. "I am sure he will not mind the intrusion." Very slowly, without taking his eyes off the sailor, Thomas stepped around the man and headed to the captain's cabin. If he were a betting man, which he was, this might be the opportune time to meet the captain.

A half hour later, Thomas exited the ship with great satisfaction. Captain Andros was a grand man and quite generous after gulping a few mugs of ale and stealing ample kisses from the buxom beauty sitting on his lap. Thomas had managed to secure a fair price for himself to the Malabar Coast and another for his dear wife who was going to Portishead to stay with relatives until his return. Thomas's only regret was that he didn't bring Anne with him to bargain. One look at her deep mahogany hair, high cheekbones, and her lush red lips, the captain might have cut the price of their passage even more. On the other hand, she might have lectured the captain on his sinful habits, which could have resulted in them being tossed overboard. Thomas winced. Perhaps he should have a conversation with her about keeping her righteous thoughts to herself once they boarded the ship. No sense in riling up the captain on their journey.

Early dawn crept over the sleeping village. They had only a few hours before the ship set sail. Best he collected the sleeping beauty. They didn't want to be left behind.

Thomas entered the quiet inn and took the stairs two at a time. A swift knock on the door caused it to open. "Be lively, madam, our ship sails soon." He looked to the bed. Empty. His gaze shifted to the table and chair. She did not sit there either. A lone tallow flickered in the dark room.

His heart raced as he glanced around the room again and again. He even dropped to his knees and searched under the bed. She was gone. Fear clenched his gut. Did her stepfather find her? Again, Thomas scanned the room, nothing was out of place. The bed had not been touched. Surely if the lout had found her, she would have put up a struggle.

And then, as if a club had been smashed over his thick head, the truth hit him. She left on her own accord. The sweet, not so innocent, conniving wench left with his golden jeweled cross.

CHAPTER 6

"Where is she?" Thomas smashed Roland's head against a timber wall at The Whistling Maiden. Finding the villain had been easy. One mention of his name and a dozen fingers pointed Thomas in the right direction.

"I swear to ye," Roland huffed. "I do not know." He sniffed. "Haven't seen her since ye clunked me head." He closed his eyes as Thomas launched another fist into the slimy innkeeper's face.

"If he says he doesn't know, then he doesn't know," the present Mistress Roland Getting added.

"Stop lying to me. You and your worthless daughter robbed me. Return my goods or I'll pummel you until your face is part of the floor beneath our feet."

Roland Getting slid down the wall and wailed, shaking his head from side to side. "Haven't set eyes on Anne since ye took her away. Swear on me love of me life's grave. Me late wife."

A gasp left the throat of the current Mistress Getting, signaling that Roland was in for a tongue thrashing after Thomas was done with the villain.

Blood oozing from his nose and mouth, Roland struggled to

his feet. "Wanted to get a healthy sum of coin . . . Anne's natural kin. They want her back." Roland wiped his mouth and held up his hands. "What if we both look for her? Split the profits." He ducked his head, clearly worried another blow might come his way. "'Tis the truth." He inched toward Thomas. "I swear on the soul of my dear, dead, lovely wife."

"I'll give you dear, dead, lovely wife." This time the assault on Roland came from his live, lethal, present wife. Pounding her fists on his back, he might just be meeting his dead wife very soon.

A skinny young lad crept forward and tugged at Thomas's sleeve. "For once me *tad* is speaking the truth. We haven't seen Anne in over a month."

"I thought she was running from a less than desirable bridegroom?" Thomas asked, taking a step away from the unhappy couple.

"Ow, leave off. Ye killin' me," Roland screeched, shielding his face from his wife's blows.

The lad slipped closer to Thomas. "Aye, she was. And me *tad* was right put out about it. Old man Bunner was going to give me *tad* a mite of coin for her, but all that changed when those fancy-dressed folk showed up. Me *tad* threw Bunner out on his ear and told him to find a new woman to beat."

So the story about marrying against her will had been true, if this young lad could be believed. Thomas looked deep into the boy's round green eyes. There didn't seem to be any deceit there, yet poverty had a way of hardening even the young. He could be as skillful of a liar as his father.

"Stop, dove. Stop bashin' me head." Roland ducked behind a table for protection.

Thomas pushed the lad closer to the inn door and knelt

down in front of him. "Do you swear on your beloved *Mam's* grave you speak the truth?"

The lad shrugged. "I do not remember her, sir." A scraggly, wet-rag-smelling, three-legged dog hopped to the boy's side. The lad put a gentle hand on the dog's back.

"What about on this beast's life? Are you telling me the truth?"

Wrapping his arms around the dog's neck, the lad nodded.

The present Mistress Getting launched a pot toward Roland's head.

Thomas shielded the boy's body with his own. "Pray tell, where do you think Anne could have gone?"

The lad gently patted the fleabag's head. "When she was upset, she always went to the Reformed Church up the street. Me *tad* said if we were Catholics, he would have sold her to the church."

"Of course he would," Thomas mumbled. He reached into his leather bag and pulled out one shiny coin. "This is for you. No reason to tell your *tad* about it."

Like lightning, the lad snatched the coin from Thomas's fingers. He then turned to his furry friend and whispered, "Come on, Twig, we have another treasure to hide."

Thomas rose to his feet and watched the dog dutifully limp after the young waif. Memories of his own childhood burying his treasures with Ma Audrey warmed his body and created a yearning for home he had not felt in years.

Roland's howls brought Thomas back to the present. "Leave off, woman." Roland held up his hands against the blows.

"Leave off? I'll leave ye off, ye sad sack of withering flesh. 'My dear, dead wife.' How'd ye like to join her?" She took another swing. Roland crouched over like a turtle trying to hide in his shell. The patrons of The Whistling Maiden hooted and hollered, egging Mistress Getting on with her physical entertainment.

Thomas slipped out of the tavern and headed toward the church. Though he doubted Anne would be there, he was running out of time. If he didn't find her soon, he would have to get on the ship and head for the Malabar Coast without a farthing to his name. He'd have to work and slave for years, all in the hopes of finding the woman who lived while his real mother died. Why, Queen Jane could very well die before he had the chance to talk to her and kill her himself. The thought curled his gut.

Aye. He needed that jeweled cross in order to swiftly carry out his plan.

The early morn's light mist gave way to a bright blue sky. Certainly Captain Andros would want to depart on time, and being paid in advance, he would not think twice about leaving Thomas and Anne behind. If he did not find the wench at the church, he would have no choice but to head back to *The Prince's Prize.*

At first, he thought he had walked in the wrong direction for the Reformed Church was nothing more than a rickety wood structure with worn stone steps to mark its entry. He pulled open the weathered door, and his heart started pounding in his ears when he saw Anne on her knees before a modest altar. The spindly lad had been right. Thomas should have given the boy more for his honesty.

Thomas raced forward and towered over Anne. "Where's my treasure? You thought to sneak away and leave me a pauper. Where's the honesty in this? I doubt all your prayers will gain you forgiveness."

She unfolded her hands and looked up at him with puzzlement. "I have no intentions of keeping your ill-gotten goods. I only seek to know if helping you keep them is the right thing to do." She turned her gaze back to the rough wooden cross standing on the shabby altar before folding her hands in prayer once again.

Irritation swept up his spine giving his body a small tremor. "I told you to stay in the room. Imagine how surprised I was to find you gone. Thankfully, your brother does not hold the same eye for greed as your stepfather does."

"Brother? You went to see Roland? Why?" Her eyes grew wide as she rose to her feet.

"Because you were not where I left you." Thomas fought to keep a tight rein on his anger.

She had the audacity to shake her head. "That was foolhardy. If there is coin to be had, Roland will follow. We'll never be rid of him."

"Not likely. Your stepmother was beating him to a pulp when I left. If it had not been for your brother, I never would have found you."

"Which one? I have three stepbrothers." Anne's arms flailed about like she was swatting a swarm of bees.

"The one with the large, innocent eyes and spends his time with a three-legged mongrel."

"Oh, that is Scrape."

"Scrape? Odd nickname for a lad."

"He has a Christian name, but that died with his mother." Anne shook her head. "To my shame, I never learned his real name. Only the name given by Roland seems to be remembered. The boy has the habit of scraping Roland's nerves. I should offer up a prayer for him."

69

"The lad could use divine help, but we have no more time to pray or do anything else. Besides, I paid him well." His words made Thomas wince. When had he become so cold? *When you lost your heart and your family back in Scotland.* With a grind of his teeth, he pushed the thought away. It was his family's lies that set him on this path. "Come. We must be going; the ship will leave the harbor in less than an hour." Thomas held out his hand, but when she dawdled, he dragged her by the arm to the entry of the church. "We'll discuss your thievery later."

She pulled back. "An hour? I came here right after you left. Surely not that much time has passed?"

Roland had been right about one thing, Anne would have made an excellent nun, always on her knees in prayer. Thomas opened the church door, and the gold chain around her neck sparkled in the sunlight. "Aye, I am sure. Now, madam, hand me my bounty so that we can be on our way."

Her face screwed up like a withered apple. She hesitated but relinquished the cross. "Someday you will learn there are more precious things in the world besides gold and jewels."

"Perhaps, but until then, I'll happily take the wealth for it feeds the belly and opens the world." He looped the chain around his neck, then grabbed her hand once again. "Now come. I fear we may have missed our passage already."

When they got to the docks, Thomas had been right. The ship was getting ready to drop its ropes and set sail. It might have departed without them had not the captain spotted Anne. He then ordered his men to hold on a few moments longer until she daintily stepped onto the ship.

"Ye didn't tell me your wife was a beauty." Captain Andros held out his hand like the gentleman he wasn't. "I am so glad you are joining us, Mistress Armstrong. Your quarters are ready, but if they are not to your liking, you can spend your time in mine."

If not for their dire need of passage, Thomas would have slugged the captain in the mouth. Anne laughed and gave the man a dazzling smile that nearly turned the seaman into a slushy puddle at her feet.

"I thank thee for giving us passage. Please call me Anne." The moment the captain looked away, she glowered at Thomas. What did she think? That he would say she was his sister or far worse tell the truth? Why, Captain Andros would have deposited her in his chamber and not let her out until they reached the Malabar Coast, forgetting to stop in Portishead altogether. The way Thomas saw it, she should be thanking him and not glaring at him as if he were some filthy mop.

Thomas wrapped her free arm around his and gently pulled her away from the captain's grasp. "A cozy cabin will serve us just fine."

Captain Andros's lustful gaze traveled down Anne's body. "It is a short journey across the channel, we should be there in a day or so."

A day or so! Why, with a good wind, they should be there by nightfall, next morn if the weather turned foul. Thomas swept his gaze around the ship. They needed a cabin to keep the prying eyes of the crew off both of them and for Anne's comfort. She had never sailed before, and she might become ill.

"Oh my, look at this?" She pulled away from Thomas and headed straight to the tall mast in the middle, thumping it with her fist. "I have never seen a ship like this up close. I am sure these masts hold mighty sails. What a grand ship you have here, Captain."

The man beamed and came to stand next to her. "Aye, *The*

Prince's Prize is quite fine. Would you like me to show you around a bit? My first mate can guide the ship out of port, and your husband can settle your possessions into your cabin." Captain Andros left his gaze rest on the paltry sack at Thomas's feet and smirked.

Thomas picked up the bag and had a great urge to hurl it at the captain's head. Instead, he nodded and headed for the small berth. He should be thanking Anne for keeping Captain Andros busy and on deck. A happy captain made a grateful captain, and a grateful captain could make the later voyage along the African coast to India quite pleasant for Thomas. However, his insides lurched every time he thought of the captain's grubby hands on the lass even during a harmless turn around the ship.

Shoving the bag into the small cabin, Thomas returned to the deck but could not find the captain or Anne anywhere. "Have you seen my wife?" Thomas asked a sailor who was uncoiling a rope, getting ready to hoists the sails.

"She went to the captain's cabin. Doubt you'll be seeing much of either of them until we reach Portishead."

Not if he could help it. Thomas stormed to Captain Andros's quarters, finding the door locked. He knocked. "Captain, I need to have a word with you."

When no answer came forth, he began pounding the wood with his fists. Anne's God would hold him accountable for any injury she might sustain at the captain's filthy hands.

"Captain, open up, please."

Did the man truly believe Thomas couldn't break a flimsy lock? He put his shoulder into the door and began slamming his full weight against it. Stepping back, he got ready to rush the entry again, but to his surprise, it popped open.

Standing there as if everything was right with the world was Anne. "What are you doing?"

"I was worried about you." Thomas peered inside to find the captain standing over his desk with a large map.

He motioned with his hand. "Come in, Master Armstrong. I was showing your wife what your journey to the Malabar Coast will look like."

Anne tipped her head to the side and put her hands behind her back. "I thought you would be disembarking with me for a while in Portishead." Her lips grew thin. For sure she would be lecturing him later on that sin. "But alas, I know you must travel on." She turned her attention back to the captain. "I am sure you will be in good hands. Captain Andros is a fine gentleman. In fact, we were just having a nice discussion about his manners."

'Twas then that Thomas noticed the red mark below the captain's eye. Why, the lass walloped him. Indeed, it did seem she could take care of herself. A surge of relief washed over Thomas. True, the captain might be a little grumpier now and may make Thomas's voyage south a living hell, but Anne was safe, and that was all that mattered. Only one thing niggled at him now—why he even cared.

She smiled at both men. "I'll be going back to the deck now. I am so excited. I do not want to miss a thing, this being my first sea voyage."

The captain mumbled something about closing the door behind them, which Thomas quickly obliged.

The rest of the morn, Anne enamored most of the crew with her questions and interest. At first, Thomas enjoyed her cheerfulness and her wide-eyed enthusiasm, but as the day wore on, his mood darkened. The crew was becoming friendlier by the moment. A sailor stood behind her, guiding her hand and arm as he taught her the proper way to coil up a rope. Another would help her adjust the trim. Even the first mate gave her a turn on the poop deck. The woman was oblivious to the danger. Did she think she could defend herself against a whole crew of hot-blooded males?

By midday, Thomas had had enough and literally grabbed Anne by the arm. "Come along, wife, you should rest awhile."

She started to protest but seemed to think better of it and allowed him to escort her to their berth. Once inside the tiny space, she whirled on him. "If you were tired, you could have come and rest on your own. There is no need for me to watch over you as you sleep like a little boy. After all, you do have a long journey ahead of you."

Thomas took off his outercoat and threw it onto the bed. She was upset he had not told her about going to the Malabar Coast. "I am not tired. But leaving you on deck a moment longer might well have caused a mutiny the way you throw your smiles around. Why, if these men were not fresh out of port, I shudder to think what would happen to you."

She dropped her chin to her chest and glared at him. "Do not worry about me. I can take care of myself."

"Against a gang of men? I think not. All you did was set them on the chase." He placed his back against the door. "After what you did to the captain earlier, this very moment the crew could decide to throw me overboard and have their way with you. I doubt Captain Andros would lift a finger to stop them."

Her shoulders slumped, and the fury left her eyes. "Oh dear, I wouldn't want them to harm you."

Harm him? He had intended to instill fear for her safety, not worry for him. Yet there it was in the sadness of her gaze that she was chastising herself for a crime that had not been committed. This whole demeanor did not suit her. Better to deal with her stubbornness and her snappy tongue than a woeful widow.

Thomas removed the chain from his neck and dropped it onto hers. "I think it best if you stay here and hold the cross, then if one of the sailors does deem to toss me overboard, perhaps you will have something to bargain with."

The fire returned to her gaze as she pointed that familiar sharp finger in his direction. "You're just trying to keep me here. You . . . you scoundrel."

He reached for the door handle. "You know that cross needs protection. It belongs to God after all. Better you feign rest and save God's holy relic than to dance joyfully above and risk your soul."

She came at him with both fists up, but he was faster. He slipped through the door and into the hallway. He held the door shut, hoping to stall her pursuit. She banged against the door once, then clicked the lock on her side. Clearly this was the calm before she unleashed her fury. He'd bet the queen's palace that Anne was planning some vile punishment for him. Whatever her thoughts, she was safe for the time being. He slumped down against the door, closing his eyes. Finally, he could get a little rest for it had been a long night and an even a longer day.

Shouts from above awoke him from his slumber and must have disturbed Anne as well for he fell backward into the cabin when she pulled open the door. "Are we at Portishead?" she asked.

Assuming he had slept most of the night and the next day, they very well could be. He rose to his feet and held out a hand. "Shall we go and see, wife?"

She blanched at the use of the familiar term but took his arm nonetheless. "Aye," she said through gritted teeth. "I will be so happy to leave this ship and start my *new* life."

Indeed. It was time they parted company. Anne would be much safer on shore, and he would get more rest. As the sun began to set, Captain Andros moored the ship south of Portishead, probably because they were either taking on or unloading contraband.

When they appeared on deck, the captain gave a curt bow to Anne and then reminded Thomas that they would be leaving early in the morning. A sailor helped Anne onto a small rowboat. Even though he was fearful Captain Andros would leave without him, Thomas decided to go into town with Anne to make sure she secured safe lodging.

"You know I can take care of myself. You do not have to come with me," she said as they rowed to shore.

"I *dinnae* doubt your capabilities, but it is late, and a lone woman finding lodgings in the dark may not be as easy as you think. What husband would let his wife go alone into a strange town? What would your wooed deckhands think if I *didnae* accompany you?"

She said nothing more on the matter, and Thomas took that as gratefulness. They said little on their walk to town, and he felt a mite of regret leaving the lass. Even with a saucy tongue, she had proven to be good company.

They found a quiet inn on the outskirts of the village that provided a hearty meal and a warm bed. During their meal, Anne talked about heading to Bristol to find work as a maid or a cook. "I've been known to make a tasty stew."

He marveled at how she enjoyed her simple life, even though she had no real kin to speak of—except those at Tretower Court.

What was her true past? Her real kin wanted her back. What he would give for such a chance. Perhaps her future would have been bright had he helped Roland. Thomas shook his head. If she was a by-blow of a nobleman, her life could still be one of servitude. A warmth sluiced through his weary bones as he listened to her chatter on about her hopes and dreams. Whatever her future, it would be on her own terms, and Thomas took solace in that knowledge.

After knowing she was secure in an inn room, he gave her the rest of his coin. "Here, you will need these."

Anne pushed his hand away. "Nay, I'm thinking you will be needing that more than me." She tapped her temple. "I have my wits."

"Are you saying I have none?" he asked incredulously.

"Oh nay. I think you are plenty smart, but you always seek the easy way out. I do not think you are used to doing hard work like I am."

He thought of his childhood and his father . . . correction, stepfather. He had been grooming Thomas to take over a whole entire keep. Being raised to become a laird could not compare to her rough upbringing. Hopefully, Gran and Ma Audrey were fine. Surely they helped Marcas with his duties as laird.

He took her warm, soft hand in his and dropped the coin bag into her palm before curling her fingers around it. "Nonetheless, I want you to have this as payment for helping me."

Her lush lips parted slightly, and Thomas almost bent his head to kiss them, but for once in his life, he acted like a gentleman and left, closing the door discretely behind him. He headed back down the coast and breathed a sigh of relief when he saw *The Prince's Prize* still moored in the dark cove. Once on ship, he made his way to his cabin and fell fast asleep, dreaming of the lovely, strong-willed lass he had left behind. Shouts of a ship ready to set sail rocked him out of his deep sleep. Going to the deck, Thomas could barely make out the shrinking land in the predawn sky as the ship sailed farther out into the channel.

"Worry not, man. I think your wife will be fine without your protection." The captain dabbed at his bruised cheek.

Thomas smiled. Aye, he need not worry about Anne. She was indeed a resourceful lass.

"I'd be more worried about those pepper growers where you are going. They'll rob you blind with their sweet tongues and shifty hands. Best you hold on to your purse strings." The captain slapped Thomas on the back and then walked up to the poop deck.

Thomas laughed, knowing his security hung about his neck. He placed a hand on his chest and felt . . . nothing. His heart thumped louder and louder as he patted his chest over and over. Nothing. The necklace was not there. He ran back to his quarters and searched his belongings, thinking he may have taken the cross off because he had been so tired. No jewel was hidden in his other clothing or coat.

Then he remembered. He had placed the cross about Anne's neck and had forgotten to retrieve it once they got to Portishead. Her words rushed into his brain. *"I have my wits."*

Undeniably she did. And she had batted her pretty lashes and warmed him with her sweet smiles. Not only had she taken all his coin, but she had his jewel as well. Oh, she was cunning. Praying all night, bah. It had all been a ruse. No wonder she made no fuss when he held the cabin door last eve or when he left her all alone in a strange town. She had what she wanted. He had been fooled a second time.

Thomas rushed to the deck and climbed up onto the rail.

"Hey, what are ye doing?" shouted the first mate.

She would not make a fool of him a third time. Burning with anger, Thomas dove into the icy water and started swimming to land.

CHAPTER 7

She should have said something to Thomas. At first, when
she had plunked the cross over her neck and raced out the
door, Anne had been furious. His ill-conceived tactics to keep
his stolen jewels safe were foolish and now led to him losing
them forever. If God deemed her to have the necklace again,
who was she to question His judgment. She had spent the time
in the ship's cabin in prayer asking for direction. The answer
had been clear—say nothing. So she sat calmly and waited for
Thomas to open the door and reclaim his possession. He did
not.

Not once did he ask for the cross as they rowed to land. Or
when he found security for her at a comfortable inn. She should
have contentment, but she didn't, believing this was God's will.
Perhaps she had made a mistake.

All night long she paced the tiny room and rubbed the cross
against her chest. At one point, the jewel seemed to burn her
neck, so she tossed it onto the bed to ease her suffering. By
morning, she was out of sorts and still did not feel at peace with
her decision. This might all change once she found the closest
church and returned the holy relic to God.

Gently, she lifted the cross from the bed and gulped before

she put the shiny jewel around her neck. 'Twas like a yoke—heavy, unbearable. "I will give it back to God," she reassured herself before wrapping her shawl around her shoulders.

As if the devil's hot breath chased her, Anne raced down the stairs only to be stopped by the inn's owner, Alvin Denbow. "Where you going, mistress? Your husband paid for a week's stay. No need to scurry away like a thief." His eyes lit up as if he knew about the necklace or doubted the validity of her marriage. She almost confessed to both for a sin of omission was just as awful as telling a lie.

How her mind played tricks. The jewel was well hidden and impossible to see. Maybe he was only concerned for her safety. "I shall return shortly. I wish to get a breath of fresh air. Perhaps you can tell me where the nearest church lies of the Reformed faith?"

Alvin's eyes widened, and he stepped back and bowed his head slightly as if his thoughts needed repentance when, in truth, she was the one who needed God's grace. "Up a short way not far outside of town. If you wait a bit, I'll roust my son. He can show you the way."

The older man's worry for her welfare, though touching, was not needed. She was on a quest to make things right, no harm would befall her. "I thank thee, Master Denbow, but truly, I will be fine. If I am not back within the hour, you can send your son to find me."

A mild relief seemed to smooth out the wrinkles on Alvin's face. "All right, mistress. But be alert. Even though day is breaking, there still can be a villain or two lurking the streets. I'd never forgive myself if any harm befell you."

Anne reached out and squeezed the older man's arm. "God's peace," she offered before slipping out of the inn.

The narrow, sleepy streets would soon be alive with noisy traders calling out their wares, town criers, and food merchants selling sheep's feet, scraps of stew meat, and fish. Anne clutched the cross tight against her chest. There would be thieves too. All the more reason to get rid of this treasure as soon as possible.

For a moment, she stood and listened and then looked skyward, not a church bell could be heard or a tower seen. Though small, Portishead had to have a house of prayer. Alvin Denbow said the church was but a short walk to the edge of the town. She raised the hood of her cape and turned left. After taking only a handful of steps, a soaking-wet figure jumped out in front of her. Huffing and puffing, eyes red with rage stood the dragon she hoped had returned to the sea.

"Thomas," Anne cried.

He circled her wrist with his hand. "Aye, madam. 'Tis I. It seems you have something that belongs to me."

She looked about and noticed a merchant setting up a table outside his shop. Perhaps they would come to her aid if Thomas would not back down. "I have nothing that belongs to you, sir," she said loudly.

Thomas glanced at the shop owner and then muttered words only the devil would use. "If you choose this course, not only will I wind up in a dark cell, so will you. For what would a poor widow be doing with such a precious, expensive relic?"

Anne bit her lip. His words made sense. Another man stopped to talk to the merchant; they both started walking toward Thomas and her. She took her free hand and put it on Thomas's shoulder. "Oh, husband," she all but shouted again, "I did not recognize ye, dripping wet like a drowned rat. What happened to you?" She smiled and leaned into him. "Hug me, you fool," she whispered.

The pair of men paused, but they did not walk away.

With stiff arms, Thomas engulfed her before he relaxed and almost squeezed her to death. "I should crush you until all the air leaves your lungs," he whispered in her ear. "Did you truly think you would get away with my gems?" He then pulled back and brushed the damp locks out of his eyes. "I took a morning swim to cool some of my wayward thoughts, wife." His voice carried across the lane where a maid just opened a door and hurled a pail of waste into the streets.

Anne's cheeks flamed, and the men laughed. They turned and stepped toward the merchant's shop. Thomas threw a soggy arm around her shoulders and began leading her down the road.

"Where exactly are you headed to?" he asked quietly.

"To the church to pray—"

"You *dinnae* expect me to fall for that trick twice, do you?" His calm mask fell away, and his lips sneered like a diseased dog.

Squishing sounds from his wet shoes accompanied them as they walked on. Anne's lips twitched as she fought to hold back a smile. "I speak the truth. I am going to the church to return what God has placed in my hands twice."

He stopped, stood in front of her, giving her countenance a thorough examination. "You are either unable to tell a lie or the best liar I have ever met. My head leans to the latter, but my gut says you *cannae*."

"Well then, your gut seems to be smarter than your head." The smile she tried to censure broke free.

His jaw slacked. "This is no laughing matter."

"No indeed. If your brain is soft, that can be quite sad." Try as she might, the last few words she uttered came out in a laugh.

He scowled and grabbed her arm as they continued to

walk toward the church. "You will return my cross before you step a foot inside. I'll not have you crying sanctuary. Do you understand?"

She paused. Did he not see? She was trying to save his soul. She shook her head. "The devil has a hard hold on you, Thomas Armstrong."

"Maybe so, but at least with him I know where I stand." He pulled her between two buildings. "Now, I will be taking my cross."

A deep sadness filled her heart. There was no help for him. If she yelled and screamed, the authorities would come, and she did not want to see him in prison wasting away. Yet, if she gave him the jewel, he would break it apart and use it for ill purposes, and his soul would be lost. What to do?

He stretched out his arm. "Now."

Before she could call the warning, a young boy jumped out at the mouth of the alley. "There he is, Father."

Alvin Denbow came running down the alley, screaming like a madman, swinging a leg of a chair above his head. A look of bewilderment registered on Thomas's face before Denbow hit him square on the noggin. Thomas fell into a heap.

"I'd crack him again if I could," huffed Alvin. He turned to the boy. "Ye did good, son. I am so glad I had the boy watch after you. I'd been right. A pretty woman like you shouldn't be wondering around on her own. I'll call the magistrate right away."

Anne dropped to her knees. She had to think fast. "Nay, Master Denbow. This man is my husband." Like a sack of grain, she rolled Thomas over. "Do you not remember? This is the man who brought me to your inn last eve."

Alvin pushed his cap back on his forehead. "Why, so it is. I did not see his face. I thought him a villain meaning to hurt ye. God forgive me." He turned a sharp eye on his son, who had the smart sense to run out of the alley.

She shook Thomas's shoulder, and he gave out a low moan. "There is no harm done. Help me get him to the inn."

"Aye." Burly Alvin Denbow lifted Thomas to his feet. "Mistress, he be all wet."

"He was supposed to sail south, but he could not bear to leave me." She sighed. "So strong is our love." If she weren't a Christian woman, she would so love to smack Thomas in the face for he made her tell a lie, not once but twice. May God have mercy on her soul.

He moaned and looked at her with blurry eyes. She wanted to poke them. Now she would have to continue the ruse. Oh, why had she not given Thomas the cross? *Because you wanted to see him again.* Anne clutched her throat, fearing she had said the words out loud. Could that be true? Was it her will she was following when she left with the cross? Did she have some fondness for Thomas?

Thomas's head lolled from side to side when Alvin picked him up. Her heart gave a definite lurch. She would have to pray on this matter some more before she lost her wits and her heart to such an insufferable rogue.

Back at the inn, Alvin Denbow, feeling a shame he should not, gave Thomas a new set of clothes and brought him a hot plate of lamb stew and a large brew. The humble innkeeper kept uttering his apologies over and over before he closed the door to their now newer, cleaner, and larger chamber.

"May God not strike us both dead," Anne said as she stood next to the table while Thomas shoveled food into his big mouth. Not a lick of guilt on his face.

"What are you so upset about? I'm the one who got clunked on the head." He smacked his lips and picked up the bowl, not leaving a drop behind.

Anne waved her hands in the air. "You're a vile man."

"We have already established that long ago." He wiped his mouth with his sleeve. A twinkle entered his eye. "But now you are just as low as me, telling such lies."

She looked away. "That is nothing to be proud of."

He tried to stifle a belch, but the disgusting sound echoed off the wall anyway. "Perhaps not, but I thank ye all the same. You could have let Alvin drag me away and taken off with my cross before anyone came looking for you."

Aye. But she had never planned to keep the bothersome jewel. "Do you not see? Only evil will befall us if we do not give the cross back to God."

Thomas rubbed his expanded belly. "There is no evil in having a good meal. Now then, hand over the necklace and then you can go and pray for both of us while I take a long rest."

She stared at him. He needed to spend a day or two in the stocks. With a huff, she removed the cross and dropped it onto the table. "May God open your eyes to where you should be storing up your treasures."

He yawned, snatched up the jewel, and looped it around his neck. "You sound like Gran." He moved to the bed. His eyelids fluttered, then closed. "Store up your treasures in heaven . . ." His breathing became heavy and even.

For all his professing against the Almighty, Thomas knew some scripture. Taught by his gran? Anne rubbed the sleeves of her dress. Oh, to have a grandmother who cared for you. Who loved you. Never had she known such affection. Perhaps

Thomas's grandmother no longer lived and that is why he is so bitter and angry at God. It would explain much.

Anne picked up her shawl and headed for the church. There was one thing Thomas was right about, she could pray for both of them. She'd pray for forgiveness, and she'd pray that someday God would give her a family to love. A family that would not throw her away like those at Tretower Court, and a family that would not treat her as a slave and beat her when they were angry. Oh, to have a family that would love her for who she was . . . Anne, a simple, God-fearing woman.

Hours later, her knees were sore and her back ached, but she prayed on and on. Anne prayed for forgiveness for the lies she told. She prayed for Thomas and even for Roland. She gave thanks for Alvin Denbow and God's wisdom for bringing her to the English shores. God was good and deserved all the glory. On and on she sent her prayers heavenward. Even the pastor seemed concerned by her long presence. He encouraged her to leave, but unlike the minister in Newport, he did not shout and throw her out.

"Whatever burdens you, God will forgive," he said kindly.

She almost told him about the cross. Not that a Reformed pastor would display the relic in the church. No doubt he would sell the jewels and use the income to do God's work. Try as she may, she could not speak of the jewel. It seemed that God had stilled her tongue and hand. Could Thomas need the jeweled cross more than this Reformed Church? Was that her wish or God's? Once, her heart was full of faith, but now . . .

Finally exhausted and with no straight answer, Anne rose and made her way to the door. She dropped one of the coins Thomas had given her into a box near the rear of the church. Her plan was to return the rest to Thomas and encourage him once again to give up the cross. With the other coins, he could get another passage to the Malabar Coast. She would ask Alvin Denbow for work. Certainly, he would have use for her once he learned about her experience in running an inn, and once she confessed her lies.

With a plan firmly fixed in her mind, she headed back to the inn as a cool wind whisked up her neck, sending a chill to her spine along with a twinge of dread. The eerie caution came too late as a thick arm twisted around her waist.

"Do my eyes deceive me, or are you the wench I was sent to find?"

CHAPTER 8

Thomas awoke to a cold room with Anne nowhere in sight. Not that he expected her to be sitting in a chair watching him sleep. She probably was halfway to Bristol by now. His head throbbed, and his heart kicked up a beat when he sat up. What if she took . . . He let out a heavy sigh when his fingers grazed the cross.

She had not taken it.

But that did not make her less of a thief. Still, he could not tamp down the disappointment he felt that she had left. Maybe she sat down below with the innkeeper, Alvin Denbow. The old man did seem quite fond of Anne. He knew naught of her cunning ways and devilish charms.

However, when Thomas opened the door and crept down the stairs, he did not find Anne talking to Denbow. Instead, a man dressed in a black cape with a wide-brim hat was engaged in conversation with Alvin. Like a swift-footed cat, Thomas crept back into the shadows. The visitor was not that big of a mystery for Thomas knew him well from the queen's court. Benedict Carlton was one of Queen Elizabeth's slimiest spies. The question was what was he doing there? Could the old spymaster Walsingham have learned of the demise of the *Lady*

Fair and had already sent out his minions to make inquiries to Thomas's whereabouts?

That had to be the answer. A satisfying pleasure coursed through Thomas's veins. The middling queen worried about him. If he announced he was quite well and healthy, she might be so grateful she would shower him with gifts and pay the rest of his debts. On the other hand, the queen might very well refuse to let him go to the Malabar Coast, worried that more disaster could befall him. Thomas had no desire to spend the rest of his days dancing at numerous queen's balls as one of her "special gentlemen" or worse, losing his fingers because of his gambling debts.

He glanced around looking for another avenue of escape. When he was ready to creep back into his room, Carlton turned and strode from the inn. Quickly, Thomas descended the stairs and walked right up to Denbow.

"Have you seen my wife?" he asked causally, not wanting to raise any suspicion. "Did she go to the church again?"

Alvin shrugged. "I cannot say. She stepped out a while ago and gave me orders to let you sleep." He paled slightly. "She was quite firm that she could take care of herself."

Another pang of loss pricked his chest. Thomas frowned. He should be happy the wench was long gone. She'd been nothing but trouble and had cost him an easy passage. Who knew when he would be able to find another ship sailing that way?

That was another worry for another day. Today he had to figure out a way to foil Benedict Carlton. Thomas cleared his throat and asked for a brew, which Alvin quickly poured. Thomas took a long drink and then smacked his lips. "I must ask, the man who just left, who was he?"

"What? Hah, you do not know?" Alvin looked at Thomas in

disbelief. "He said he was kin to your wife. Too many relatives for a newlywed to remember?"

"I had my mind on other things." Thomas winked, hoping the innkeeper would not become suspicious.

What the devil would Benedict Carlton want with Anne? Roland's words niggled. *Her relation wants her back.* Thomas rubbed his jaw. That would be a strange coincidence if Carlton was related to Anne or would be on the hunt for her true family. Nay, 'twas a trick. From the way Thomas saw it, word in Newport had gotten out that Anne Howell was seen with a man that matched his description. Finding out their destination, Carlton probably came to Portishead on a later ship. There he most likely learned that Anne was left behind while Thomas sailed away on *The Prince's Prize.* Carlton doubtlessly wanted to question Anne. To find out the truth about the voyage.

The truth!

The devil's laughter rang in Thomas's ears. Anne would not blink an eye to speak truthfully. She'd point her long finger right in his direction. With the speed of an evil demon, Thomas raced out of the inn and toward the church, hoping she was not there. Hoping she was far, far away. Safe from this fellow's claws.

A woman's screams spurred him on, but all he found was another maid with a man, and her screams were those of delight not of fear. His breath burning in his chest, Thomas continued his quest. When he pushed open the church door, he found it deserted. He leaned against a cool wall and might have offered thanks that he was rid of his conniving partner if he were a believer. Surely she had left on her own or had something more nefarious happened to her? He may never know the truth, and blasted, that made him mad. She did not give a fig about him. And he . . . Thomas clenched his teeth and his fists. Since he didn't know where she was, he would have to do the next best thing. Make plans.

Carlton would certainly return to the inn to chase other leads once he could not locate Anne. The chance of finding a ship that sailed south in the small harbor had just disappeared. Best he headed east to Bristol. Certainly, Carlton would travel south. From there, in time, Thomas knew he could find a ship to the Malabar Coast or at least to Portugal.

He debated if he should return to the inn for his other clothing. Anne had all of his coin. Returning to the inn could be perilous. There was only one thing he could do, sell off one of the cross's jewels, but that would take time. Wealthy buyers did not stand in the middle of the square shouting their desire to buy stolen gems. He had to go east, staying off the main roads. In Bristol, he would have a better chance at selling the jewel and keeping his freedom.

Before he could leave the church, a young pastor casually strolled to the back of the church. "Truly God is smiling on our humble sanctuary this day. For you are the second patron to enter this day."

"Second? Was the first a woman?" A prick of fear needled his back. Thomas pushed off the wall and shortened the distance between him and the reverend.

The man's eyes widened. "Aye, and so deep did she pray I feared she had a heavy weight on her shoulders."

So then Anne had not immediately left town. "Did she leave alone? Do you know which way she went?"

"Nay, I did not see her leave." He paused. "I am not sure, but I thought I heard a woman's shout and a man's voice." Then he shook his head. "I hope she did not come to harm."

Thomas tore out of the church and contemplated which way

to go. If Carlton had her, they would surely head for Bristol. Breaking out into a run, he raced east.

At the edge of town, he saw a familiar maid with unique strands of red running through her mahogany hair. A wave of relief mixed with joy swept through him. Part of him had grown fond of his witty minx, a part he needed to tamp down by focusing on his mission.

'Twas then he noticed her bruised lip, dirty face, and torn clothes. Had someone taken advantage of her?

"Lass. What happened to you? Did someone hurt you?" If anyone touched her or had their way with her, he would find them and beat them into the ground.

"Nay. Nothing I could not handle." She waved him off.

"What happened?" He reached out and gently made to take her hand, which she pulled away.

"I was praying in the church. I thought about leaving and going to Bristol, but I feared God wouldn't let me rest until I saved your soul."

Thomas wasn't sure if he should feel humility or worry. Was she trying to cover up what really happened to protect him? Perhaps he could get the truth by applying a different tactic. "Or perhaps you carry a wee bit of affection for me."

Her lips rounded in a perfect *O* as she stepped back. "What a prideful thing to say."

"Well then, why would you be this far from town in such a rumpled state if not harm came your way or you changed your mind and fell out of a wagon because you missed me?" He wiggled his brows.

"I wasn't leaving town, you oaf."

Oh, she was hot now, and he would have the truth.

"A strange man slugged me in the face, dragged me out of

the church, and threw me on his horse. How brash. At first, fear ruled my mind, but then I gave up a prayer for boldness. When courage settled in my being, I flicked my head upward, catching him in the chin." She rubbed the top of her head. "And while he wailed, I took my fist and punched him hard in his middle. He went falling from the horse." She dropped her gaze. "I did not stay to see if he lived. I just rode off."

"You rode off?" He wanted the truth, but none of this was making sense. Few, if any, ever escaped Benedict Carlton once he found them. "And where is the horse now?" The beast would have brought a fair sum.

She lifted one shoulder. "I gave the animal a good slap on the rump once I got near town. I am no thief. Hopefully, he will find his owner not too broken and bent."

If the horse had found Carlton, then he wouldn't be far behind. Thomas pulled Anne off the road into a copse of oaks. Once Carlton found them, he wouldn't think twice about killing Anne after what she had done. "A horse would have been helpful right now. You *werenae* stealing but saving yourself. Did this man say what he wanted?"

Anne became still and kept her gaze tight on her toes.

Carlton told her something, but she was not ready to tell. A threat? If he did, someday he would pay for his transgressions. If he still drew breath. Now was not the time to needle her with queries. If Carlton lived, he would return to Portishead expecting them to flee south, which meant they had to go to Bristol immediately.

Thomas grabbed Anne's hand. "Come on. We shall head north through the trees and fields, staying off the main road. Together we will have protection and a guise. Hopefully, we will fool the villain."

Anne pulled back, her eyes full of tears. "My thanks. I do not deserve your help."

A tight clench held Thomas's gut. He should be drawn and quartered. Anne wouldn't be in this predicament if it wasn't for him. She had her own worries with her contemptible stepfather. Now Carlton's wrath stood at her door.

A journey that should have taken them a day turned into several as they hid from just about everyone they encountered along the way. Taking the few coins they had left, they managed to buy some cheese and bread. They slept out in the open field or near any trees they could find. Anne had been unusually quiet during the journey, which suited Thomas. For once, she wasn't squawking about giving the cross back to God or about his soul being damned if he did not stop his evil ways. Something troubled her, but when he asked, she said nothing and turned the discussion to how long it would take them to get to Bristol or how lovely the countryside was in these parts.

In his opinion, the land looked almost the same as where they had been. Nothing held the beauty as his early home in Scotland. But not since that first night when she aided him on the beach had she asked about his past. At first, he had thought that to be a boon, but now he had to wonder if it was because she really didn't care about him. Or was she hiding an even deeper, darker secret than a worm of a stepfather?

They were both dusty, thirsty, and tired when they made their way to an inn in the heart of Bristol. "'Twill be safer here," Thomas said after they were given a room. "I'll see about having a meal sent up and a bowl of fresh water for you to wash before I make inquires at the docks. The sooner we part company, the better for you."

She stepped quietly into the room and looked about before she raised her head, her eyes glistening with tears. Small drops of blood still caked her bruised lip. Her slim shoulders trembled. "I can understand your hurry to be rid of me. I have caused you nothing but trouble. I am so sorry."

Thomas felt something he had not felt in years—guilt. The lass thought all that had happened had been her fault. So this was the reason for her silence. How could he let her flay herself for his transgressions? Gently, he reached out and took her hands in his, leading her to a small chair. He then knelt in front of her.

"Anne, none of this was caused by you."

She vehemently shook her head. "Nay. Roland said my true relatives were looking for me. They would pay him much for my return to Tretower Court. I did not tell you because I feared you might not take me to Portishead if you knew the truth."

"Or that I would split the coin and help return you to Tretower," Thomas added, reading her thoughts.

She flinched at his words. "You know?"

"Aye. Roland was keen to make the deal. I thought many a time to leave you, not knowing if you played me false or true. But I would never join up with a despicable man like Roland Getting no matter how shiny the coins he waved in front of my face. Though I do wonder, perhaps you would like to meet your true family?" In his heart, Thomas would love for his real family to be so close and alive.

Anne pulled her hands from his. "Ha, true family. I lived at Tretower Court for ten years, and though I was educated when very young, not once did I receive any affection from a single soul in that keep. Not even my nurse. I thought my name was brat until I was tossed to Roland like a dried bone. So I ask you, what could they possibly want of me now?"

At that moment, Thomas wanted to throw his arms around her and give her a great hug for all the pain she had endured as a child, but he feared his action to soothe would be construed to mean something else. He had no wish to add to this lass's suffering by toiling with her affections. And yet the desire to do so quaked him to his core.

"I know not, but I do understand turning away from them." He thought of his Scottish family who had deceived him for eighteen years. Some hurts were hard to forget. He reached over and took her hand. "A change of heart perhaps?"

She rolled her eyes and huffed. "They have no hearts." A swift knock at the door stopped her protest.

"Beggin' your pardon, but I thought ye would like somethin' to warm your bellies." The innkeeper slid a trough of food onto the small table and then fixed his gaze on the chain of gold peeking out from under Thomas's doublet. Quickly, he adjusted his collar to hide the jewel.

Earlier he had thought the chain had been noticed, and now he knew for sure. The innkeeper probably thought they were wealthy nobles traveling in disguise and expected better treatment. Or the man hatched a plan to lift the prize from Thomas's neck. Either way, he would again be sleeping with one eye open this eve.

Thomas thanked the innkeeper, then pushed him out of the room. Turning to Anne, he said, "Eat. I must leave for a short time. Do not let anyone in. If the innkeeper comes around—"

"I have no fear. I can take care . . ." She rose and wiped her eyes.

Of herself. Thinking of what she did to Carlton, there was no doubt. Still, he wasn't sure if leaving her alone was prudent. Scouring the docks could wait until later. "The more I am thinking on it, perhaps we should eat first. What needs to be done can wait until the morrow."

A stunning smile split her lips. "If you think it can?"

He glanced away from her beguiling eyes and rose-colored mouth. "A satisfied belly will help me think better to keep us safe." A hunk of meat might settle its toss too.

They both ate in relative silence. Talk of Benedict Carlton forgotten for the time being. When the meal was finished, Anne yawned and took to the bed. Thomas lay on the floor, using his coat as a pillow. When he heard her soft, delicate breathing, he slipped out of the room. He needed to find a buyer for one of his gems, and those things were done best at night.

CHAPTER 9

A nne woke up to a quiet inn. The scant light from the window meant dawn was breaking. A quick glance around proved she was quite alone. Had Thomas taken his leave of her for good this time? She wouldn't blame him. Though he believed the man wasn't after her, she knew differently.

You're the wench I sent my men to find. Her captor's words rang in her ears over and over. And so did Thomas's. *Perhaps you would like to meet your true family?* His eyes held a deep longing. There was so much about him she didn't know. He never spoke of his family, nor of his past. She had always thought that meant he was hiding a life of crime and deceit. Now she wasn't too sure.

She freshened up a bit before opening the door and proceeding to the large gathering room. The only one about was any elderly woman she had noticed briefly serving ale yesterday. "Did ye sleep well, mistress?" the woman asked politely as she continued to sweep the floor. "The innkeeper will be abed for some time yet. Would you like something to eat? I am sure I can find ye some cheese and milk that might not be too stale."

"Would not the innkeeper be cross?" Anne didn't need

more enemies. "I am sure he keeps an eye on his food." Roland marked every barrel and sack that came through The Whistling Maiden's door. He would let his whole family starve than lose a few precious coins to feed them.

The old woman huffed. "He better not. I be his mother, and I would take a hard stick to his backside if he questioned me."

"Then this is your inn?" Anne asked as the woman put down the broom and went to retrieve the meal.

"Nay. I used to live on a farm with me husband, but the fool lost the land in a wager along with his life. But me boy is a strong man, and a smart one too." She tapped her head. "First, he used his bulk to work at the docks. Then he used his mind to buy this inn." The old lady nodded. "He's a good man."

If what this woman said was true, then their fears of last eve were unfounded. But could this woman and her son be truly trustworthy?

"My name is Edith Blythe. My son's name is Henry." Edith then paused and looked on expectant, but Anne did not know how to answer. Giving her true name might bring her abductor to her door. Surely the man who kidnapped her would make his way to Bristol, which meant she could not stay here either.

Anne sat at one of the tables and took a sip of the milk. The warm liquid didn't contain a hint of being sour. "I'm Anne."

Edith nodded and did not seem to mind that a last name was not offered. No doubt she was accustomed to evasive people. "Are ye from London, then?"

London. How perfect. What a wonderful place to hide, so many lanes, so many buildings, so many people. Anne took a small nibble of cheese. "Nay. But we are going that way. Or at least I am."

A grunt left Edith's throat. She sat down across from Anne.

"If ye be going around telling the truth, ye'll not make it halfway there. My son saw that chain your man wears around his neck, and from your humble clothing, I figure he nabbed it." Anne put a hand to her breast. "I am not a thief."

"Maybe not, but your husband is." Edith's eyes narrowed.

Anne had no intentions of telling this woman anything. Gad, another sin of omission.

The old woman sat back. "Now ye are learning." Edith nodded, knowing Anne had bit her words. "Do ye have any more coin? Cause if you do, Henry can get ye to London."

All their coin was gone. Thomas was going to sell one of the jewels from the cross, but Anne did not know if he would return. "You'll have to ask . . . I do not carry our valuables. You'll have to take that up with . . . when he returns."

Edith raised her eyebrows as if she already knew the answer. "I will then." She returned to her sweeping and did not say another word. After breaking her fast, Anne climbed the stairs to the room she shared with Thomas. If he did not return by the time the sun had risen, she would have to go in search of him. She'd have to find work if he had left her for good. Hopefully, the man in black would not discover her whereabouts. Certainly, she had no wish to go back to Tretower Court for as sure as she stood in this room, only heartache would be waiting within those walls. She would never go back to being their slave or pawn.

Thomas made sure his jeweled artifact was hidden when he stepped into the inn. He had been well aware of the keen eye of the innkeeper last night, and Thomas didn't want to raise any more suspicions. He made his way to the room above the inn. The moment he opened the door, Anne rushed into his arms.

"I thought you had left me." She drew back; fear rested in her eyes.

Annoyance and guilt rolled in his gut. "I will not do that again, not until I know you are safe from any harm I have caused."

"But—"

"I'll not hear differently." He then pulled out a healthy bag of coins and jiggled it. "The ruby I sold was worth more, but I still got a fair price." With his other hand, he pulled out the cross, which was now missing a small ruby at its base.

She frowned and sat down. "God might well strike us dead for selling one of His precious stones. I knew you were going to do it, but now seeing the cross . . . May God have mercy on us."

Thomas threw the money bag onto the table and joined her. Why was she always woeful when she should be happy? "Lass, we have enough to buy a passage for me and enough to get you to the next town."

"London. I want to go to London."

Thomas's spine snapped straight. Why on earth would she want to walk into a den of vipers? The past poked into the present. He too had run to the great city to escape his past, only to find the past could never be forgotten. Plenty of vultures in London longed to scavenge fresh meat. Anne wouldn't stand a chance with no money and no protector. "That is a very dangerous place and none too friendly to strangers."

Anne rose and puffed out her chest. "I can take care of myself. I want to go to London."

He leaned back in his chair and kicked out a boot. "So you

have said many a time, but London has a way of bringing down even the strongest of men, or in your case, women." He rubbed his forehead. "Trust me, I know how that town can drain the life from you."

She stepped close, examining his face. "May the Lord help you, that is where you stole the cross, isn't it?"

He held up his hands, wondering how she managed to always dig out the right assumptions. "Nay, well aye. I mean, the cross was nabbed by the captain of the *Lady Fair*, not me. I only thought to take it when the ship was ready to sink."

She shook her head. "Your last act before you could have died was to steal God's cross?"

He shrugged before a brilliant idea filled up his thoughts. "Perhaps the Almighty gave me the idea to save the holy relic."

"A holy relic that is missing one of its jewels." Anne pointed to the hefty coin bag. "Mark my words, nothing good will come from that lucre."

Thomas laughed. "What is done is done."

Anne pushed past him and headed for the door.

"Where are you going?"

She gave him an exasperated look. "Where God is close to me."

"Benedict Carlton will find you there."

Slowly, she turned and tipped her head. "Who?"

Blast. Why could he not keep his mouth shut? He sighed and sat down on the bed. "The man who abducted you. His name is Benedict Carlton. He came to the inn in Portishead and talked to Denbow. That is how Carlton found you. I believe he was looking for me."

At first, he thought she would riddle him with questions, but she did not. Nor did she chastise him for bringing the spy to their door. If anything, she became thoughtful as if trying to solve some difficult puzzle.

She sat back down by the table. "I do not know him."

"Of course you *dinnae*. I told you, he is after me not you. Nor does he know about the cross. 'Tis a long story and a laborious one. I am almost sure he seeks to take me back to London."

"And why would he wish to take you back there?"

Thomas squirmed. He had no desire to go into his relationship with the queen. Why, that might very well scare Anne who seemed to see ghosts and demons around every corner. "I owe his employer coin."

Anne brow scrunched. "You lie. Though I do not doubt you have sold your soul to every cheat and crook in London, you are lying about this man." She rose and made for the door once again. "You just do not want me to go to London."

"*Dinnae* go to the church," he warned.

She spun around. "I'm not. Good day to you, Master Armstrong. We'll not be meeting again."

With that, she was gone, and Thomas sat there staring at the tempting coin bag. She'd be back. Where could she possibly go? He rubbed the back of his neck and eyed the inviting bed. He could use a bit of rest. She couldn't get into that much trouble while he caught a few winks. He lay down and closed his eyes.

In his dreams, he saw Anne fighting with Carlton as he dragged her away to London. There he handed her over to Queen Elizabeth who ordered Anne to be tortured. Her cries could be heard throughout the kingdom.

Thomas thrashed and bolted upright. His heart racing, his back full of sweat. The devil take him. She even haunted his dreams. He grabbed the coin bag off the table and headed for the door. It hadn't taken him long to learn Anne's whereabouts. She waltzed around the Red Rascal Inn serving ale and food to everyone who entered. Everyone, except him. That pleasure was left to the innkeeper's mother, Edith, who seemed to enjoy Thomas's misery.

"I gave her work after hearing what a scoundrel ye are." The woman slammed a mug of ale on the table in front of him.

Thomas grunted, never taking his gaze off Anne.

"She's a sweet girl. My son, Henry, thinks so too. I wouldn't be surprised that within a few weeks he might suggest a more permanent arrangement."

Edith tried to raise Thomas's ire, but he truly doubted Anne would settle down with an innkeeper. Nay, the lass had much bigger plans. Blythe had supplied that information. After hearing Anne's sad story, the old woman offered her work.

Thomas drained mug after mug, his mood growing darker and darker when Anne refused to glance in his direction. Finally, he could take no more, and he left the inn. He staggered down the street with his money bag tucked in his belt and the cross swinging openly around his neck. A crowing of roosters caught his attention, and he followed the call to a familiar game. A group of shouting men stood around a man-made dirt ring. Two large roosters strutted about measuring each other up. "Has the game begun?" Thomas asked one of the betting men.

The man spat on the ground. "About to."

Thomas opened the bag and took out a handful of coins just as a rooster crowed three times. "Then I would like to make a wager."

CHAPTER 10

Anne sat down at one of the deserted tables in the pub room as the last of the embers glowed before fading away in the hearth. Most of the patrons had retired to their rooms or gone home for the night. How fast she had forgotten a tavern maid's hard life. She slipped her foot out of her shoe and rubbed her aching toes.

"Workin' here ain't a dance around the queen's ballroom, is it?" Edith slid into a chair next to Anne and plopped a tray of empty mugs on the table between them.

"My feet will get used to the long hours fast enough." Anne wiggled her toes and wished she could soak them in a cool stream.

"Quite so." Edith stretched out her legs, giving out a heavy sigh. "I cannot tell ye how grateful I am ye are here." She gave Anne a sheepish look. "I am sorry about yer troubles with Master Armstrong."

"There is nothing to be sorry about." Anne dropped her hands to her lap, hoping the nosy matron would move on to other lively conversation. "We were thrown together by accident, and now we both are going our own way."

How true her words. She really knew nothing about

Thomas. Though he tried to speak perfect English, he was not an Englishman by birth. She knew a Scottish accent when she heard one. He wasn't born to the sea even though he planned to sail to the Malabar Coast. He claimed to be a pepper merchant, but never once did he talk about the trade. She had seen his type before while working at The Whistling Maiden. The shiny eyes with a faraway look. He was a man on a quest filled with secrets. All the more reason not to let her desires stray in his direction. A man on a mission never could fully give his heart to a woman.

"Mmm. I'm not thinkin' your meetin' was an accident." Edith puckered her lips. "I think the divine hand of God was in it."

The absurd thought almost made Anne laugh. There was nothing Godly about Thomas and her. They joined forces for survival, nothing more. If only he hadn't stolen that cross, then perhaps there could have been more . . . What an absurd thought! There was no they. Both would survive on their own now.

Anne rose and placed a hand on her aching back. "I'll bid you good night."

Edith nodded. "Then I shall see ye in the mornin'."

Anne shuffled to a small pallet in the rear of the inn and lay down, thankful that hard work brought pure exhaustion. 'Twas the only way she could rid her mind of Thomas.

Before she closed her eyes, she asked God to protect him on his journey. Perhaps in time she would forget all about him. The silly notion was her last thought before slumber overtook her body.

A forceful shove to her shoulder brought her to full consciousness. "Wake up, Anne. Wake up," Edith shouted.

Could it be morn already? Anne's eyes adjusted to the blackness of the room. She had risen early before, but no light of dawn peeked through the small tavern window.

"Wake up. Yer needed in the inn." Edith shook Anne's shoulder once again.

Slowly, Anne sat up and arched her back, stretching her neck from side to side. "Why?"

"Master Armstrong is callin' for you. He's in a bad way."

Worry followed by a quick admonishment ran through her thoughts. What care she if Thomas was in a bad way? Who cared if he had his teeth bashed in or got his clothes torn?

But she did.

Thomas had saved her on the docks, and she knew behind the mysteries and questionable habits lay a heart worth redemption. With haste, she scrambled from the bed and followed Edith into the pub room. There sitting with his head on the table was a bloody and rumpled Thomas. As expected, the fool had gotten into a fight. The old gash on his head was split wide open, and one of his eyes would be black as night come morning. His upper lip was caked with blood and so was his nose. She had a mind to turn around and head back to bed.

But she didn't.

His moans drew her closer to his chair. His head wobbled as he tried to lift it. "Anne . . ." With a *thunk*, his forehead hit the table.

Anne winced. Her heart started to ooze with sympathy as she knelt down next to him. "Oh, Thomas, what happened to you?" she whispered.

Henry Blythe wiped his hands on his apron and came

to stand next to his mother. "What should we do with him, Mum? I do not want any trouble here."

Edith just shook her head.

Thomas groaned before he drifted off. His hand unfurled to show his torn coin bag.

A gasp escaped Anne's throat. His neck was bare too. The cross was gone. "May God save us." She took the cloth offered by Edith and gently dabbed his brow. The poor man. Had she not ignored him this eve, perhaps he would have stayed at the inn. Any town was dangerous by night. "He must have been set upon by thieves."

Edith gave out a cackle. "Not likely."

Anne paused in her care and looked at the insensitive woman. "How can you say such a thing? Look at him. Only thievery would trigger such violence." She waved his empty coin bag before Edith's face.

"I say such because I know who brought him here." Edith smirked.

Fingers of dread scraped down Anne's back. She lowered her hand, squeezing the bag tight. "What do you mean?"

"Rat Richard dragged him in," Edith said with a firm nod.

"Who?" Anne asked, fearing the answer.

"He runs the cockfights near the edge of the wharf. Said Armstrong bet more than he had and then lost all his wagers. He put up his own fight when they went for his chain." She shook her head. "Some men just can't resist a bet."

Anne threw the coin bag onto the table along with the cloth. The man found trouble like fish guts all over a fisherman's boat. Everyone had their vices, but Thomas had a bag full. She should go to bed and let him bleed to death. Or better yet, help drag his body out into the filthy street.

But she didn't.

Standing straight, Anne looked to Henry and Edith. "Help me get him upstairs."

Henry scratched the back of his head. "I want no trouble here."

"You can take the cost of his care from my wages." Anne glared at the innkeeper.

Henry continued to scratch his head. "Well, he is paid through week's end."

Indeed, and he would barely be healed by then. She saw a healthy amount of her wages dissolve before her eyes. She didn't have the coin to call for a healer, so she would have to manage on her own and pray that God would aid in Thomas's recovery.

With much effort, Anne, Henry, and Edith managed to get Thomas to his room. Anne spent the rest of the night trying to make him comfortable and stitching up his wounds. By morning, she was tired and spent and not in the least ready to start her busy day at the tavern, but she did.

By week's end, Thomas was sitting up and taking solid foods. "I am sorry for all this. Please forgive me."

"Do not be asking me for forgiveness." Anne checked his wounds and then stepped back with a critical eye. "You sinned against God by gambling good money after bad, and now you have reaped what you have sowed."

He shook his head and held up a weak hand. "I promise I will make it up to you. I'll pay back every farthing."

Aye, when she became the queen of England. Such rot. "You can pay me back by drinking your broth and getting better. Once you are well, I'll help Henry throw you out of the Red Rascal myself."

With that, she quit the room and made her way down to the boisterous pub. By her way of thinking, Thomas would be in bed perhaps another few days, and it would be another week before he would be able to leave the inn. She had made up her mind, she would pay the Blythes for his keep, but she would not give Thomas a smidge of sympathy. He'd only get her prayers. She'd hope and pray that he would keep himself out of trouble until she had saved up enough to travel to London. Alone. Knowing Thomas, this could become a vicious circle—her almost earning enough to leave and him getting into another scrape. She would just have to be firm next time and look the other way.

Scripture from her youth burned in her mind. *Therefore all things whatsoever ye would do that men do to you: do ye even to them.* And then another passage crept in. *Give to every man that asketh of thee; and of him that taketh away thy goods asketh them not again.* Anne groaned. Sometimes the Lord asked too much, but then Jesus did die for her sins and for the scoundrel in the room above her.

The tavern was loud and overcrowded as Anne weaved through the tables to Edith's side. Frazzled, the woman grabbed Anne's arm. "I'm glad ye are back. A bunch of ships just came into port with rowdy, thirsty sailors. Plus, there is the stranger in the corner. He's been asking for the pretty wench he saw here yesterday." Edith rubbed her chin. "But I do not remember his face. Ye should serve him first but be careful. He could be up to no good."

Anne pushed up her sleeves before picking up a mug of ale. "Worry not. I can take care of myself." She could handle one lustful merchant. Why, she was hot enough from conversation with Thomas to handle the unruly sailors as well. Ready for a battle, she turned toward the corner and stopped. Dressed in black with a groomed goatee, the man's dark eyes locked with hers. A slow breath of relief left her lungs. This was not the man who had abducted her back in Portishead, but nonetheless, she approached him with care. Slowly, she squeezed through the tight tables to where the stranger sat. A deep ruby shimmered in his earlobe, and a gold band graced his left hand. A married man or a ruse used to give his black soul a hint of honesty?

"Good day to you, sir. Would you be wanting some of the innkeeper's lamb stew? 'Tis quite tasty." Anne slid the brew onto the table and waited. The man assessed her from head to toe and then dropped his gaze to her bare forearms. The skin on her back crawled as his stare burrowed into her flesh.

"That would be fine," he said with a smooth and even timbre. "But tell the innkeeper to make it a small portion, my stomach irritates easily." He removed his hat to show a head of glossy black hair peppered with grey. Upon closer look, his eyes were creased with heavy lines of fatigue. Either the man had traveled far or he was ill. "And also ask if there is a room available. I shall be here for a few more days."

Anne nodded and made her way back to the bar where Henry stood. "That man there wants a small amount of stew and a place to stay."

Henry plopped a ladle of stew into a bowl. "That be fine, but the stew will cost the same price. Tell him I will need to see his coin before I give him a room."

Of course, Henry always had his mind on his gold. She was the only one showing a measure of charity here by losing weeks of wages to Thomas's care, which the oaf probably didn't appreciate. But like the good Samaritan, God would expect her to care for him without thanks.

Picking up the stew, Anne wormed her way through the maze of sailors, ignoring their lewd remarks and wandering hands. She plopped the stew onto the stranger's table and brushed the back of her hand across her sweaty brow. "There's a room for you if you can pay Master Blythe. He'll be coming over shortly."

The man dropped his gaze to her forearms again. Instinctively, Anne crossed her arms behind her back. She should have kept her sleeves down; some men couldn't accept a small mark of any kind. Perhaps this man was a zealot preacher and might call her out as a witch.

He pulled his gaze upward. "That would be fine, Mistress . . . Do you have a name?" His question came out easy as if he was used to making queries.

"Anne," she said curtly, not wishing to give him too much information. For some odd reason, she gave a small curtsy and then scurried away. The less contact she had with this man the better for she was sure wherever he traveled, he bode no good.

By midweek next, with careful steps and with Anne's assistance, Thomas made it to the pub room at the Red Rascal. He offered his thanks, but she spun away without a word.

"Would ye like a brew?" Edith asked, following his gaze to Anne's back. "She won't serve ye."

"I am thirsty, but I *dinnae* have the means to pay for anything, and I *dinnae* want to add to Anne's burden," he answered, watching her scurry around the room, casting lovely smiles to all the patrons.

"This one I'll pay for. I had a wager with Henry. He said that those who beat ye would come and finish ye off. But I said they were satisfied with yer fancy chain and they wouldn't be back."

"Methinks the verdict on that is still out." Thomas winced when he tried to stretch out his leg.

Edith shook her head. "Nay, them that pummeled ye are done with ye, unless ye go back for more of the same."

"I will never set foot in that establishment again." Thomas squirmed in his seat, trying to relieve the kink in his back and the aches in his bones. This wasn't the worst beating he had ever had, but it was the first one where someone else had to pay for his healing. He tipped his head. Well, the queen had sent him a healer once, but she had the means, Anne did not.

A chuckle left Edith's throat. "Nonetheless, Henry loosened his tight purse strings, and I have a few new shiny coins." She gave him a crooked smile. "I'll get ye some food and a brew." Edith hobbled away, mumbling and laughing under her breath.

Not being able to gain Anne's attention, Thomas focused on the patrons in the inn. A few dusty travelers, many boisterous sailors, and a man . . . staring straight at him. His gaze was sharp and full of secrets. Could this be one of Walsingham's spies? Yet, Anne served the man with a warm smile. She lingered by his table and laughed when he spoke. She swung her hips back and forth. This blackguard might misconstrue her actions. Anne should be more careful.

Edith returned with his brew and stew. "Here ye go. Eat hearty."

Thomas's eyes never left Anne and the gentleman. "Who is that over yonder speaking with Anne?"

"Him?" Edith followed Thomas's gaze. "That be Master Antonio Santos. A Portuguese merchant. He's been here at least a week. Claims to be selling spices from the east." Edith frowned.

"You doubt him?" Thomas asked, fearing the man was a bigger scoundrel than himself.

Edith shrugged. "There is a Portuguese caravel harbored in the port, and many a spice merchant do choose to stay at an inn once their ship is docked, but there is something different about him."

"What is that?" Thomas leaned over the table.

"He doesn't spend much time in the markets like most merchants. He spends most of his time here. I think he fancies Anne."

Her words all but confirmed Thomas's suspicions. He had to be a spy. Santos's smile vanished when Anne left his table. Aye, this merchant was not who he claimed to be.

"Are ye all right?" Edith asked. "Ye look a little peaked. Do ye want me to help ye upstairs?"

"Nay, I am fine." Thomas took a swallow of his brew.

"Well then, I'll leave ye to yer meal." Edith hurried to another table.

"I thank thee," he called out before digging in to his food. Once his plate was clean, Thomas turned his attention to Santos, who gave a lazy salute when he caught Thomas looking at him. This was all a game to this supposed Portuguese merchant. If Thomas were capable, he would march over to the rogue's table and demand an explanation for why he was here.

The thought had barely registered in Thomas's brain when Santos started making his way toward Thomas. Without asking, the man sat down. "It is good to see you up and moving about, Master Armstrong."

Thomas's suspicions were right. The blackguard was a spy. "So you are one of Walsingham's men, then?"

The man let loose a hearty laugh. "Hardly."

"Well, you are not a Portuguese merchant. I have dealt with many, and you are not known to me," Thomas countered.

The smile fell from Santos's face, and his lips drew a grim line. "I assure you, by trade I am. Your reputation is well known in my circles."

Thomas squirmed. Indeed, he had no qualms of selling goods to anyone, be they friends of the Crown or not. He only hoped that Santos's business partners were not some of the men Thomas had cheated by adding more weight to his scales. "All that you may say could be true. But that *doesnae* explain how you found me or what you want from me."

Santos sat back in his chair. His lips kicked up into a small smile. "I am a very resourceful man. One only needs to keep his ears and eyes open to learn many things."

The villain held his secrets close, all the more reason for Thomas to stay clear of him. "Sir, we have nothing further to discuss. I have no intentions of returning to London and my warehouses anytime soon. I suggest you find another to do business with."

The merchant snickered. "I am not interested in selling my goods. I have come to you for another reason." He reached into his doublet and pulled out the golden jeweled cross—with all of its jewels?

"How did you . . . I sold—"

"It matters not how I came to own your prize possession. Nor how I managed to buy back the jewel you sold. What matters is you are impoverished and on the run."

If Santos wasn't a spy of Walsingham's, he should be. The

man clearly had ties in London and somehow had managed to track him here. Thomas leaned back in his chair. "I suggest you leave and tell Benedict Carlton to come and do his own dirty work."

Santos rubbed his belly and winced. "You speak foolishly. A blind man could have tracked you here. There were few who survived the *Lady Fair,* but there were some. One by the name of Harthal remembered you well. He said you were always sneaking around the captain's cabin." Santos waved the cross in front of Thomas. "I am assuming that is where you found this."

With a flinch, Thomas pushed back from the table. "The ship was sinking. I only meant to save the relic."

With a snicker, Santos tucked the cross back into his doublet. "I have not come to judge you but to help you."

No wonder the man's gut ached. His words were laughable and hard to digest. Yet, Thomas was intrigued. "What do you want?"

"I wish to travel to your homeland in Scotland. If you take me there and introduce me to your family, when the time is right, I will give you back this precious relic and take you to the Malabar Coast at no cost to you."

Excitement, fear, and caution coursed through Thomas all at once. Free passage to the coast with ownership of the cross, but at what price? Why did this villain wish to travel to Warring Tower? Though he had disowned his family, he did not wish to see them harmed. There was no doubt that Santos was a dangerous man.

"I assure you. I mean no harm to your family," the merchant said.

"Then what do you want with them?" Thomas folded his arms over his chest.

The older man's eyes misted over. "To fulfill a promise made long ago."

"A promise?"

"Aye, to a love I left behind."

A love? Just when Thomas was ready to ask who, Santos rose to his feet.

"Know this, I shall make my way to Warring Tower with or without your help. I will give you a day to decide. But I will not tarry longer for there is danger here for all of us." Santos paused and looked around the inn until his gaze caught a fetching maid's. "But most definitely for Mistress Anne."

CHAPTER 11

"Such nonsense. I do not want to go to Scotland. I want to go to London." Anne stood with her arms crossed, creating a barrier from the two men.

"Perhaps we should have this discussion elsewhere." Antonio glanced around the Red Rascal before stepping closer to Anne. "We do not need to draw any unwanted attention."

As if anyone cared about a serving wench. "And you are going along with this foolery?" Her hard glare pinned Thomas where he stood.

"We shall not stay there long. I'll introduce Master Santos to my family, and then we shall return to England." Thomas gently touched her elbow, guiding Anne to the door. "But we must leave now."

She locked her legs and refused to budge. "Your family? You have said nothing about a family." She had been right about his accent, but something still niggled her. *Do you have a wife?* She swallowed those words and came up with others. "You're going to introduce Master Santos to your family? Why? You do not even know him." She tilted her head and thinned her lips. "What profit is there in this for you?"

Thomas's eyes widened with false hurt as he placed a hand

over his heart. "Why, none. I think only of your safety and Master Santos's broken heart. It seems he knows one of the cottars who lives on my family land, a love that he left behind long ago."

One of the cottars who lives on my family lands. Then Thomas was a gentleman? A second son perhaps? Or this could all be more lies. "A Portuguese merchant left his heart to a Scottish maid?" This had to be the worst lie he had ever told. Or the man was losing his ability to be a proficient liar. She turned her attention back to Antonio. "And I was beginning to think you were an honorable man."

"I am, madam. I assure you. My heart is in Scotland." Antonio's gaze slid around the inn again. "But we must leave now for all our sakes."

His speech seemed forthright. The story was so preposterous it could be true. But alas, that might be what they wanted her to believe. Anne threw up her hands. "I am working now. We can discuss this later, or both of you can leave without me."

Thomas shook his head. "I'm not leaving you behind."

"Why?" Anne placed a hand on her hip. This was all so absurd. Her heart could not take one more of his schemes. Why could he not stop and settle down? *With whom?* her mind teased. *With you?*

"I have a confession to make." Thomas rubbed a hand behind his neck. "The queen of England is quite fond of me, and she wishes to have me back at court. The man that kidnapped you works for Walsingham, her spymaster. His name is Benedict Carlton. He thought I left on *The Prince's Prize*, and he hoped to get information from you about me."

Well, she had been wrong. He could come up with bigger, worse lies. "You're telling me you are one of the queen's 'special gentlemen'?"

Thomas nodded eagerly.

Anne picked up an empty mug and debated if she should slam it into the side of his head. Did he not know that such words tore her apart? "Of all the vain, silly stories I have heard . . . God should strike you down right here, right now." She turned her wrath onto Antonio. "And you believe this?"

Antonio remained stoic. "Whatever is true, you are not safe. Best you come with us." His gaze shifted about the room once more before he lowered the brim of his hat over his forehead. Obviously, it was not her the villains were after but these two.

Her grip on the mug tightened. "I'm not leaving." She held up the tankard and waved it between Thomas and Antonio. "And if I were, it wouldn't be with either of you." She spun about and returned to her work. For all she cared, they could stand there all day and gape. Going to Scotland, such rot. Not even if the Archangel Michael suggested such a thing. When she had the means, she was going to London.

Once both men left, her day went surprisingly fast even though her mind kept wandering to Thomas's preposterous words. *The queen of England is quite fond of me.* Such drivel. True, Thomas was handsome in his own way, but to think she would believe such a haughty, conceited notion was more than arrogant, it was ridiculous. He must think so little of her to offer such an outlandish tale. Her heart ached. After all they had been through together, he still saw her as a naïve ninny.

When her workday finally ended, she skipped her evening meal and went immediately to her pallet in the backroom. Before lying down, she prayed for forgiveness of her anger and malignant thoughts. She also prayed for safe travels for the two rogues and blamed the rumblings in her stomach on skipping her evening meal, though her mind screamed it had nothing to do with food and everything to do with the russet-haired Scotsman who had brought adventure to her life. Now those times were over, and she would carry on alone.

With a long yawn, she closed her eyes and floated into a deep sleep. Wonderful dreams of riding horseback with Thomas at her side glided through her mind. Sweet heather filled her senses as they galloped over the glen. But the fancy didn't last long when a foul odor shook her from her dream. Something or someone tugged on her hands. When she tried to scream, a greasy rag was jammed into her mouth. Her wrists were bound with tight rope. Was this real or some ghoulish nightmare?

Her body was slung over the shoulder of a man. Doubts scrambled her mind. Where was she being taken? By whom? With care, she was placed in the back of a wagon. Her eyes tried to adjust to the dark, but she could not make out her kidnappers before the cart rumbled out of town. Antonio had been right; her life was in danger. How did he know? Fear infused her body, and she could think of nothing to do. She could not even formulate a prayer in her mind.

Divine hand of God. Edith's words punched a hole into the mad blackness. Anne hung on to those words. *Your divine hand. Hold me in your divine hand. Protect me in your divine hand.* Over and over her mind sped along until God reached down and, with his divine hand, gave her blessed sleep.

Anne awoke with a start as sunlight beat on her face. The gag had been removed from her mouth, and her hands were no longer bound. One villain drove the wagon while the other sat in the back searching the countryside. She sucked in her breath as his features took focus—curly auburn hair, merry copper eyes, and a firm chin. Was the devil playing a trick on her? Nay, the devil's minion was sitting in the wagon. And he was well known.

"Thomas?" she asked through dry lips. "Is that you?" All fear vanished as the anger she prayed to leave her last eve grew like a hot wound in her gut.

A flash of white teeth and a devilish wink confirmed her assessment.

She struggled to sit up. Heat spiked up her neck. "Of all the . . . Why would you do this? Turn this wagon around and take me back."

"We cannot. I am sure Carlton is not far behind. Santos and I spotted the fellow near the wharf not long after we left the Red Rascal."

Anne grabbed at the sides of the wagon to steady herself. "So? If what you said is true, then all I would have to do was point him toward you and Scotland."

Thomas visibly winced. "I'd happily allow you to do so, but Santos thinks the man is after you and not me. Either way, we didn't have the time to sort out the truth."

Crawling over to Thomas's side, she whispered, "Why would a merchant leave his boat in a harbor and decide to take a cart to Scotland? Did it ever occur to you that this so-called Portuguese merchant could mean us both harm? Sometimes I think your head is made of wood."

The Scottish oaf looked at his hands.

"You have." She slugged him in the arm. "Then why are we going on this silly chase?"

"He holds the necklace with all the jewels, even the one I sold," Thomas mumbled.

She slugged him in the arm again. "You put our lives and that of your family's in harm's way for a handful of jewels?" She started pushing hard against his shoulder. "Get out of this cart. Get out of it now," she all but shouted.

"You do not understand. You are in danger because of me. Carlton will use you as a pawn to get to me. I am trying to protect you at the expense of myself and my family."

Anne paused her onslaught. Could he be telling the truth? Why would he place her above his own kin unless he did care about her? But he had left his kin and never spoke of them. Why were there so many mysteries to this man? Her patience was worn thin as a spider's silk. "You care about no one but yourself."

Antonio turned on his perch. "Ah, you are awake and arguing. How delightful."

"I want off. You cannot keep me. I have no desire to go to Scotland or anywhere else with either of you."

The merchant chuckled. "Unfortunately, you have no choice. You may be in serious danger, and until I can figure out which is the best path to take to keep us all alive, you will remain in our care."

Thomas shook his head. "Perhaps she is in more danger staying with us. Carlton *widnae* bother her if I give myself up. The queen may be upset I tried to dupe her spies, but in time, she will relent. Though I *cannae* say I will be happy to be back in London."

Anne pulled back and stared at him in disbelief. "I am exhausted by your lies."

With a scoff, Antonio shook his head. "Do you truly believe you are the reason the queen's spies lurk about?"

Thomas puffed out his chest the best he could as the wagon

hit every rut in the road. "But of course, what other reason could there be? The queen would not send spies for Anne, that would be absurd."

"Perhaps," agreed Antonio. "But then again, perhaps not."

Anne fell silent. The logical explanation was that Carlton was not a spy or connected to the queen at all. The man must be working for her kin at Tretower Court. She knew it and so did Antonio Santos, who was probably a fortune hunter. But if that were true, why head to Scotland? She needed to change tactics to get her answers. "Surely your ship cannot stay in Bristol's harbor forever. Why are you not sailing north to a closer port?"

Santos tapped the side of his forehead. "Ah, the lady is using her wits. My ship has already sailed south."

"Without you? I have never heard of such a thing. I do not believe you. You are as big of a liar as Master Armstrong." She lifted her chin and sniffed. "I am in the hands of two bumbling cutthroats."

Antonio chuckled and turned his attention back to the road. Thomas looked positively stricken. The sheepish look in his eyes beseeched her to behave. She had no intention of granting him such a wish. Before she could rail on him some more, Thomas turned away, but not before she saw the concern in his eyes.

A new thought dawned on her. She inched closer to him so the Portuguese merchant could not hear. "You are going with Antonio to Scotland because you fear for your family, aren't you? You want to protect them. Not because of the cross."

The truth glistened in his eyes, but he said nothing.

Could it be that Thomas Armstrong wasn't a scoundrel, a rogue, a liar, a cheat, or the thief she thought him to be? Would he risk his life to save his family? He had risked his life to save

125

hers, and she was all but a stranger. A dip in the road made the wagon rock. Thomas reached out a protective hand, securing her seat. Had she misjudged this man? If so, she had fled her seaside cave with one of the most compassionate and caring men she had ever met.

CHAPTER 12

In a fortnight, the rickety wagon stood at the gate of Warring Tower. Thomas swallowed hard as he viewed his childhood home. Not much had changed in ten years, and yet many things had changed. There were fewer Galloway ponies grazing in the fields and fewer cottages nestled nearby. The stone tower still stood protected by the low fortress wall. The battlements held the iron baskets used for signal fires, but many stones had disintegrated, and every basket was in need of repair.

His father, Gavin Armstrong, had taken pride in rebuilding the landmark tower and the nearby town, but clearly Thomas's brother had turned a blind eye to such things. *You were groomed to run this keep, not Marcas.*

Thomas gave himself a mental shake, the past could not be changed. He called to the guard, but the iron-latticed yett did not open.

"Who do ye say ye are?" the guard asked.

Not at all surprised by the question, Thomas lifted his head so his features could be seen. "I am Thomas Armstrong, son of Gavin Armstrong." *Liar, he is not your real father.*

No answer came forth for quite a while. Anne and Santos sat quietly. Thomas fidgeted, and his breath hitched when an older woman with streaks of grey through her dark hair appeared on the battlements. Hands shading her eyes, she stared at the gate and at him. At first, he believed it to be Gran for this woman was frail and could not possibly be the robust Ma Audrey. His mind stepped back to when Ma Audrey would race through the yard and throw a blade better than most men. Nay, this woman was not she.

"Thomas, is that truly you?" The woman's delicate voice floated on the soft wind and warmed his soul like a soothing balm. His pulse rose, and his heart jumped. *'Twas his ma.*

Immediately, Santos perked and squinted his eyes, gazing upward. "Is that your mother?"

Without answering the merchant, Thomas jumped down from the cart, lifted his chin, and stretched out his arms wide. "Ma Audrey, 'tis me."

"It is you. Praise God," she shrieked and then disappeared. The gate began to creak and rumble open.

A deep yearning rolled in Thomas's gut. Would she welcome him with open arms or slap him across the face for his desertion? One never knew where Ma Audrey's thoughts roamed.

"Santos, bring the wagon," Thomas called as he stepped toward the gate. "And say nothing. I will make the introductions when the time is right."

The merchant nodded and lowered his wide-brimmed hat over his forehead. "I see this is an emotional reunion. I shall see to the horse and wagon. You can introduce me after you've been received."

Thomas paused and stared at Santos's back as he guided the horse and cart toward the stable. Were there tears in Santos's voice or had the rumbling of the cart scrambled Thomas's hearing? The man was an oddity at best and a danger that would have to be reckoned with soon enough.

Anne walked up next to him and gave Thomas a weak smile. "For once I do not believe you are shoving a sack over the truth." She had been unusually cordial after the first night they had kidnapped her. Why, he could not say. Not once from that moment forth did she complain or ask why he was dragging her along. Even when they slept in the woods or on a grassy hill, her countenance remained calm and cheery. She offered to prepare meals, prayed often, and asked many questions about his home in Scotland, of which he was quite evasive. The less she knew the better. However, he could not help but wonder at her change and feared she planned revenge in her bonnie head.

For the first time in years, Thomas almost had the urge to drop to his knees and pray. Was he doing the right thing coming here? He might be bringing a dragon to Warring Tower. More than once he thought of subduing Santos and leaving him tied to a tree. Anything that would keep his family safe.

When they entered the gate, Ma Audrey greeted them with her hands clasped in front of her. She eyed him up and down before running toward him, throwing her arms around his neck, and kissing his cheek. "Oh, Thomas, it is you. I always knew you would come back to us."

He wrapped his arms about her thin waist and cringed at the frailty of her body. Her round curves were gone, and the signs of age were upon her. "It is good to see you again," he whispered through a clogged throat.

She pulled back; he took a sharp breath when he saw the wrinkles that creased her forehead and cheeks. Everyone aged, but Ma Audrey's lines were deep. Lines of sorrow—of which many he had carved.

"I see you have not come alone." Her gaze rested on Anne. A warm smile lightened Ma Audrey's weary face. "Have you come to tell us something?"

Thomas laughed. Some things never changed. "Nay, this is not my wife. She was in need of aid, and I could not think of a better place to come to keep her safe."

Ma Audrey tipped her head, and merriment danced in her eyes. "Pray tell, what type of trouble could the maid possibly be in that would make you bring her to Scotland?"

Still astute as ever. Thomas glanced about as Anne quickly approached. "Let us just say, her troubles are of my doing," he murmured.

"Oh?" Ma Audrey's peppered eyebrows shot heavenward.

Anne dropped into a deep curtsy. "My lady."

"This is Widow Anne Howell of . . . Wales," Thomas said dryly, trying to hide a smirk.

Ma Audrey nodded. "Of all of Wales?"

"Not all of Wales, my lady. I hail from Newport." Anne straightened and lifted her chin.

"Newport in Wales." Ma Audrey turned back to Thomas. "So not only did you spend time in England with the queen, but you managed to get yourself to Wales too."

Anne gasped, perhaps finally realizing he had spoken the truth about Queen Elizabeth.

"You seem surprised by my words, Widow Howell. Why is that?"

"I-I . . ." Anne's cheeks pinked, and she dropped her gaze. "I did not believe Thomas when he said he knew the queen. I now see the guilt is mine."

"Guilt?" Ma Audrey laughed, reaching out to Anne. "Child, Thomas was always a rascal as a young boy, so your doubt is understandable. Please do not chastise yourself." She then took Thomas's arm. "Come. The family is within. There will be so much joy tonight in the old hall."

They walked past the block kitchens where the aromas of familiar foods whetted his appetite. It had been a long time since he had a tasty rabbit or, in good times, a slice of rich meat from a boar. However, from the looks of the keep, they would not be eating a king's feast this eve.

They walked toward the tower, through the wide stone-arched entry, then a sour smell of neglect assaulted his nostrils. Few barrels and molding grain sacks were stacked in the cool cellar indicating a harsh winter. No wonder Ma Audrey had heavy, dark circles under her once sparkling eyes. To his knowledge, there had not been any border wars for some time. How had things gotten this bad at Warring Tower?

A twist of guilt coiled up his spine. He had left a lad and two aging women in control. None who were groomed to take over as he was. If poor management had caused this blight, then his desertion was to blame.

Ma Audrey led the way up the spiral stairs to the hall. Thomas gave out a sigh of relief when he noticed the hall was still orderly. The rushes were clean, and the furnishings were in good repair. Light streamed through the narrow windows making the room merry. A newer wooden screen hid the small scullery that had been added during richer times. He'd bet all of his coins that he had tucked behind the stairs in the modest chapel remained untouched. A favorite place to hide all of his treasures as a youth. How good it was to be home.

Blair, the servant that had seen to his many needs when he was a lad, came out of the scullery. Her blond hair was now tucked under a matron's cap. She no longer swished her hips like a seductress but stood firm and stout as a woman of middling years should be. "Well, it is about time ye come home."

Thomas bowed slightly. "Mistress Blair, as beautiful as ever."

She rolled her eyes and folded her arms under her heavy breasts. "Still the charmer."

He strode forward and squeezed her tight. "I am so glad you are here."

"Pff. And just where would I be goin'? I have five of me own to feed now and a shiftless husband who hasn't plowed a decent crop in years."

"Oh, she exaggerates." Ma Audrey waved her off. "He is a good man."

Untangling herself from Thomas's embrace, Blair craned her neck. "I see ye have brought a maid. I'll fetch ye some food and drink." Her brows rose as her gaze swept cautiously around the hall. "If I can find some," she mumbled before stomping off to the scullery.

Thomas took a deep breath. Aye, indeed, it was good to be home. In those days, he was as bold as a brandishing sword. Full of confidence and bluster while his brother, Marcas, was meek and quiet. Thomas scanned the hall. Where the devil was his brother? And Gran? No doubt, she was resting. He remembered she had been known to do such in the afternoons.

Out of the corner of his eye he caught sight of another woman standing by the long table. Young, perhaps seventeen or eighteen summers, dressed in a green gown that accentuated her emerald eyes. She reminded Thomas of a praying mantis. Reed-thin, but not from lack of food, but from a gift given to her by her parentage. Comely, but not overly so. Soft brown hair framed her elongated face. If they were outside, she would blend in like a stick of grass in a muddy field.

Thomas tipped his head in acknowledgment. "And who might this be?" he asked Ma Audrey.

The gentle smile fell from her face, and her gaze turned hard. "This is Lady Cecilia."

The young woman stepped forward meekly. "I have heard much about you from my husband."

"Husband?" A heavy silence ensued. Ma Audrey did not enlighten him on who this woman could be. Anne averted her eyes, obviously feeling the tension in the hall. The fire crackled in the hearth, but no responses came forth.

Finally, the woman in green answered his query, twisting her hands in front of her. The blue sparkling ring caught Thomas's attention. 'Twas Edlyn's ring. The ring he had given Marcas long ago. "Your brother is my husband."

Joy coursed through Thomas. Marcas had taken a wife, which meant the Armstrong line would continue. Gavin Armstrong could rest in peace knowing his true son carried on the family legacy. Thomas looked to Ma Audrey. This was grand news, so why the stoic face?

The past crept over his shoulders. This was always a house of secrets. So then, what was the mystery surrounding Lady Cecilia? He searched the hall. Where was Marcas? He must be out riding the marches—something every good laird did daily. Hopefully, he was searching for game to fill the bellies of all within the tower.

Thomas turned his attention back to Cecilia. "And where did my brother find you?"

"I am of the Elliot family." Her long lashes fell over her green eyes. "We met at a Truce Day."

Though she resembled a mantis, her voice purred like a cat.

Oh, Thomas could see why his brother was attracted to this woman. What he couldn't understand was why Ma Audrey was not. The Elliots had allied with the Armstrong family more than once over the years. Had something changed within the last decade to disrupt that alliance?

"Ah, Truce Days. I used to love them as a lad. I could run like the wind and was fair with the bow," he said, trying to lighten the mood.

Cecilia laughed. "I remember."

She remembered? But he didn't know her.

"I was but a child. Everyone knew the Armstrongs of Warring Tower." She backed away as if she feared him.

Yet, Ma Audrey bristled. Did she not like this gentle woman? And if not, why?

Audrey's gaze held a plethora of questions. Needles pricked Thomas's neck. It seemed the fly had just flown into the spider's web. Clearly all was not well here. What would happen when he introduced Santos to his family? He let his gaze roam the hall once again. Where was the man? No doubt he had wisely settled in the stable or gone to look for the sweetheart he claimed lived nearby.

Not wanting to add to this already stressful situation, Thomas turned to Ma Audrey. "We have traveled long and far. I am sure Widow Howell wishes to rest a bit. Is there a place for her to rest here?"

"I am fine," Anne protested. "I have been sitting in a wagon all day and need to stretch my legs. I am fit to do any task that would ease your burdens."

Ma Audrey affectionately slipped her hand into the crook of Anne's arm and tossed a smug look at Cecilia over her shoulder. "I am sure you are, but you might want to freshen up a bit. There is a small chamber above that you may use. I shall bring up a trencher of food. You must be famished from such a long journey." She then called to Thomas. "We will have to find a place to put you and your servant as your old room is full of Cecilia's clothes and things from her father's home. I can send some food to the stables as your servant must be hungry as well."

The last thing Thomas wanted to do was take food away from the starving mouths at the tower. Since Ma Audrey thought Santos was a servant and not a guest, perhaps there could be a delay in his introduction. "Worry not about me and my man, we shall sleep in the stables, and we still have plenty of food in our bags. We'll not starve."

Wisely, Anne did not correct his words. A hard thing for a woman who could not stand a lie.

Ma Audrey patted Anne's hand. "The chamber is small, but it is next to mine. It used to belong to Marcas's mother."

Immediately, Thomas could see Anne's mind spin with more questions, which he knew he would have to answer later.

The pair made their way to the spiral stairs. "Do not tarry long, Thomas," Ma Audrey called over her shoulder. "I am sure Marcas will want to see you."

Indeed. His brother would sort out this mire that had Ma Audrey and the servants tiptoeing around his bride. Without another word, Cecilia glided to a chair near the hearth where she picked up a piece of needlework and began to hum an eerie tune.

Right now he had to settle with the problem waiting in the stables. Bringing Santos into his family home had Thomas's bones chilling as if they rested in his own father's grave.

CHAPTER 13

The friction between the two women sent quivers down Anne's spine. Lady Audrey loved her son, but the wariness she held for Cecilia was also obvious. Something was terribly wrong here. A rivalry between the past lady of the keep and the new lady of the keep? Possibly.

Many other questions needed answering as well. The first being if Thomas was the eldest, then why was he not laird of Warring Tower? What caused him to leave his duties to his brother?

Anne followed Lady Audrey into a small chamber where a narrow bed hugged one wall and a simple table with one chair sat under an arrowslit window. A modest tapestry of children dancing in a circle hung above the bed, giving the room a little merriment.

"I know it isn't much. My husband always planned to add to the tower for future children, but unfortunately, he died before that could happen." The telling of the past seemed to drain Lady Audrey of what little strength she had left.

Apologies were not necessary. Anne had never had a room of her own. Even before living in a cave, she rested her head on a bit of floor at The Whistling Maiden. At Tretower Court, she slept in the women's quarters. She had to fight the desire to run her fingers over every piece of furniture, so excited was she to have a room of her own even if it might be for only one night. "I assure you, this is more than fine."

Suddenly Lady Audrey rushed forward and gave Anne a hug. When she pulled back, there were tears in her eyes. "Thank you for bringing Thomas home." She stepped toward the door. "I shall send up a tub and some hot water so you may take a bath. After you have bathed, eaten, and rested, we shall have a nice talk." A weak smile lifted her cheeks before she closed the door quietly behind her.

The moment Lady Audrey figured out Anne was nothing more than a serving wench and not the love of her son's life, she would be tossed into the slop. Anne bit her lower lip. She could ask Lady Audrey for work in the kitchens. Scotland didn't seem to be any worse than England, and for certain, Roland and Carlton wouldn't find her here. Anne sat on the edge of the bed when a knock on the door brought two burly men carrying a half-barrel. A serving maid followed with two buckets of hot water.

"Lady Audrey said ye be needin' a bath." The maid filled the barrel. Once finished, she followed the men to the door. "I'll be bringin' ye more water right away. Would ye need help with your bath, mistress?"

Help with her bath! Anne had not had such luxury even when she was a little girl at Tretower. Back then, if she were lucky, she would bathe in a cold stream or use a wet rag to wipe the grime away. Her body shivered at such an extravagance of taking a real bath. Anne looked to the waiting serving maid. "Nay, I will tend to my own needs."

After the maid left, Anne stripped off her clothing and eased into the warm water. She closed her eyes and envisioned herself a grand lady dressed in a fine gold dress. What a life that would be. But then reality settled in. She was not a fine lady, and the only clothes she owned lay on the floor.

Another knock forced Anne to sink farther into the tub. The maid was back again, this time with a trencher of cheese and nuts and a carafe of goat's milk. Over her shoulder was a simple blue gown and a white shift. "Lady Audrey thought you might like these as well."

A sluice of joy rushed through Anne. The gown may not be as fine as a queen's, but even from where she sat in the tub, she knew it to be the best she would ever own. The maid scooped up Anne's old clothes and gave a quick curtsy before she scurried away. Anne's cheeks grew warm. No one had ever curtsied to her. What would it be like to not have a care for one day? To be treated like she mattered to someone . . . Oh how she could get used to this life.

When the water grew cold, Anne let out a heavy sigh and reached for the drying cloth. She wrapped the cloth around her body and pulled her fingers through her wet hair. It would be a while until the locks would dry, but she was not in a hurry to vacate her dwellings. With a delicate touch, she ran her fingers over the soft wool gown and smooth shift. Though the gown was far from new, it was still beautiful. The modest neckline was covered with a fine trim of lace. Thankfully, the sleeves were long and would hide her dark mark. She held out the gown, examining it from top to bottom. The frock would fit her perfectly. Excited, Anne quickly donned the clothing and then dove into the cheese and nuts. She finished off her meal with the goat's milk and then brushed the back of her hand across her mouth. A satisfying "ah" left her lips. She fell back onto the bed and rubbed a hand over her flat belly. This had to be one of the finest days of her life. A heaviness weighed upon her eyelids.

When she opened her eyes, dim light shone through the narrow window. She yawned and thought of rolling over to continue her rest, but then the face of Lady Audrey swam in her mind. "I really should go and thank her for her kindness," Anne said to the wall. Thomas must be downstairs reminiscing about old times with his family, and she did so want to know more about the man's past.

Just as she sat up, an agonizing moan drew her attention to the floor above her. The sound was raw and full of woe, and it continued over and over. Was someone ill or injured? The sound of soft feet slipped passed Anne's door and continued up the stairs until she heard a door scrape open, followed by a flurry of murmured voices. As quickly as the moaning started, it stopped, and not long after, the same set of footfalls descended the stairs.

Anne crept to her door, and as quietly as possible, she opened it. No one was in the narrow hallway. Her gaze traveled from the steps that led to the hall below and then to the steps that led above. What lay up there wasn't any of her concern. She made a mental nod, closed her door ready to descend the stairs, but then another groan split the air. Someone was in pain or grave danger.

As if her feet had a mind of their own, she began to ascend the stairs. God would want her to aid someone in need. *He would also like you to keep your nose out of other's affairs.* She paused. *God, what should I do?* The answer came in another soft, agonizing moan. Jesus would want her to love her neighbor. Anne threw back her shoulders and raced upward to the chamber.

When Thomas entered the stables, he found Santos finishing up the simple meal Ma Audrey had sent to him. "My thanks to your *mãe*, she is very thoughtful to send such a meal to fill my belly."

"Ma Audrey thinks of all. In truth, she is not my mother. My mother is dead," Thomas said bluntly.

Santos placed the trencher on the floor and stood. "I know. Your brother has a different *mãe* as well."

How true. Santos seemed to know everything. Or at least everything concerning Thomas and his family. Where he got the information from only the devil knew. "Is that what brings you here? One of my *da's* wives?"

A flash of white teeth accompanied Santos's laugh. "You are such a cynic. You see misery and misfortune around every corner. 'Tis why your life has been so wanting."

Thomas curled one hand into a fist and raised it in front of Santos's face. "You harm a hair of anyone in this keep, and I swear, I will slit your throat."

The merchant laughed again, wrapping his hand around Thomas's fist. "I am not the evil which plagues your soul. If anything, I may be the answer to your prayers."

The flash of gaiety in the man's eyes curled Thomas's gut. How he would love to punch Santos until his face was bloody and Thomas's strength was spent. Squelching his anger, Thomas dropped his arm and uncurled his hand. "I *dinnae* pray." He then began to saddle one of the Galloway ponies.

"Aye, it is apparent. Might be why your life is in a dismal state."

"I need no lectures from a shiftless snake as you." Thomas

glared at him. "From where I am standing, your life is not a bed of heather either."

Santos shrugged. "Where are you going?"

"To find my brother. I am sure he rides the marches. 'Tis what all good lairds do."

The firmness left Santos's jaw. "You would leave me alone . . . here?"

"Nay, you are coming with me. Put this on." He threw Santos a canvas jack with metal plates sewn within.

"What is this?" Santos asked, holding up the jack.

"'Tis a jack of plate. The marches are not always a safe place." Thomas pulled a dirk from his belt and waved it in front of Santos's face.

The Portuguese merchant chortled again. "You think to quell me with such a little knife?" Santos pulled out a wheel-lock pistol and a dagger of his own. "Think again, Armstrong." His gaze then slid to his bundle beside the empty trencher. "I have a sword as well. Unlike you who has lost most of his possessions to a game of chance."

Thomas's back muscles tensed. The man could gloat all he wanted, being at a disadvantage didn't mean a thing. If Santos so much as lifted a finger against any in this tower or Anne, Thomas would rip the merchant apart limb by limb. He pulled on the horse's reins. "Let's go. We *dinnae* have much daylight, and we have much ground to cover."

Once they left the tower, the pair rode over the meadows, up the hills, and along the river. They covered as much of Warring Tower's land as they could before the sun faded away. Not once did they spot other reivers or his brother. Either they kept missing him or he was not on the marches. Then where could he be? Visiting the Maxwells or his cousin Jaxon Armstrong? If this was so, then why didn't Ma Audrey tell him? Reluctantly, Thomas and Santos headed back to Warring Tower where they dismounted in the courtyard.

Santos grabbed the reins of both horses. "I shall tend to the beasts. You go and see to your family."

The act of kindness made Thomas pause. "You *dinnae* want me to introduce you to them now?"

The Portuguese merchant shook his head. "Nay. This is your first night home. It belongs to you and your kin. I have waited a long time." He paused and left out a rough cough, his gaze darkening. "I can wait another day."

The man was a mass of contradiction. Just when Thomas believed him to be the enemy, Santos acted like a friend. No doubt his actions were done on purpose to keep Thomas spinning like a hung corpse in the wind. Either way, the man was ill. If anyone could set him to right, it would be Gran.

Leaving the stable, Thomas entered the tower and took the stairs two at a time. Once again, he found Ma Audrey sitting by the hearth with Cecilia. They all greeted him warmly, but he was not in the mood for pleasantries.

"Where is Marcas?" he asked.

Ma Audrey stood, her needlework dropping to the floor. "He is upstairs."

The hollow look in her eyes sent a shiver up his spine.

"I meant to tell you right away, but I was so jubilant you had returned I wanted to hang on to that joy a little bit longer." Her fingers shook, and a tight, grim line captured her lips.

Thomas held up a hand, hoping to ward off any evil she would utter next. Without a word, he turned and headed straight for the stairs, not stopping until he reached the top floor. His hand froze above the latch. The last time he had entered this chamber, his father was dying. What would he find now? Taking a deep breath, Thomas opened the door.

Within, his brother lay prostrate on the bed with Anne at his side. Her eyes glistened in the candlelight. Anne's mouth gaped as she glanced at him. "Thomas, come quick. I fear he is dying. Though I do not know of what."

CHAPTER 14

Thomas rushed to his brother's side and beheld his ashen face. The Marcas he remembered had vanished, and now all that remained was an emaciated body. Flesh covering bones. Gone was his muscle and sinew. How could this be? His brother was only two and twenty. He should be strong and virile, chasing maids around the tower, drinking ale at the nearby tavern, and riding the marches with vigor. Yet he lay groaning and thrashing on a bed.

Thoughts of their father withering on his deathbed squeezed the air out of Thomas's lungs. He noticed his father's large seal ring on Marcas's skeletal finger. Could his brother suffer from the same malady? "Marcas," Thomas whispered, taking his brother's cold hand in his. "It's me. Thomas. Do ye not hear me, lad?"

A soft, aching moan slipped from Marcas's lips before his purplish-rimmed eyes fluttered open. He tried to lift his head, but he did not have the strength. "Thomas." His threaded voice tore Thomas's heart asunder.

He glanced at Anne. "Is there naught we can do?"

"I am not a healer," she said with woeful eyes.

Gran. Gran would know what to do.

A flutter of footsteps drew his attention to the door. Ma Audrey and Cecilia entered the room. "Where is Gran?" he asked the pair.

At first, they remained mute, turning to each other like mindless fools. Finally, Ma Audrey came to his side. Her lips trembled as the truth transformed her face.

Thomas dropped his brother's hand and placed his hands on Ma Audrey's shoulders. "Where is Gran?" he shouted. "She can help Marcas."

Ma Audrey shook her head as tears ran down her cheeks. "Oh, Thomas, she died six months past." She paused and shook her head. "I wanted to tell you . . . but Marcas listened to . . ." Her gaze drifted to Cecilia. "But others did not hold my thinking. In the end, the decision was made not to tell you."

Cecilia took a deep breath and stood as tall as possible, towering over Ma Audrey. "'Twas my husband's wishes not mine."

Thomas was beginning to see what caused the rift between the two women, but their woes did not concern him now.

Gran was dead.

The chamber turned into a hollow tomb, Ma Audrey's voice echoing off the stone wall. Thomas squeezed her shoulders, hoping he could make her words change. She crumpled into a weeping mess. He drew her into his arms and tightened the embrace, kissing her temple. "It's all right. Everything will be all right."

As if the will of every demon vied for his attention, Cecilia drew his gaze with her steady stare. "Marcas needs his medicine. It is the only thing that gives him relief." She rushed to a nearby table and grabbed a small jar. "This will help him." Slowly, she came to the side of the bed.

Thomas released Ma Audrey, noticing the fear in her eyes. The look propelled him to smack the jar out of Cecilia's hand. The pottery smashed into pieces when it hit the floor.

Cecilia glared at him and backed away. "Look what you did."

"What poison are you giving him?" Thomas spat.

"Poison! I have no cause to poison my husband." She bent down and began picking up the broken pieces. "Leave us as you did before. You're nothing but a coward who deserted his family."

The rage that had driven him to lash out vanished. Is this what his family thought of him, a coward? Thomas took in the features of Ma Audrey. Nay, she did not think so, but she knew the truth of his birth.

Anne's gaze held questions but no condemnation.

Thomas brushed a hand through his hair, looking toward his brother once again. Did Marcas believe such? A deep, dark hole grew in Thomas's heart. He had left them when they needed him most.

But not now. "I'll not leave until I know what ails my brother. We may not be of the same flesh, but we are of the same heart." He knelt down next to the bed on the opposite side from Anne. "Is there naught we can do for him?"

"If his wounds were external, I might know, but this . . ." She shook head. "Perhaps a warm broth. If we can get it between his lips."

Ma Audrey stepped to the edge of the bed. "He fell ill not long after Gran died. At first, I thought it was just melancholy because of her death. They were so close." Her gaze then slid to Cecilia who quickly scooped up the broken pieces. "But then I wondered if it was something else."

So Ma Audrey believed Cecilia held some blame. Smashing the pottery could have destroyed any evidence. Unless the pottery still held some proof of the poison.

Thomas rose to his feet. "Stop, Lady Cecilia."

She looked up at him with venom in her eyes. "Would you like me to throw the piece back on the floor so poor Marcas can cut his feet if he chooses to rise?"

Rise! The lad could hardly lift his head. "Place the pieces on the table. I will see to them myself."

Cecilia paused, but she did not follow his orders. She looked to Ma Audrey but found no support. The young woman's gaze narrowed, and her jaw tightened. She rose to her feet and dropped the pieces on the floor. "Fine. You take care of the mess you made." She then gave them her back. Like a regal princess, she strode from the room.

Thomas turned to Ma Audrey. "Tell me truthfully, is she poisoning him?"

"I do not know." Ma Audrey moved to place a hand on Marcas's brow. "The jar does not contain a poison, or at least that is what the old cottar healer from the local village said, but Cecilia may have skills beyond what is known in the region."

"How long have they been married?" Thomas asked, suspicion nibbling at his mind.

"A year within a fortnight. She quickly pushed her father to seek the marriage. Some say your uncle Jaxon Armstrong was seeking her hand as well."

"Jaxon! He is old enough to be Cecilia's father. No wonder she dashed into the marriage, but what about Marcas, did he want the marriage as well?"

"Aye, he was enamored with her. They seemed happy. I should have listened to Blair. She seems to see things other do not. She said Cecilia would bring no good to this family." Ma Audrey pulled her hand from Marcas's forehead. "Though I do not understand, what could Cecilia gain by poisoning Marcas? She isn't with child. She would have no hold on this keep."

An excellent point. A widow with no child would have no say on her dead husband's estate.

There were many questions that needed answers, and he was certain he would not find them here now that Gran was dead. Thomas walked over to the smashed jar and lifted a broken piece to his nose. It had a familiar smell like one of the potions Gran used when an illness took hold of the household. His old nurse, Hetta, used it to, but she was long gone. Died when he was twelve summers old. She had been a part of their household forever except for a brief time when she lived with the Maxwells.

"Does Rory Maxwell still live?" Thomas asked Ma Audrey.

"As far as I know. Though I have heard his health has been failing." She cocked her head to the side. "Why do you ask?"

Thomas knelt down and began to pick up the pieces. "I need a small bag." His gaze searched the room until it locked on a leather pouch. He rushed forward and dumped the contents onto the desk, then placed the pottery within the bag.

"What are you planning to do?" Ma Audrey asked, her voice full of concern.

"I'm going to find out the truth. I will be leaving for the night." He looked to Anne. "I want you and Blair to keep an eye on Marcas at all times. Do not let Cecilia give him anything."

Ma Audrey grabbed his arm. "You can't leave. Your brother needs you."

At first the wild notion to shout that he was not his brother swept over Thomas, but then an act of birth did not change the fact that Thomas did love Marcas as if he they were blood family.

Anne rose and came to Thomas's side and placed a tender hand on his forearm. "We will take good care of him."

Her firm touch soothed his ire and rallied his determination. Anne would guard and watch over his brother as if he were her own kin. Thomas wanted to give her a hug, but he didn't want Ma Audrey to get the wrong impression. Instead, he gave a tight nod. "I leave him to your care."

Over Ma Audrey's protests, Thomas strode from the room and exited the keep. He entered the stable to find Santos stretched out on a bale of hay. "I did not expect to see you so soon, my friend."

There were many things Thomas thought to call Santos, but friend was not one of them. "Get up. We are leaving."

The merchant rose. "Tonight? What is the urgency? Has an evening with too many women forced you to flee?" Santos was too sharp for his own good.

"Nay, my brother is ill, and no one seems to know why." Thomas paused. "You *dinnae* have a healer's skill, do you?"

Dusting off his hat, Santos shook his head. "My wife was the healer, but alas, she is not here." He coughed, wiping his perspiring brow.

Clearly, she must be dead for Santos sputtered and coughed more than an obstinate mule. His wheezing grew on their way to Scotland. Another more appealing thought sat in Thomas's mind. Unless there was no love in their marriage and Santos's wife wished him dead. After all, he claimed to have come to Scotland to find an old love. Whatever the truth, now was not the time to worry about Santos. His ailments weren't as severe as poor Marcas's.

Thomas began saddling up his horse. "Then we better be going for it is unsafe to ride the marches alone." Nor would he leave Santos with the women. Though possibly Cecilia would finish him off, saving Thomas another problem.

"But of course," Santos said smoothly. "We would not want anything to happen to you on your journey . . . where?"

The older man could not be fooled, but it didn't matter. Hopefully, word had not reached far that Warring Tower's laird had fallen ill. Such news always brought trouble. Thomas looked up at the battlements. There were enough men on guard to keep all within safe. "We ride to Maxwell land. I need to speak to its laird."

Blair offered to watch over Marcas but promised to call for Anne and Lady Audrey if there were notable changes in his condition.

They proceeded to the hall where they found Cecilia drinking heavily with a few of Warring Tower's moss-troopers.

"Is this common practice for her?" Anne asked Lady Audrey while they sat near the hearth.

"Only when she is upset, which seems to be often lately." Lady Audrey's shoulders sagged. "Their marriage was forged on lust, not on love, and fear of her being married off to an aged laird. Once the passion died, resentment took hold. Then Marcas fell ill."

If this were true, and Marcas was indeed poisoned, then Cecilia would seem to be the guilty party. Anne watched Cecilia laugh and giggle with the moss-troopers. Did she cuckold Marcas with one of these men? Most looked to be twice her age, nor did she favor one over another. She seemed more interested in the drink they offered than the men themselves. The young lady might only be trying to drown her sad life in a mug of ale.

Anne turned back to Lady Audrey. The woman spoke impeccable English, and she held herself as if she perched on a throne in a royal court. "You were not born in these parts, were you?"

Lady Audrey chuckled. "No indeed. I hail from London and was sent here, believe it or not, by Queen Elizabeth to spy on Gavin Armstrong of Warring."

"Your husband?" Anne gasped. She placed a hand to her lips. "Forgive me."

The wrinkles on Lady Audrey's face smoothed. "We did not start out as allies, but adversity bloomed into love." Her gaze became misty. "We had ten beautiful years together. Thomas and Marcas are not my natural children. Marcas was born to Gavin and his first wife. And Thomas . . . he is quite special."

Quite special? What did she mean? Had he not said earlier they were not of the same flesh? Was he a bastard? That would explain why a first son did not inherit. Were they alike, both illegitimate? Had he not once said Anne might be better off going back to Tretower Court? Did he believe a loving family would be waiting if she returned?

She gave herself a mental shake. Nay, if her so-called family wanted her back, it was for their profit not her own. Anne remembered the night her "good aunt" dragged her to the kitchen and handed her over to Roland. Her aunt's words stung. *"Her father is dead. No reason to keep the whelp now. She's yours to do with as you wish."* Pain dug a hole in Anne's heart.

But Thomas's family accepted him as one of their own. Then

why would he leave? Could he not rejoice in his brother being laird over him? If that were the case, then he would not care if Marcas was dying, but Thomas had been thoroughly distressed. Oh, there were so many questions that had no answers, but she had no right to pry into this family's affairs. Her own affairs were hidden under lock and key.

Realizing Lady Audrey had not stopped talking, Anne tried to focus. Certainly the tale from spy to lady of the keep was an interesting one.

"I was pregnant once but lost the child." Lady Audrey gave a heavy sigh. "I carried the child in my womb for about four months. Marcas was about twelve, and Thomas ten and eight." A deep sorrow floated in Lady Audrey's eyes. "No one knew I was pregnant."

"Not even your husband?" How awful to lose a child, but to grieve alone? That didn't seem right.

"Nay, he died before I had a chance to tell him. Another sorrow I carry deep within." Cecilia let out a bawdy laugh, and Lady Audrey frowned. "We should pull her away from that bunch. She is well into her cups."

The frail Lady Audrey wouldn't be pulling anyone anywhere. She had suffered enough for one lifetime. Anne rose. "I shall help her. Perhaps we can place her in the room you have given me since she can't be near Marcas."

"Good heavens no. I will sleep on the small pallet in Marcas's chamber. The one Cecilia had been using. We shall put her in my room. She has had an eye on it ever since Marcas has fallen ill. One night in my chamber will make her think she has gone to heaven." Lady Audrey rose to stand next to Anne. "I hope she wakes with a devil of a headache."

Anne had to censure a smile. How she wished she had a

stepmother like Lady Audrey—fast witted, full of warmth, and a dash of humor.

The pair, with the help of one of a moss-troopers, managed to get Cecilia to Lady Audrey's chamber. The room was spacious and decorated with tapestries and needlepoint pillows. The bed was not what Anne expected. Large, it looked to be something you would see at a palace. It did not fit with the other simple furnishings in the room. Two modest chairs sat next to an iron brazier. At the foot of the bed lay an exquisite yet frayed exotic rug. On a corner table below the arrowslit window sat an inkwell and a piece of parchment, giving truth that Lady Audrey was an educated woman.

"I know what you are thinking," she said as she helped undress her daughter-in-law. "This room is a mass of contradictions. The ornate bed was Lady Francis's who Thomas calls Gran. So is the rug. This used to be her room."

A Scottish grandmother had such elaborate furnishings?

"She was English too." Lady Audrey covered Cecilia and made her way to the door.

Anne followed close behind. "There seems to be more English blood in this tower than Scottish."

Lady Audrey let out a snort. "So true. The rest of Gran's things are in the cells below. I should have given them to the poor, but I could not bear to let them go."

An idea pricked Anne's mind. "Gran was a healer, right?"

Lady Audrey nodded. "Indeed. Many from all over would come and seek her care and wisdom." A sadness crept into Lady Audrey's eyes. "But she could not save her own son's life. It bothered her fiercely. She would scour her apothecary book from morn to night looking for the answer to what killed Gavin."

"Could her book be down in there?" Anne asked.

Lady Audrey placed both hands on her back and rubbed. "It is not. We have searched her things many times over. There is nothing. Not even in her trunk's secret compartment."

They entered the hall to find that most of the servants and some moss-troopers had retired to their own homes or found comfortable corners to rest. Anne sent up a prayer that she would not be sleeping there this eve.

"Perhaps someone else took the book?" Anne said, not wanting to give up on finding something that would help Marcas.

"We have often thought Cecilia may have taken it. She was always lingering around Gran's chamber. But we have searched her things when she was as you see her tonight." Lady Audrey shook her head. "We found nothing." She yawned.

Anne held out her hand to the older woman. "Methinks you should rest, my lady. As far as the apothecary book, only God knows where it may be. I shall pray it will be found."

Lady Audrey's dark eyes grew wide. She squeezed Anne's hand. "That's it. That is where the book is." The older woman rushed away with Anne quick on her heels. They entered a small, musty chapel that held a simple stone altar. "I should have known she would hide her book there."

With quick steps, Lady Audrey went to the back of the altar and removed a weathered stone to reveal a small compartment. With a gasp, she reached in and pulled out a small book folded in half. A bright glow lit her dark eyes. "This is it! Gran knew Thomas would return and search his old hiding places. She wanted him to have her most precious possession."

Lady Audrey handed the worn book to Anne. Carefully, she unfolded it. The book was full of words and drawings and possibly the key to unlock what ailed Marcas. Anne handed the book back to Lady Audrey. "I hope you find the answer within. I shall help you if you wish, but my skills with the written word are limited."

Lady Audrey covered Anne's hand with hers. A hopeful smile filled her face. "While we search the pages, I shall teach you the words. Together we will find the answer and petition God that it is not too late."

CHAPTER 15

The grand Maxwell fortress had not changed since Thomas was a youth. Three times the size of Warring Tower, Maxwell's keep had always been the finest in the lowlands. The bright torches illuminated the heavily guarded ramparts, and his iron gate was impossible to penetrate.

Santos fidgeted in his saddle. "I am hoping this man is a friend of yours."

"The old laird, aye. His son . . . well, let us say we have had our differences." Thomas guided his horse closer to the stone fortress and looked up to the guard. "I am Thomas Armstrong come to see Laird Rory Maxwell." Years ago, the simple pronouncement would gain him entry. A chill tore at his back. However, time had its way of changing many things.

No answer came over the high stone wall. Thomas sat patiently. Rory Maxwell's rutty, scarred face popped up over the battlements. "Is that truly you?"

The old man's rugged features drew the past close. "Aye, Laird, 'tis Thomas come home at last." A squabble could be heard before the gate opened allowing Thomas and Santos entry.

He had barely dismounted and handed off the reins of his horse to Santos when an out of breath old man came running toward them. In some ways, Rory Maxwell looked the same; in other ways, he was quite different. The long, jagged scar still ran from his brow to his cleft chin. Now grooved by many wrinkles, the scar did not seem as ominous as when Thomas was a lad. His eyes were still brown but watery and rimmed with dark circles. His body held some girth, but his shoulders were round and his back humped. The bear of a man was gone, and all that remained was an aged goat. Nonetheless, he was the closest thing Thomas had to a *grandda*.

The elder gave the younger a hearty hug. "I heard you had returned. Me men said ye were riding the marches. I thought it to be a fairy's tale, but now I see it is true." Rory stretched out his arms to have a better look at Thomas. "It seems ye have grown a little more around the middle." A robust laugh left the older man's lips before it turned into a laborious wheeze.

"I shall leave you to get reacquainted, *meu senhor*. I shall see to the horses." Santos gave a quick nod in Thomas's direction and then followed the groomsmen to the stable.

Thomas affectionately squeezed Rory's shoulder. "I had heard ye were ill, but here ye are standing before me." He let his Scottish brogue have full reign on his tongue.

"Aye, 'tis so. Me heart all but gave out when I heard me Francis left this earth."

He spoke of Gran. Rory Maxwell had always had a deep affection for her. Their friendship blossoming after Thomas's *da* and Ma Audrey married. However, a friendship it remained, it never became more as far as Thomas knew. Yet they seemed to share many secrets, which were now dead with Gran.

"I miss her too. Had I known she was in ill health, I would have come home earlier," Thomas lamented, wishing he had given up on his stubbornness and anger long ago.

"There is the thing, she never was ill. She just gave up the ghost and went to meet her maker." His gaze became distant. "Such is the life of the old."

"Well, well, well, the prodigal son has returned." Out of the shadows of the courtyard stepped Ewart Maxwell, Rory's son. His once red hair and beard now sprinkled with grey. A rotund gut all but hid his scrawny legs, and his bulbous nose told of his nefarious drinking habits.

"Eventide to you, Ewart." Thomas tipped his hat in greeting. He grinned, tamping down the glee he realized from goading his old foe.

The grind of Ewart's teeth could be heard even though they stood a good four hands apart. Being older, Ewart never enjoyed the familiar use of his name by a younger lad.

"The whelp has finally come home." Ewart strolled around Thomas as if he were inspecting a prize pig. "Come to challenge your brother for that broken-down keep?"

"Shut yer mouth, Ewart," Rory bristled. "Why ye always have to shove a hot stick into things?"

Ewart wrinkled his nose. "I care not for these Armstrongs and miss the days when ye hated them as well." He pulled on a pair of riding gloves. "But worry not, *Da*. While ye entertain this dreg, I will be on the marches, making sure no more of his kind ride our lands."

The younger Maxwell showed his back and headed toward the stables. If Ewart's tongue remained bristle, Santos might take offense and cut it out. Thomas readied to follow, but Rory held fast to Thomas's arm.

"Let's venture inside. There is a mite of a wind out here," the old man pleaded. The laird might be aged, but he was still wise. Better not to poke a snake.

"Aye, 'tis a strong wind. We can talk within." With slow steps to keep pace with Rory's shuffle, Thomas helped the matured man into the keep. The hall was dim and dreary and not as clean and grand as he remembered. Only a few servants scampered about while many moss-troopers watched them with keen eyes. The shine of their swords and dirks sent a strong warning. Ma Audrey had said they were in a time of peace, but this room made Thomas think of war.

They took a seat at a long table where two mugs of ale were placed before them. "Are you gearing up for a fight?" Thomas watched the sorrow and exhaustion pass across Rory's visage.

"Nay. 'Tis Ewart's doing." The older laird took a drink. "When I took to me bed after hearing about Francis, the buffoon panicked and hired these men. Like we can afford to feed all these mouths."

Indeed, they could, but Rory Maxwell was never one to throw away his coin needlessly.

The old man took another healthy drink of ale and then shook his head. "Yer *da widnae* have done such a stupid thing."

There stood the rod that had driven Ewart's hatred. Rory Maxwell had constantly compared the shortcomings of his son to Gavin Armstrong. Obviously, the comparing had not ended once Gavin had died. Ewart's deficiencies remained cast in iron to the ghost of Gavin Armstrong.

Thomas pushed his ale away. "As much as I would like to talk about old times with you, I have come here for a reason."

"Figured ye had since ye come at such a late hour." The elder rubbed a veined hand over his beard. "Out with it."

"Marcas is ill."

Rory Maxwell's eyes widened. With the speed of a youth, he grabbed Thomas's arm. "What ails him?"

"We are not sure. Since Gran's death, we *dinnae* have a healer. That is why I am here. Hetta always said you had the finest healers in the land."

"Aye, we did." Rory Maxwell slammed his hands on the table. "But that was long ago. Hetta is long dead, and those who came after her are not worth a man's spit."

His fingers began to drum the table rapidly as if the motion could trigger the needed help. The fast beating eased, and the older man lifted a finger.

"Ewart sent for a crone when I was low. I am not sure she can help as I am sure I healed meself. Yet, ye are welcome to her. Mind ye, she is old, and ye'll need a cart." Rory paused and shouted to one of the servants. "Tell the stable master we will need a cart ready in the morn."

A wave of relief washed over Thomas, an old healer would surely know if Marcas was poisoned or not. "I am in your debt. I will return her as soon as possible."

"Worry not about it." The old man drained his mug and slammed it on the table, calling for another. "We shall set off at first light."

"We?" As if punched, a cramp formed in the middle of Thomas's gut.

"Aye, I'll be goin' with ye. Marcas is like my grandson. I'll not rest easy until the lad is healthy again."

And there was the other reason Ewart Maxwell hated the Armstrongs.

The next morn, Anne sat on her bed with the apothecary book on her lap. Some of the words were easy to figure out, while others were strange and foreign. Luckily, there were many pictures that helped explain the various potions, poultices, and treatments. She'd do anything to help the brother that Thomas clearly loved. In truth, she would do anything to make him smile. No longer was she interested in censuring his wayward habits. For in reality, since they started their travels north, he did nothing to warrant her censure. He had been polite and cordial, seeking to her every need. At other times, he fell deep into thought.

What then was this turn of events that made him more somber and caring? How she wished she knew. Maybe he had found a new opponent to occupy his worry. 'Twas obvious he did not trust Antonio Santos. Yet often Thomas did the merchant's bidding. He claimed it was to earn the cross back, but the words rang false. Not once did his eyes gaze at the chain Santos wore around his neck. Thomas, the former scoundrel, was turning out to be a complex man.

With a heavy sigh, Anne turned her attention back to the book. She must focus on the task at hand, the healing of Marcas, not the conduct of his handsome brother. Her heart quickened. What would it be like to snuggle in Thomas's embrace, his eyes beholding her lips with passion?

The book fell from her fingers. Those wanton thoughts could not be tolerated. She rose and hid the apothecary book in the bottom of the trunk across from her bed. She brushed out her dress, admiring the soft blue color. Did Thomas like the look of her figure in this fine dress? Her hands stilled. *Get behind me, Satan.*

With quick steps, she made for the door. She needed to go to the chapel to pray. She could not lose her heart to a man who was frivolous and chasing . . . what?

Her feet stalled on the stone stairs. He did not wish to go to the Malabar Coast because he was a merchant, he wanted to go there for some other reason. She tapped her foot on the step. What drove him away from his family? What made him put up stone ramparts around his heart?

She continued her descent and hurried into the chapel, relieved to find it empty. She fell to her knees in front of the weathered wooden cross and clasped her palms together. "Dear Lord, you know all things. Your wisdom is greater than any man's. You have brought me here for a reason. If it be thy will, give me the understanding to find a cure for Marcas. Lord, heal Thomas's soul for I know he hides his pain behind a rogue's mask. Send me the answers so that I can help them heal. I ask all this in your Son's name. Amen."

The prayer had barely left her lips when a flurry of voices filled the hall. Anne strained to listen but could not make out a single word. She rose to her feet and crept out of the chapel and peered into the hallway. Her breath caught in her throat at the sight.

Next to Thomas stood an old man stooped and bent. His unwashed grey hair framed a face only the devil could have created. A scar stretched across his left cheek from forehead to chin. His muddy brown eyes settled on her. With great effort, he straightened his shoulders and began to shuffle forward.

"Well, well. What do we have here?" the demon asked with a gravelly voice.

Her throat all but closed as her stomach grew tight. She stepped back.

"Laird Rory Maxwell, let me present Widow Anne Howell." Thomas strode to her side, and with a reassuring smile, he gently guided her toward the beast.

"Widow ye say." His murky eyes twinkled with mischief. "Would she be lookin' for a new husband? If so, I might be tempted."

The demon cackled while Anne fought the urge to run back into the chapel, bolt the door, and vomit.

CHAPTER 16

Anne jerked back, and Thomas swiftly put his hand on her lower back. Was this the reason he had been so kind to her on their trip to Scotland? Her temples began to pound as her thoughts spun deeper horrors. Might this be where Roland and Carlton wanted her to be all along? Were Thomas and Santos in league with them? Had the pair outwitted all the others? She was a fool to trust them. She should keep her wits in case she needed to flee.

Behind the old man stood an equally old woman in soiled, tattered clothing, clutching a leather bag to her breast. She leered at Anne with milky eyes and a toothless grin.

Thomas's hand slid from Anne's back. He clasped his fingers firmly around hers. "Widow Howell is a guest in our home. Please treat her with the same respect you would give Ma Audrey."

Her shoulders relaxed a smidge. His strong words and firm touch gave her a bit of relief.

Laird Maxwell's gaze began to dart around the hall. "Where be the lady? I hope she is well?"

The turn of his attention quelled Anne's earlier apprehension. 'Tis possible her mind went galloping wild for no reason. Yet another peek at the woman sent a shiver down her spine.

Thomas turned to Anne. "Worry not, he is all bluster and no bite. Behind him is Healer Tibbie. I have brought her to see Marcas."

Anne exhaled as her heartbeat slowed. Thomas had not been in league with her stepfather.

"Lady Audrey is resting as she was at Marcas's bedside all night." Blair stomped into the hall and skewered Laird Maxwell with a wary eye. "I hope you *didnae* bring yer son with ye."

A grainy laugh left the older man's lips. "Ye lookin' for him, lass?"

"Ye know better than that." Blair placed her hands on her hips. "He's a cur with no soul, but I'm not tellin' ye anything ye *dinnae* know already."

Though Laird Maxwell hooted again, there was no mistaking the wound that lingered in his gaze. The son must be a disappointment to his father. Even worse, everyone seemed to know it. Her heart ached a little for his son. She knew what it felt like to be a disappointment. To be unwanted and unloved.

"If you are here and Ma Audrey is in bed, then who is with Marcas?" Thomas's eyes darted around the room; obviously, he was looking for Cecilia.

A hint of fear entered the servant's eyes. "I have my duties in the hall and the kitchens. I searched for Anne earlier but *couldnae* find her. 'Tis her turn to watch over him." Blair's quick retort rolled easily from her lips and set the guilt at Anne's feet. "I left him with another servant."

And now it seemed she was disappointing those at Warring Tower. "I shall go to him forthwith." Anne tried to pull free from Thomas's grasp, but he held her firm.

"Nay. Laird Maxwell's healer will see to him." His stormy gaze locked with Blair's.

Laird Maxwell plowed through all of them and headed toward the steps with more exuberance than expected for a man of his age. "Let me see the lad. No doubt ye all have bungled things up."

The healer mutely followed, casting a shifty glance first at Blair and then at Anne.

"Come with us," Thomas said softly to Anne. "Your honesty on Marcas's situation will be appreciated." Bleary-eyed and weary from lack of sleep, Thomas looked to Anne for judgment. Why was her opinion important to him? Did he not trust that healer? Surely the woman had more experience with potions and cures.

He trusts me. A warm satisfaction coursed through Anne. She was wanted and needed. Thomas treated her as if she had value. "I will try my best, but remember, I am no healer."

The moment the healer entered Marcas's chamber, she pushed away the servant and ordered Anne to find a cover for the narrow window that gave only a smidge of sunlight to the room. "The sickness can sense the light."

Her words sounded foolish, but Anne followed the old healer's instructions before lighting a few more tallows.

Laird Maxwell sank down on a chair near the side of the bed, ignoring the healer's complaints. "How be ye, lad?" he asked Marcas, who let out a groan in answer. His eyes were closed, and perspiration covered his head. "Ye *cannae* die. I *cannae* lose ye too."

Touched by what she saw, Anne still wondered who else the old laird had lost. Thomas stood sentinel near the door, his gaze keen on the healer.

The old woman walked around to the other side of the bed and bent over Marcas and sniffed. "*Cannae* smell any poison."

She raised his eyelids. "His eyes are rolled back." She looked to Thomas. "What's he been takin' other than that potion in that broken jar ye showed me?"

"Nothing to my knowledge."

The healer harrumphed and turned back to her patient and then rummaged in her bag. She pulled out a grimy knife. "Get me a bowl. If he be sick, a little bleeding might set him right. If he be poisoned, it will have little effect on him."

Immediately, the servant left to seek out a bowl.

Anne covered her mouth with a hand. She had seen bleedings in the past, and often it would send the ill to the next life. Then again, she did know a few who had recovered after such a practice. The servant quickly returned with a wooden bowl and a clean cloth. The healer adjusted Marcas's arm over the bowl, looking for the right place to cut him. With an eerie leer, the old woman slid her tongue out of the side of her mouth as she readied the knife.

"Stop," cried Anne.

Healer Tibbie paused. A cold, condemning censure entered her gaze. "Hush, girl, me hand could have slipped, and I could have cut him clean through."

Besides the old healer, two other sets of stony eyes glared at her. Laird Maxwell and Thomas did not approve of her interference. Marcas's labored breathing wore through the silence.

"I have heard the new practice is to clean the knife before using to ward off the evil spirits," Anne implored. The excuse was foolish, but without being able to read the words that accompanied the pictures in the apothecary book, the explanation would have to serve.

A puff of air left the healer's lips. "'Tis nonsense." She held up the jagged, filthy knife. "This tool has served me well over the years."

And how many have died from its use? Anne sucked in her breath and sent up a quick prayer. *Please, Lord, intercede.*

Turning back to Marcas, the healer felt for the right place on his arm. A feverish glint glowed in her eyes. Again, her tongue slid out of the side of her mouth.

"Halt!" This time the cry came from Thomas. "Best we listen to Widow Howell and clean the knife. We *dinnae* want an evil spirit to enter Marcas." He stepped forward and took the dagger from the healer's hand and held it out to Anne. "See that this is cleaned properly."

The Lord did hear her feeble prayer. With a quick nod, Anne raced from the chamber, down the stairs, and into the kitchens. There she found the cook with an equally dirty hatchet chopping heads off chickens on a blood-soaked table. A putrid order of guts and dung hung in the air. Gad, no wonder Marcas was sick and Lady Audrey looked so pale.

The cook slammed the cleaver into the wood when he saw Anne standing in the doorway with hands over her nose and mouth. "Quit ye gaggin' or spill yer guts in the yard if ye goin' to be sick."

Anne tried to breathe in the fragrance from her bathed and perfumed hands. Nothing that was happening before her was new. Nor was she unfamiliar with dirt. Had not Roland's kitchen been just as revolting before she scrubbed it clean? She lowered her hands and stood erect. "I need to clean this knife. I need boiling water, quickly."

"Hey? Ye come here to order me about? I only take me orders from Lady Cecilia." The cook wiped his bloody hands on his soiled apron.

"This order comes from Laird Warring's brother, Master Thomas. If you do not believe me, then go and ask him yourself, but do not blame me if he chastises you for wasting time while Laird Marcas's healer is delayed."

Pondering her words briefly, the cook nodded, no doubt realizing that if Marcas died, Thomas would become the new laird of the keep. On the cook's call, a young maid appeared in the doorway and quickly stoked the fire in the kitchen's hearth. A pot of water was placed above the flame. Anne took the knife and held it to the flame before dropping it into the water.

The maid looked at Anne as if she was daft. Anne raised a finger. "You shall see, much of the grime will come off. Find me a clean cloth to remove what remains."

The maid scurried away and returned just as the water started to bubble in the pot. Bits of grime and dirt floated in the once clear water. "Well, I *widnae* believe it if I *hadnae* seen it with me own eyes," she called to the cook, who looked into the pot and grunted.

When the blade looked fairly clean, Anne drained some of the hot water onto the dirt floor, she then took the clean cloth and reached into the pot, grabbing the dagger. Quickly, she wiped off the knife before hurrying back to the laird's chamber. Testing to make sure the blade was not too hot, she held out the clean blade to Tibbie who huffed before jabbing the tip into Marcas's arm.

Anne didn't know if the cleansing would truly help, but it couldn't hurt either. *God, let this work. Give Marcas complete healing.* Hopefully, the Almighty heard her prayer for Marcas did not look long for this earth.

Later that day, Anne sat in her room trying to figure out the words in the apothecary book. Lady Audrey had planned to come by, but her other duties had kept her so busy, and she tired easily.

A swift knock interrupted Anne's study. The latch slipped open, and there stood Thomas. "I wish to have a word with you."

With nimble fingers, Anne tried to hide the apothecary journal under her bedding. Lady Audrey did not mind that she possessed it, but Thomas might have a different opinion. After all, the book was found in his old hiding place. "Oh, come in. I pray that your brother is feeling better."

Thomas frowned and rubbed a hand through his unruly russet hair. "He is much the same. I fear the healer has come too late."

"Then we shall have to pray all the more." Her heart drumming, Anne glanced at her coverlet to make sure the book was well hidden. She quickly stood as Thomas approached the bed.

"If you think that will help." His gaze dropped to the coverlet as he shrunk the distance between them. His warm breath teased her cheek and neck. "You know, I *dinnae* believe the Almighty gives us a second thought. We are but playthings for his amusement."

She placed a hand on her throat to shield herself from the pleasant balm. "Of course, I have to disagree. God is always with us. Helping. 'Tis man that refuses to see."

He touched a wayward strand of her hair and tucked it behind her ear. "And pray, what *dinnae* I see?"

His nearness clogged her throat, and her head started to spin. She took a deep breath, trying to clear her senses. "His goodness and his protection. He saved you from the sea while others perished. In my heart, I believe you have been saved many a time, but you do not see it."

Thomas shrugged, then took her hands in his. "I *didnae* come here to talk about God, I came here to thank thee."

"Thank me?" He rubbed his thumbs over her knuckles, and her knees began to quake.

"Aye. I have seen the method of cleaning healing tools before. By someone very dear to me. I *dinnae* know why I *didnae* think of it earlier."

"Oh," Anne squawked, her gaze dropping to the bed.

With lightning speed, Thomas dropped her hands and flipped the coverlet. The apothecary book lay exposed like an army with an open flank. He picked up the book and started to flip through the pages. "I knew you were hiding something . . . Where did you find this?"

"I found it with Lady Audrey. In the chapel behind some loose stone." She began to rub her upper arms. "We were going to go through it together, but she has been busy and . . ."

Thomas studied the book. Anne could not tell if he was happy or angry with her. "Gran must have left it there for me to find." He looked up, his eyes full of bewilderment. "She must have known I would always return. Have you found anything that would help Marcas?"

A shameful heat coursed through her body. She took a thick swallow. "I had some education when I was little, but I cannot read all the words."

His gaze met hers. He looked intrigued, like he held a palm of valuable jewels. His cheek twitched. "Would you like to learn?" His tone held a note of truthfulness.

Anne dropped her chin to her chest. "Aye, but Lady Audrey is occupied elsewhere."

Thomas placed the book in her hand. "I will teach you to read this and other things as well. Together we will solve what ails Marcas."

If she had wings, she would be soaring with the angels. Thomas offered to teach her to read. He was willing to spend time with her when there clearly were more pressing problems at hand. "All right. If it will not take all your time. When?"

"Why, now." He sat down and patted the bed. She gingerly sat down next to him, hoping he did not hear the drumming of her heart. He flipped open the first page. His gentle fingers briefly touched hers. "Can you read any of these words?"

Anne tried to focus even as his earthy scent invaded her senses. She scanned the page. "The, a, can, be, sm-all, and k-kn . . ." She lifted her head and shrugged one shoulder. "That is all."

"That was very good." He pointed to the page again. "This says, 'a small knife can be a healer's best tool.' Now you try."

She mimicked him and pointed to each word.

"That was beautiful."

Anne warmed, relishing in his praise.

They spent the good part of the afternoon reading through the book. Thomas patiently pointed to every word so she could follow his phrases. By the end of the day, she had learned a few more words but had yet come upon an answer to Marcas's illness.

A knock on the door ended their lesson as Thomas was wanted below. He closed the book and handed it to her. "We shall continue on the morrow."

Anne watched his strong back as he strode to the door. *Thank you, Lord, for placing such a patient, kind man in my life. Please do not let me lose my heart to him for I know there is no future for me here.*

CHAPTER 17

Thomas entered the hall to find Rory Maxwell pacing back and forth. His heavy footsteps stomped the floor like a restless bull. As frail as the man had seemed earlier, the adversity and gravity of Marcas's situation seemed to invigorate him. A true Scotsman dug deep when things looked grim.

"I'm not sure that hag Tibbie knows what she's doin'," he bellowed. "I sat by the lad's bed all day, and there is no change. If anythin', he seems worse not better. All the bleedin'. Bah." He stopped and shot a fist in the direction of the stairs. "I swear, if Marcas dies, I'll have the witch drawn and quartered."

With swift steps, Thomas ushered the old laird to a chair near the hearth. No need to have the old laird rupture the red veins in his neck. "Calm yourself. The last thing you want is to be in her care as well."

"Argh," Rory growled and slammed a fist on the arm of the chair. "Francis would have known what to do."

A warm memory of his Gran flooded Thomas. "Aye, she did have a talent for healing." He signaled to a servant to bring forth a beverage. A spindly lad served up two mugs of small beer.

Laird Maxwell took one sip and spat the drink out onto the

floor. "This retched weak water. Why *cannae* an Armstrong make a proper drink?"

Thomas took a sip to hide his smile. "Not all in these parts can afford fine ale like the Maxwells."

"I'll send over a few more kegs," Rory grumbled. "I'd send over every barrel I had if I thought that would heal the lad."

Thomas held his tankard on one knee. "Drink *widnae* do it, but we have found Gran's apothecary writings."

"Ye have Francis's healing book?" Maxwell straightened in his chair. "Did ye find anythin'?"

"Nay, not yet, but An—Widow Howell is examining it very closely."

"She seems to have more sense than that crone waddling about in Marcas's chamber." Maxwell raised his eyes to the ceiling. "Ye are quite keen on the widow? She is very comely, but can she be trusted? The Welsh are not much better than the English."

Thomas took another drink as he watched the flames pop and crackle in the hearth. "She is devoted to her prayers."

"Ack." Rory Maxwell threw his head back against the chair. "The pope in Rome claims devotion to God, but that *doesnae* make him a trustworthy man. Ask any Reformer."

There lay the problem. This land had seen much blood spilled in the name of one religion or another. When in truth, power and greed were the roots that twisted the vine. "I know not much about her. She saved me after I was shipwrecked off the Welsh coast. Her stepfather is an innkeeper in Newport. A man of poor character who seemed to beat her often."

"Stepfather?" The old mad rubbed a hand on his beard.

"She claims to be a by-blow of some lord at Tretower Court." The flames leapt in the hearth.

Maxwell leaned forward. "Do ye believe that to be true?"

Thomas took one more sip and let the liquid glide down his throat as his mind sailed back to the past events. "Not at first, but it seems her relation is now looking for her." He pulled his gaze from the fire and filled Maxwell in on all that had recently transpired.

The old man shook his head. "I *dinnae* blame the lass for turning her back on a family that threw her away."

Or a family that lied to you. Thomas inwardly grimaced. This was not about him.

"I *widnae* want to go back either." Maxwell leaned back and rubbed his eyes. "A sad tale to be sure, but that *doesnae* answer my question. Do ye trust her?"

The events of the last few weeks marched through Thomas's thoughts. Even though she had run off with his jeweled necklace, he did trust her. More than the Portuguese merchant who had just entered the hall. Thomas's lips thinned. Santos had promised to wait for the right time to give his introduction. Blast the man! But what could one expect from a scoundrel?

From the corner of his eye, Thomas saw Ma Audrey enter the hall. There was no turning back now. He rose to his feet and straightened his doublet. "Excuse me. There is something I need to attend to."

Thomas had not gone far when Ma Audrey stopped short. She clasped her chest, staring at Santos. A weak smile lifted the merchant's cheeks. "Greetings, Audrey."

"Can it be?" Ma Audrey's weak voice floated across the hall. Tears welled in her eyes.

"You know this man?" Thomas asked.

Ma Audrey ran into Santos's arms.

Rory Maxwell rose. "What the devil is goin' on here?"

"I have no idea," Thomas answered. Santos knew Ma Audrey? Was she the maid he lost his heart to? A possessiveness swam in Thomas's gut. He strode over to the couple with his hands fisted, pausing a breath away from them.

"I can't believe it. You said you would come back." Ma Audrey lovingly stroked every line in Santos's face. Then to the surprise of all, she kissed him on his cheek. In turn, the filthy merchant kissed Ma Audrey's brow.

White-hot rage bubbled within Thomas. Who really was this man? Had she known him before coming to Warring Tower? Or did she cuckold his father? *He's not your father*. The dead deserved honor. How dare she. The woman was nothing but a walking bundle of secrets.

"I demand to know what's going on here," Thomas roared.

"Aye. Open yer lips, Audrey, and tell us who this pirate be?" Maxwell added, shuffling to Thomas's side.

Pirate! Thomas took a hard look at the Portuguese merchant, the well-trimmed dark goatee, the studded ruby on his earlobe, the two large gold rings on his left hand. The jeweled cross under his doublet. All the signs were there, except one. Now Santos sported a fine Portuguese *colhona* sword, long and black, designed not to reflect the sunlight or rust when exposed to salt water. Indeed, this man had to be a pirate.

A series of wretched, gravelly coughs exploded from his mouth. Ma Audrey cradled Santos with a look of concern. "Fetch him some water," she cried.

Immediately, Thomas grabbed a pitcher from a servant's hand and held it steady to Santos's lips. The man might hack up his lungs for all Thomas cared, but the villain best not die before explanations were given. "Here. Drink."

Santos clutched the pitcher with shaking fingers and raised his watery dark gaze to Thomas in thanks. When the attack passed, they helped the pirate to a near bench. Ma Audrey sat down next to him and began rubbing his back.

With heavy breaths, Santos gulped for air. He nodded. "My thanks."

Thomas grunted and folded his arms, towering over the rogue. "Out with it, Santos. How do you know Ma Audrey? Is she your lover?"

"Lover!" Ma Audrey shot to her feet. "What would make you think such a vile thing? The only man I have ever known was your father."

"He *wasnae* my *da*." Thomas gritted his teeth.

"Oh, Thomas, after all these years, you still reject us. Why? Have we not always loved you?" Ma Audrey began to sway, the color leaving her cheeks. She placed her palm against her aching forehead before her knees gave way.

"Audrey," Santos cried, coming to his feet.

With speed, Thomas reached out and caught her before she collapsed. His heart raced as her breathing became shallow. "Ma Audrey, Ma Audrey, can you hear me?" He turned and shouted to the servant. "Quick, fetch Tibbie the healer."

Maxwell loomed above them. "I swear the devil must live in this place, for everyone within seems to be cursed."

Under Thomas's order, Ma Audrey was taken to her chamber while Santos and Maxwell stood in the doorway like two lost sheep. Thomas knelt silently by her bed as the old healer lifted Audrey's eyelids and poked around her body. She ended her examination with a sniff. "This one be poisoned for sure."

"Poisoned," all three men said in unison.

"Aye, foxglove, I think." Tibbie took another sniff and then put her ear to Ma Audrey's chest. "Her breath smells fowl, and her heartbeat is slow."

Blair pushed through the two men at the door and rushed to Ma Audrey's bed. "Foxglove! Will she live?"

The healer shrugged. "Depends on how much runs through her body. Most live, but I have a feeling she has had contact with this poison before. I can see it in her eyes, and there be a red rash on the inside of her arm."

"Who would do such a thing? She is kind to all." Blair grabbed her other hand and began to sob.

Who indeed. Thomas gritted his teeth until they ached. What he took as starvation was probably an effect of the poison. What evil lurked in these walls? There was no reason to poison Ma Audrey. Warring Tower belonged to Marcas. Why poison a woman of middling years who did naught but try to make a comfortable home? She was harmless. A chill swept down Thomas's back as Ma Audrey took a ragged breath. She looked too peaceful in her torment.

Tibbie pushed him out of the way and frowned at Blair. "Ye all need to leave. All this weepin' and wailin' is upsettin' Lady Audrey. I'll keep watch over her. I am sure Laird Armstrong is in good hands under the watchful eye of that widow."

Thomas jerked. In all the turmoil, he had forgotten about his brother and Anne. Plus another, where was Cecilia? Being new to the family, she was the reasonable villain in all this mess. Yet, much of this started years ago. The horrific memory of Gavin Armstrong withering and foaming at the mouth stabbed Thomas's heart. Could he have been poisoned too?

"Get yer howlin' servant out of here," Tibbie ordered, breaking Thomas's thoughts.

Gently, he helped Blair to the door where Santos and Maxwell stood like guards at the queen's palace. "Best we wait below."

Santos narrowed his eyes. "How do we know that hag won't finish her off? Not all healers are honorable. I have known some that are happy to help the ill along to the next world."

Maxwell raised a fist to the old healer. "If she dies, so will ye," he pronounced.

Tibbie huffed and gave Maxwell her back. "Get out. All of ye."

Another ragged sob flowed from Blair's throat.

None were thinking with a right mind. "Perhaps we should all go to the chapel and pray. Ma Audrey would want us to do that," Thomas said, surprised at his own words since he had not prayed in ten years.

A black eyebrow shot upward. "Have you found your faith now?" the pirate asked.

"*Dinnae* take to prayin' with a bunch of Reformers. I'm still part of the True Faith," Maxwell added.

Thomas almost laughed. There were many words to describe Maxwell and his faith. Being a good Catholic was not one of them. "I think Ma Audrey would find comfort in such thoughtfulness." Thomas ushered the group out of the room and then tipped his head toward Blair. "I think we would all find solace in talking to God."

Maxwell caught Thomas's meaning and carefully placed a hand on Blair's shoulder. "Come along, lass. Ye need to pray like a good Reformer, and I'll pray as a member of the True Faith; surely the Almighty will hear one of us."

Maxwell and Blair led the way to the chapel. At the door, Thomas stopped. Ten years ago, in this very chapel, he took his anger out on Ma Audrey. Now she lay at death's door. How could he have been so cruel? Why had it taken him so long to return home? Hell did wait for him.

"The woman was like a mother to you. Surely even you can find some words to speak on her behalf," Santos whispered.

A hardness swept into Thomas's heart. He had known two mothers, Ma Audrey and Edlyn Armstrong, and neither were his true *ma*. She was buried in a queen's grave, while the dethroned monarch still roamed this earth. Everywhere he turned there were secrets. Lies and half-truths had a way of destroying everything.

That was it! That had to be why Ma Audrey was poisoned. She knew a secret that someone wanted to keep hidden, but who?

The Portuguese pirate gripped Thomas's shoulder. "Shall we go in?"

Perhaps the old healer had been wrong. Perhaps Ma Audrey had been poisoned recently. Perhaps the would-be killer stood right next to him. Thomas shook off Santos's hand. "Pray tell, just how do you know Ma Audrey, and what do you want from her?"

A look of astonishment filled Santos's gaze. He laughed. "What is your thinking, Armstrong? That I came all the way to Scotland to kill your stepmother?"

"I have seen people go through great lengths to kill for revenge."

Again, Santos let out a nerve-grating howl. "So have I, but I can assure you that is not why I have come."

Thomas stepped closer and pulled out a dirk from his

doublet, placing it against Santos's chest. "I swear to you, if you poisoned Ma Audrey, I will kill you."

The pirate pushed the blade away. "I assure you. I am not the master of this deed, but when we do find who it is, I will cut him or her in two."

"Oh, and why is that?" Thomas ground out, holding his position.

"Because Lady Audrey, your Ma Audrey, is my beloved sister."

CHAPTER 18

Anne leaned forward in her chair, hands clasped tight. Shouting and commotion from the floor below traveled to Marcas's chamber. Lady Audrey was sick as well. To be sure, evil lurked in this keep. Anne desperately wanted to find out what was going on, but she had promised Thomas she wouldn't leave his brother's side. All through the long night, no one else came to see how Marcas fared, which could mean only one thing—Lady Audrey fared worse than her son.

Anne replaced the dry compress on Marcas's head with another damp, cool cloth. Falling to her knees, she folded her hands and began to pray. "Please, Lord, heal this young laird and Lady Audrey as well. You are victorious over death, both physical and spiritual. Do not let the evil one win. Please, God, Thomas has suffered enough. Show him that you still care about him by saving his family."

The door latch clicked, and Anne swiped a lone tear from her cheek. Quiet footsteps crossed the floor and stopped near the bed.

"How is he?" Thomas said softly.

Anne stood. The sight of him lifted her spirits and awoke her tired mind. "I think he is much improved. Color has returned to his cheeks, and the wrestling has left his body. Now let us pray that he will wake." She frowned when she saw the heavy shadows under Thomas's eyes. "It is all in God's hands."

Heaving out a halfhearted laugh, Thomas brushed his fingers through his hair. "If He exists, then He has certainly outdone himself this past eve."

Thomas's angry words sent Anne's stomach into a tumble. "How is Lady Audrey?"

"She will live. Seems she has been poisoned."

"Poisoned!"

"Aye, or at least that is what the healer Tibbie says. She thinks it was foxglove." Thomas set his gaze on his brother. "If her words are true, then I believe my brother has been poisoned as well."

"But the healer wasn't sure about Marcas." Anne thought about the words and pictures she had been trying to decipher in the apothecary book. "Foxglove has an awful odor, does it not?"

Thomas nodded. "So the healer says."

"But no such odor has been present here." A weave of foreboding twisted up Anne's back. "Could it be possible that another poison was used on your brother?"

A grim line settled on Thomas's lips. "I had the same thought."

"But who would do such a thing?" She wanted to touch and soothe the worry lines that creased Thomas's strong brow. He claimed he did not care about his family, yet he wore his heart openly. He loved them all. Oh, that someday he would hold some affection for her as well.

"I have my suspicions. Lady Cecilia has fled the tower." A darkness flickered in his gaze. "Blair told me that she and Ma

Audrey have been fighting for the control of the lady's duties of the keep. A truce was made, and Ma Audrey oversees the hall and tower, while Cecilia manages the kitchens. Perhaps the compromise was not to her liking."

Anne remembered the filth of the kitchen compared to the neatness of the hall. Indeed, the two women had different views on how a household should be run, but was that enough of a reason to poison a person? "I cannot believe Cecilia would try to kill both. I feel we are missing something that is right before our eyes."

"If they were dead and I had not returned, my cousin Jaxon would claim control of Warring Tower. But he is as old as Ma Audrey, and I am certain if he wanted the land, he would have claimed Warring Tower long before now. Nay, it must be Cecilia. Otherwise, why would she leave?"

His words could be true; however, Anne could not shake the feeling that Cecilia would have nothing to gain by the death of her husband or mother-in-law, unless the young wife was pregnant. So many unknowns kept them in the dark. Acquiring land and power might breed several villains. Even make traitors out of loved ones. From her own past, Anne knew that not all families were rooted in love.

She bit her lip, voicing any objections or opinions now would only disrupt Thomas's fragile trust. "Have no worries, I will keep watch over Marcas while you search for Lady Cecilia."

His shoulders relaxed as the angry censure fled his body. "You need sleep. Tibbie will be coming along soon. After she takes a short rest."

"Then who will tend to Lady Audrey?"

"Santos."

The lack of sleep and worry must have clouded Thomas's judgment. "You trust him with Lady Audrey?"

"I better, he is her brother."

The pronouncement hit Anne like a slap to the cheek. "Lady Audrey has a Portuguese merchant for a brother?"

"Aye, nay." Thomas shook his head. "The man is as English as they come. His name is Asher Hayes, and he fled England years ago. At first, I *didnae* believe him, but when Ma Audrey awoke this morn, she claimed all to be true."

"Did she say how he wound up masquerading as a Portuguese merchant?"

Clouds entered Thomas's eyes once again. "Nay, something to do with his marriage, I think. Worry not, I intend to find out the truth. However, that will have to wait until I find Cecilia. Methinks she could still be in the tower. I have asked the servants and guards to search once again." His gaze flipped to his brother. "I need to know what she gave Marcas. It is the only way we can save him."

Anne nodded. In her heart of hearts, she knew something more sinister weakened the young laird. What ailment she did not know, but surely the answer was in the apothecary book.

"If she is not here, I'll take Santos, I mean Hayes, and search the marches for her. Maxwell and Blair can keep an eye on Ma Audrey." Thomas reached out and squeezed Anne's hand. "Please be careful. Cecilia could be anywhere, and like a caged animal, she could be dangerous. *Dinnae* confront her on your own with our suspicions."

The concern in his voice and his apprehensive gaze touched Anne deeply. "I promise. I shall not say anything that would alert her or cause her to flee."

Thomas gave a quick nod. His fingers slowly slipped

from her palm. "Then I shall go." He started to turn away, then stopped. Leaning over her, his lips briefly touched hers, sending a flash of fire from her mouth to her belly. "Take care, sweet Anne."

His kiss lingered long after he had left. A familiar longing settled in the middle of her chest. She dared not give in to the desire. As a child and a youthful maid, she had searched for love, only to be disappointed. Anne placed the palms of her hands over her chest. Nay, not again. She would guard her heart from the wretched pain. Love was for poets and dreamers, not for a barmaid and a son of a laird.

Thomas descended the stairs and paused outside Ma Audrey's chamber. The door was partially open, and he could hear soft voices. He darted to the entry, then paused, falling back into the shadows. Hayes sat on the bed next to Ma Audrey. Her hand in his.

"I never believed I would see you again, Asher. How did you find me?" Though her face was pale and drawn, a warm smile lifted her cheeks.

"I went first to London. I made a few inquiries of old family friends. 'Twas then I found out that our parents were dead and you were taken back to court. There I used some of my old contacts who told me that once a year you would return from Scotland with a young lad by the name of Thomas Armstrong. According to my friends, Queen Elizabeth was devastated and the whole court was abuzz with his shipwreck off the Welsh coast. The queen sent out Walsingham's spies. From there, I only had to stay one step ahead of them."

A weak laugh left Ma Audrey's lips. "And we both know you are very good at that."

There was the proof that Thomas needed. Hayes had more underhanded deals than . . . himself. Clearly there was more to this tale, and Thomas intended to get the rest of the truth.

Ma Audrey touched Hayes's cheek. "You do not know how I have prayed that you would return. 'Tis a miracle. I am so blessed. God has granted me two miracles at one time, both you and Thomas have returned."

Miracle. God had nothing to do with it. Hayes dragged him home with threats. Why had the man not been honest? Why the pretense? Thomas searched his mind. Ma Audrey had told many fanciful tales of her brother being a spy for Queen Mary. Stories to entertain a child. Now he knew they had to be true. She had said her brother had left England to marry some mysterious woman and would probably never return.

Yet, here he was, in the flesh, holding his sister's hand.

Hayes let out a hard, jagged cough. "I promised I would see you again."

Ma Audrey lifted a stray lock from her brother's forehead. "Are you ill?"

He pulled his hand away. "Worry not about me. Sleep now. We can talk more later. 'Tis your well-being that is of everyone's concern."

"Aye, I shall, but, brother, you must take care too. You must seek out Healer Tibbie. I am sure she can find a cure for what ails you."

Hayes bent down and gently kissed his sister's forehead. "Anything for my dear sister. Peaceful dreams."

Ma Audrey's eyes closed.

He rose and turned toward the entry. His eyes narrowed

as he came to the doorway, spotting Thomas. Hayes pulled him farther into the hallway. "So, I am sure you have many questions."

Thomas nodded. "Aye, but they will have to wait. We need to find Lady Cecilia for I am certain she carries the answers we need to all the chaos that has happened here."

After Thomas had left and the healer came to sit with Marcas, Anne wanted to check on Lady Audrey. If she was feeling well, a discussion on poison would certainly take Anne's mind off of Thomas's kiss. However, when Anne peeked into the room, Lady Audrey was fast asleep, and Laird Maxwell sat dutifully at her side. He put a finger to his lips when he spotted Anne. Better to let Lady Audrey rest.

Anne returned to her own chamber and flopped onto the bed. Her head filled with thoughts of Thomas. The kiss still tingled on her lips, and his gentle touch warmed her skin. She rolled over onto her belly and closed her eyes. Think of something else. Thomas's words twirled in her mind. *"Take care, sweet Anne."* Nay, not those words!

She must focus on other things. *"I believe my brother has been poisoned as well."* There, that was better. Concentrate on helping Marcas. What could she do? With a grumble, Anne sat up and reached for the apothecary book. Again, her traitorous thoughts drifted to Thomas. *Stop, O fickle mind. Let me think of healing Marcas, not his brother's kisses.*

Setting her resolve, Anne flipped to the section on poisons. There were indeed some toxins that left no smell, but wouldn't Tibbie know of them, and wouldn't she be able to use other signs besides smell to discover the poison? The words blurred in front of Anne's eyes, and her mind drifted to Thomas's kiss. She groaned and let the book drop to the floor. If only she could read more words, then perhaps her mind would not wander.

With no other ideas brewing in her mind, she rose to retrieve the book. She could study the pictures. Some of these plants might be found near the tower. Some might be as red as Thomas's lips. Anne slammed her palms on the book and puffed a stray strand of hair out of her face. Her mind would not stick to her task.

A knock on her door drew her attention. "Enter."

Tibbie poked her head into the room. "Beggin' yer pardon, I meant to talk to Master Thomas, but he's gone with that Portuguese fellow. Lady Audrey and Laird Maxwell are sleepin' like *bairns* . . . the old laird is something fierce when he is suddenly woken."

The worry in the healer's eyes set Anne on edge. "Is Laird Armstrong all right?"

"Oh aye, that is what I wanted to tell thee. Come, come." Tibbie flailed her hands. "He's awake."

Anne jumped off the bed and rushed up the stairs. "Praise the Lord."

When she entered the chamber, two ghostly blue eyes stalled her steps. Dare she approach Marcas or wait for Thomas to return? "Laird Armstrong, I am Anne Howell, a friend of your brother, Thomas. I—"

"Thomas." The word seeped out of Marcas's mouth like a steady stream of smoke floating on a breeze. "Here?"

Squaring her shoulders, Anne stepped closer to the bed. "Aye." She paused, trying to choose her words carefully. "He is riding the marches at the moment."

Marcas briefly closed his eyes and winced. "Good." When he opened them again, his gaze was drawn to the window. "Where's Cecilia?"

God only knows. Anne bit her tongue. She couldn't say that, nor did she wish to add another lie to her already growing list. "She is somewhere. As soon as she can be found, we'll let her know you have awakened."

"You a healer?" The sweat on his pale brow seemed to grow with each word he tried to utter. Too much exertion could send him back into the heavy mist of his mind.

"Nay, just a helper. Laird Maxwell's healer is watching over you." Anne looked about, but the woman was nowhere to be seen. Perhaps she went to check on Lady Audrey again.

"Want no healer." He gasped, his breathing becoming irregular. "Where's Cecilia? Potion. A little more."

A little more? By the man's own words, Cecilia was giving him some concoction that was indeed killing him. Though Anne hated to admit it, she owed Thomas an apology.

She gently went to the pitcher and poured Marcas a cool mug of water, helping him to sit up a bit before holding the drink to his lips. He drank steadily and then fell back, exhausted from the simple act.

"I do not know of any potion, but you must drink plenty of water. That is Mistress Anne's potion." She placed a gentle hand on his shoulder. Bone poked at her flesh. "Rest now. Soon your brother will be here, and everything will be all right."

Marcas's lips trembled. "Thomas true laird. Finally." He then closed his eyes and drifted off.

True laird? Either his words were the ravings of the illness or Thomas was not illegitimate as she had once believed. If that were the case, then why did he leave his family ten years ago?

Someone here knew the answer. No doubt more than one.

But who else besides Thomas? Lady Audrey would know for sure and quite possibly Laird Maxwell. If asked, would they speak the truth? Anne wiped her brow. Was it really her affair to pry? The past could hold the keys to the present. Though, it wasn't her past to meddle in.

Another thought twisted her stomach. Was she falling in love with a laird? All bonds she held with Thomas began to dissolve and disappear. Best she forgot his gentle touch and kisses. A laird could never love a commoner. Not one as tainted and plain as she.

CHAPTER 19

"A beastly night to be traveling, do not you think?" Rain pelted Hayes's back and dripped off the large brim of his hat.

The squeak of Thomas's saddle added to the storm's melody. Searching the mud for Cecilia's tracks had been all but impossible. "Marcas's life hangs in the balance. We dare not tarry."

In spite of the weather, they had managed to get ten moss-troopers to join them. Some would say this was a blessing to have the loyalty of the men to Warring Tower. Thomas believed it to be a testament to how much his brother was loved by the people.

Hayes halted his mount and scanned the wall before them. "It is a godsend we were able to track your sister-in-law this far. Do you know whose keep this is?"

Again, Thomas didn't agree with his partner's assessment. The few muddy hoofprints and broken branches they followed could have been made by others. "This place belongs to my cousin, Jaxon Armstrong. Methinks she may have found refuge here when the storm broke." Thomas pointed to a hedge of small hills. "Her father's lands rest beyond the yonder hill."

"Surely your cousin will turn her over to us." Hayes adjusted the sword on his hip. "We could have waited until morning to give this chase."

Not so. If Ma Audrey spoke truth, then Jaxon was already besotted with the girl and would do anything to protect her. Thomas tapped the dirk tucked in his belt, hoping he would not have to use it this eve. "Nay, I have been told my cousin has turned into a bitter man. Even more so since Cecilia snubbed him in preference to Marcas."

"That is what you were told but not what you believe." Hayes gripped the pommel of his saddle. "What do you fear?"

"I believe this was their plan from the beginning. Concocted by the both of them, my uncle and Cecilia, to get their hands on Warring Tower. If Marcas dies without an heir, Jaxon would inherit the lands."

A hiss of air escaped Hayes's lips followed by a mirthless chuckle. "Then you returned to Scotland and foiled their plans. You would inherit the lands." He nodded slowly. "It would explain why she ran away not long after you arrived."

Indeed. Marcas was Gavin Armstrong's true son. The rightful heir of Warring, no one else. Thomas's father—stepfather—had always spoken of the deep friendship he had with his cousins, Jaxon and Fraser, when they were young. Somewhere along the way, that friendship eroded after Fraser left Scotland and Gavin made a truce with Rory Maxwell. Jaxon had been furious.

Something still niggled Thomas. "Ma Audrey said Marcas and Cecilia seemed very happy right after they got married."

"Never trust outward appearances. They usually are false. Unfortunately, I did not have the privilege of studying the couple's mannerisms before your brother became ill. If I had, I am sure I would have been able to discern the truth."

Hayes was quite observant and seemed to see things others did not notice. He tracked Thomas to Bristol and even managed to recover all the jewels for the cross. Ma Audrey's brother or not, the man was a mystery. Once again, Thomas wondered the real reason why Hayes left England. Whom did he marry? And why did he leave his wife to traipse all over Scotland? The past and his questions would have to wait. They had to find Cecilia for Marcas's sake.

A series of wretched coughs caused Hayes's shoulders to shake. "I care not to sit out in this damp rain all night."

"Half the men will stay back here while the others will come with us. Hopefully, everything will work to our advantage." He glanced at the men behind him. "I have no desire to tell some lass her sweetheart *didnae* make it home this eve."

"All is set. Let us enjoy your uncle's hospitality without raising suspicion." Hayes flashed a smile, then gave his horse a good kick in the flanks and galloped toward the keep.

Surprisingly, Thomas only called to the guard once before Jaxon stood on the battlements. "Ye can enter, but yer men have to stay where they are."

Arrows pointed down on the moss-troopers, and a hot fear chased away the icy chill on Thomas's back. "Aye, I'll bring but one man with me. Tell your men to ease their weapons. We are not here to skirmish but to talk peacefully."

At consent, the gate opened, and Jaxon's men eased their bows. Thomas and Hayes guided their horses forward while the other men dismounted and huddled together under a broad oak to ward off the damp night.

Once inside the courtyard, two guards flanked them. Quickly, Thomas and Hayes dismounted and were ushered into the hall where Jaxon and a wet-eyed Cecilia sat.

The wench sat like a queen in a dry bright-green gown, drinking ale and nibbling on cheese like a shifty rat. Thomas's uncle had indeed aged. Instead of the toothy grin that broke many a maid's heart years ago, his parted lips showed a dark tunnel. His red hair had receded, and his face bore pockmarks, a sign of his loose living.

Jaxon rose from his seat and gave Thomas a hearty hug before casting a wary gaze on Hayes. "I am so glad you have returned. The lowlands have not been the same since ye left." With a wave of his hand, he offered them to sit. "I would ask what brings you out this beastly night, but I already know the answer. I expect even tempers as you promised and an acceptance of my words."

A flush of color entered Cecilia's cheeks when Jaxon offered her a besotted smile. You would have to be daft not to see how much Jaxon Armstrong loved the lass. Whatever story she spun he would readily accept. Getting Jaxon to give up Cecilia would not be easy. However, they could not dally here long for as soon as Laird Elliot heard that his daughter was traipsing across the countryside in the middle of the night, alone, he'd be on the steps of Warring Tower with an army in tow.

Thomas placed a hand on his chest. "First, let me introduce Lady Audrey's brother, Master Asher Hayes."

Jaxon's brows shot upward before he took the man's hand in friendship. "Then ye are more than welcomed. Come, rest yer bones." His uncle waved them to a bench near the table before he motioned for his servants to provide drink.

Hayes gave a cordial greeting but didn't say more. His gaze shifted around the hall, probably assessing every possible means of escape. He sat to Thomas's left and nudged him in the thigh with the hilt of his sword. The message was not lost. They had their weapons. Another blessing from the Almighty? Or an oversight by an aging laird? Thomas chose the latter, while he was certain Hayes would choose the first.

Once they were settled, Jaxon did not waste time. "So tell me, Thomas, why have you returned, and why are you out chasing poor Cecilia at this ungodly hour?"

Thomas splayed his fingers on the table. "I have not come to claim rights to Warring Tower if that is what you are thinking. I only came home to unite the family." He nodded to Hayes before he fixed his gaze on Cecilia. "And I am also here to reunite a laird and his wife."

"Nay, that is not so," Cecilia cried, grabbing Jaxon's arm. "He comes to take me back to Warring Tower and throw me in chains." She inched closer to his uncle. "Thomas believes . . . they all believe, I poisoned Marcas." The crafty lass then dropped her hand to Jaxon's shoulder. "*Dinnae* let them take me."

His uncle patted her hand. "There, there now, Lady Cecilia. *Dinnae* worry yer bonnie head over this. Ye go and rest while I have a nice conversation with yer husband's brother." He lifted a chin to one of his female servants.

Any show of fear and woe fled Cecilia's countenance. With a flutter of her lashes to chase away her false tears, she rose and followed the servant. Jaxon ogled the sway of her hips as she took to the tower steps. Cecilia would not be able to keep that wolf at bay for long. Laird Elliot would not take a liking to having his daughter ravished by Jaxon Armstrong. A dung heap had a better reputation. This keep held the tinder for a full-scale border war, and Thomas didn't have a clue on how to defuse the situation.

Suddenly Hayes rose to his feet, clutched his throat, wheezed, and coughed until sweat poured from his brow.

Truly the devil was having a merry time this eve. Thomas gave himself an inward kick. He knew Hayes was ill and getting sicker by the day. He should have left him at Warring Tower with Ma Audrey.

"Master Hayes, are you all right?" Jaxon rose and called for a pitcher of water, but Hayes fell to the floor, a fit of hacks wrenching his body.

Thomas knelt next to him. Hayes lolled his head to the side and gasped for air. Thomas fought to hold back a curse. Ma Audrey would kill him if her brother died. "Do you have a healer about?"

"We have a maid with some skill. Find Sorchae," Jaxon barked and then ordered two servants to take Hayes to a private chamber.

"I should see to him," Thomas said, rising to his feet.

"Nay, not yet. Not until we have settled our dealings." Jaxon pointed at the bench. "Sit."

Slowly, Thomas made his way back to the table. A yellow-haired maid scurried into the hall clutching a bag to her chest. Jaxon made a slash with his hand to where the servants had carried Hayes. The healer rushed away as if a fairy nipped at her heels. What had happened at this keep that all within feared their laird?

Thomas waited until his host sat across from him once again. Gradually, the anger receded from Jaxon's eyes. "Uncle, I am not your enemy, I just want answers, and Lady Cecilia has them."

Jaxon drained his mug and held it out to be filled again. "The lass claims innocence, and I believe her. What would she gain by poisoning Marcas? The lad has always been weak and worrisome. That's what happens when ye are raised by a bunch of hens."

The words were meant to cut. Jaxon didn't need to remind Thomas that he had quit his responsibilities to the family. Never more than now had Thomas regretted letting his anger get the better of him that fateful night his father died. "Aye, you speak truth. I should have stayed until Marcas was older."

His uncle leaned over the table. "Why did ye leave? Yer father was so proud of ye. Ye *couldnae* even stay to see him buried."

The truth lingered on the tip of Thomas's lips, but he could not bring it forth. His throat closed, and he shook his head.

"Ack, ye are as weak as yer brother. How could Gavin Armstrong have raised two feeble sons?"

Aye, his uncle spoke the truth. Thomas rubbed his turning gut. He ran and laid the blame on others. His life consisted of one failure after another. Did the past hold the blame or himself?

Jaxon took another long pull of his drink before slamming the mug on the table. He wiped his mouth with the back of his hand and stood. "When Lady Cecilia is well rested, she'll answer yer questions. Here, where she is protected." He called over his shoulder as he strode from the hall. "Good night to ye."

Thomas rubbed his eyes and forehead before he lay down on the bench. After a bit of sleep, he should check on Hayes; hopefully, he was not as ill as he appeared. They had a plan to carry out. If they *didnae* act soon, when morning came, they might have to take Cecilia out of here by force. War was never pleasant before breaking your fast.

A large, sweaty palm covered Thomas's nose and mouth

and brought him fully to his senses. "Shh, we will have to be quick," Hayes whispered before removing his hand.

Thomas sat up and adjusted his eyes to the dark. He gave a sigh of relief when he found his dirk safely tucked within his belt. "I take it you are feeling better?"

"Aye, more of a ruse to get the lay of the keep. Sometimes my illness comes in handy."

Hayes held his sword in his right hand.

The man's cleverness and stealth raised more questions, but at the moment, his actions were welcomed. "What of the healer Jaxon sent you?"

"A few coins had silenced her lips and softened her feet as she crept away." Hayes pointed to the stairs. "Lady Cecilia is in a small chamber next to your uncle's. I fear he wishes to make mischief with her this eve, so we must move quickly."

If the soiled heap touched Cecilia, her father would have every Armstrong head that occupied the lowlands. Thomas rose and started following Hayes. They paused in the dark hallway near her chamber. "I am surprised he *doesnae* have a guard at her door."

"Your uncle doesn't think you are foolhardy enough to try to abscond with the girl right under his very nose." Hayes's voice dropped yet another decibel. "Earlier, he called for a pitcher of wine. Then he called for two more. No doubt trying to work up the nerve to have his way with Lady Cecilia. The chamber has been quiet for some time. Methinks he is in a drunken stupor. We must act now."

Both men crept past Jaxon's chamber until they stood before Cecilia's door. Hayes pulled a rag from his doublet. Inside, they heard a loud shriek followed by a scuffle. Thomas quickly opened the door. There they found Cecilia with a wooden bowl in hand. Jaxon lay in a heap at her feet.

"He tried to . . ." She dropped the bowl, and long jagged cries left her throat.

"We best act," Hayes whispered to Thomas before stepping toward Cecilia. "Now, now, no tears. We are here." With deft fingers, Hayes dabbed at her eyes with the rag.

"I *didnae* poison Marcas. I *widnae* do such a thing. I love him," she wailed.

Hayes jammed the cloth into her mouth and wrapped his arms around her struggling body. Was there nothing this man could not do? His quick action made Thomas pause. Had Hayes performed such rescues before?

"Either tie her hands or take hold of her and I will do the job," Hayes snapped. "If we do not secure her quickly, the whole keep will come and seek out what ails the lovely Lady Cecilia."

She squirmed and stomped on Thomas's feet, breaking his hold when he tried to tie her hands with a piece of rope. "We mean you no harm, Lady Cecilia," he whispered. "But you must calm down."

Her eyes grew wide like a pair of full moons. Jaxon started to moan. Pushing Cecilia toward Thomas, Hayes pulled out his sword and clunked Jaxon on the head with its hilt.

"See there," Thomas whispered, still struggling with Cecilia. "If Laird Jaxon awakes and we are taken away, what will happen to you?"

Instantly, Cecilia stilled.

Thomas frowned as Cecilia's muffled screams started up again. "Perhaps the hand tying is a bit much."

"Nay, it is not. Now hoist her over your shoulder. We must leave now." Hayes headed for the door.

Thomas picked up Cecilia and followed Hayes, praying he knew what he was doing.

They ran down the stairs and out to the courtyard, hiding in the shadows while shouts rang out. Someone must have found Jaxon, or he had already managed to shake off Hayes's blow. Their chances to escape were growing slimmer every moment. His uncle would skewer them where they stood if they were caught.

As if he did this all the time, Hayes pointed to a rope hanging over the back wall. "Our moss-troopers are on the other side."

Thomas nodded. "I cannot believe this, your plan worked. You must be a magician of some sort."

"We can discuss that later." Hayes raced over to the wall. Tightening his hold on Cecilia, Thomas followed him to freedom.

CHAPTER 20

Thomas and Asher congratulated themselves as they entered the hall like a pair of crowing roosters. Anne wanted to throttle both of them for placing their lives in danger. Cecilia was a weeping mess, and Maxwell wanted to throw her into Warring Tower's cells. Anne intervened and offered her room instead.

"I can sleep upstairs on the pallet in Laird Armstrong's chamber. I'm sure Tibbie won't mind sharing. I fear Cecilia needs more rest than anyone."

"Ye can sleep there by yerself. I'll give Lady Cecilia a draught. She *willnae* be a bother until mornin'. My work is done here. I'm returnin' to me home." Tibbie folded her arms across her chest and glared at Maxwell expecting a fight.

Laird Maxwell opened his mouth to argue but then shrugged instead. "Do what ye want. Now that the lad is on the mend, there is no reason for ye to stay. Nobody wants yer sour looks around here anyway."

"What?" With the drop of his jaw, Thomas grabbed the healer by the arm. "Is it true? Is Marcas gaining strength?"

"Aye, he awoke earlier and talked to Widow Howell before he fell back to sleep. Methinks the worst is over." The healer lifted her chin to Anne. "She can take care of him. She seems to have the touch."

Anne's stomach clenched. Tibbie gave her too much praise. If Marcas recovered, it was because of the healer's skill and God's grace.

Thomas gave her a smile. An unspoken thanks softened his eyes and warmed Anne all the way through, but his admiration was misplaced. She had done nothing. Tibbie should be the beneficiary of his appreciation.

"What caused his illness?" Asher asked.

The healer's frown deepened. "I *cannae* say for sure. Some things are in the Almighty's hands. I did nothin' special. Anne did most of the fussin'."

"Or perhaps the absence of Lady Cecilia had something to do with it," Thomas countered.

"Methinks the lass *doesnae* have the wit to manage such a feat." The healer tapped her temple. "But think what ye want. I'm goin' home." She hobbled to the spiral stairs, then paused and gazed at Maxwell. "After I get me things, ye will prepare a cart for me."

Maxwell tipped his head at the demand. "Yer payment will be placed within."

The mass of wrinkles on her face deepened as she glanced at Laird Maxell over her shoulder. "I'm too old to be beggin' for coins."

Anne rushed to the healer's side and tenderly touched her arm. "Much thanks, Tibbie. I wish you would stay . . ."

The healer shook her head. "Nay. I am finished with these Armstrongs. Ye take care of them."

Her coarse words made the hair on Anne's arms rise. Granted, taking care of the ill was hard work, but was that not what the woman was trained for? Perhaps she was just tired. Anne touched the older woman's shoulder. "May God bless you and always be with you."

Then Tibbie paused, her watery eyes opening a window to her suffering heart. "Ye do not know how much yer words mean to me. I could use the Almighty's help once in a while." She then straightened her shoulders, and her steps became less wearisome.

A sense of calm filled the air for a brief moment, but the peace did not last long. Thomas and Asher jumped to their feet.

"I want to see my brother," Thomas said.

"And I wish to see my sister." Both men sprinted past the healer and disappeared up the stairs.

"I think ye should go with him, lass. We *dinnae* want him upsettin' the lad." Maxwell spoke of Marcas. True, he had only awoken once and was as weak as a newborn calf.

In her heart, Anne wished the healer would stay a little longer. If Marcas took a turn for the worst, who would Thomas blame? 'Twas a selfish thought, but one she could not tamp down. Without knowing the cause of the illness, she would have a hard time combating any relapses. *Dear Lord, please do not let that happen. If it be your will, make Marcas stronger every day.*

"Come on, lass," Maxwell called over his shoulder as he dashed after the others, leaving Anne no choice but to follow.

Maxwell and Hayes stopped at Lady Audrey's room while Anne trudged upward, hoping Marcas was still sleeping peacefully. When she entered his chamber, she found Thomas kneeling at the bedside, holding his brother's hand.

"He still looks so pale. Perhaps you should—"

"I've done all I can," Tibbie jammed all of her belongings

into a small bag. "He'll be fine now." She winked at Anne. "You'll see. So stop yer frettin'."

Her overconfidence was more than a little unsettling for Anne. As a child, she had been around enough ailing folk to know that anything could happen. More than once she had seen a man laughing and smiling after coming off the sickbed, only to fall back into the same illness the very next day. Never to recover again. How could Tibbie be so confident?

"How can you be so sure? He has the look of a . . ." Thomas dropped his head into the hand he held. The uncertainty in his voice ripped at Anne's soul and mirrored his fears. Did she have the skill to heal the young laird, or would he flounder until the angel of death came knocking on his door? She couldn't bear the loss of Thomas's brother and what he would think of her if Marcas died.

Tibbie grunted and left the room, not giving Thomas or Marcas a second look. Her flippant ways nagged Anne. What did the healer know that made her so certain the young laird would recover? Or did she flee because she saw imminent death in his eyes and didn't want the blame to fall on her head?

Not knowing which question held truth, Anne quietly stepped to Thomas's side, placing a hand on his shoulder. "I think we should pray."

He raised his head; his eyes filled with hesitation and doubt. Finally, he nodded. Anne knelt down next to him and folded her hands. "Lord God, we humbly come before you today with thanksgiving and praise. Thank you for lifting Laird Armstrong from his illness. We ask that in your mercy and kindness you continue to heal him until he is able to praise you with his own lips. You are all powerful, and we know your power is wiser than any man's wisdom. We ask all this in your Son's name, who died for our sins. Amen."

A tiny amen croaked out of Thomas's throat and caused Anne's heart to ache. She offered up one more silent prayer. *Please, Lord, allow this to happen so that Thomas might learn how great thou art.*

With his free hand, Thomas reached out and grabbed hers. "I know you will take good care of him. Promise me you will?"

Her lungs deflated, and she swallowed hard. She wanted Thomas to trust God and also trust her as a friend, a healer, and something more. Her chest grew tight. "I will try with all my heart, soul, and mind."

. "I know you will." He then took her hand and brought it to his lips.

Her stomach tumbled, and her knees quaked. He had so much faith in her she dared not fail him. *God, give me the wisdom I need to heal Marcas.* As by God's direction, she thought of the apothecary book. *It sits in my chamber where they have taken Lady Cecilia.*

A new fear squeezed Anne's heart. Gently, she wiggled her fingers from Thomas's and stood. "Stay with your brother. I will be back shortly."

Thomas did not question her, his gaze floating back to Marcas's ashen face. With lightning speed, she flew down to her old chamber only to find a gruff guard standing at the door.

Anne squared her shoulders and stepped forward. "I have need of my things."

It took but a moment for the guard's brain to catch up to her words. He stood aside. "Of course, Widow Howell."

To her relief, when the door opened, she found Cecilia

sound asleep. The book still sat undisturbed on the small table under the narrow window. Quietly, Anne tiptoed into the room and picked up the book and a few belongings. She had almost made it to the door when Cecilia's eyelids opened. The woman sat up, loathing and anger twisting her features. Fear punched Anne's spine.

Anne stilled. Her feet were like anvils. Fright held her fast.

"All this is your fault. Yours and Thomas's. I was helping Marcas, trying to make him better. You wait and see. He'll die for sure now," the young lady slurred.

Could she be right? Anne's pulse quickened. Would Marcas die under her care? Doubt mounted and clouded everything she believed. Anne closed her eyes. *Please God, let her words be false.*

A faint voice answered her plea. *Have no fear, I am with you.*

Her eyes flew open. Peace and courage rushed through and filled her soul. She met Cecilia's cold stare. "I do not know what transpired here before we came, but I know Marcas would not be alive today had we not entered this home. So save your venom and lies for later. You will have much to answer for. We only seek the truth."

A small gasp left Cecilia's throat, and her lips trembled before she rolled over to face the wall. "You'll see. I am not the evil you seek."

With her feet lighter, Anne fled the room and raced up the stairs with a new confidence. Marcas would improve because God was on her side. This time when she opened the door to the laird's chamber, she found him awake, talking to Thomas.

Anne clutched the apothecary book to her chest while raising her eyes heavenward. *Thank you, God. May Marcas continue to grow strong and may harmony reign in this house once again. Your harmony.*

Hours later when Blair came to sit with Marcas, Anne stepped into the hall to find a cozy group sitting by the hearth. Lady Audrey sat with a coverlet wrapped around her legs. Her cheeks had a rosy glow, and she seemed so much more alive than the ghastly grey woman who greeted Anne days ago. Laird Maxwell and Asher jovially sat on either side of the matriarch. Thomas sat across from Lady Audrey, a look of pure admiration on his face.

Joy flooded Anne's chest. All were on the mend just like Healer Tibbie predicted. Anne approached the group with hesitant steps; after all, she had no history with this happy family. Oh, that her life had been different. What would it be like to be loved and cherished?

"Ah, Anne, come join us," Thomas said, patting the bench next to him. "Look, Ma Audrey is well."

The elder woman's cheeks glowed. "I was a little sick, but I am far better now."

Anne eased onto the bench, careful not to touch Thomas's thigh with hers. Her heart tumbled over. "I give thanks to God for your quick recovery."

"Are you comfortable, sister?" Asher tucked the coverlet firmly around Lady Audrey's legs.

"Aye, brother. All is fine now." The strong bond between the siblings sparkled in their deep smiles.

Love never seemed to wan when blood was involved. An emptiness settled in Anne's chest. She had never known such family affection and devotion. Roland's shouts and slaps had been her upbringing. Never did anyone show her a mite of affection . . . until Thomas. Best not think on him. His kindness of late grew out of gratitude for helping Marcas.

Maxwell leaned forward. "Now tell me, lads, how did ye get the lass away from Jaxon Armstrong? Ye only had ten men."

Thomas and Asher exchanged a hearty look of admiration. Their lack of trust had dissolved like a thin mist on a warm summer's day. "'Tis quite a tale," Thomas began. "Hayes here planned it all. He is quite cunning."

Taking a drink from his mug, Asher laughed. "I had no clue if it would work. I have no soldier's training, but I do know how to sneak about."

Thomas slapped his new friend on the back. "I tell you, with all of Lady Cecilia's weeping and wailing, I thought all was lost."

"Fortunately, Armstrong knew the lay of the keep and where our men could successfully toss the rope over the wall." Asher flexed his arm producing a large muscle. "He's also one of the strongest men I have ever met. He was able to climb the wall after I plopped Lady Cecilia on his shoulder. Once on the other side, I could barely keep up with him when he sprinted into the forest. Arrows flying everywhere." Asher flailed his arms around to add flavor to his words.

"When Thomas became old enough, he won all the Truce Day footraces," Lady Audrey interjected.

"He also was good with the ax," Maxwell added. "That's where he gets his strength."

From all the praise, Anne expected Thomas's head to swell. Instead, his ears pinked up, and his gaze found his boots. "Most of the praise should go to our moss-troopers at the gate. They kept the guards occupied while the other half circled around to toss the rope. Once we were out of danger, those in front of Jaxon's keep mounted their horses and galloped away, flummoxing the guard."

"'Twas risky, but the plan worked. We rode off and met the other moss-troopers in the forest." Thomas slapped Asher on the back. "This man is quite bold and brilliant."

"More like cunning and crazy," Maxwell added. "Jaxon will be here in the mornin' with an army behind him."

"I'm thinking not," Thomas said. "If word got out what almost happened to Lady Cecilia while under Jaxon Armstrong's protection, the whole Elliot family would be at his door. That's something Jaxon *widnae* want to face without support." Thomas stretched his arms above his head and gave a yawn. "On his own, he is a weak *bairn*."

"What do you mean? What almost happened to Lady Cecilia?" Anne asked.

Asher took a drink of ale and cleared his throat, shooting Thomas a warning gaze.

Thomas waved off Asher's concern. "Jaxon wanted to become intimate with her."

Lady Audrey gasped and placed a hand on her chest. "At her approval?"

Waving his arms, Asher shot to his feet. "Nay, not at all. In fact, I have to say Lady Cecilia fought him by whacking him over the head with a bowl."

"Good for her." Lady Audrey slapped a hand on her coverlet. "He's been a real bear since she chose Marcas over him as a husband. Why Jaxon would think she would want an old, broken-down goat like him is beyond me."

Laird Maxwell frowned and puffed out his chest. "Hey now,

old men need a little affection too."

"Pffsst. Men. Your lustful minds get you into trouble far more than reivering ever did." Lady Audrey pinned Maxwell with a hard look.

A small, sad smile touched Maxwell's lips. "Aye. That is true. We have all fallen prey to a beautiful woman at some point in our life."

Flames licked around the dry wood in the hearth causing the timber to crackle and pop as the group became quiet and slipped into their own thoughts. Comfort and balminess seeped into Anne's body. In her security, she could not help but peek at Thomas. The warmth in her belly blossomed like a water lily in full sun on a tranquil pond. Thomas returned her gaze, his eyes steadfast and glistening. Had she finally found a home, a future, a true bond with her mesmerizing scoundrel?

CHAPTER 21

Galloping hooves and the nicker of horses drew Thomas to the battlements the next morn. Surely news of Cecilia's wanderings last night could not have reached the Elliots already? No doubt it was Jaxon come to seek revenge for last night's escapades. As the riders drew closer, Thomas gave out a long and weary sigh. Jaxon did not approach the tower, but on the horizon came Maxwell's disgruntled, selfish son Ewart.

"Jaxon would have been preferred," Thomas grumbled as he slowly descended the stairs he had hastily climbed. In the hall, he found Maxwell slurping the rest of his potage with a bit of dried bread. "Your son is approaching our gates."

"Good." Maxwell wiped his mouth with the sleeve of his garment and stood, patting his stomach until a loud belch soiled the air. "I sent word for him to come last night. 'Tis good the lad listened for once."

Placing a hand on his dirk that had recently become a familiar part of his apparel, Thomas walked toward the entry. Ewart never brought good. Thomas bit his lip to hold a curse. He might well have to lock up Ma Audrey and Anne to keep them safe. "We have no need of him. I told you, Jaxon will not come."

"That is the problem with you Armstrongs, ye always believe that there is an abundance of good in people when there is an abundance of evil." The older man limped toward the entry. "I never make that mistake."

Quite so. Thomas remembered the feud between his father and the elder Maxwell as if it had happened yesterday. Then Thomas had been taught to hate the Maxwells with all his heart. In fact, it had been Maxwell who kidnapped him and threatened him as a young lad. However, after Queen Elizabeth ascended the throne, things slowly changed. A strange bond developed between Gavin Armstrong and Rory Maxwell, so tight that as a child he came to call the crusty old laird uncle. But time does not heal all wounds. Time could not change your parentage. Time could not change a lie and make it true.

Ewart Maxwell entered the courtyard with all the pomp of a king. He wore shiny black boots over woolen breeches. His black jack had silver buttons instead of the common wooden ones. A crisp, white linen shirt with a ruffled collar puffed out over the top of his jack. A chain of fine gold hung from his neck to his navel. He looked like a man who was about to have an audience with a queen not ready to fight a battle.

His father spat onto the ground. "What ye gussied up like a peacock for? There be no royalty here, unless yer plannin' on makin' another go for Lady Audrey's hand."

Thomas's insides began to wither. Ewart and Ma Audrey a couple? A nightmare that must never happen. The image sickened his belly.

With assistance, Ewart slipped from his mount. "Have no fear, *Da*. Neither of us seek such a union. I just wish to be presentable when I meet her." He threw back his shoulders and straightened his jack. "I brought me fightin' clothes too."

"Aggh." Maxwell waved a hand in disgust. "Me wealth has made ye soft. Or perhaps it was that last wife ye had. She was always putting on airs. What good was she? She *couldnae* birth me one healthy grandson before she gave up the ghost."

Ewart sniffed into a lace hankie the likes of which Thomas had not seen since his days at court. The irony was not lost; Ewart would have loved the life Thomas had at court, while Thomas had always craved the life of the rough and rugged Scotsman.

"Put that thing away. Ye look like a fancy Englishman," Maxwell growled.

Immediately, Ewart tucked the cloth into his sleeve and followed his father around the courtyard.

"How many men did ye bring?" Maxwell clomped toward the open gate and shaded his eyes inspecting the men. "Looks like not enough. Jaxon Armstrong could be heading here with the might of the Elliots behind him."

"I brought all that we could spare without leaving our own keep defenseless," Ewart countered, finally beginning to grow some semblance of a spine.

On this point, Thomas agreed. Another war could start if other reiver families or the English discovered the Maxwells were left without adequate protection. What drove Rory Maxwell's bizarre desire to protect Warring Tower at all costs?

Thomas gazed out over the field of a hundred moss-troopers. "I think we have more than enough men. Besides, I think you worry without reason."

Maxwell puffed out his burly chest, placing his thumbs in his belt. "Nonetheless, I am glad you are here. I hope you have brought plenty of supplies."

"We are a tad short," Ewart responded. "I plan to send some

of the men to town to purchase more."

In other words, rough up the cottars to sell what goods they had at a pittance of a price. An army of stomping horses and moss-troopers could destroy Warring's crops. All at the tower would fare better in facing the Elliots alone.

Hearing enough, Thomas started striding for the tower. Unwittingly, Maxwell might be the one who started a war. It wouldn't take long before Jaxon and the Elliots learned about the army forming outside Warring Tower. A fragile peace had always been the lowland's legacy. Gavin Armstrong had secured this ground for his family, and Thomas wasn't about to let a pack of inflamers spark a fight.

When he entered the base of the tower, he found Hayes rolling some of the barrels of grain to the back of the cellar. "I know Maxwell is a family friend, but what lies outside will only bring trouble to your home. Forgive me, but I have asked your cook and servants to hide the food."

"Aye." Thomas pushed up the sleeves and began helping Hayes. "That is why I want you to carry a message to Laird Neal Elliot. I wager that by nightfall he will know of the troops outside our gate. If Jaxon speaks to him first, he will turn the blade of gossip against us and will push for war. I aim to stop the fight before it has begun."

Giving out a grueling cough and swiping the sweat from his brow, Hayes leaned against a barrel. "Give me a few men and we will leave posthaste."

Considering his health, all this might be too much for Hayes, but there was no one else Thomas trusted. "All right. I shall meet you in the stables within the hour. Take whomever you wish. Say it is upon my orders." Thomas paused at his statement. Were his words true? Had not everyone turned to him for guidance the moment he arrived home? Was this his rightful place? Or was he just an impostor, stealing what belonged to his brother?

His blood thumped in his temples as he made his way up the stairs and did not stop until he was in Marcas's chamber. Heavy in sleep, his brother looked like a cherub resting before he awoke to strum his harp. Marcas had always been a tender soul. A man for the church perhaps, certainly not for the harsh Scottish marches. *Am I to blame for your poor health? Had I stayed, would you be robust and healthy?*

Anne crept out of the shadows. "He was awake but then fell back to sleep and has been so for a number of hours." She tenderly brushed back a blond curl from Marcas's forehead. "Hopefully, all the racket will not disturb his slumber."

A large lump settled in Thomas's throat. With a quick nod, he strode to the laird's desk and pulled out a piece of parchment. Picking up a quill, he dunked it into an inkwell and then quickly wrote out a message to Laird Elliot. Gritting his teeth, Thomas walked to his brother's bedside and wiggled the laird's ring from his hand.

"What are you doing?" Anne rushed forward and grabbed Thomas's arm.

"What I should have done years ago." Thomas jammed the ring onto his finger, returned to the desk, and melted a bit of wax over a lone tallow. He then curled his fingers and thrust the seal into the soft wax. Without looking back or saying a word, he rushed to the door and down the steps, twirling the heavy hunk of jewelry on his finger.

Though he meant to help all within Warring Tower, Thomas could not help but think hell certainly waited for a man who stole his brother's birthright.

Hayes and five of Warring Tower's men managed to slip away without Maxwell or Ewart giving notice. From that point on, the day had been a rotten mess. No matter how many arguments Thomas made, Maxwell would not send his moss-troopers home. His men made a camp within the gate, and they made another outside the gate. They fought with the cottars, stealing sheep and stored grain. They trampled and decimated the young crops. When Thomas pointed to the folly, the older Maxwell just shrugged.

"I'll take care of those at Warring Tower just like I have always done since your father died."

And then the devil took Thomas as he folded his arms over his chest and let the sunlight glisten off the laird's ring.

Maxwell's eyes bulged. "So ye will take what is yer brother's?"

Aye, Thomas wanted to growl, but instead, he pulled back as if Maxwell had slapped him. *It was his brother's right, not his.* Did Maxwell know the truth as well? If so, then who else? Who else besides Ma Audrey knew he was not Gavin Armstrong's true son? "For now, while Marcas recovers, I will watch over our lands."

Without waiting for Maxwell's thoughts, Thomas strode back to the tower barking out orders to any who would listen. Maxwell had pushed his weight around here for the last time. This was Armstrong land, not Maxwell land. If Thomas stayed or if he left, best the old man learned his place and focused on his own family.

But he was here when you were not.

Thomas fumed at his thought. He fought the urge to shake

his fist at the heavens. His life seemed to be a constant battle. Fighting to earn his father's love as a child, only to discover the man was not his father at all. Fighting to find his real family, only to learn he had none. Fighting to seek answers to his past, only to wind up where he started. Truly he had asked for so little. Did he deserve this?

Did Ma Audrey? Did Marcas? Thomas swallowed hard. They trusted him to always be there, and he had run away. Now he had come back and had taken control. He ground his teeth. If this was God's punishment, then so be it. He had trampled God's commands before, and still lived.

Once evening came, Thomas sat by the hearth drinking tankard after tankard of ale. From the corner of his eye, he saw Anne enter. She greeted Ma Audrey who sat by a long table with the Maxwells. Earlier, Ewart had given Ma Audrey a bottle of fine French wine. Costly to be sure, but the Maxwells' wealth could provide many things. Even fancy wine to impress a lady.

Thomas swallowed his spit. May the devil take all the Maxwells.

"You look quite sour this eve." Anne pulled up a chair and sat across from Thomas. "Is that why everyone else chooses to sit away from you?"

He licked the ale from his lips. "Let them sit in the cold. Ewart can warm them with his French wine and his foolish words."

"Far better than your chilly stares." Anne smoothed out her skirt. "Why are you so cross?"

"Maxwell will start a war that Warring Tower can ill afford."

"Perhaps." Anne lifted one shoulder. "Perhaps not."

Thomas cocked his brow at her cheery voice. "Ye *dinnae*

understand. What little wealth Warring Tower had died with my *da*. A war would cause this tower and this family to be beholden to the Maxwells for all eternity."

Ewart leaned over and whispered something into Ma Audrey's ear, producing color to her cheeks and a laugh from her lips. What change of events was this? She had always despised the man. Gavin Armstrong would sit up in his grave if he saw such a display.

The warmth of Anne's touch stopped his dark thoughts. "Do not spin a tale in your mind. Your mother has no affection for that man."

He pulled his hand away, letting the cold of the laird's ring chill his fingers. "*Dinnae* think ye know my thoughts, *wumman.*" Thomas slurred. "My eyes can see what is going on here."

"And what is that?" Anne glared at him as if he were a petulant child. "Lady Audrey has been brave a long time. She tried to run this keep with little assistance. Now you have come home, and her younger son is on the mend. A little merriment will do her well. Can you not be happy for your mother?"

The half-filled mug slipped from Thomas's fingers as he rose from his seat. "She is not my *ma*," he shouted from the top of his lungs.

The hall grew silent. He turned away from the pity he saw in Anne's eyes, but he could not turn away from the pale gaze and the tears pooling in Ma Audrey's eyes.

How he hoped there was a hell, and he hoped the devil would swallow him up soon.

CHAPTER 22

Anne watched Thomas stumble from the hall. She should have given him aid, but a man deep in drink needed only one thing—time to sleep off the effects of his folly. 'Twas obvious a part of him died earlier when he took Marcas's ring. A month past she would have claimed that all Thomas wanted was riches and power, but now, knowing him better, she knew the truth. He despised both and had spent a good part of his life running away from such things. His gambling was just another way to sabotage his life.

As she glanced around the room, she wondered why he wished to throw this all away. He had a loving family. True, Lady Audrey wasn't his mother, but she wasn't Marcas's either. That could not be the cause of Thomas's distress. What demon dug at his soul?

A gruff laugh drew her attention to where Lady Audrey sat with the two Maxwell men. The elder one was well into his cups like Thomas, but the younger was clear-eyed and keen on Lady Audrey. Rumor at the keep spoke of an affection Ewart had for her when she was young, before she married Gavin Armstrong. But that was twenty years ago. Could the man still desire the lady?

Nay, Ewart's look didn't hold desire, more to the opposite. He kept pushing the wine goblet in her direction. "Come, Lady Audrey, you have barely touched your wine. Cost me a great deal of coin and trouble to obtain it, but I would do anything for you. I know how much you love French wines. This bottle is far better than the last one I gave you." Though his words dripped of honey, the hard lines of his face oozed with malice.

Cheeks already flushed and a rash creeping up her neck, Lady Audrey took a small sip from her cup. Her eyes hazy and distant like when Anne had met her. . . could it be possible?

Like a stampeding horse, Anne rushed next to Lady Audrey's side. "My lady, you look tired. You are just out of the sickbed, and I am sure you need rest."

Lazily, Ewart dropped his arm from the back of the chair to Lady Audrey's shoulder. "She is fine. She only needs a little more wine to ease her malady."

"I believe she has had enough this eve." Swiftly, Anne pushed the goblet away, causing it to spill.

Ewart jumped to his feet, glaring at Anne. "Now look what ye have done." He turned a simpering smile toward Lady Audrey, righting the cup. "We shall have to give ye another."

Anne moved her hand above the goblet, hindering the pour. "She needs rest not wine. I have sat by Marcas's side and seen illness firsthand. Lady Audrey needs her sleep."

"I agree with the lass," piped in Rory Maxwell. "The wine seems to have an ill effect on her. See how she is wobblin'? Take her upstairs. She can try more of the drink tomorrow if she wishes."

A shake of anger overtook Ewart's body. The elder Maxwell laughed at his son's fury. Anne had no intentions of seeing how this scene would play out. She helped Lady Audrey to her feet and gently began to guide her to the stairs.

"Tomorrow then, sweet lady," Ewart called from behind them.

Anne picked up her pace. Lady Audrey let out a faint burp, and a rank smell like urine seeped into the air. As she suspected, the wine was tainted with foxglove. Much more of the wine and they would be digging a grave come morning. Without a doubt, they had found their villain. The question was why. Could Ewart be holding a twenty-year-old grudge? 'Twould seem unlikely. Then why now after all these years would Ewart wish to poison Lady Audrey?

The answer would have to wait until the morn when Thomas had a clearer head. Another worry struck Anne. What would come of the alliance between the Maxwells and the Armstrongs once the truth was told?

To Anne's relief, a guard still stood at Cecilia's door. The man offered to stand between Lady Audrey's and Lady Cecilia's chambers. Ewart wouldn't dare come near either room with this burly fellow in place.

After spending a few hours at Lady Audrey's bedside, helping her to vomit out the poison, Anne made her way up to her own pallet off the laird's chamber. The day had been long and full of surprises. She would need some rest for tomorrow would bring more trials. Kneeling and folding her hands, Anne closed her eyes.

"Heavenly Father, I fear on the morrow I will add to the strife at this keep. Please calm everyone's spirit. Open our hearts and minds to your purpose. Let peace reign that all within these walls may give you the honor and glory you deserve. In your Son's name. Amen."

Anne crawled into bed and continued her prayers until God

in his mercy gave her sleep. The next morn, when the sun crept through the tiny window above her pallet, she stretched her arms high and wide before offering a prayer of thanksgiving. When finished, she placed her feet on the cool floor and hurried to see how Marcas fared. She found the laird sitting up in bed, his gaze casually examining his fingers. His cheeks held a healthy color, and his eyes were bright.

"Seems I am missing a piece of jewelry," he said calmly.

Anxiety plucked at Anne's spine. This was one problem she did not wish to contend with this morn. Not when she had a powder keg waiting for her in the hall. "My laird, knowing you were ill, your brother temporarily took over your duties. I daresay he resented you for making him to do so."

Marcas nodded as a small smile crept to his lips. "As he should. Where is my brother? I wish to speak to him."

As did she. "He is sleeping out in the stables, but I will happily get him when I fetch something to break your fast."

"That would be wonderful." He paused and cocked his head. "Are you a new healer? What happened to Tibbie? I wanted to speak to her about something."

He probably wanted to thank her. "She has quite the healing skill."

"Aye." His gaze drifted away as if he were catching a memory. "Among other things." His vison cleared, fixing Anne with a penetrating stare. "Can you bring her back?"

The woman was in such a hurry to leave, Anne doubted that a queen's fortune could tempt her back to Warring Tower. "I could ask Master Thomas his thoughts on the matter."

"Do that."

His answer was sharp and quick. Anne wondered if there was more than thanks the young laird wished to offer the old healer.

"What is your name?" Marcas asked as she made her way to the door. "I should know the name of the angel who nursed me to sanity."

Slowly, she turned. She could not claim to be an angel. Well, maybe a fallen one. "I am Anne Howell. I came here with your brother."

Again, Marcas's gaze floated away. "Aw yes, now I remember. You are the woman he fancies."

Heat rose from her toes and burned through her body. "You are mistaken, sir. We are naught but acquaintances."

"I doubt that. My brother would not drag you to his home if you were just acquaintances." His eyes closed, signaling the conversation had ended.

Anne crept out of the room. Marcas clearly felt the effects of his illness. Yet his words filled her heart with hope. Perhaps, just maybe, Thomas held more than a friendly affection for her. For she could not envision a life without him and his silly antics. Her feet stalled on the upper-level steps. There it was, the man had wormed his way into her heart. How then would she survive once they parted ways?

A cry rang out from below, hastening her descent. Lady Audrey stood in her shift outside Cecilia's chamber. "She is gone again and look what she has done." The door lay open, sprinkles of sunlight illuminating Lady Audrey's bare feet. Where was the guard?

A sorrowful moan floated from the room. Anne crept in to find the guard lying on the floor rubbing his bloodied head. "The wench tricked me. Hit me with her chamber pot and then bashed me in the face with that candlestick."

Just like she had done to Laird Jaxon. Anne helped the guard to his feet before turning her attention to Lady Audrey.

"Sound the alarm. She could not have gone far."

The older woman dashed to her room and shouted out the window, awaking all within the tower. With his arm around her shoulders, Anne guided the guard down to the great hall before ordering the servants to bring water and cloths. By the time they had reached a bench by the table, Blair had returned with her requested items.

"I'm sorry, mistress." The guard winced as Blair was none too delicate with his care. "She was weeping so. I thought she might be ill, so I opened the door—"

"And let the banshee out," Blair finished.

The elder Maxwell stomped over and washed a hand over his face. So far gone was he last eve that he slept in the hall all night. "What? Cecilia has vanished again."

Where was his evil son? Anne glanced around the hall. The villain was nowhere in sight. However, a loud thumping on the stairs gave way to a welcoming sight. Thomas entered the hall with a sword buckled at his waist.

"What goes here?" he asked, a red curl falling over his wrinkled brow.

"It seems Lady Cecilia has flown her perch again," Maxwell answered while Blair continued to dab and clean the guard's wound.

Thomas threw back his head, running his hands through his hair. "God's teeth."

"Ye should have thrown her in the cells below like I told ye." Maxwell poured himself and the guard a tankard of ale. "Here, man, this will take the sting out of yer noggin."

To Anne's vexation, the guard greedily gulped down the drink.

"You were right, the lass is slipperier than an eel. She could not have gone far. The gate is closed. Methinks she is still inside." Thomas strode back to the spiral steps, barking out orders. Moments later, the long room emptied except for Anne, the guard, and Laird Maxwell.

Refilling his and the guard's cup again, the old laird smiled. "Well, lass, how are ye enjoying yer stay in Scotland?"

What manner of questioning was this when Cecilia was missing? Could he too be involved in Lady Audrey's poisoning? Anne hesitated before providing a polite reply. "'Tis a nice change to the Welsh and English countryside." A crusty laugh followed by a loud cough echoed off the walls. "Is it not? Well, ye better get used to the dampness and the constant strife of its people. Methinks Thomas will be wantin' you to stay for more than just a little while."

Laird Maxwell's words were meant to tease, but deep down, Anne hoped the man and his ale had not spoken a yarn.

Once the guard was back on his feet and Laird Maxwell had joined in the search, Anne headed back up the stairs. Her heartbeat picked up when she found no one in Lady Audrey's chamber. Did Ewart use the ruckus in the hall to make off with the poor woman? Wouldn't someone notice Lady Audrey in her shift being dragged out of the tower?

A thump above perked Anne's ear.

Marcas.

He had been left unattended, and Cecilia roams free. Anne raced up the remaining stairs. *Please, Lord, keep the young laird out of harm's way.*

Opening the door, she breathed a sigh of relief when she

found Lady Audrey sitting at the foot of Marcas's bed. "Oh, I heard a noise and thought Laird Armstrong needed my help."

Lady Audrey pointed to a chair in the middle of the room. "The chair fell over when I moved it away from the bed. But as you can see, it has been righted, and my son is just fine." She patted Marcas's leg. "More than fine."

He looked at Lady Audrey with affection. "And how are you this day, *Ma*?"

"I have a slight headache, but all in all, I have been feeling better every passing hour."

Indeed, both were quickly becoming the picture of health thanks to keeping a villain and a temptress away. How then would Marcas and Lady Audrey take to being betrayed by family and friends? A revelation that would not be uttered until Thomas was present.

"We can thank Widow Howell for both. For she stayed by your side until you were better." Lady Audrey reached out her hand to Anne. "She took care of me too."

A deep frown creased Marcas's mouth. "Healer Tibbie was here to take care of me."

"Aye, but she was so impressed with Anne's ability that once you were on the mend, she left you in capable hands."

Anne bit her lip. Her skills had nothing to do with Tibbie's quick exit. There had been relief and fear in the healer's eyes when it became clear that Marcas was on the mend. Something else made the healer leave quickly.

"Still, I just wish she were here now." Marcas rolled his head from side to side, stretching his neck muscles. "I could use something for these kinks in my neck."

"I do not understand what your fascination is with that woman. You spent so much time with her when you should have been paying more attention to your wife." Lady Audrey let go of Anne's hand before leaning over to adjust Marcas's coverlet.

Foreboding skittered up Anne's spine. Why would a handsome young laird spend time with an aged healer? "Are you interested in apothecary, my laird?"

"Only for one thing . . ." Marcas's gaze slid to the empty goblet that used to hold his medicine, the poison Cecilia dutifully gave him every day.

Lady Audrey inched her way up the bed, her eyes soft and tender as she looked at her son. She brushed a loving hand over Marcas's shoulder. "Let us speak of something else. We must celebrate that you are better. Soon you will be able to take over your duties as laird."

The color in Marcas's cheeks receded. A stony mask descended. "Where is Cecilia? I have not seen her in a long while."

Both women looked at each other. Lady Audrey shook her head slightly in warning, but the small motion was not lost to Marcas.

"What?" He sat up straight. "What is wrong? Is my wife ill?"

Anne swallowed hard. He had the right to know the truth. "Your wife is missing."

Like a spry youth, Marcas threw back the covers. "Where are my jack and sword?"

Rising, Lady Audrey placed her hands on Marcas's chest. "Cease this. You are not well enough. I'm sure it is all a misunderstanding that will be laid to rest now that you are well." She turned and cast Anne a knowing look. "Thomas and Laird Maxwell are looking for her. She may be in the kitchens or anywhere for that matter. Warring Tower is not a small keep. I am sure she will turn up."

Marcas pushed Lady Audrey aside as if she were a feather. "Nay, *Ma*. Something has happened to her, or she would be at my side doing my bidding. Giving me my medicine."

Anne stepped in his path as he stumbled toward his sword. "Stop. Lady Cecilia left of her own free will. Your worry is misplaced." His wild actions propelled Anne to speak her mind. "She does not deserve your devotion. She has been poisoning you."

The fire abated from his eyes as he fell back onto the bed. "Ye are wrong. She *wasnae* poisoning me." He raised his sad eyes. "My wife would never do such a thing." The truth shining through. Cecilia had been a pawn. She thought she was aiding in her husband's recovery when she administered the poison.

Everything became crystal clear. Healer Tibbie had coiled like a snake when she saw the broken pieces of the medicine jar. She had lied when she said there was no smell of poison. No wonder the healer had hovered over the young laird's bed until he was better.

Marcas's lower lip trembled. "I poisoned myself."

CHAPTER 23

Cecilia had vanished like mist under a warm morning sun. None of this surprised Thomas. Undoubtedly, Marcas had shown the lass the hidden tunnel under the tower, and she had fled long before anyone noticed. She would make her way east to Elliot land. If she left on foot, they would be able to find her quickly. However, if she had an accomplice and left by horse, she could reach her kin and spin a tale of lies in no time. Neal Elliot would want blood if he found his daughter wandering the countryside alone and frightened.

Hopefully, Hayes had reached the Elliots already and had been able to reason with their laird. Thomas shook his head as he exited the stables leading his Galloway pony. What amount of reasoning could get a man to accept that his daughter tried to commit murder? Nay, it was hopeless. Elliot would want vengeance.

Thomas's gaze drifted up toward Marcas's chamber. With his brother growing strength daily, perhaps some agreeable solution could be negotiated with Neal Elliot. Maybe returning her to her father for a quick and quiet annulment. Again, Thomas's spirits fell. When had anything been kept quiet on the Scottish marches? Bah. One would have better luck uniting the English and Scottish crowns.

"Where ye goin'?" Laird Maxwell lumbered into the stables with a furrowed brow. "I hope not to chase down that pirate brother of Lady Audrey's."

"Nay. I plan to scout the marches." Thomas wanted to add, "and to inspect what new damage Maxwell's moss-troopers were inflicting on Armstrong cottars." Instead, he adjusted his saddle on his horse's back.

"Good. Lady Audrey has suffered enough over the years, and if the wretch is gone for good, all the better."

"Hayes searches for Lady Cecilia." Thomas gave the saddle strap a tight tug.

"A wench who has caused nothing but conflict. I had first thought that when Marcas married her, she would be a replacement for the daughter Audrey lost, but I have been wrong there too."

Thomas's hands stilled on the saddle. "What do you mean the child she lost? Did she have a dalliance with someone else after Gavin died?"

"Nay. Francis told me she was with child when yer *da* died. The loss of him and ye leavin' had all been too much for her. In her grief, the *bairn* slipped out of her belly too early." The old laird shook his head. "Your gran thought Audrey would soon follow your *da*. Took her a long time to come around."

Blood drained downward and pooled in Thomas's gut. Ma Audrey had been pregnant, and Gran knew. He had left them alone in their grief. Another sin to lay at his feet.

"Laird Armstrong," a servant called, rushing from the tower. "Lady Audrey would like ye to come to Laird Marcas's chamber, posthaste."

The urgency in the man's voice chilled Thomas to the core.

He handed the reins of his horse over to Maxwell and rushed into the tower taking the steps two at a time. In his brother's room, he found Ma Audrey and Anne helping Marcas dress.

"Are you that well, brother?" Thomas strode to Marcas's side and gave him a great hug.

Pulling back, the young laird raised a hand to his throat. "Somewhat."

A fit Scotsman would beat his chest and call for ale. Stepping back, Marcas sat on the chair near his bed.

"Then should you be up?" Thomas asked, trying to tamp down his worry, but like a cramp that vexes a muscle, he couldn't relax.

Anne stepped forward holding his brother's boots. "We wanted him to rest, but he demanded to speak to you . . . fully clothed."

The edge in her voice only enhanced his uneasiness. Thomas flexed his fingers at his side to control his growing apprehension. *You abandoned them.* "What is the matter?"

As if rehearsed, both women looked away while Marcas inhaled his breath. "Brother, there is no need to shout. My hearing is as good as always." His words came out barely above a whisper.

"Then pray tell, why are these two playing the part of mourners instead of rejoicing that you are up and well?"

"Because they have just learned the reason for my malady."

A painful pause crept over the room. The weight of this predicament rested on Thomas's shoulders. *You abandoned them.*

He wanted to shout. Why all the mystery? Was Healer Tibbie wrong when she said Marcas was getting better? Would he always be weak and frail? Thomas relaxed his stance and dropped his arms to his sides. "What do you wish to tell me?"

Like an arrow tip, his brother's gaze sharpened. "I poisoned myself with a potion that has no smell. One that would kill slowly as not to raise suspicion. I believe it came from Italy."

What foolery was this? "What are you talking about? Why would you seek out poison?" A muscle in Thomas's cheek began to twitch. "You say such to protect your wife." He looked to Anne and Ma Audrey, but neither woman gave their support to his claim.

"Thomas, Thomas." His brother shook his head. "Why would she poison me? What would she gain?" Marcas's lungs seemed to deflate as a slow, steady stream of air left his lips.

"A cold heart, an evil bent, a lover. Who knows what makes women do what they do?" Thomas wiped his sweaty hands on his thighs, trying to brush away the absurd lie. "Fleeing her home twice is proof enough that she is guilty."

Marcas leaned forward in his chair. "Twice? What do you speak of?"

Thomas winced. He had no desire to go into Cecilia's uncanny ability to slip through their fingers.

"Methinks she left because she knew if I died, she would not be welcome here." Marcas turned an accusatory gaze on Ma Audrey.

The older woman's lower lip wobbled. "I know I could have been kinder to her, but her ways of running the tower were so contrary to mine. She is so messy; the kitchens are filthy. I feared your illness was caused by spoiled meats or curdled milk."

"Perhaps you could have guided her into learning these skills." Marcas shifted his attention back to Thomas. "All of us benefit from guidance. Is that not right, brother?"

There was the conviction. Thomas had left his brother to train himself. Certainly Maxwell helped, but the old man had a keep to run and a wicked son to control. Thomas left Gran and Ma Audrey. Even a spear through the heart could not atone for what he had done.

The disbelief and denial that coursed through Thomas's veins evaporated. The clarity of the situation shined as bright as the Star of Bethlehem. Marcas's rash act was a cry for deliverance from a life he was ill-equipped to handle.

"This is my fault," Thomas whispered, dropping his chin to his chest.

Ma Audrey touched his shoulder. "Son. Do not punish yourself."

You abandoned them to languish in poverty. A storm of white-hot self-loathing rushed through him and shredded his heart. He gritted his teeth as the dark frenzy overtook him. "If I weren't a pigheaded fool, none of this would have happened. I am not worthy to be your son or anybody else's." He turned and stormed out the door.

"Thomas, Thomas, stop." Anne called, rushing after him.

Without pausing, he hurried down the stairs and out of the tower like a madman hell-bent on destruction. The ominous clouds overhead bellowed. The winds picked up. A heavy drop of rain fell on his cheek followed by another and another until the sky wept with him. Thomas brushed the tears from his eyes and stormed to the stable where he found his horse tied up outside.

"Wait, Thomas," Anne shouted just mere steps from him now. "Your family loves you and needs you. Why do you push them away?" She grabbed his shoulder and whirled him about, waving her hand around the courtyard. "What man here would not kill for such love? Blood or not, we just saved your brother, and you turn your back on him?"

The rain pelted his back like a hard lash. He pulled and turned away, slapping his feet in the mud. Thomas unhitched his horse from the stable wall and led him to the gate. He could not let her see his tears, his despair, his shame. Beyond the gate, he tried to mount the beast, but he slipped and fell. Brown ooze splattered his clothing and face. His sodden hair hung like a soiled rag. He beat his head with his fist and let out an agonizing howl. His whole body rocked like a ship being tossed on a chaotic sea.

A slopping of feet reached his side, and a hand reached in front of him. "Let me help you up. You don't belong in the muck. You are not a perfect person, Thomas, lo, I should know. But you have good in you. I have seen it and so have the people at this tower, your family." She pushed her hand closer. "Come now, we've traveled this far together. I'm not letting you go. You have grown on me like a knotty vine."

Even though the whole keep looked on, he could not control his weeping. He grabbed Anne's hand and stood. "God, forgive me. For I have caused the woe that plagues this tower."

The last thing he remembered was Anne barking out orders to moss-troopers to carry him inside. Thomas winced. How long before the whole countryside spoke of him losing his wits? Further, she ordered others to draw him a bath and take it to his childhood room. Now clean, wearing fresh clothing, Thomas sat in the chamber staring at a lone tallow.

The door swung open, and Anne entered carrying a plate of

mutton and a mug of ale. She slid the drink and plate onto the table. "Eat. You need to renew your strength."

"I need to hang my head in shame," he retorted. "I broke down in front of the whole tower."

Bland as an oat cake, she gazed at him. No look of judgment or disappointment showed on her face. "If that will give you solace, then do so, but get done with it quickly. I know you are a quick-witted, intelligent man. All here look to you for guidance."

A shallow, gritty laugh left his raw throat. "If they want me to lead them, then they are fools for I have a habit of giving up on people. I abandoned my family when they needed me the most."

She rushed to his side and knelt down. "What Marcas did was not your fault. He suffers from a melancholy that is beyond normal thinking. Such things are in your gran's apothecary book."

Thomas gave out a mirthless laugh. "This tower has a way of ripping the soul out of people. Did you know his mother killed herself? Jumped from the battlements. All because she loved another."

"Stop. The past is gone." Anne squeezed his hand.

Another dark night ten years ago swirled around Thomas's body. "You *dinnae* understand. The past is not gone. It lives in this tower. I had believed she was my mother too. The night I left I found out the truth—that I was not related to any Armstrong." His chest grew tight. He had not spoken the whole truth to anyone since that dreadful night. "I am a son of a whore. A woman who bartered her life to keep a queen alive."

Bewilderment replaced the kindness in her eyes. "I do not understand."

"Believe me, I fought the truth as well. Do you know about the English woman, Lady Jane Grey?"

Anne nodded slowly, looking at him as if his head was full of straw. "The heir who sat on the throne for nine days and soon after was beheaded for treason."

Thomas snorted, oh how he wished it were truly so. "My true mother resembled her. Being poor with a young *bairn* to feed, she traded her life for mine. She died on the block while the queen was whisked away. I wound up near the Scottish border in an English noble's home. His daughter, Edlyn, became my mother." With the whole story out, the tight band around his chest loosened a little. He breathed deep. "There *isnae* a drop of Scottish blood in me. I'm as English as they come. And if that *wasnae* enough, Ma Audrey was with child when I left. Had I known . . ." Thomas shook his head. "I must be honest; I might have still left."

He had expected many things—her to shrink away, to give him pity, to slap him in the face. Instead, she sat back on her heels and beheld him as if her were a cherished childhood friend.

"You and I are cut from the same cloth. Neither of us know our real parents. We both took flight to hide our pain and sorrow. But that is where the similarity ends. No one ever wanted me for anything more than a servant or someone to beat for their woes. No one ever cared about me. No one ever loved me. Not like I have seen the love poured out for you." Anne placed her hands on his cheeks and dried his glistening tears with her warm gaze. "But you were raised in love from the moment you were born. Your real mother died so you could have a better life. Your stepfather was willing to make you laird of this tower over his own true son. Lady Audrey loves you and does not blame you for what happened. I would fight for a love like that." She dropped her hands and rose to her feet. "Now, you can let the guilt of the past eat you up, or you can ask God to give you the strength to become the man all who love you know you can be." She bounced her head with such determination, he'd be a fool to debate her wisdom.

Holding out his dirk and his sword, she took a deep breath. "So what is it going to be, Laird Armstrong? Are you going to wallow in shame and self-loathing, or are you going to stand up and take care of your family?"

This woman who lingered in fear in a cave, who followed him into danger, believed even at his lowest there was good to be found in him. No longer would he flounder in self-pity because he didn't believe he deserved God's forgiveness. The band around his chest snapped. He would thank God for His mercy and become the man all here at Warring Tower wanted him to be.

"You should have been born a man. You would have been a fine laird." Thomas rose and took the dirk and sword and slid them into his belt. "But I am glad you are not."

With wide arms, he engulfed her, taking in her sweet scent of floral earth and clean sea. Mimicking her actions, he cradled her head in his hands. Her beautiful face spirited him away on angels' wings. The moment their lips touched, the pain of the past began to ease, washed away by her tender kisses. He marveled in the healing strength of it. The blessing God was giving to him even when he didn't know he needed it.

He broke the kiss but held her tight. "Anne, I—"

A firm knock on the door broke his words. "My laird, riders approach."

The urge to sigh welled up in his chest, but instead of giving out the weary noise, he took Anne's hands and brought them to his lips. "When this is settled, we shall have a long, long talk."

He turned, threw back his shoulders, and opened the door. "Ready the men on the battlements. We may have a fight on our hands."

CHAPTER 24

Anne wanted to run after him and badger him until he spoke his thoughts, but Jesus did not say in the beatitudes blessed are the naggers. Nay, he said, blessed are the meek. An attribute she failed to have. She took a deep breath and smoothed her hands over her skirt. *Blessed are the meek, blessed are the meek, blessed are the meek.*

Even as calm washed through her, the whole tower vibrated with vigor and tension. Moss-troopers and guards rumbled up the battlements. Shouts echoed in the courtyard as the gate was closed. When she gazed out the window, she saw thick smoke bellowing from the kitchens. A heavy smell of burned peat rose in the air. She shuddered at the thought of black tar being poured over invading troopers.

With her heart hammering, she raced up to Marcas's chamber hoping to get a better look at the activity in the courtyard. There she found the young laird wearing his jack of plate, his shiny boots, and his sword strapped to his side. "I must go help my brother."

Anne blocked his exit. "My laird, do you think you're well enough?"

"Save your breath. I have already tried to talk him out of

his foolish plan." Lady Audrey stood near the window holding a long, wicked-looking dirk. "If Laird Elliot wants a fight, we shall give it to him."

What was this? Since Anne's arrival, Lady Audrey had always been the picture of blessed are the meek. The effects of the poisons were gone from both of them. They stood like two angelic warriors. She should try to talk some sense into them, but even the fear of the Almighty wouldn't prevent them from their task. Suddenly the words that Roland always spoke when he was in a fix rattled in her brain. *"If you cannot take down your foe, then you had best join him."*

Anne walked over to the small table and picked up the golden candlestick. "Where shall we make our stand?"

"I know my brother; he will meet them head-on. I plan to be at his side." Marcas took the candlestick out of her hand. "You two should stay here where it is safe."

Lady Audrey raised her dagger. "I'll not stand by. I aim to aid my children."

Marcas headed for the door before turning back. "*Ma*, you are so stubborn." He then gave Anne a pointed look. "Take her to the battlements so she can see what is happening. Otherwise, I fear she will ride out and join us on the field." He then flipped his attention back to Lady Audrey. "Please stay there. Neither I nor Thomas need to worry about you." Without another word, he was gone, along with the feeble young man who had tried to kill himself.

"Marcas," Lady Audrey cried, racing toward the door.

Anne quickly caught her by the elbow. "Let him go. This may give him the strength he needs to live on."

As Anne's words sunk in, Lady Audrey stopped her struggle. "You are right. If he is ever to be the laird of Warring Tower, he must learn to stand firm in a fight. Though I do not know how that will be possible. Marcas has always been more of the scholarly type."

"Perhaps his astute mind will serve him well today. One cannot win a fight with only brawn." Anne fished her arm through Lady Audrey's.

"A Scotsman would strike you dead for such words."

"So would a Welshman, and I wager an Englishman too. Come, let us go to the battlements and plan our next course of action. For a woman's cunning can also win the day."

Once above, the pair found Rory Maxwell and a slew of archers perched on the west battlement, readying their bows. Lady Audrey pushed next to the old laird and peered over the edge. "I thought you would be out there by Thomas's side."

He motioned with his chin to the field. "Ewart stands with him. If the man ever plans to be laird of Maxwell lands, he had best show his character now."

Anne squeezed next to Lady Audrey and examined the scene below. Thomas sat on a Galloway pony with a handful of moss-troopers at his side, strong and determined. He would not let his family down. A flutter of pride filled her belly.

Ewart sat with a line of Maxwell men behind Thomas. Galloping toward them was Jaxon with Laird Elliot, plus a small contingent of troopers. No doubt, the rest of their men lay over the hill.

"Where is my brother?" Lady Audrey asked, scanning the approaching riders.

"Hayes, more than likely, hightailed it out of here this morn. Probably heading back to England." Maxwell bumped his elbow into Lady Audrey's side. "Ye know how delicate the English can be." A chuckle of mirth spread through the archers.

The humor did not decrease the lines of concern on Lady Audrey's face. Anne placed an arm around the older woman's shoulders. "Worry not, I am sure he will show up."

"Look there." Maxwell pointed. "There comes Marcas. He cuts a fine figure ridin' that Galloway." Instead of a close friend of the family, Rory Maxwell preened like a proud grandfather.

Blond and blue-eyed, Marcas didn't look anything like the old, rugged laird. Yet, Anne could not shake away the absurd thought.

He leaned his head toward Lady Audrey. "Ye have done well with him."

The poor woman's whole body stiffened, no doubt thinking of the poison Marcas inflicted on his own body.

"My so . . ." Maxwell started.

Anne could feel Lady Audrey shudder before giving him a look of censure.

"I mean, his father would be proud of him," Maxwell's voice hitched . . . with tears?

As if seeing the workings of Anne's mind, Lady Audrey quickly added, "He looks just like my dear departed husband."

Indeed, his resemblance to Gavin Armstrong had been established long ago. Something else wormed its way around these two. When this conflict was over, she would have to dissect the meaning. Anne turned her attention back to the field. Jaxon and Laird Elliot brought their horses to a stop, a fair distance separating them from Thomas and Marcas.

"Where is my daughter?" Neal Elliot shouted, leaning forward in his saddle.

"Laird Elliot, please. Let us lay down our arms and settle our differences over a mug of ale." Thomas's plea was met with a loud roar.

"You keep my daughter as a prisoner, and you expect me to sit down and drink with ye?" Elliot's horse pranced beneath him. "Then you be as big of a fool as yer brother."

Marcas edged his horse forward. "How wonderful to see you, Father." The familiar usage made Elliot bristle and sit straighter in his saddle. "You wish to see my wife, and I long to be reunited with her again as well."

"What's he doin'?" Maxwell whispered. "He shouldn't be sayin' that. Elliot will rip this place apart if he finds out the lass is gone. Ye should have taught him not to be so honest."

Lady Audrey waved off. "Give him a chance."

"Are you trying to tell me my daughter is not here?" The moss-troopers next to Laird Elliot raised their spears. Jaxon drew his sword.

Thomas edged his mount forward. "Think what you are doing. Look about." He waved at Ewart and the Maxwell men. "You will be struck down before you can call your troopers from the hills."

"Not so," said Ewart, moving his mount and men forward. He nodded, and his men drew their swords and raised their weapons, pointing them at Marcas's and Thomas's backs.

Anne's heart fell to her toes as Lady Audrey's fingers curled around the stone battlement to steady her stance.

"What's the fool doin'?" Rory Maxwell roared.

"Methinks it would be wiser if the Maxwell family stands with the Elliots and Jaxon Armstrong against these vile fiends." Like a penitent sinner, Ewart clutched his chest. "Ye have no idea what wickedness dwells in this tower. Yer daughter fled for her life."

Laird Maxwell slammed the battlements with both fists. "I'll run his sorry hide through." He grabbed an archer's bow and aimed it at his son's head. "Ewart, ye pile of dung," Maxwell yelled. "Ye be orderin' my men. Stand down or I swear yer next breath will be yer last."

Ewart swiveled and looked up at his father. "Perhaps not, *Da.*" With a quick signal, a Maxwell trooper lunged and smashed the old laird in the head. The bow slipped from his fingers as his legs crumpled beneath him.

"What are you doing?" Anne scrunched down next to the wounded laird. Her gaze swept over all the men on the battlements. "You're all filthy traitors. How could you take that Judas's side? Thomas and Marcas are the lairds of this land. Where is your God-fearing allegiance?" Her words sent a rumble through the men, and pretty soon they were fighting among themselves.

Lady Audrey punched one of the archers in the nose and grabbed his bow. Taking Laird Maxwell's dagger from his belt, Anne popped to her feet and stood back-to-back with Lady Audrey. She raised her weapon. "If anyone so dares as tries to hurt Lady Audrey, I will gut you alive," she growled. Many of the troopers and archers lowered their weapons.

"Ewart," Lady Audrey cried, aiming the bow at Ewart's head. "Think again what you do. For I have practiced many a year to improve my skill. I shall not miss."

Not a trooper bellowed nor a weapon clanked. Even the dark smoke that filled the air dissipated. An eerie stillness filled Warring Tower, making Anne want to hold her breath and drop to her knees in prayer. Lady Audrey eased the bow string back. Thomas and Marcas sat on their mounts with swords drawn. Laird Elliot's fist hung midair ready to signal the attack.

None would win this fight.

Anne looked heavenward and sent up a quick prayer. *Dear*

God, show your might and stay the hands that wish to cause mayhem this day. Cool their heads and hobble their feet so that they may not be able to harm a soul.

The rumble of three horses approaching from the west paused the attack, releasing a mite of tension.

Lady Audrey relaxed her fingers on the bow. "Asher," she called.

Indeed, it was the merchant-pirate with Healer Tibbie and Cecilia. The young lady rode right up to Marcas's side, leaned over, and kissed her husband's cheek. "You look well, my laird."

Laird Elliot lowered his fist. "Cecilia, what goes here?"

Taking up her reins, Cecilia guided her mount between both factions. "Much. And if you can remove yourself from that vile man's side." She pointed her finger at Jaxon. "I will be happy to tell you."

Jaxon raised his sword ready to call the attack.

Anne sucked in her breath as Lady Audrey now fixed her bow on Armstrong kin.

However, before the order could be given, Laird Elliot jabbed the hilt of his sword in Jaxon's side, unseating him. "Hold. I wish to hear what my daughter has to say," he bellowed.

"*Da*," she matched his roar. "All will be explained if we can discuss this peacefully."

"Lower your weapons." On Laird Elliot's nod, all moss-troopers sheathed their swords and lowered their spears.

Laird Maxwell moaned, and Anne helped him to his feet. "What's happen'?"

"Cecilia has returned, and Laird Elliot has ordered his men to stand down."

Seeing Jaxon on the ground, it didn't take Rory Maxwell

long to figure out the lay of the land. "Lower your bows," he hollered to archers on the battlements. "Or ye'll be sleepin' in my cells this eve."

Once the order was followed, Anne rushed down the stairs with Lady Audrey on her heels. They may have averted a fight, but the war was far from over.

CHAPTER 25

The air crackled with tension as the hall filled with eager moss-trooper ears. Thomas had to tamp down the desire to throw Ewart into the cells below, but peace was needed to sort out this mess not hot heads and terse words.

Rory Maxwell wasn't inclined to oblige. He stormed over to his son and punched him in the nose. The younger Maxwell howled and cupped his wounded snout. "What's the matter with ye? How could ye turn on yer own kin?" Rory shouted, and the room grew quiet.

Kin? The Maxwells were close to the Armstrong family, but they did not share blood. In fact, the only relative present outside the immediate family was Jaxon Armstrong.

"Ye love these fifthly Armstrongs more than me," Ewart growled, dabbing his nose.

The elder Maxwell tightened his hands into fists once again and lunged toward his son.

Thomas quickly stepped between the pair, stretching out his arms. "Cease this. Nothing will be resolved with fists and heated words. Let us sit and calmly work out our differences."

Anne nodded her agreement, and Thomas threw his shoulders

back at her approval. His Anne stepped closer to Blair.

He shifted his gaze to the maid. "Some drink perhaps to cool our dry throats and soothe the high tempers?"

She flopped her hands on her apron. "I'll have to send a lad to get some clean mugs from the kitchen. We *dinnae* keep such a large supply in the hall scullery." She shook her head. With a glare to the Maxwells, she added, "Might need more small beer too. We *arenae* as high and mighty as some who are flushed with coin and ale." On that, she gave the assembly her back and disappeared into the scullery.

"Now then. Let us take a seat." Thomas winced, there weren't enough chairs or stools within the hall to accommodate the families and their moss-troopers. "Or find a comfortable spot to stretch your legs."

Mumblings and grumblings reverberated off the stone walls as most found a place to stand or sit. Laird Elliot took a seat at the table with Jaxon and Rory Maxwell. Cecilia sat next to her father with Marcas on her other side. Hayes dragged a chair from the hearth to the table for Ma Audrey and then stood sentinel behind her. Healer Tibbie stood close to Hayes while Ewart sulked against a far wall.

"I shall go help Blair," Anne said. "This is a family matter."

Thomas caught her arm. "Nay, stay. For you are as much a part of this family as I am. I need your calming wisdom and your keen eye."

Her warm smile and glistening eyes eased the knots in his stomach. "You are a good man, Thomas Armstrong. Heal your family . . . there will be plenty of time for us to talk later, and I fear Blair will never return with enough ale." She gently removed his hand from her arm and entered the scullery.

"Armstrong, explain what is going on here," Neal Elliot

bellowed in Thomas's direction. "Was my daughter a prisoner here or not? Why did she feel the need to flee to Jaxon Armstrong's home?"

Thomas straightened, ready to give an answer when Cecilia placed a hand on her father's arm. "*Da*, methinks I should answer these questions."

Heaven help them, her words would only inflame the masses. After all, they did lock her up. Thomas stepped forward. "My laird—"

"Let her speak," Hayes interrupted. "Her words and those of Healer Tibbie will enlighten us all."

"And just who do ye be?" Neal Elliot asked.

"He is my brother," Ma Audrey answered, lifting a bright smile toward Hayes.

"By all that is unholy. There be more Englishmen in the Armstrong household than there are Scots." Neal Elliot shook his head.

"Here, here," Ewart piped in from his corner. "A lot of mongrels."

"Shut yer mouth," Rory Maxwell roared. "Nobody wants to hear from the likes of ye."

Feeling a fever of fury escalating, Thomas held up his hands. "Come, come. Let us discuss our concerns in a civil manner."

"Agreed," echoed Hayes. "So let Lady Cecilia speak."

A murmur went through the hall as all heads turned to the young woman. With an appreciative nod toward Hayes, she began her tale. "I know many here thought I was trying to poison my husband, but I *wasnae*. I simply followed his wishes by giving him the potion he wanted to take. There really was no reason to lock me up."

The whole room erupted. Neal Elliot shot to his feet and drew his sword. "I have heard enough. How dare ye imprison my daughter."

Before Thomas could even call for calm, Cecilia equally rose and placed a hand on her father's sword. "Stop, *Da*. Ye *dinnae* know all of the story."

The hall slowly grew quiet once again. A war of emotions broke out on Laird Elliot's face. Finally, the tenderness for his daughter won out, and he placed his sword back in its sheath, taking his seat once again. "Ye better give me a reason why I shouldn't slit every Armstrong's throat."

Jaxon bristled. "Not all Armstrongs are of the same bent."

Cecilia leaned over her father and pointed an accusing finger at Jaxon. "Aye, not Marcas and Thomas, but ye are. When I came to ye for help, ye tried to help yerself to my body."

With a lion's roar, Laird Elliot jumped from his seat and wrapped his hands around Jaxon's neck, lifting him from his chair. "How dare ye try to put yer soiled manhood—"

"Laird Elliot, your anger will not help anyone here." Ma Audrey rose and banged a tankard on the table. The loud voices fell to mumbling and grumbling. "We shall deal with Laird Jaxon after we have heard Lady Cecilia's account."

With a healthy shove, Laird Elliot pushed Jaxon to his guards. "Watch him closely. *Dinnae* let him out of yer sight."

The guards pulled their dirks from their belts and held them to Jaxon's side. "The girl lies," he protested, but the red of Laird Elliot's face and the shaking of his body quickly ended Jaxon's complaint. Wisely, he held his tongue, or it might just have been cut from his head.

"*Da*." Lady Cecilia gently reached with her hand, dragging her father back to his seat for the second time. "He *didnae* touch me. Thomas Armstrong and Master Hayes came and rescued me."

Thomas's shoulders slumped as he blew out a breath of relief. Thankfully, Cecilia left out the details of her rescue.

"When I returned, I learned that Lady Audrey had been poisoned too. I knew all would suspect me. That is why I fled again."

Laird Elliot slammed his hands on the table. "What goes on in this tower?" He looked from Marcas to Thomas. "Does no one here protect their *wummin*?"

Ma Audrey bristled. "I need no man's protection, sir."

"Well, me daughter does." Laird Elliot grabbed Cecilia's arm and started to stand for the third time. "Let us go and leave these fools to their folly."

"Nay, *Da*. I aim to stay now. When I escaped the second time, Master Hayes found me. I told him where the jar of poison came from." Cecilia struggled against her father's pull. "Ye need to hear from Healer Tibbie."

"Clear the hall," Thomas shouted. The last thing they needed was for all in Warring Tower to learn of Marcas's attempt to end his own life.

The grumbles intensified, but Warring Tower's moss-troopers followed Thomas's orders. Close-lipped, Laird Elliot's troopers did not move.

"Please, sir." Hayes stepped forward, his demeanor tranquil yet firm. "I can confirm that what you will learn, you will not want shared with the rest of your people."

Laird Elliot weighed Hayes's words carefully. Like it or not, his family was connected to the Armstrongs by marriage. Begrudgingly, he ordered his men to leave. He then turned his wrath on Jaxon. "And throw that heap of dung in the cells below." His hawk-like eyes challenged every remaining Armstrong in the hall. "And no man best gainsay me on this."

No Armstrong lifted a voice or a finger in protest as Jaxon was taken to the cells below, yet others remained who did not need to hear about Marcas's deeds.

"I think it would be best if the Maxwells leave as well." Thomas motioned to the guards to take Ewart away.

"If it concerns the lad, it concerns me." Rory motioned his head toward Marcas, then folded his arms over his chest.

Laird Elliot raised his brows. "How so?"

"I am sure Laird Maxwell will not be opposed to having Ewart wait with his men in the courtyard," Ma Audrey interjected.

"Nay," Anne called, walking from the scullery with mugs in hand. She placed a tankard before Laird Elliot and Laird Maxwell. "Ewart must stay for he is important to what has happened at Warring Tower."

Thomas wanted to pull his hair out. What the devil was she doing? Ewart Maxwell didn't need to know about Marcas's desire to take his life. Why, Ewart would mass an army with or without his father's permission. Thomas was ready to override her words when Ma Audrey stood.

"The Maxwell moss-troopers will leave, but Laird Maxwell and his son can stay. The truth has been hidden long enough." Her words echoed off the hall walls. When only few remained, Ma Audrey sat down. "Now then, perhaps we should hear from Healer Tibbie before we decide how to proceed."

The old healer twisted her hands in front of her as she stepped toward the table, her gaze darting from one face to another before resting on Thomas's. She wetted her trembling lips before she spoke. "I *didnae* know what he was goin' to do with the poison. If I had, I *widnae* have given it to him."

"What's she blubberin' about?" Rory Maxwell asked before taking a quick swill of his drink.

"Hush up and let her speak," Ma Audrey chided. "Go on, Tibbie."

The healer nodded. "Laird Marcas visited my hut often. He had a keen desire to learn the healin' arts. Said he acquired some skill from his old nurse. Bein' I remembered the woman, I figured I would share some of my skills. I thought nothing of it when he said he wanted some arsenic. To kill rats, he said. I swear I *didnae* know how he would use it."

"What's the hag gettin' at?" Maxwell interrupted again.

This time the correction came from Hayes. "My laird, if you would listen."

"I gave Laird Marcas a bottle of the poison. When I come here and saw the broken jar, I knew what he had done. I got scared ye would blame me if he died, so I healed him as best I could." She shook her head. "For a while, I thought he *widnae* recover."

"Wait, are ye sayin' Marcas tried to kill himself?" Laird Maxwell lunged at Tibbie, wrapping his fist around the top of her tunic. "Take them words back. Ye are just tryin' to save yer own withered body."

Laird Elliot threw his head against the back of his chair. "Heaven help us all. My daughter is married to an unbalanced man."

Ewart cackled. "Oh, this is all so delicious. See, *Da*? See what ye love so much?"

Thomas called for calm, but every tongue wagged, and no one listened. Finally, a sharp whistle pierced the air.

All turned to stare at Anne. "Close your lips and sit back

down. I am sure Laird Marcas has something to say on this matter." She stomped her boot. "Go on now, sit."

Indeed, he did, but Thomas wasn't sure his stepbrother's malady was the wisest thing to be shared with the Maxwells and Elliots.

Thomas lifted a brow when Marcas kissed Cecilia's fingertips. Perhaps the couple did hold some affection for each other.

"My sweet, if I would have known you would take the blame, I never would have asked you to help me." Marcas stood and straightened his jack. "Since my *da* died and Thomas left, there always seemed to be a darkness lurking in this tower, but I promised Thomas that I would take care of the family, and I tried." He smiled down at his wife. "Marrying Cecilia was one of the best decisions I ever made. I know Ma Audrey and Cecilia *dinnae* always get along no matter how I tried to mend their differences. When Gran died and the keep still seemed to be in disarray, I felt like I had let everyone down." He held up a hand when protests arose. "I failed to live up to the Armstrong standards. I knew Thomas would return home once he learned of my death. He was always destined to be the laird of Warring Tower. Not I."

A trickle of guilt slid down Thomas's back. Oh, if Marcas only knew the truth. Laird Maxwell was vehemently shaking his head. Cecilia was crying, and Ma Audrey's eyes held a deep sadness. Thomas wanted to wrap his arms around his brother and confess his parentage, but not in front of the Maxwells . . . unless they already knew.

"But now I see the error of my actions, and I want to live." His sheepish look held worry. "Truth be told, I want to be laird of Warring Tower. I *dinnea* want to leave any of you."

Thomas rushed to Marcas's side and gave him a firm hug. "Brother, I want you to be laird too." He pulled the signet ring from his hand and handed it to Marcas.

From his corner, Ewart whooped. "Look at the loving family, a cabbage head and a coward who ran away." Having him witness all of this had been a mistake, but that could be easily rectified.

Thomas strode over to Ewart's side and lifted him by the front of his jack. "I think it is best ye leave."

"Wait," Anne shouted again. "We still have one poisoning to account for."

The anxiety on Anne's face caused Thomas to drop Ewart in a heap. Thomas went back to his seat on the other side of the table. The further Thomas was from Ewart the better, for the desire to pummel him was great. "Aye. I doubt Marcas could have done so being ill himself."

"I had nothin' to do with poisonin' Lady Audrey, I swear." Tibbie dropped to her knees and folded her hands.

"Nobody is accusin' ye. Stop yer snifflin'," Rory Maxwell growled. He fixed his gaze on Anne. "What do ye know, lass?"

For a moment, Anne stood and said nothing. Finally, she resolutely straightened her shoulders. "The wine that Ewart gave Lady Audrey was laced with poison."

On her declaration, Laird Maxwell roared once again. "Where's yer proof in this?"

"She lies," Ewart hissed, jumping to his feet, inching closer to Anne. "Why should we believe her words?"

Thomas curled his hands into fists but held his position. Cool heads were needed no matter how much he wanted to slug Ewart in the face. How dare he try to soil Anne's reputation.

Anne lifted her chin and threw back her shoulders. Her stare pierced Ewart's scowl. "I do not lie."

Indeed, she didn't. Yet why would Ewart poison Ma Audrey? What would he gain from such an act?

"Send Blair to get the wine from Lady Audrey's chamber," Anne countered. "You'll see I speak the truth."

Marcas called for Blair, who quickly went to get the wine.

Ewart pointed a finger at Anne. "I'll not stand here and be accused by this whore."

Thomas launched himself across the table and began pummeling Ewart's face. Anger ablaze, he ignored the cries from Anne and Ma Audrey to stop.

Suddenly a dagger zinged past Thomas's ear and landed in a wooden painting behind Ewart.

"Stop this," Ma Audrey yelled. "This fighting solves nothing."

Thomas froze. He had forgotten Ma Audrey's skill with a dagger. In the past, she had won many a contest with her blade skill. His anger ebbed, but he still took great pleasure in seeing the blood ooze out of Ewart's crooked nose and broken lip. Perhaps the rearrangement would be an improvement to his grizzly looks.

Picking up a stool, Thomas offered it to Ewart. "Here, Maxwell, sit."

Anne gave him a fresh cloth to hold against his bleeding face. "Perhaps we should wait until later to discuss this matter. When we all have cooler heads."

"Indeed, I think you are right." Ma Audrey came to Ewart's side. "Laird Elliot and Laird Maxwell, can you help Ewart to one of the chambers above?" Both men immediately lifted Ewart up by his shoulders and headed for the stairs. "Tibbie, please see to Master Ewart's injuries."

With a nod, the healer followed the others.

Just as swiftly, Ma Audrey turned back to Thomas and Anne. "We shall give Ewart a few hours' rest, but then both of you shall come to his room and the whole truth will be uncovered." A shadow of the past hung over Thomas's shoulder. Ten years ago, he had learned a truth that made him flee the tower. Ma Audrey's words echoed through his mind. *The truth has been hidden long enough.*

CHAPTER 26

Anne quickly answered the knock on her chamber door. "Mistress Anne, you are wanted in the chapel below." A servant delivered the message in a low voice.

The hours of waiting had been nothing less than a torment. Lady Audrey had purposely found an excuse to get Ewart out of the hall, but why? Truly she had seen other men take worse beatings, and yet they were expected to carry on. Nay, something else drove her on. She had insisted that Laird Maxwell take Laird Elliot aside for a private talk with Asher. Then she quickly dismissed Anne to her chamber. Either Lady Audrey thought Anne was a liar or she knew the reason why Ewart would use the poison. Whatever the case, Anne quickly followed the servant.

In the chapel, Lady Audrey stood near the altar between Thomas and Marcas. Making the most of his injuries, Ewart sat on a stool against the far-left wall, moaning as if in great pain. No doubt hoping he could sway his father's opinion. Maxwell stood by his son, but his eyes held no certainty of Ewart's innocence.

Asher, Laird Elliot, and Lady Cecilia were nowhere to be found. Here then had to be the reason why Lady Audrey called for the delay. She did not want them present.

On the altar stood the bottle of poisoned wine. Anne's stomach lurched when no greetings were offered, not even from Thomas. She folded her hands, squeezing her fingernails into her palms. Her testimony would either draw this family together or split them in two.

Dear Lord, please let my words ring true in their ears. You know this family has suffered greatly over the years. Heal them. Renew them that they may see the truth. Taking one more confident breath, Anne stood in front of her hosts.

"I want you to know that no one has tampered with this wine since Blair brought it into the hall. I posted two guards to watch the bottle at all times." Lady Audrey's gaze shot around the chapel, challenging anyone to gainsay her.

Coming to his feet and leaning on his father, Ewart picked up the invisible gauntlet. "I gave that wine to you in good faith. Widow Howell could have poisoned it while it were in your chamber. All here know this commoner was given free rein of the Armstrong household. What do we know of her? She tries to lay blame on me to hide her own guilt."

Thomas stepped to Anne's side, his fingers grazing hers. "And why would she do such?"

Ewart snickered. "Why, a blind man could see the reason. The lady has been assisting Tibbie with Marcas's healing. By the healer's own words, she thought he would die. If that happened, then Thomas Armstrong would become laird at Warring Tower." He waved his hand at Anne. "Anyone who has eyes in their head can see you are smitten with the lass."

A scarlet streak shot up Thomas's neck as he raised a fist in Ewart's direction. "You know nothing of my relationship. Keep your foul tongue in your mouth."

Though he tried to defend her, Thomas's words cut deep. True, in the beginning they were adversaries, but they had become friends, confidants. A flush warmed her skin as she remembered the kiss they had shared. And deep down she did want him to be smitten with her.

"Look." Ewart was waving his arm between the both of them. "*Cannae* ye see? They are a pair of lovesick *coos*."

Thomas roared and leapt toward the younger Maxwell. Rory drew his sword, but just as quickly, Marcas blocked Thomas's path, pushing him back. "Cease this, brother. He means to bait you. We all know the type of tapestry he weaves."

"Tapestry?" Ewart cackled. "Nay. Hear my words." Heavy folds creased his forehead while evil slithered across his face. "She aims to be the next lady of the tower."

If they stood before a magistrate, she could very well be condemned. But here, in God's chapel, no one passed sentence. Biblical words rang in her ears. *For my mouth will utter truth; and the wickedness is an abomination to my lips.* Anne fell to her knees before Lady Audrey. "Though it is true I do hold some affection for your son, I would never dishonor this family by coming up with such a devious plan." She did not plead for belief. If God willed it, she would be vindicated.

"Where is the proof?" Ewart spat.

Rory Maxwell rubbed his beard. "The lad makes a good argument. Where is the proof that she or Ewart tampered with the wine?"

"You forget. I was being poisoned long before Anne came to Warring Tower." Lady Audrey inched forward and jabbed a finger at Ewart. "You gave me other bottles of wine. You encouraged me to drink last eve."

"That *doesnae* make the lad guilty. It only removes the blame from Anne." The elder Maxwell stood with sword in hand as an avenging angel between the Armstrongs and Ewart. "It could very well have been Tibbie. At times, I believe the woman is a witch. Where is she anyway? Why is she not present?"

Lady Audrey strode to the chapel doors and flung them wide. She cast a sideways glance at Rory. "Enter."

Asher, Laird Elliot, and Tibbie marched to the front of the chapel. In Tibbie's hands, she held a clay jar. Ewart visibly paled. Rory's grip tightened on his sword. Marcas looked puzzled, and Thomas shielded Anne with his body.

Lady Audrey strode back to the front of the chapel. "Tell us what you have learned, Laird Elliot."

"Well, Healer Tibbie swore she sold Ewart a bottle of foxglove and instructed him on how to use it sparingly."

"That's right," the healer piped in with a nod. "He said he was havin' troubles with his bowels. Bought the bottle over two months past."

Laird Elliot stepped forward. "Upon hearing Tibbie's story, I asked Laird Maxwell if I could go to his keep and search his son's chamber."

Ewart gasped. "*Da,* ye *didnae?* How could ye not believe yer own son?"

Laird Maxwell tapped his sword against his legs. "Because since I have met this lass"—he waved his sword to Anne—"she has not spoken a false word. But ye, I am hard-pressed to know when ye *dinnae* lie."

"Continue on, Laird Elliot. What did you find?" Lady Audrey encouraged.

He motioned to Asher. "We tore Ewart's chamber apart and found nothing, but then Master Hayes accidentally kicked a candlestick across the room. It hit a lower panel near the bed.

As if the Almighty wanted us to find it, the panel popped open. Inside, I found several bottles of wine and a jar of foxglove and other poisons. Healer Tibbie confirmed some were very deadly, and others could kill over time if properly administered."

Laird Maxwell placed his sword back in his sheath, his face awash with misery. "Why, lad? Why would ye do such a thing? What has Lady Audrey ever done to ye that ye would poison her?"

As if the devil had entered his body, Ewart's eyes darkened, and a predatory smile flashed, revealing his yellow, canine teeth. "Ye know why?" He poked his father hard in the chest.

Before Ewart could speak more, Lady Audrey raised a hand. "That is all we need, Laird Elliot. What follows now is private. If you do not mind, please leave with Tibbie."

A dark cloud settled on Laird Elliot's face. He wanted to give protest, but the offense had been against Lady Audrey and not his daughter, so he did not have the right to stay. With no other recourse, he turned a pleading gaze to his son-in-law. "Marcas?"

"This is an Armstrong matter. I thank thee for your help. Please see to Cecilia. I am sure she needs your support."

The decision made, Laird Elliot nodded and left with the healer right behind him.

Asher made to leave too. "Halt, Asher." The elder brother turned and faced his sister. "You are family. What happened here is as much your concern."

Asher raised a disagreeing eyebrow, but he did not speak. Instead, he nodded his head and leaned against the back wall of the chapel.

Anne pulled away, not wishing to interfere in a family matter.

Thomas reached out and grabbed her hand. "Stay." His gaze beseeching, his tone soft.

Though she wanted to acquiesce to his request, the choice rested with Lady Audrey.

"'Tis all right. I believe you know most of the tale anyway," the matriarch said.

Anne tried to digest what she had learned. She knew Thomas was not the true laird of Warring Tower, that Laird Gavin Armstrong was not his father, yet how any of this was related to Lady Audrey's poisoning remained a mystery.

Laird Maxwell leaned against a wall near his son and crossed his arms over his chest, his gaze floating around the chapel. "I always hated this place. Nothin' but bad memories lurk here." With a long sigh, he locked his gaze on Ewart. "Tell us. Why ye poisoned Lady Audrey?"

The pretense of being a weak-willed disappeared, and Ewart strode back and forth in front of all of them like a wolf who didn't know he was being barred from the pack. His gaze lit on Lady Audrey. "Yer life would have been so much better had ye accepted my proposal after Gavin died. But no, ye chose to remain the suffering widow."

"So you waited ten years to take your revenge? But that isn't the reason, is it?" Lady Audrey stepped closer to Marcas.

"So ye have figured it out." Ewart scrutinized her face. "I thought so."

Lady Audrey squared her shoulders. "I always had my suspicions and so did Gran, but we had no proof. So when did you learn the truth?"

Marcas scratched his head while Thomas looked askance. Anne was just as flummoxed as to what was going on between the swan and the jackal.

Laird Maxwell pushed off the wall. "Perhaps this best be left unsaid."

Ewart spun about. "Why? Ye loved Gavin more than me." His eyebrows dropped as they shifted to Marcas. "And ye loved this whelp more than me too."

"Stop now," Rory cautioned.

"Nay. Look at them. Look at all of them. None know the truth except ye and Lady Audrey." He thumped his chest and raised his voice. "And me. The one ye all thought was too thick in the head to figure it out." Ewart circled his father like a buzzard seeking fresh meat. "I always wondered why after years of hatred ye finally decided to make peace with the Armstrongs." Ewart let a finger slide down the side of his father's face. "I know how ye got that scar. Ye and that old hag, Lady Francis, had whelped another son."

Thomas's body became ridged against Anne's side, either Ewart had gone mad or Ma Audrey held another secret. He swung his gaze to her. The truth flashed bright like a star in the heavens.

Laird Maxwell's face shot molten red. He waved a fist in Ewart's face. "Watch yer tongue."

Ewart stepped back away from the threat. "Why, so ye can keep the truth from comin' forward? I wager Laird Jaxon would be interested in what I know."

"Hush up." Rory's hands shot out and grabbed his son's shirt, but Ewart easily lifted his arms and broke the hold.

"'Twas obvious. The truth was in the way ye walked and the way ye laughed. Ye and Gavin the same. Ye were both stubborn, built to fight." The anger faded; deep sorrow engulfed Ewart's face. He fell back and stood in front of Marcas and Thomas. "Do ye not know? *Didnae* yer ma tell ye?" A hysterical laugh left his lips. "Yer *Da*, Gavin Armstrong, *isnae* even an Armstrong. He was sired by my *da* and that whore, yer gran, Lady Francis."

Thomas's mouth fell open, and his whole body relaxed. Anne took hold of his arm to brace him. Never had he suspected that Gavin Armstrong, the man he had called *Da*, was not the legitimate heir of Warring Tower. He knew his grandfather had been a cruel man, but he always thought Gran had been faithful to her husband. Deep, dark sins abounded in this family, and yet Gavin had tried to bring in some light by making Thomas his heir. He chose to give the title to someone else's illegitimate son instead of his own blood child.

Marcas lurched forward with a loud roar and wrapped his hands around Ewart's throat. "You lie. I will have my satisfaction."

Thomas and Asher rushed forward and pulled Marcas away. "Methinks this is the truth, brother," Thomas whispered.

The young laird's legs buckled. He stumbled back and sat down on the floor by the altar, waving a lone finger at Rory Maxwell. "Then ye are . . ."

"Aye, lad, yer *grandda*. Francis and me tried to remain apart, but we *couldnae*. That's how I got this scar. Her husband *wasnae* too keen on what we had done. She never told me or yer *da* the truth until long after ye were born."

"Until Truce Day when I was six summers old." Thomas sat down next to Marcas and reached out. "Everything changed after that day. I thought it was because . . ."

"Ye *werenae* Gavin's seed?" Maxwell shook his head. "Aye.

That be part of it. Yer *da* be just like ye. Sired by one man and raised by another."

Marcas gasped. "You *arenae* my natural brother either? But he was training you to be laird of Warring." Marcas shook his head. Dawning settled on his face. "No wonder you left. That night when *Da* died. That's when you found out."

"Aye, by accident. I left in anger, but I have returned to support my brother. Forgive me, Brother." He touched his forehead to Marcas's, grabbing him around the neck.

The more truth that flooded forth, the more Thomas felt free. No longer would he need to lie to protect his family, and they were his family, if not by blood, then at least by heart. He turned to Anne as Biblical words rushed through his mind. *And the truth shall set you free.*

No wonder she clung to God and the truth. For in both, a man or woman could find rest. He smiled at her, and she tipped her head in perplexity. Unknowingly, she had saved his life. His soul. Just as he reached out to take her in his arms, Ewart arched his back and let out a howl.

"Do my ears deceive me? Not even the eldest Armstrong is a real Armstrong. My, my, what will Jaxon do when he hears of this?"

Thomas didn't care if all of Scotland learned of his parentage. Let Ewart crow as much as he wished.

But Ma Audrey was not done fighting for her family. She stepped in front of Ewart. "But that was not the plan to tell Jaxon. Was it?"

Like a thief who had just stolen the crown jewels, he danced about. "Nay. Though in truth, I only intended to murder Gavin."

Both Marcas and Thomas sprang to their feet. "Ye killed our *da*!" they shouted in unison. Immediately, Hayes and Rory

Maxwell dashed in front of them. Thomas let out a howl to ease the pain inside him.

"Killing him now will not bring your father back." Hayes pushed on Thomas's chest. "Let him finish his tale and then you may seek justice."

"Hayes makes sense." Thomas pulled on his brother's sleeve. "Let Ewart's last breath be giving testimony to the truth."

Hayes and Maxwell moved—one next to his friend, the latter next to his son.

Marcas shook off Thomas's grip, revenge flashing in his gaze. "But he killed our *da*. What more could he say that we would care to listen?"

"I want to know why Ewart killed my husband." The anguish in Ma Audrey's voice took the fight out of Marcas. He reached out and took her in his arms.

"Oh, look at the sad, pathetic Armstrongs, mourning a man who harbored more secrets than Satan himself. I wager I will meet your *da* in the fiery pit."

Thomas swung about and backhanded Ewart, producing a new ooze of blood from an old wound.

"Here now," Laird Maxwell wailed. "Enough. Have we not all suffered enough?"

Anne stepped forward and placed a calming hand on Thomas's shoulder. "Please. This anger solves nothing."

Her soft eyes and gentle touch vanquished the beast that had ruled his soul for ten years. Thomas raised his gaze upward. *Lord, give me patience.* A rush of peace replaced the old aches and hurts. No matter what vile words left Ewart's mouth, Thomas would let them bounce off his chest as if he wore armor. He covered Anne's fingers with his and gave them a squeeze. "All right. Let the serpent continue."

Ewart slunk back, dabbing his nose. "Ye will be on yer knees before I am finished."

Another fiendish cackle sliced the air, goading Thomas. *Please, Lord, give me strength to not act out of rage.*

All remained calm, though most wanted to slit Ewart's throat. "Even after Gavin's death, Audrey still would not marry me." He shrugged. "No great loss. I had my revenge. The son my father loved was dead." The wrinkles on Ewart's face began to coil. "But even in death, Gavin haunted me. That hag, yer gran, finally figured out the truth. So I killed her too."

A long, eerie wail filled the chapel. "Ye killed my Francis?" Rory beat his chest. "How could ye do such? *Wasnae* the blood of yer brother enough?"

Marcas fell back against the altar. Thomas leaned into Anne for support. No man could be this wicked. Ewart had to truly be the devil's own. Switched at birth with Rory Maxwell's true son.

"Had to." Ewart lifted his chin in defense. "She knew what potion I used and found my writings when she came to visit ye. She aimed to take the proof to the magistrate. I *couldnae* allow it." He looked about as if he could find a confidant to understand his blight. When all eyes held him in contempt, he let out a long, laborious breath and continued. "Since I had been conveniently widowed, I offered Audrey one more proposal. She was so weak and fragile."

"From the poison you gave her." This accusation came from Anne.

Thomas squeezed her shoulders. "Patience," he whispered, "this goat is not worth your anger." Her cheeks flamed.

"It was all too perfect." Ewart rubbed his hands together,

his evil eyes glowing. "Marcas had fallen ill and was close to death with no heir, and Audrey was in such a delicate state. She would have turned to me. I would have become laird of Warring Tower, uniting this land to Maxwell land." He turned to his father. "See? I would have accomplished what you planned to do over twenty years past."

"Lad," Rory choked, "that plan was always rotten. Look what it has brought."

Ewart's face turned hard as his words became brittle. "All would have worked out perfectly, then ye showed up." He thrust a finger in Thomas's face. "The white knight come to his brother's rescue. Pfft." He strode back and forth between his father and Thomas. "That meddlesome woman ye brought found the hag's apothecary book. Marcas became stronger, and I knew it *widnae* be long before Audrey learned the truth."

"So you planned to finish her off quickly." Thomas could feel his anger bubbling even as he struggled for patience.

Ewart sniffed. "What choice did I have? You would have done the same had the tables been reversed."

Not even if Queen Elizabeth offered him half of her kingdom. Thomas shot his gaze around the chapel. "What say you all to his fate?"

With painstaking breaths, Rory Maxwell shuffled before Ewart. "He is no heir of mine. Do with him as you please."

In a flash, Ewart reached for the dirk in Rory's belt and planted it deep in his father's stomach. The old laird gurgled. Blood spurted from his mouth. "I should have done this years ago."

Ewart pulled out the blade and turned, lunging toward Anne. In a flash, Ma Audrey dragged a blade from her sleeve. The dagger hit Ewart in the chest. His eyes bulged, and his lips parted before he landed in a heap near his dying father.

Ma Audrey strode to his side and removed the knife from Ewart's chest. "I took to wearing it again once I learned of the poisoning." She turned to face Rory Maxwell. "I am sorry."

He waved her off, then held out a hand to Marcas. "Lad."

The young laird rushed to his grandfather's side, clasping his hand.

"Hear now in the presence of all . . . in my chamber . . . be a parchment . . . with me seal. If both me sons are dead . . . Maxwell land goes to ye. Since Ewart has sinned against me and God, I disown him. The land is yers."

"*Granda*," Marcas cried, curling into the old man as he took his last breath. "*Dinnae* leave me. *Dinnae* leave us."

His words were an echo from the past when a young lad asked his brother not to leave. Pain pierced Thomas's heart. He knelt down next to Marcas, cradling him in his arms. "I am so sorry, brother."

CHAPTER 27

A week later, Thomas entered the laird's chamber to find Marcas dressed in a crisp white shirt. Black leather boots covered the shins of his breeches. On his finger, he wore Gavin Armstrong's ring. He cut a fine noble figure. He tapped the ring on the table before him while he gazed down at the testament of Rory Maxwell. "I *cannae* accept the land without causing a war."

His weak, insecure brother had finally become strong and wise. "Agreed. The Maxwell family will not accept you. They are already blaming the Armstrongs and the Elliots for Rory's and Ewart's deaths."

"Aye, but it is all bluster. Their cousin, Heath Maxwell, is secretly gloating over his good fortune. According to Healer Tibbie, he is already moving his possessions and family into the Maxwell keep." He turned and gazed at the document. "I have told Laird Elliot everything, and he is willing to keep the Armstrong secret."

Indeed, he would for Cecilia's sake. What father would want a scandal of illegitimacy and murder placed around his daughter's neck?

Thomas picked up a lit tallow and held it out to Marcas. "Then it's best we destroy it."

Rolling up Rory Maxwell's letter, Marcas picked up the parchment and placed it in a metal bowl. He then took a lit candle and set the truth on fire. "For the well-being of all the Armstrongs, we will carry yet another secret."

They watched the parchment edges curl and sizzle as the fire consumed the last wishes of Rory Maxwell. When the letter was nothing but ash, Marcas looked up with a softness in his eyes. "Though Cecilia and Ma Audrey have made amends and are working out their differences, I still could use your guidance. Will you stay?"

The tragic deaths of Rory and Ewart had woken up Ma Audrey and Cecilia. Instead of criticizing her management of the kitchens, Ma Audrey had taken to giving helpful suggestions. In fact, the pair had become inseparable and a force to be reckoned with. Thomas shook his head. "You have Ma Audrey, Cecilia, and your father-in-law to help you. I would only be in the way. But know this, if you are ever in trouble, I will come to your aid. You have only to send word."

"Then where shall you go?" Marcas asked.

"I have one more promise to fulfill. To take Anne to London."

"Methinks you should make that woman your wife. She is intelligent and probably the only one who can tame that wild streak that always got us in trouble."

Thomas cocked a brow, thinking about his youth. "Trouble? Never." He laughed, thinking of how he had coaxed his brother into doing some very mischievous deeds.

Marcas wagged a finger. "I remember when Cook was preparing a feast for Truce Day, and you made me remove the rabbits from the pot and fill it with snakes and frogs. I had to sweep and clean the kitchens for a month."

"I'd rather clean the kitchens than sit, stretching out my

arms so Gran could wrap thread about my hands while she sewed and weaved." Thomas groaned.

"You made such a lovely maid." Marcas batted his eyes. They chuckled until they fell into each other arms and shared a brotherly embrace.

When parted, Marcas's words hung between them. *Methinks you should make her your wife.* "You have spoken forthright, brother. I have much left to do in London before I can take anyone as a wife. It *widnae* be fair to the lady."

Marcas leaned against his desk. "Asher told me there are many who want your head in London."

Thomas grimaced, thinking about his gambling debts. "I *didnae* lead a pure life."

"Few do." Marcas folded his arms over his chest. He looked every bit refreshed and the handsome laird. "So then, what do you plan to do after you have taken Anne to London?"

The thought of revenge, of going to the Malabar Coast with Hayes to find Lady Jane Grey and finish her off for his mother's death no longer held the appeal it once did. Anne and her prayers had managed to erase his anger. Somehow his heart of stone had truly become a heart of flesh.

What had transpired here taught him that a family's love did not grow out of flesh and blood but from the hearts that bonded loved ones together. This was his real family, and unbeknownst to Anne, she had made him see the truth. Perhaps he could get his affairs in order in London, and once done, maybe he could persuade her to become his wife. A darkness swept over his soul. If she would have a scoundrel like him.

He bowed to Marcas. "I have a few matters to settle that *cannae* wait."

A twinkle of mirth filled Marcas's eyes. "By all means, set

straight your affairs." He took a deep breath and looked at the other scrolls on his desk. "I have my own duties to attend to."

"Ah, the life of a laird, so filled with adventure." In two steps, Thomas was at the door. "I leave you to the excitement."

Marcas balled up a piece of parchment and threw it toward the door. Thomas exited the room, the wad hitting the doorframe before dropping to the floor. Elation filled Thomas's chest. All would be fine at Warring Tower. And if God willed it, all would be fine between him and Anne. But before he talked to her, he had one more lady he needed to see.

Thomas skipped down the stairs and stopped at Ma Audrey's chamber. He knocked on the door and stepped in. She sat in a chair with mending on her lap. "Oh, Thomas, please come and have a seat." She reached for a pitcher. "I have some cool water if you are thirsty."

Instead of taking the other chair, he pulled a stool from the corner and sat down in front of her. "Nay, I am fine." He gently took her mending and placed it on the small table. "I have come to ask for your forgiveness."

"Forgiveness for what?"

He took her hands in his. "For leaving you all those years ago." His throat clogged as his eyes burned with unshed tears. "Had I known you were with child—"

"Stop, Thomas. Even if you had stayed, I might have lost the babe. There were problems with the carrying long before Gavin died. In truth, I had lost a child a year before. That is why I didn't say anything to anyone. What was lost once could be lost again. And that is what happened. 'Tis not your fault."

Thomas shook his head. "Still. Perhaps if I had stayed . . ."

"Perhaps what? You would have become laird of Warring Tower?" She pulled her hands from his and cupped his face.

"Knowing the truth, you never would have accepted it. Nay, you did what you thought was right and so did your brother. What the devil intended for evil, God has turned to good. The suffering has changed Marcas into a fine laird, and we have been united as a family again. Old wounds have been exposed and healed." Her eyes grew soft and tender. "Even if you must leave us again. I know nothing stands in your way from returning."

"You were always a wise woman." He took her hands back in his and gave them a kiss.

"Not always. But time is a good teacher, and God is patient."

Indeed, He was. He had waited a long time for Thomas to give up his anger and resentment. Now he had one more promise to fulfill. "I promised to take Anne to London."

"Aye, and she might not want to go now. I think you need to speak to the girl and learn her desires."

He pulled back and looked into Ma Audrey's kind gaze. "Why would she want to stay?"

"Methinks she would go wherever you are."

Thomas wanted to argue while hoping Ma Audrey's words were true. He wrinkled his brow. "I—"

"Go and find her. Learn her wishes." She patted his cheek. "Speak your heart and she will show you hers. I think ye both be patterned from the same cloth."

Could Ma Audrey be right? Would Anne be willing to take him as her husband? There was only one way to find out. Thomas rose and kissed Ma Audrey's cheek. "We will talk later."

"Aye. Go on now and find your future." She picked up her mending and began to hum.

A tune Thomas carried in his heart all the way into the hall.

When he did not find Anne there, he headed to the courtyard only to find Hayes seated on top of a pile of molding hay.

"Surely you could have found a better place to take rest? You are family. I am sure your sister would want you to reside within," Thomas said, itching his nose.

Hayes looked about. "Sometimes the place you rest should fit your mood."

The blue sky, the chirping birds, and the easy sounds of a keep at work would brighten anyone's day, but Hayes's dark looks resembled a storm's wind before it blew away a man's crops. "Are you not feeling well this day?"

"Quite the contrary. Mistress Anne has concocted a potion that has set my lungs at ease." He pulled out a small bottle that held a yellow-brown syrupy mixture. "It's made with carline thistle, among other things. I had her write down the ingredients so that I could give them to my wife. I came to see my sister because I believed, very soon, I would be at Saint Peter's gate. My wife will be pleased that I have not died. She will have many more years to scold and chase me around the house."

"I *cannae* see a pirate like you with a wife, living a quiet life." Thomas chuckled. "No doubt she is most happy when you are at sea."

Hayes's mood sobered even more so. "She has been trying to heal my ailment for some time."

Thomas stepped back from the offensive smell of the decaying hay. "Then you should be joyful, yet you are not."

Hayes removed the golden cross from his neck and held it in his hand. "I believe this is yours."

With all the woes at Warring Tower, Thomas had forgotten about the cross. He took the necklace in his hand and felt its weight. At one time, it had been the center of his life. Even though the jewels would settle all of his affairs in London, the relic meant nothing to him. Thomas tossed the chain over his head. The heavy cross hung as a symbol of his atonement. Maybe he would give half the jewels to the Reformed Church and half to the Catholics. That would make Anne very happy and lighten his steps.

"Do you still wish to travel with me to the Malabar Coast?" Hayes asked.

The pointed questions curled and churned like soft butter through Thomas's chest, plugging all the holes that had once existed. He kicked a pebble near his boot. "It all depends on Anne. I promised to take her to London. And if she *doesnae* wish to go, then I will stay here with her if she will have me."

"I thought as much." Hayes stood and brushed the fermenting hay from his clothing. "Come. The sun is high, and the air might have a sweeter scent if we take a walk in the meadow."

As much as Thomas had come to appreciate the man, he would rather seek out Anne. "Could we not do that later? I wish to find—"

Hayes grabbed Thomas by the upper arm. "We must talk now, and definitely before you speak to Anne."

The forcefulness of his friend left Thomas mute. He let his new family member drag him past the gate and out to the yonder fields. The miracle cure had made the man stronger than any moss-trooper riding the marches. Once there, Hayes dropped his hand and pointed to a copse of trees. "There. You will wish to sit down once you hear what must be said."

Either the man had lost his wits or the elixir Anne had made was bruising his brain. With a nod, Thomas followed, wondering if Anne could fix his broken mind.

Once in the shade, Hayes paced, his brow rolling and curling like a violent sea. Finally, he stopped and glared at Thomas. "You are in love with Anne, are you not?"

Why would his feelings for Anne cause Hayes a problem? Unless he held some affection for her too. Nay, he spoke of his wife with great gentleness and care.

"My intentions toward Anne are none of your affair," Thomas answered coolly.

"That, my friend, is where you are wrong. They are the whole of England's affair."

His cryptic words crawled up Thomas's spine like a tiny worm. "What do you mean?"

Hayes locked his fingers and stretched out his arms as if he were stretching for a fight. "You know I was a spy for Queen Mary."

Thomas only knew the fanciful tales Ma Audrey had told him, but it would indeed explain how easily he tracked him and Anne from the Welsh countryside and his ability to carry out secret plans and plots. His observation skills were second to none. "So the stories your sister told Marcas and I were true?"

"Aye, I did her bidding in many things. I spent many an hour in the queen's private chambers."

Had Hayes dragged him across the fields to unburden his conscious about an affair with the former queen of England? Thomas held up his hands. "I *dinnae* judge you for your past deeds. God will judge all of us soon enough."

Hayes shook his head. "You do not understand. What I am trying to say is she was comfortable with me, and often I would see her in different forms of dress."

Truly, it had to be Anne's potion addling his mind. Thomas shortened the distance between them and placed an arm around

Hayes's shoulder. "Perhaps we should seek out Anne, and she can help you. Methinks that elixir you have taken has befuddled your mind."

He shrugged off Thomas's arm. "Queen Mary had a strange birthmark." He pointed to his left forearm. "Right here."

Thomas chuckled. "Queen Elizabeth had over two hundred pairs of gloves to hide the same type of mark."

"I never met Elizabeth, but the pieces are starting to come together. Why Walsingham, the chief spymaster, had sent Carlton to find Anne."

The man's mind truly was disjointed. Thomas took a deep, patient breath. Getting Hayes back to the tower would not be an easy feat. "Walsingham's men were after me not Anne. She is just a peasant maid, a by-blow of some Welsh lord."

Hayes placed one hand on his hip and washed the other over his lips. A snake of sweat slid down Thomas's spine as he tried to ward off his deepest fears. Hayes turned dark and direct. "What I am trying to tell you is Anne carries the same mark in the same place as both queens. She may very well be Queen Elizabeth's daughter."

Thomas guffawed, then stopped. Could it be true? She had been educated for the first six years of her life, but then the father she had never met died. The wind echoed through the trees. A hot sweat broke out on his back. Nay, not Anne. Not his Anne. God would not play another cruel joke on him, not after his faith had been rekindled.

The dark pain he thought he had put behind him oozed and swept through his body. "How long?"

"What?" Hayes cocked his head as if listening for a storm to erupt.

"How long have you known?"

The Adam's apple in Hayes's throat bobbed. "Since the day I met her."

Whatever trust Thomas had in the man evaporated. What did he expect? Asher Hayes was first and foremost a liar and a spy. "So the woman I love is the daughter of the queen? Is there anything else you *havenae* told me?"

The deceiver rubbed a hand over his throat before taking one step back. "Only one small thing."

"Out with it," Thomas roared, his calm destroyed by the storm of deception.

"Queen Mary orchestrated the death of your true mother. Lady Jane Grey wanted to stay and die, but the queen didn't want Jane's blood on her hands . . . well, not right away anyway. Queen Mary drugged Jane and sent her away. Over time, she wound up in Germany."

Thomas let out a shallow breath. Even though he wanted to pummel Hayes for not telling him about Anne's parentage, he was glad he no longer sought to kill Jane Grey. She had been a pawn in a royal's game just like his true mother.

"I care not about the woman, nor do I seek revenge. Her life no longer fuels my anger. What is done is done. Though I do wonder how she wound up living off the Malabar Coast."

Hayes fidgeted and picked at the bark of a tree. "Years later, Queen Mary heard rumors that Jane Grey was massing an army to retake her English throne. The queen was not a well woman. Her mind became tormented. She sent me to find and kill Jane Grey."

Thomas's mouth fell open. Not only was Hayes a spy and a liar, but he was a murderer as well. How could he be related to Ma Audrey?

Hayes put up his hands. "I did not kill her. In fact, she saved the queen's life instead. Do you understand?"

Thomas nodded, and his hands curled into fists. "So she sent her far away."

"Exactly," Hayes said quietly. His eyes took on a sheepish look as he tucked his neck to his chest. "She's a wife of a pepper merchant. You see, Lady Jane Grey is my wife."

The Spirit of the Lord that had given Thomas such peace departed. Rage sluiced over his shoulders. His heart exploded in his chest. A guttural cry tore from his throat and sent the birds in the trees to flight. His fist flashed outward and connected with Hayes's chin, sending the man to the ground. Madness. This was all madness.

Thomas stomped back to the tower with the whispers of the devil in his ears.

Though early in the season, Anne still managed to harvest a few herbs. Her ability in apothecary grew daily as did her love of this countryside and the people. The rolling hills, soft meadows, and kind folk made her wish this place was her home. She rolled some of the herbs between her fingers to weigh their texture. Most would be used to dry and grind for healing potions. In a strange way, she had found purpose for her life that did not include mopping and scrubbing an inn. Planning her speech well, she would ask Lady Audrey and Laird Marcas if she could become Warring Tower's healer. If they consented, then only one more thing would have to be remedied—her feelings for Thomas.

For certain, he would want to stay and help his brother manage the tower. Perhaps in time Thomas would find some quality in her to love. Then again, if she did not make her feelings known to him soon, he might find some other maid to turn his fancy. Anne bent down to gather another young herb. What to do? She didn't want to be too bold, or any affection he held for her could wane.

Out of the corner of her eye, she saw the man who plagued her thoughts come marching through the fields. She straightened, wiped her hands on her skirt, and tried to put on her brightest smile. "Good day, Thomas."

He stopped and stood close, shoulders tense, his body blocking out the sun's rays. His brows furrowed. His lips hung like a weeping woman's. He reached out and gently took the basket from her hands, wedging it at his side.

"Anne, there is something we must speak about."

Her heart shot to the heavens. Could this be the declaration of love she so desired? If so, then why did he approach her with such angst? Another thought bubbled forth. Perhaps he thought she would reject him, or worse, see his affection as some cruel jest. She fought to keep her lips somber.

"Then speak your words for I am listening."

His tortured gaze searched her face. She wanted to console him, to tell him all would be all right. That their hearts were on the same course.

His brow relaxed. "Had I not returned home, I would have never reconciled with my family. This *widnae* have happened if it had not been for you."

Her cheeks heated from his praise. He need not utter any words of flattery to win what was already his. She gently touched his chest. "Thomas, please. Do not give me praise for what God put into motion. The Holy Spirit touched your heart because He willed it to be so."

Like ashen sack cloth, his cheeks fell. He shook his head. "Nay, I war with my faith again, but I know I must accept God's will. 'Tis Him who chooses our rulers, and my selfishness *shouldnae* stand in the way."

What was he babbling about? He must have read the perplexity on her face because he grabbed her arms and pushed up her sleeves. A raw, ugly scowl marred his face when he saw her birthmark. Her insides ruptured and oozed. Misery spread through her chest like a deadly poison. She tried to pull her arm away, but he held it fast, staring at the mark.

"I am sorry what you see repulses you," she spat. "'Tis just a mark. An accident of birth. But I can see from your face you believe it to be the devil's mark." He let go of her arm, and she quickly pulled her sleeve down.

"Quite the contrary. Your mark does not come from the devil but from a queen."

A queen? She scrutinized his face, looking for the answer of a cruel jest. She found none. Was he ill? Her anger fled. "Are you feeling all right? Does something ail you? Your words are quite confusing."

Thomas shook his head. "Nay, I *dinnae* jest, but I wish I did." He gently took her hands in his. "Sweet Anne, you were right. Carlton *wasnae* after me, he wanted you."

This revelation had him thinking of the queen? How odd. "Aye, but they are working for my former family at Tretower Court. That has nothing to do with any queen."

"That is where you are wrong."

A fortnight pause hung between them. Pinpricks danced down her spine. She swallowed hard, waiting for his explanation.

"You said your true father was a noble, and when he died, you were tossed out, but recently the family seemed to want you back. There is a motive for their actions."

The muscles in her legs began to weaken as Thomas's features grew grave. She pulled away from him. "I care not what they want with me. That was the past. I would be happy to stay here if your brother would allow it."

The cords on Thomas's neck grew tight. "You *cannae*."

"And why not?" she shot back, done with his leaden tone and cryptic words.

"I have seen that mark before. It is the mark of royalty. There is a strong possibility that you are Queen Elizabeth's daughter."

She waited for him to laugh, to tease, but his face remained grim, washed with grief. A cool breeze kicked up on the early summer air and twisted around Anne's body like a serpent's coils. As a child, she had dreamed about being a princess, but now all she wanted was to live out her days in obscurity.

This could not be true. She sunk to the ground and beat her chest. *Make this all a lie, Lord. Please, make it to be a lie.*

CHAPTER 28

The longest days of her life had been the days traveling to London. A few months ago, she dreamed about the place. She'd closed her eyes and dreamed of the smells, the sounds, and sights of the grand city. Now as she rode down the muddy streets, her nose took in the rank odors, her ears heard the cries of anguish, and her gaze beheld the filth. The city's blight matched her mood. They entered a narrow street and stopped by a stone building with a heavy, worn wooden door.

"We are expected." Benedict Carlton dismounted his horse. The shifty, vile man had shown up at Warring Tower exactly one week after Thomas's big revelation. It had been decided that Anne would go see Queen Elizabeth's head spymaster, Francis Walsingham at his shop of spies. He would discern the facts and truth. Anne had prayed continually that Walsingham would find her lacking the Tudor traits and call off his dogs. A week had not passed when Carlton had shown up at Warring Tower demanding that Anne return to England or the queen would send troops north to take her by force. A war was the last thing the good people of Warring needed, so Anne consented to return.

She swallowed hard as Thomas helped her dismount her

horse. "Worry not. Hayes and I will be at your side at all times."

His encouragement did not ease her growing fears, nor did it settle the rapid beats of her heart. Nonetheless, she managed to put one foot in front of the other and entered the dark, dank building. Men dressed like merchants, villains, and sailors scurried through the rooms. A few others sat at rickety tables scratching out notes or deciphering messages.

Anne, Thomas, and Asher were ushered into a room where dim light streamed through paned windows, illuminating a large desk piled with parchment and ciphers. The air smelled of vinegar often used in the making of invisible ink. Carlton motioned her to sit on a chair in front of the desk. Thomas and Asher stood against the back wall.

"He should be along shortly," Carlton said, crushing his cap between his fingers. "Make yourselves as comfortable as possible but do not touch anything." The man slipped out of the room before a query could be made. Obviously, Francis Walsingham would not tolerate the two *i*'s—interference and incompetence.

Anne firmly planted her feet on the ground. Whatever they believed to be true, she would not go merrily to the queen's court without a fight. "If the sod is not here soon, I shall leave."

Thomas pushed off the wall. "Anne, be reasonable. He is a busy man."

"Only because he has his nose in other people's affairs." She pulled her shoulders back and sat up straight.

"His work protects the queen," Asher added, trying to defend a sneaky practice.

"Tell me, what protection does a queen need against a Catholic innkeeper or a scullery maid?" Anne twisted in her seat to glare at Asher. "They carry no power. How is their faith a danger to anyone? Yet Walsingham sniffs them out and throws them into prison." Anne shook off a shiver. What fate awaited her?

Asher grimaced. "You forget. I used to find Protestants for Mary Tudor, but like the Apostle Paul, I have changed and am saved by grace. However, you must remember, the queen has many enemies, the Spanish, the French, and her own cousin, Mary Queen of Scots."

"All the more reason I want no involvement in her life." Anne rubbed her forehead when the door popped open and in came a man dressed in black. His long face resembled a mourner at a funeral. His body was neither lean nor necessarily large, his footfalls quiet. When he sat, he blended into the dark wall behind him. No doubt that was by choice rather than by accident. He carefully folded his hands on his desk as he set his dark eyes on Anne.

"Hmm, I see some resemblance. Pale skin, brown eyes, the hair is a bit too dark, but then that could be a trait from Dudley."

Anne's tight lips loosened. "Good sir, I have never heard of a man named Dudley. I began my life at Tretower Court in Wales. If it is this man's child you seek, then perhaps I am the wrong woman."

"Wrong?" Walsingham coughed. His eyes all but bulged from his oblong head. "How impertinent you are." He leaned over the desk. "Madam, I can assure you that all of my facts have been checked before I sent good men in search of you." He waved a hand at Thomas. "The situation you see before you would never have come to light had it not been for Armstrong getting shipwrecked."

Thomas looked positively ill at the mention of his

involvement. "I'm sorry." He took a step forward, which immediately made Walsingham clear his throat.

"Hold your place, Armstrong, or I will have to have you wait outside."

Thomas froze but never took his gaze from her. How she wanted to rise and wipe the worry from his brow, but she did not need to give this bland little man any weapons to use against her.

"The queen was quite distressed when your ship went down along the Welsh coast. She immediately ordered me to send out men to gather information in the hopes you might still be alive." Walsingham's chair creaked as he sat back, fixing his gaze on Anne once again. "They landed in Newport and heard the tale of a widow who had run away to avoid an undesirable marriage. Nothing new there, but while some of my men searched the coast, a few others went to Tretower Court on the chance that if Armstrong were alive, he might seek out the local nobles." Walsingham's gaze slid to Thomas once again. "He usually migrates to the wealthy. Gets them into his confidence by spinning some grand story about his unusual closeness to Queen Elizabeth. I cannot tell you how many times he has procured large amounts of coin using her name."

Thomas frowned, folding his arms across his chest. "I only told such tales in London."

"Indeed. I gather when you met Widow Howell, you realized you had in possession a far greater gem."

Shortening the distance, Thomas leaned over the desk. "I *didnae* know who she was until a fortnight ago when Hayes told me."

With a short raise of the head, Walsingham let his gaze travel over Asher. "Ah yes, Queen Mary's master spy. I do so hope Queen Elizabeth will allow me to interrogate you. I am dying to learn all your secrets."

Being more cunning than Thomas, Asher gazed down at his fingernails. "You may try, but my words will only be spoken to the queen."

"Mmm." Walsingham rustled some papers on his desk. "The moment I mentioned your name, the queen seemed quite keen on meeting you." His hands stilled. "But that does not mean she will be happy with what you say."

Asher's expression remained blank. 'Twas clear he was used to playing games of intrigue.

Walsingham flipped his feline gaze back to Anne. Her heart raced and echoed in her ears. "I can see the doubt and fear in your eyes, my dear. If you are ever going to survive at court, you must learn how to school your features."

Her palms grew slick, and her whole body seemed drenched in fire. "I am not related to Queen Elizabeth. You are mistaken."

"Nay, I am not." He exhaled a heavy breath and lifted a piece of parchment from his desk. "Hearing about Tretower niggled something in my mind. It took me awhile to unearth, but now it all makes perfect sense."

He gave a dramatic pause, and Anne wanted to reach out and shake him until his beady eyes rolled from his head. If she gave the word, she knew Thomas would join her in the delectable act. "Do get on with it," she snapped.

Walsingham lifted a finger. "Tsk, tsk. That is not how a lady of breeding acts."

Thomas launched himself over the desk and grabbed Walsingham by his doublet. "But it is exactly how an ill-bred Scotsman would act."

Immediately, Asher pulled Thomas back. "Pummeling him

senseless will not get us the answers we seek. Let him finish."

The air in the room cooled, and Thomas shoved the little man back to his seat. Aye, perhaps he should start with Hayes. Thomas was far from forgiving his deception. Walsingham quickly adjusted his clothing, his gaze firm on Thomas. "Someday the queen will reject you. And when she does . . . I will be right there, waiting."

Thomas lurched forward, but Anne stopped him with a touch of her hand. "Please. I wish to hear."

Pain erupted across his face and split her heart asunder. They both knew their desire for one another ended there. He eased back to the wall and closed his eyes and probably his heart to her as well.

Fighting the sting of tears behind her eyes, she took a deep breath and lifted her chin. "Continue, sir."

Walsingham sniffed, mumbled under his breath, and then returned his gaze to the parchment in front of him. "Now where was I, oh yes, Tretower Court, which happened to be the home of Henry Vaughan."

"Who? I do not remember him." Though she did hear of the Vaughan name when she was a child.

"Of course not. I presume he was long dead before you arrived." Walsingham waved him off and returned to his story. "But I am sure there are some in this room who might have heard of his son, Thomas Parry." His words were met with blank faces. "Well, perhaps you are all too young to remember him."

Or we do not care, Anne thought. However, Asher shifted his feet.

"He was quite close to Queen Elizabeth long before she became queen," the spymaster continued. "After Wyatt's Rebellion, Queen Mary imprisoned the then Princess Elizabeth in the Tower. Robert Dudley was a prisoner there as well because of his father's plot to overthrow Queen Mary and put Lady Jane Grey on the English throne." Again, Walsingham paused as if debating on how he should proceed. "Princess Elizabeth and Robert Dudley were quite fond of one another."

Thomas let out a huff. "That is one way to put it. There isn't a courtier that doesn't know that—"

"That is enough, Armstrong." Walsingham's pale cheeks reddened. "The fondness of the couple will come out quick enough."

The room grew still, and Anne fidgeted, certain she did not wish to hear the rest of the story.

"Months later, Queen Mary released Princess Elizabeth from the Tower and sent her to Woodstock in Oxford under the care of Sir Henry Bedingfield. He was the captain of the guards and loyal to Queen Mary, though he really didn't have the stomach for the task of handling the princess." Walsingham flipped to a different parchment. "Thomas Parry, a close confidant of Princess Elizabeth, badgered Bedingfield and gained permission to remain with the princess as a guard and confidant. It was quite valiant of Parry. After all, most believed the young princess would lose her head within a sennight." Walsingham stopped and tilted his own head. "Are you well, my dear?"

Anne's throat became dry. Her head began to spin. Parry's name was familiar. Old words sprung to life again in her mind. *"Parry won't like it if she isn't educated properly." "Parry is dead. No need to treat the by-blow as anything more than she is."* Could this Parry be her father? Her stomach rolled and twisted like a rocking ship on a tumultuous voyage. She swallowed hard and nodded.

Walsingham licked his lips and resumed his story. "I have

it right here, found these writings in Parry's old things. I will say his wife was not happy when we went rummaging through his works. She had them all sealed away after his death in an ornate box, like some blasted shrine." He shook his head. "What people will do to hang on to their loved ones." Shifting his gaze around the room, he turned his attention back to his pages. "Anyway, according to his writings, Princess Elizabeth wasn't the only one to leave the Tower on May 19, 1554. She carried a little package in her belly courtesy of Robert Dudley." He paused and looked up, his eyes practically glowing with glee. "Seems they were given a little freedom while they were in the Tower. How foolish."

Heat slowly rose up Anne's spine as she counted down the months to her own birth. She did not know the exact date, but she knew it was either late December 1554 or early January 1555. However, she had been born in Wales not in Oxford, hadn't she?

Unbeknownst to the battle of doubt waging in Anne, Walsingham continued with his tale. "Parry, being a sharp though a somewhat disagreeable man, kept Bedingfield and his spies away from Elizabeth's chamber. In truth, I wonder if he knew about her condition and hoped that Queen Mary wouldn't find out. After all, he was the lieutenant of the Tower when Dudley and Elizabeth were . . . well, you understand." He lifted his gaze for agreement, but no one uttered a word. "Parry made up stories about Elizabeth's poor health and her inability to travel. Thankfully, she wasn't released from Oxford until April of 1555. Long after the birth."

Anne's shoulders began to shake as anger turned inside her. "If what you say is true, then how did I wind up in Wales at Tretower Court?"

"Ah." Walsingham raised a finger, a sinister smile settling on his lips. He glanced back down at the pages. "According to Parry, the birth was hard. The princess was quite delirious and had lost a lot of blood." He dropped the pages and leaned back in his chair, his gaze fixed on Anne. "Parry instructed the midwife to tell Elizabeth that you were born dead. To save your life and Princess Elizabeth's, Parry whisked the babe to his ancestral home, Tretower Court in Wales, with the strict instruction to raise you as a lady."

Though her chest rose and fell, Anne labored to breathe. All he said could be true. But it couldn't. She wasn't a lady. She had no talents of a well-bred lady. She was just a tavern wench, a servant. "I'm not a lady. And have never been."

"But you were for a few years. Mary Tudor died in 1558, and Queen Elizabeth took the throne. She immediately made Thomas Parry Comptroller of the Household. Many grumbled at the appointment. As I said before, the man was not well liked at court or anywhere else for that matter. But he didn't have his duties long. He died in December of 1560. The queen didn't know of your existence, and those at Tretower Court thought they were raising Parry's by-blow. With him gone and no coin coming in for your care . . . well, why waste the time and money on a child nobody wanted."

Anne's heart cracked. His stinging words held truth. She had every comfort until she was about five. Then one morning she was torn from her bed and given to the Tretower's cook, Roland Getting, to do with as he pleased. She could not stop the tears that fell from her cheeks for the sad and unwanted child who prayed daily for her true parents to come and take her away. How desperately she wanted a real family. Now, she had one, and she so desperately wished she did not.

Thomas pushed off the wall and came to stand behind Anne, gently placing his hands on her shoulders. "You speak falsely. Anne is deeply loved and wanted by many."

He meant to soothe, but she could not stop the flood that flowed from her eyes. She didn't need many. She only needed one. She needed him.

"Indeed." Walsingham stood. "Well, loved or not, Widow Howell right now has an audience with the queen."

CHAPTER 29

Over Thomas's and Asher's protests, Anne left them in the palace gardens while she was taken to the queen's private quarters. The massive hallways and the whispers of exquisitely dressed nobles turned her firm resolve into a dung heap of doubt. She brushed her hands over her simple blue gown and hoped her lack of grandeur would set the queen's mind in a different direction, away from wanting a daughter. When the door slammed, leaving her quite alone in an eloquent sitting room, Anne sent up one last prayer. *Please let the queen be mistaken. Please let me be nothing more than a poor widow.*

Time trudged along in the warm room. She paced back and forth in front of a large window wondering why she was being made to wait. The queen had an excellent view of her gardens. Down below, she spotted Thomas wearing his own path thin, pacing like a trapped tiger. Asher sat, his legs leisurely crossed, taking in the sunlight. He was used to the games of the royals. Anne turned away. What kept Queen Elizabeth?

A mass of scrolls lay on the floor next to a small reading table. Anne clasped her hands behind her back to avoid the temptation to take a peek. She bent down as the door abruptly opened.

"Curiosity is not a good trait if you cannot do it without getting caught."

Anne straightened and swung about. Her heart hammered before taking a dive to her stomach. The middle-aged woman was dressed in a simple green woolen gown. A wig of red curls sat on her head in an unflattering fashion. She wore not a bit of jewelry except a diamond and ruby ring. White makeup was smeared across her forehead and chin. Her lips and cheeks were covered in a red rouge. This woman was nothing like the beautiful queen who filled the stories that swept the Welsh countryside. If not for the expensive ring on her finger, Anne would have thought someone was playing a cruel joke.

"What's wrong, girl? Am I not what you expected?" The queen smoothed her hands on the plain gown. "Did you think that every day I dressed in fashionable gowns and wore coiffed wigs?"

Anne quickly swallowed the *aye* that formed on her lips. She dropped into a deep curtsy only to be pulled up by the armpits. The queen cocked her head as if examining a leg of mutton. Of course, the royal only saw the truth. A peasant. Anne's cheeks burned as her throat grew tight.

"Well, that is one skill you have in your favor, say little and curtsy. Someone raised you well enough." The queen stepped back and eyed her from head to toe. "Blast, I knew it. You have his good looks. If the peacock learns of you, he'll be crowing for months."

Anne dropped her gaze to her toes. Could all this be true? She fought desperately not to ask a single question about her past and this mystery father . . . At least, not yet.

"Turn around," the queen ordered. "Slowly."

A niggle of temper began to flare in Anne's belly. Queen or

not, she had no right to treat her like an oddity from a distant land.

As if reading her mind, the queen lifted one heavily painted eyebrow.

Oh, all right. What good would come from raising royal hackles. Anne placed foot over foot and turned in a small circle.

"You do carry the same shape I had when I was young." The queen rushed forward and grabbed Anne's arm, yanking up her sleeve, twisting her forearm left and then right, examining the mark. "Hmm . . ."

Would she now be accused of being a witch? What a perfect way to get rid of an unwanted child for the second time. With a quick jerk, Anne tried to pull her arm away, but the queen held fast.

"Come now. Do not be ashamed of what makes us great." Queen Elizabeth smirked, released Anne's arm, and pulled up her own sleeve, displaying an identical mark of a lighter hue.

Anne's lips fell open as she gazed at the birthmark she has keep hidden for a life time. 'Twas not from the devil, but from a queen. Her legs became weak as she gazed at her true mother.

The royal spun about and headed for the small reading table, pulling down her long sleeves. She picked up a small brass bell and gave it a ring. Immediately, a servant popped into the room.

"Wine. For both of us." The young woman gave a small curtsy and left. "Come, sit. We have much to discuss."

Anne complied eagerly, sitting across from Her Majesty. What would her standing be in this court? Would she be accepted with open arms or hidden away once again? Anne gulped. Or would this be the last day her body held breath?

With a swift knock, the servant rushed back in with a flagon of wine and two goblets. She set the wine on a side table and picked up a glass to pour when the queen waved her off. "That will be all."

The servant scurried away like a well-trained pet. When the door had closed, the queen picked up the decanter and filled the goblets. She handed one to Anne before sitting back in her gilded chair without taking a sip.

The goblet shook in Anne's hand. *Was it safe to drink?*

"Oh come, give it a try. If I had wanted you dead, I would have told Walsingham to kill you long before you came to my chambers. Killing you here would cause a great scandal."

Anne worked to hold the chalice firmly. Safe for now, but what about later. Would she be a target for every power hungry noble?

The queen sighed, leaned forward, and took a drink. "There. Are you satisfied?"

"Aye and nay, Your Majesty. I have never had a queen serve me before. May I speak freely?" Not waiting for consent Anne rushed on. "I do not know what to think about this new revelation. I feel I do not know who I am or what is expected of me."

Elizabeth let out a grand hoot. "Oh, my dear, you are a fresh breath to this dodgy place. What is expected of you remains to be seen."

'Twas not the answer Anne was looking for, but one she would have to accept, for now.

With a warm smile, the queen lifted a plate of sweet cakes. "Here, have some of these. They were baked this morning."

Anne wanted to grab the whole tray, but with great control, she only took two. She lifted the treat to her nose and instantly smelled cinnamon, a spice that rarely came into the ports in

Newport. Unable to control herself, she popped the whole treat into her mouth. The flavor exploded, warm and spicy mixed with a delicate, flaky crust. Oh my, how she would love to eat these daily.

The queen gave another robust laugh. "Be careful, my dear. They can become habit forming and over time can add a little more girth to the middle."

Like she cared. Anne spent most of her life scrounging for food. A diet of cakes sounded wonderful no matter where they would settle on her body.

Elizabeth pushed the plate forward. "Have more if you wish."

"Do you not like them?" Anne asked around a mouth of sweets.

"I do, but I enjoy watching you eat with such gusto."

Anne stopped chewing and gulped. The treat bumped down her throat. "I am sorry. I must look greedy. And unlike a lady at court."

"Heavens, not at all. I am more upset at myself at not questioning Parry more after you were born. He lied to me about my own flesh and blood. My infant child."

The pain in the queen's eyes tugged at Anne's heart. "You were young, and you trusted your advisor."

The queen looked away. "Indeed, I did. To be honest, I was both relieved and sad. Your death allowed me to ascend the throne three years later. Had I known you lived . . . I wonder what life would have been like . . . for both of us."

So did Anne, but dreaming would not change either of their lives. "Your Majesty, I pretended I was a princess often when I was young. It made the time washing pots in the kitchen go fast."

Elizabeth placed a hand over her chest. "The kitchens! My heart swoons. How dare Parry let this happen?"

Anne reached over and stretched out her hand, placing it close to the queen's. "It wasn't all bad."

The queen's thumb twisted the ruby ring on her finger. "I only wish Parry were alive so that I could wring his thick neck with my hands." The royal took a deep breath. "Pray, tell me all."

With temperate words, Anne spoke of her time before Parry died and the time after. She spoke of the skills she had learned while working at Roland's tavern, her first marriage, and fear of her second betrothal. "But then I met Thomas. At first, we were at odds." Her cheeks warmed under the queen's sharp eye. "But then he treated me like I was a . . . "

"You are fond of that rascal, aren't you?"

Anne gave a timid nod. "Very, my queen."

Elizabeth sighed and gazed out the window, years away from where they were now. Slowly, she turned her attention back to Anne, pointing to the ring on her finger. "I want to show you something." She pushed a lock, and the ring popped open, revealing two miniature pictures. "This is a picture of my mother, and this is a picture of me. I always wear the ring, but no one knows about the secret compartment."

Anne looked at the young woman who had sacrificed her life because she refused to give up Elizabeth's claim to the throne. "She is beautiful." Anne surveyed the other picture of the present Queen Elizabeth. "You are quite grand."

The queen chuckled. "You bend the truth with flattery." She looked at the pictures. "I once was young and pretty, but smallpox took my beauty, and the years have swallowed up my youth."

Anne's body burned under the queen's scrutiny. Scorched by the royal's stare.

"You are named after her. Even though I thought you were dead, I told Parry to name you Anne after my mother, Anne Boleyn." The queen's eyes became glassy, and she dropped her gaze with a small sniff. She closed the ring, hiding the past once again. "At least that was one thing the fool did right. I swear I would flay the skin from his bones had he lived."

"I am sure he would have told you about me eventually," Anne soothed.

Elizabeth tapped the table with her fingers. "You give him more credit than he deserves. Thank God, I have a better advisor now. Do you know of my good man, William Cecil? Would you like to hear what he thinks about you?"

All in the queen's kingdom knew of the man. Some loved him and said he was sent by God to aid the queen. Those outside of England had a different opinion. They claimed he was ruled by greed and wanted nothing more than to expand the kingdom's power. Whatever was true, Anne did not care to meet him.

When she didn't answer, the queen carried on. "He thinks you have made a very delicate situation worse."

"Delicate situation?"

For a moment, the queen said nothing. "Some say Robert Dudley killed his first wife with the hope that I would marry him."

The grisly sentence drained the blood from Anne's face. Could the man who had sired her be a killer as well? Roland Getting was beginning to look like the far better parent. "Did he?"

The queen shrugged. "Who knows a man's mind." She rose

and turned away from Anne. "The death of his wife may have left him free to marry, but the secrets and gossip that swirled around the death left it impossible for us to ever be together. And after being loyal for eighteen years, he snuck behind my back and married again. So I banished him from court."

"But at one time you did love him? If he had not married his first wife—"

"I am married to England." The queen spun about and pinned Anne with a ferocious stare.

A shiver ran through Anne. She clasped her hands to keep them from shaking. "Forgive me for being so bold, Your Majesty."

The fire left the queen's eyes, and her shoulders relaxed. "Do not apologize, I am pleased you have some spirit." She took her seat again and picked up a sweet, eating it gingerly.

Seizing the moment, Anne rushed on. "I would so like to meet him."

Color flooded the queen's pale cheeks, her eyes filled with water, and she began to cough and choke. Anne jumped out of her seat and began slapping the queen's back. Elizabeth's arm shot out, waving Anne away.

Queen Elizabeth's attack continued. Anne feared the queen would expire. However, after a few moments, her breathing eased, and the high color in her cheeks receded. She became pale and cool once again. "Oh my, that cake meant to kill me."

A cinnamon assassin. Anne tried to hide her smile. "Are you all right, Your Majesty?"

The royal stroked her neck. "Quite recovered." After clearing her throat countless times, she continued. "You shall never meet your father. Though he acts like a dunce, he can be shrewd. I can see his beady brain bouncing the dates in his mind. No, my dear, you shall never meet him. Unless he divorces and I marry his wicked hide." Love, betrayal, and hurt raced across the queen's countenance. She patted her own cheeks, looking around. "My, it is warm in here. Where is my blasted fan?"

It was warm, but Anne guessed the pain searing Queen Elizabeth's heart flamed like stoked coals. Anne dropped her chin to her chest. "My presence has caused some difficulties."

"That is a mild way of putting it." The queen spotted her fan next to the scrolls on the floor. She picked it up, flipped it open, and frantically waved it through the air. "Walsingham thinks I should slit your throat. Cecil thinks I should cut out your tongue and place you on an island far, far away."

Anne's throat all put closed, and her stomach rolled. Death or no tongue. Her head grew light. "Surely you would not do either."

The queen's fan stalled. "I'm not going to kill you. Nor take your tongue. Good heavens, at your birth, you ripped me wide open. Why, the midwife claimed it would be almost impossible for me to have another child. And now, well, it is quite obvious the bloom has not only withered, it is fighting the winter chill that is nipping at its stem."

"My queen, anything is possible with faith." Anne boldly reached out and grabbed Elizabeth's hand. "You are God's child. He would love to bless you."

The royal jerked, her gaze fixed on their locked hands. "It has been a long time since anyone has reached out to me with true kindness." The queen's cold hand warmed. "This is quite delightful. I wish I could have watched you grow up."

A whirl of love and sadness splintered Anne's heart. "I wish you had too."

Abruptly, the queen pulled her hand away, No doubt sniffing back the years that had been taken away. Perhaps thinking about the happy times, the sad times, the easy times, the tough times, all the times a parent and child enjoy.

Anne let her tears drip from her chin, and descend deep into her soul.

"Stop that." The queen held out a cloth. "This won't do for either of us. I am England, and you could very well be the next queen if I marry Dudley."

"But I am illegitimate," Anne stammered.

"What has that got to do with anything? I was legally born and then declared a bastard when it suited my father. Now I am quite legal, and I would remove the head of any man that would say I am not."

When Henry VIII wanted to marry his mistress, Queen Elizabeth's mother was accused of many crimes, including adultery and witchery. Elizabeth and her half-sister Mary were classified as illegitimate when their half-brother Edward was born. Their lives had been a constant reminder of the king's treachery and tyranny. Anne might have weathered a few beatings as a child, but she never thought Roland would kill her. Queen Elizabeth spent her life constantly looking over her shoulder, wondering when an assassin would strike.

"Do you want to marry?" Anne asked.

The queen's lips thinned. "I want no man to rule me."

And there was the answer. The queen may love Robert Dudley, but she was not willing to share her crown with him. Nor should she sacrifice her crown because of an act of passion that happened a long time ago. Anne had been in Scotland long enough to know many believed Mary Queen of Scots was the rightful English heir. This scandal would split old wounds wide open. The last thing Anne wanted was to start a war.

An idea sprung into her head and took hold. "Your Majesty, if I may be so bold, I might have a solution if all parties are agreeable."

The queen's brows shot up before her eyes narrowed. She leisurely sat back in her chair, assessing Anne from a distance. "Oh, but I dare say my daughter is conniving as this regal." She gave a long sigh. "Something tells me I will have to put on my finest gown today."

CHAPTER 30

Thomas had been reduced to counting his steps as he trudged back and forth across the same plot of soil. Every so often, he would raise his gaze and look to the windows of Queen Elizabeth's compartments. At least Anne hadn't come sailing through the panes. "What could they possibly be talking about for so long? A half a day has passed."

Lying in a prone position on a bench, a long, loud yawn escaped Hayes's lips. "I believe they would be catching up on years of missed history."

"Or while we lull in this garden, Anne could be in grave danger."

Hayes sat up. "You know the queen, do you truly think she would kill her own daughter?"

Nay, he did not, but Elizabeth had a fiery temper. Plus, she had been fighting for her own life from the moment she was born a female instead of a male. Would she sacrifice her own flesh and blood to save her crown? A creeping chill swept through Thomas's bones. Aye, she would.

He glared at Hayes. "I have not forgotten your deception no matter how hard I have prayed; I have no other ally. We have to save Anne. I *couldnae* bear to live if she was tormented and murdered." Thomas strode over to the heavily guarded door. "I demand to see the queen."

The guards shifted their long spears to block his entry.

Hayes shook his head. "We must be patient. There is naught we can do but wait."

"Wait! We have been in the detestable garden for hours." Thomas marched over and stationed himself under the queen's windows. "I'll not stay here while you torture Anne," he shouted.

A firm hand on his shoulder yanked him back. "Stop you threats at once. For there are more detestable places to cool your heels than this lovely garden," Hayes whispered.

A retort died in Thomas's throat when the garden door opened and a servant announced the queen was ready to see them. He followed the servant with Hayes close behind. Thomas finally pushed the servant out of the way and stormed into the queen's chambers. There he found Queen Elizabeth dressed in a fine gold and black gown with an eloquent red wig sitting on her regal head.

"Wine, Thomas?" The queen poured him a goblet of red wine, but he left it on the side table.

Thomas scanned the room. "Where is she?"

"Calm down. She will be along shortly. She's just taking a bath."

"A bath?" he croaked. *Thank you, God. She lives.* "What is she taking a bath for?"

"So she doesn't smell like a plough horse." Elizabeth placed the cup back on the table and dabbed her nose with a cloth. "Something I think you would benefit from too."

Thomas ran a hand through his rusty, matted hair. "For the love of—"

"None of your Scottish vulgarity will be tolerated here." The queen waved a finger.

A chuckle at the door drew the queen's attention to Hayes. "Ah, the elusive Master Asher Hayes. Pray tell, how is our Lady Jane?"

On quiet feet, he stepped into the room and bowed. "My queen, my wife is happy in the life she has chosen and wishes to stay in our new homeland forever."

"A lesson her husband should have learned as well. I do believe you told my sister you would never return. And yet, here you are." Queen Elizabeth eyed him like a vulture ready to savor his bones. Thomas stood stock still. He didn't want that look transferred to him. Was it a mistake to bring Hayes?

Not a line of worry creased his brow. Hayes eased forward. "I only returned to fulfill a vow to my sister, Lady Audrey of Warring Tower. I promised her I would see her again before I died," he said smoothly.

"So you keep a vow to your sister but not to mine?" The vulture circled her prey.

"Nay, Your Majesty. I kept that vow as well. I promised Queen Mary, your sister, I would not step foot in England as long as she was alive."

Queen Elizabeth stepped back and placed one arm around her bodice while the fingers of her other hand played with the pearls around her neck. "How clever you are. Why, I think you would make a better spymaster than Walsingham." She dropped her hands to her sides. "Let us make short of this. Why are you really here?"

Anger heated Thomas's back. The queen was playing her games again. "I want to see Anne," he roared.

No matter how much paint the queen put on her face, the

mask of civility slipped away. "You can either drink your wine here or you can drink it in the dungeons. Sit down and behave. I will deal with your antics after I have a nice conversation with Master Hayes."

Thomas wanted to push past her and search the private sleeping quarters, but such an action would only rile Elizabeth to fulfill her promise to throw him in the torture pit. All her finery could not mask the hurt and longing Anne's resurrection had brought. He had always taken advantage of the queen's good will. Perhaps it was time to give her the respect she deserved. He took the goblet off the table and sipped.

"There. Isn't this much better than roaring and thrashing about?" the queen asked.

Thomas nodded and took another drink, erasing quick words that he would later regret. It took all his strength to sit down and once again wait.

Elizabeth returned to her original course. "Now, Master Hayes, I have only one question. Why are you here now?"

Hayes never wavered. He met the queen's hard gaze with one of ease. "I thought I was dying. My wife being a healer could not cure my long-suffering cough. As the days rolled by, I became weaker. I knew the time to see my sister was running short."

"And you had made a promise." Elizabeth took in his measure. "There is only one problem. You look to be in the picture of health."

"He was sick," Thomas piped in, hoping to save Hayes's life just so he could pummel him later. Besides, Ma Audrey would never forgive him if something happened to her precious brother.

The queen waltzed toward Thomas and patted his shoulder. "And only words of white truth have ever left your lips."

He deserved her doubt. He placed the cup back on the table. "Anne healed him. With some herbs that only grow in Scotland."

"Indeed?" The queen looked back and forth between the men. "I will have to ask her about this miracle cure." Disbelief laced her tone. "In any case, what am I to do with you now, Master Hayes?"

Asher cupped one of his wrists with his other hand. "I have seen my sister, and she is well with her son in Scotland. With your permission, I would like to return to the Malabar Coast and my wife. Never to be seen on these shores again."

"Mmm." The queen folded her arms and pursed her lips. "Oh, if I could believe you."

Hayes boldly stepped closer. "My queen, my word is my bond. I stand on English soil because of Mistress Anne. Whatever you decide to do with me, the girl deserves your protection."

"How honorable your words. Yet you used Thomas and Anne to get to meet your sister," the queen retorted.

"True. Once I saw the mark on her arm, I always knew either Thomas or myself would have to bring Anne here. A life should never be lost out of convenience."

Thomas scrambled to his feet. He'd do anything that would save Anne from the queen's wrath. "Listen to him. Please. A life should never be lost. Either reclaim Anne or set her free to live as she chooses."

"Set her free?" The queen stepped back and placed a hand over her heart. She looked as if she had swallowed her pearl necklace. "I can't have her prancing around England as if she were some commoner. Think what my enemies would do with such knowledge. With her!"

Was all lost? Elizabeth had spent years trying to preserve her life as well as run a country. Her will would be followed over anyone else's. Thomas's chest deflated. He had always been a pet to her. A plaything. Someone who made the gossiping tongues wag but never taken seriously. Would the fire he played with claim Anne's life?

He placed the wine on the table and dropped to one knee in front of his queen. "I know you *dinnae* take me seriously, and I have given you good cause not to, but believe me now. Anne is a marvel and can do many things. Even though she has had a rough life, she never bid anyone ill. She is smart and witty. She never tells a lie unless forced by others to do so. She prayed until my faith was restored. She would be loyal to you. Her loyalty knows no bounds. You *dinnae* know what a gem you have in your hand."

"I do not?" the queen asked coolly.

"Nay. Please take care of her and love her as I . . ."

"As what, boy?"

Gazing up into Queen Elizabeth's eyes, the slippery words that he had always used to get around her disappeared. Anne had taught him to be honest. "As I love her." The simple phrase freed his heart. "I want to marry her. To be her husband. And I want your blessing."

The queen laughed until she almost cried. She bent down until they were at eye level. "Do you speak these words knowing she is my daughter or is your heart truly committed to her?"

"You know me. Examine my face, my voice, my words." He laid his heart and gaze open to her. She bore into him searching, weighing, deciding. He only hoped that God would let her see the truth.

Abruptly, she stood. "Get up, Thomas."

The harsh tone of her voice spoke of rejection. He stood. Hayes stepped close and opened his mouth to give a defense. A quick raise of a royal hand stopped his speech before it had begun.

"What of your adventure to meet the woman who lives while your mother died? The revenge that ruled your heart for so long?" She pointed at Hayes. "This man can take you to her. Is that not what you always wanted?"

Since he had seen eighteen summers, that had been his goal to find the connection to his true family and then destroy the woman who had taken it away from him. But now he did not care. Slowly, he shook his head. "All I want is Anne. Even if you *dinnae* allow the marriage, let me stay by her side and protect her."

"Oh my. Do you really think I am that dim-witted to lay the wolf at the dove's door? Ye gads, that would be the worst solution." Another hoot escaped her lips.

Trembling—all was lost. Anne would be taken from him. "My queen, please then, hide her away. Spare her life."

"Spare her? Over me?"

And there lay the choice. The queen and her power over Anne's existence. Why? Why couldn't both be saved? "My queen, hear me out. Take my life instead of Anne's. Send her to the Malabar Coast with Hayes. My death will send the tongues wagging in a different direction while Anne slips away to a new life." Boldly, he reached out and placed his hands on the queen's elbows. "This way you still have your daughter, and you have removed a rogue from your life."

The queen stepped back. "Take your hands off of me. Your charms no longer hold my fancy. However, someone else has put forth a similar plan." She looked over her shoulder. "Come in, dear."

Behind the queen, a door opened and in walked a woman dressed in a blue silk gown trimmed with a fine lace collar. A pile of mahogany curls graced her head. Anne's alabaster skin glowed. His heart flayed in his chest. She had never looked more beautiful.

She bowed and gracefully walked to the queen's side.

Thomas leapt forward, but the queen blocked his progress. "Hold your place. My daughter has no desire to be mauled by you."

A blow from a sword could not have cut him quicker. The truth lay before him. He desired Anne, but she did not desire him. And if the queen acknowledged Anne as her daughter, the suitors would be crawling out of the Thames. He stepped back and lowered his gaze. "I am sorry, my queen."

Ignoring him, Elizabeth swept past and stood in front of Hayes. "As I said, a similar plan has been mentioned, to send Anne to the Malabar Coast with you." Her gaze swept over Hayes. "However, you are quite handsome and of the same age as me. I have a mind to keep you here."

"My wife would not like that," Hayes answered smoothly.

"What care I about your wife? It was because of Lady Jane's father and Wyatt's Rebellion that turned my sister's suspicious nature on me. Because of them, I was a prisoner in the Tower, expecting to die at any moment." She waved toward Anne. "'Twas where my daughter was conceived." The queen paced back to Anne's side. "Lady Jane's family cost me much. And now all of you want me to give the very woman I have come to despise my most precious possession."

The room grew quiet and cold. Looking at mother and

daughter standing next to each other, the resemblance was remarkable. How could he never have noticed. The same nose, mouth, and chin. It wouldn't take long for the court to come to the same conclusion.

"If she stays," Thomas said softly, "you both could be in danger. Once the truth is out, there will be loud cries to remove you from the throne."

"Do not you think I know that?" Elizabeth snapped. Her features softened as she looked into Anne's face. "That is why I will let Master Hayes take my beautiful daughter to where that vile woman lives."

"Jane is not vile," Hayes defended.

"Do not question my words or I will have your head and hers." A cloak of sadness descended on the queen as she smoothed a palm over Anne's cheek. "I have just met you, and now I must give you up again."

Thomas's own sorrow mixed with theirs. So much happiness had been sacrificed to save a crown.

Eyes moist, the queen's gaze remained fixed on Anne. "I wish to keep you with me longer, but Walsingham stresses the need to be swift. The longer you stay here, the more danger for all of us." She closed her eyes, and when she opened them again, they were steeled. "You best take care of her, Hayes. Or I shall strip your bones clean."

The former spy placed a hand on his heart. "I shall. I promise."

With a swift nod, Elizabeth turned back to look at Thomas. "Now what shall we do with you?"

Thomas gulped. Someone would have to pay for the queen's misery.

Her stern look softened slightly. "Under different

circumstances, you would not be my first choice, nor the last choice. You would be no choice. However, without your ridiculous antics, I would have never found Anne. She has some fondness for you. Therefore, I have no choice but to sanction a marriage between you both."

A shout shot from his heart and filled the room. "Anne is to be my wife?"

The queen lifted a brow. "Please tell me you are not that thick. What did I just say?"

"Anne is to be my wife!" He pushed past the queen and lifted Anne into the air and twirled her around. "We are to marry."

"Aye. We will not have to traipse this earth alone." Anne laughed as lovely as a song bird. Thomas's broken heart fused together at the sound.

The queen picked up her fan and whacked him on the arm. "Stop that. Put her down. There will be no dancing and wandering fingers until after the wedding."

Thomas immediately complied but did not take his arm away from Anne's waist. "Elizabeth, I mean, my queen, you have made me a happy man."

"Have I? Do not thank me, it wasn't originally my plan. I shall not only have to bear losing her, but the gossips will think I have sent my son away because he married some common woman I do not approve of." A wide grin rose on her lips. "The jest shall be on them. How fun."

Thomas cringed at how many times he had created the illusion of being the queen's illegitimate son to gain coin or credit from others. Another thought plagued him. "I have many debts—"

"And many who want your hide," the queen finished. "When I thought you had died, I paid all your debts. I was so distressed, but I got over it quickly enough."

It was nice to know the queen had held some affection for him, even if she did not fully favor him now.

She touched a gentle finger to Anne's chin but addressed Hayes. "Come along, Master Hayes. You and I will take a turn in my garden while these two make a few plans." Her gaze then snapped to Thomas. "You will be honorable?"

"I promise." Thomas thumped a fist to his chest.

Her gaze narrowed. "Why do I not trust those words?"

Thomas let go of Anne's waist and grabbed the queen's. "I promise. I will give my life to keep her safe." Elizabeth's eyes moistened, and a small quiver crossed her lips. She pulled away with a nod and turned to Hayes, who ushered her toward the door. "You will meet us by the rose garden. Do not tarry. Have I made myself clear?" the queen called over her shoulder.

"Aye, very," Thomas answered before taking Anne's fingers in his and kissing them.

When alone, Thomas grew quiet. He loved Anne, and he knew she was fond of him, but she had never professed a measure of love for him. His heart squeezed. Was he trapping her into another loveless marriage? His palms began to sweat, but he did not release her hands. "When I met you, you were running away from the prospects of a terrible marriage only to be thrown into another unwanted union. I am heartily sorry for that, but I promise—"

Anne pulled her hand free and placed a finger to his lips. She had heard enough of his pleas. "What makes you think I do not want this?"

"I know I have stolen a few kisses from you, but I never, ever wished to force you into any marital situation."

How true. At Warring Tower, was she not the one who

wanted the kisses, the love? He was the one who had always pulled away. "Did you not hear the queen's words? The plan you came up with was an echo of hers. Where do you think the idea came from?"

"Walsingham, who else?"

Anne stepped back and turned to the window, watching the queen strolling arm in arm with Hayes through the rose garden. How he would love to take such a leisurely stroll with her every day. Perhaps on a faraway beach or down a wooded path.

"The queen is right. You are indeed thick at times." She faced him. "The plan was mine, and she was not so convinced until she heard your words of affection for me."

His shoulders slumped. Defeat slacked his jaw as his gaze dropped to the floor. He had been a fool. She held no favor for him. "So once again, you sacrifice yourself for another."

. "I sacrifice nothing." She stamped her foot. "Look at me, Thomas. Are the words you spoke to the queen true? Do you truly love me?"

His chin snapped up, and he stepped forward.

She held out at hand. "Answer me. I need to know."

He took one step closer. "Aye, I do. I *didnae* know I could love someone so much. When I met you, I aimed to use you to get what I wanted. But somewhere along the way your safety mattered more than my life. I was lost, but you led me back to God, and you won my heart. In truth, I believe my love started with that cold swim from *The Prince's Prize* to the Portishead coast." He opened his palms, his face, and his heart to her. "However, I have no intentions of forcing myself upon you. Even if we marry, once we arrive at the Malabar Coast, I will not force you to be my wife. I will freely let you go if that is what you want."

A bright joyful smile graced her beautiful lips. An ember of fire sparked in his belly. He would protect her forever if she would have him.

Boldly he took a step forward and took her into his arms, kissing her forehead. "I am sorry. I am sorry I have caused you such distress. I should have left you in that cave."

She shook her head. "Nay. Had you done so, I would never have known what love is." She wiped her eyes. "Thomas, I wished to open my feelings to you long ago. I am certain my opinion of you began to change while we traveled to Scotland." She placed her hands on his shoulders. "Somehow I fell in love with a scoundrel, a rogue, a liar, a cheat, and a thief." She sealed her scandalous list with a long and ardent kiss. Her hands patted his chest, but she felt no chain or jewelry. "Where is the cross?"

He took her hands in his and held them tight to his chest. "The former scoundrel, rogue, liar, cheat, and thief gave the relic to the first church he saw after entering the city. So, my lady, you will be married to a worthless man once again."

"Nay, not worthless. My life will be filled with a glorious love, and that is something I have wanted since the day I was born."

They then bonded their love with another passionate kiss. No matter where they ended up, in a cave, a keep, or a castle, he 'd make sure their family would have a bounty of love that would last from generation to generation.

EPILOGUE

L ady Jane Grey shielded her eyes from the noonday sun as she looked out over the horizon, searching for a man who might not ever return. Day after day, she stood on the docks and remembered the wonderful life she had with Asher. He gave her a second chance at a new life. She had become a healer, a scholar, and a mother to a beautiful son. Her blessings were abundant. Her life had been perfect until Asher became ill.

But God did not promise an easy life, just freedom in the Spirit through the death and resurrection of Jesus Christ.

"Mother, I think that ship is one of ours." Her tall, handsome son, Nathan, quickened his steps to the docks. Asher had groomed him well. He had taken over the pepper business with few trials.

Their ships would sail to Portugal and back carrying valuable spices. The only ship that would never return was the one that carried her husband away months ago. Yet slowing into the bay came that very ship.

Hope rose in Jane's chest causing her heart to awaken, but the beat quickly slowed. There was no way Asher could have survived the return voyage. She raced forward. Could he be alive? When the ship docked, Nathan shouted out a greeting to the captain. Jane's breath grew short, and her heart flipped. The captain removed his hat to show a head of black hair sprinkled with grey.

"Asher." The name came out in a gentle whisper as her feet rushed to the edge of the dock.

He scanned the dock. Their eyes met. She clutched her chest. *Thank you, Lord for bringing him home.*

Once the gangway was in place, her bright smiling husband made his way into her arms. "I'm home, my dearest Jane." His arms enveloped her, their lips meeting and reveling in the sweetest of reunions. Asher slipped out of her embrace to hug his son.

"Father. 'Tis a miracle," Nathan said.

"My prayers have been answered." Jane examined him from head to toe. His broad form and sun kissed face surprised her. "But how? How are you here with us?"

"I am healthy. Though you are the wisest healer I know, there is a herb, a carline thistle, found in Scotland that has set me to rights."

She could not deny his words for her strong, virile husband stood before her. He called to a couple who stood near the gangplank.

The young woman was quite pretty and had a familiar look, but it was the man who held her attention. His russet hair and copper eyes reminded her of . . . herself or the woman who took her place in the block so long ago. Could it be? Even though they had never met, she knew him.

"My dear," Asher said, "this is Master Thomas Armstrong and his lovely bride, Anne. They have come to live in this beautiful country."

"I am so pleased to meet you." Her greeting went to both,

but her gaze never wavered from Thomas. "Your mother must be very sad that you have left your home."

"My mother died when I was a babe," the young man answered, taking her hand in his.

Jane's breath caught in her throat. Then it was true. This was the son of the woman who sacrificed her life all those years ago so that she might have a new life. "Please tell me your mother did not die in vain. Did her son thrive and live well?"

"Aye, Mistress. He was well loved and still is to this day."

Tears of joy, not dampened with regret, sprung from her soul and wet her cheeks. "I am so sorry for the pain I caused you. The death of your mother . . ."

Thomas pulled a cloth from his doublet and handed it to her. "My lady, your tears are unnecessary. I would not trade a moment of my life. Its path has given me Anne and restored my faith. If anything, I should be thanking you for taking a stand for your beliefs when you were so young."

Jane released his hands as her heart wrenched. "Daily, I prayed for you. I have tried to live a good life so that I would not dishonor the sacrifice your mother made for you and me." Sniffing back her tears, Jane placed an arm around Thomas's back, ushering him along the walk. "Welcome to our home. I hope you and Anne will find as much joy and love here as I have."

Anne took Thomas's other side, looping her arm through his. "Something tells me this is the home we have been searching for all along. Isn't it, my dear husband."

"I believe it is." Thomas bestowed a firm kiss on Anne's cheek.

A passage of scripture entered Jane's mind and took hold as they strolled from the docks. No matter what the future would bring, God's truth would always be her anchor.

But the fruits of the Spirit is love, joy, peace, patience, kindness, goodness, faithfulness, gentleness, self-control; against such things there is no law. Galatians 5:22&23.

Dear Reader,

Thank you for reading *A Life Reclaimed*. It's always hard to write the last book in any series, but this one was especially difficult as I truly feel I've left a part of myself with these characters. I'm looking forward to expanding my horizons by writing a sequel to my inspirational contemporary book, *Joshua's Prayer*. I hope you'll join me on this new endeavor.

Do you want more historical fiction? Try reading the award-winning, **Sword and the Cross Chronicles**. All six books are rich in history and flavored with a hint of humor. Each story is a clean read, carrying a Christian message.

Finally, as always, I make a humble plea: if you enjoyed this book, please leave a review wherever you purchased it. Authors work long and hard on their stories and a little positive encouragement goes a long way.

May the love of God encourage you in all that you do.
Until next time . . .

Abundant blessings,
Olivia

Excerpt from

Joshua's Prayer

GOLDEN RIDGE SERIES

OLIVIA RAE

One

Sam Morgan stared at the shabby sign outside the old dilapidated Victorian. In peeling paint it read:

GRACE HOUSE WOMEN'S CENTER
Giving women a fresh start during troublesome times.

A fresh start. That's what he wanted for himself and his son, Joshua. But he worried he'd had more than his fair share of fresh starts . . . How many fresh starts could a person, a family be allowed to have? One? Two? An unlimited number?

Apart from college, Sam had lived in Golden Ridge, Missouri, all his life. He'd met his wife, Vicky, there and they had their son in Golden Ridge. He thought he'd die here in this small town nestled close to Big Golden Ridge Lake. Years ago any person who spent a pleasant sunny afternoon in Golden Ridge would have thought, what a wonderful carefree place. The people are so friendly with their easy talk and warm smiles. And the homes in this town are so well-kept. What a delightful place to live in and raise a family.

Those used to be his thoughts and dreams. To live a perfect life in this perfect town. But he'd been wrong. Now this place brought him nothing but sorrow. This town reminded him of failed promises and death: the death of his parents, death of his wife, and the death of his dreams.

His spirit was as worn out as the broken-down house and neighborhood before him. It was time to collect his son and try to piece together their lives elsewhere. Away from the painful memories Golden Ridge held around every corner.

A gentle clinking sound drew his gaze to a small wooden sign swinging on metal chains below the larger one. In bold black letters the words leapt off the stark white sign:

Now Open
GRACE HOUSE PRESCHOOL
Serving the Community of Golden Ridge
All Children Welcome

Sam looked at his watch. Five o'clock. School should be out and hopefully most of the kids had gone home. Well, at least those who didn't live there with their mothers. Sam walked up the path to the house. He paused at the steps and clutched the railing. The time had come for him and Joshua to start anew.

"No, I won't go!"

Sam's gut wrenched at his son's panic-filled cry. He'd known this wouldn't be easy for Joshua, but he didn't think getting his son to leave Grace House would be this hard. Like a recurring nightmare, he was disappointing Joshua again. Huge tears spilled from his son's eyes as he clung to the hem of his caregiver's skirt. Sam had tried to cajole Joshua out of Grace

House and into the car. They'd gotten as far as the foyer when everything stalled.

A more direct approach was needed. He took a deep breath and took hold of his son's arm. "Joshua, I'm sorry. You can't stay here. Mommy doesn't live here anymore. It's just you and me, buddy. We're going to be okay. I promise." He buffered his gruff actions with a smile. Unfortunately, Joshua wasn't buying any of it.

"No. No. No. I want to stay with Miss 'Cole." Joshua turned his tear-streaked face up to Nicole James. "Tell him. Mommy wanted me to stay with you while she's in heaven."

Sam's heart constricted. No child should ever have to lose their mother. And no child should have to carry the weight of such a loss alone. Especially not alone. Sam had known that and thought of his son while he worked overseas, but at the same time he'd grasped at reasons not to return and face the reality of his wife's passing.

Some father you are.

Miss James rubbed a gentle hand over the boy's curly, dark honey-colored hair. "Joshua, your daddy wants to take you home, but I'm sure he'll bring you back for preschool tomorrow."

Her green-flecked eyes narrowed as she lifted her chin and glared at Sam, challenging him to defy her words. "Won't you?"

She had to be kidding. He had no intention of bringing his five-year-old son back there tomorrow or any other day. He had a realtor to contact and movers to talk to. Regardless of whether or not their house sold right away, he planned to roll out of Golden Ridge, Missouri as soon as possible. He postponed several surgeries in Guatemala after he'd learned of Vicky's death. People were counting on him to return, ASAP.

With Vicky gone there was nothing left for them in Missouri. He had responsibilities and Joshua—even with his disability—would adjust in time. His son would be fine once they got away from all the misery and sad reminders Golden Ridge had to offer . . . and the iron-spined redhead standing in front of them.

Though he didn't know her well, Sam had exchanged a few pleasantries with Miss James at church. He knew the attractive twenty-something-year-old was co-owner of Grace House, which apparently just opened a preschool. But beyond that he knew little else. In letters she wrote and during phone calls, his wife had raved about the support she and Joshua received there when they returned from Guatemala. He didn't care if Miss James was the best preschool teacher in all of Missouri. Right now she was the roadblock that stood between him and his son. Sam gritted his teeth. "Come on, Joshua. Daddy is going to take you back to Guatemala. You remember. You and Mommy were there for a month. Remember Jario? The man who made the wooden flutes? You liked the songs he played."

Joshua yanked his arm from Sam's grip and seized Miss James' legs like she was a buoy keeping him afloat during a dangerous ocean storm. "No. I don't 'member. I don't. I don't. I don't." There was no negotiating with him now. Once his son hit the "fit" stage, Sam knew it was all over.

"Dr. Morgan, please," the teacher said. "Joshua is having a hard time dealing with change. Most young children with his condition do. And because of his short-term memory problems, and his mother's accident and death, he's even having problems remembering you."

My God. they hadn't been apart that long, had they? Sam's mind ticked away the months. Could five months erase a child's memory of their father? Not normally, but a child with severe

Fetal Alcohol Syndrome might forget. Guilt tightened its band across his chest.

Sam rubbed his aching forehead. "Look, Miss James, I appreciate all you've done for my son, but now it's time for Joshua and me to make a new life." *Away from Golden Ridge.* "There are only bad memories for us here."

She squeezed Joshua closer. "I mean no disrespect, but I was working with Joshua and his mother while you were gone. Joshua has made excellent progress at Grace House's Preschool and since your wife moved here she . . . was working very hard too."

The pause in Miss James sentence was worth a thousand words. Though this young teacher didn't want to admit it, in the end, Vicky had fallen off the wagon again. All the years of therapy hadn't changed the outcome. Vicky's alcoholism had finally killed her, albeit with a car and a tree. Had she stayed sober, she wouldn't have hit that maple tree and Joshua would still have a mother.

Miss James lifted her pretty chin another notch. "I think you should consider enrolling him in the kindergarten program we're starting this fall. The more things stay the same, the better off Joshua will be. Trust me."

I love my son and am not doing anything wrong. Why should I trust a stranger with his welfare?

No way. He was done with those words. He'd trusted his wife would remain sober. He'd trusted God would help her stay that way too. His gut tightened. He'd trusted everyone else— his whole life. And look where that had gotten him and Joshua.

"I don't think that's going to happen." He clenched his teeth.

Why had Vicky started drinking again? Going to Guatemala had originally been her idea.

She'd been so enthusiastic when they thought about giving a year of service to the International Surgical Christian Outreach Program. She'd said it was God's will, His plan for their family. She'd thought a year in Guatemala would do their marriage a world of good too. Sam had hoped she was right, for their marriage could use all the help it could get after years of lies and deceit.

He'd wanted a new start just as much as she had. He wanted the fun-loving, caring wife he married years ago and he was willing to do almost anything to have her healed of her addiction. Even if it meant spending a year away from his home. But a month after arriving in Guatemala, Vicky had packed up and left with Joshua, blaming his son's FAS for why they couldn't stay. However, Sam had signed a year's contract with ISCOP. They desperately needed his services and before she left, Vicky made it pretty clear she didn't want him back home right away either.

The move hadn't changed a thing. She was still unhappy and he hadn't a clue about how to change her attitude. So he honored the terms of his contract and made a decision he'd regretted every day since Vicky's death.

The air seeped out of Sam's lungs as he eyed the young woman pensively. "Come on, Joshua."

Miss James' hand covered his. "Please, Doctor Morgan."

At one time, he'd believed this woman could keep Vicky sober in his absence and change her back into the woman he'd married long ago. He'd believed Grace House offered the answer to his prayers.

Some answer. He hadn't even been gone four months when Vicky served him divorce papers. To top it off, she had moved into Grace House with Joshua. Her letter had been pretty clear:

"I hate everything about you. Even your house." He couldn't get rid of the niggling feeling that Miss James had something to do with that. Sam knew he should have come home as soon as he was served the divorce papers, but he thought helping a kid who had been waiting for eighteen months for a new jaw was more important. Besides, deep down, Sam knew his marriage was finished. Returning to Cedar Ridge wasn't going to change the outcome for any of them.

Clearly his decision to stay overseas had been wrong and Joshua was suffering as a consequence. Sam pried Joshua away from the not-so-tender grip of the delicately built Miss James. "Sorry, we have to go."

His son kicked and shrieked, his wide-open mouth displaying his crooked baby teeth; that too was caused by FAS. Well, at least that was fixable—if Joshua would sit in a dental chair. At the moment, his son twisted and turned, flailing his limbs. Sam mentally sighed. He could straighten teeth, but he'd never be able to fix Joshua's mind or change the past for either of them.

A second later that set of tiny teeth latched onto his hand. In surprise and pain, his grip loosened and Joshua made a beeline for the stairs and his bedroom. His son was out of sight in less time than it took a hummingbird to blink.

Beads of blood left an imprint of uneven teeth on the side of Sam's hand. The wound stung, but not as much as the pain in his heart. He'd known things would be tough when he returned home, but he hadn't expected his son to freak out at the sight of him.

Miss James took his hand in hers, examining the slight injury. "You're hurt."

Her hands were warm and soft as she gently touched the side of his hand, running her fingertip over the wound. She had all the earmarks of being a caring, loving person, but he knew better than to believe that. If it wasn't for Nicole James, he'd probably still have a wife waiting for him at home. Not to mention a son who didn't screech at the sight of him.

He pulled his hand away. "It's nothing major."

Her brow wrinkled. "I don't know. Bite wounds can cause serious infections. You really should—"

"I'm an oral surgeon—I got it."

The metal rod returned to her spine. "Of course, you know best."

Now she got it. He did know best. This town was bad news with its reminders of his parents wasted lives and his dead wife. If he had gotten his family away from this town years ago maybe things would be different now. He should have insisted that Vicky and Joshua stay with him in Guatemala. But he had trusted Vicky's judgment. He had trusted God. He had trusted the good people of Golden Ridge. Trusted all of them to watch over Joshua. But no more blind trust. No more bad decisions. He couldn't handle making even one more mistake.

Looking up to where his son had retreated, Sam took a deep breath and made for the stairs, but Miss James stepped in front of him.

"I think you should leave Joshua here for the night. This has been his home since before his mother's death. Don't you agree we should try to keep things as normal as possible for him?"

Of course he didn't agree. He'd managed to make it back for the funeral, but obviously not fast enough. Pastor Martin said Joshua was in excellent hands. At the moment Sam felt that statement was up for debate. "I know this is hard for Joshua," Sam inched toward the stairs, "but staying here longer than necessary will only make things worse. You've known him for five months. I'm his father. I've known him his whole life."

Miss James didn't back down. Instead she rose up on the bottom step and looked him in the eye. "He's still very shaken up from losing his mother. Uprooting him before he can come to terms with her death could mentally scar him for life. I am sure all he needs is a few more months of stability—in Golden Ridge."

Heat rushed over Sam's body and he broke out into a sweat. "I disagree. The sooner Joshua forgets this place, the better." Sam winced at the forcefulness of his voice. *Was he mad at her or at himself?* He should have been here for Joshua when Vicky died rather than leaving his son with a stranger. Things seemed clearer on this side of the equator, away from so much need.

"I'm sorry, Dr. Morgan, w-we all think it is important for Joshua to stay awhile longer," she stammered.

"We? Who's we?" He clenched his hands at his sides, controlling the urge to push her out of the way and make his way up the stairs to his son.

She shot a glance at his fists and then put a hand to her throat. "Why Pastor Martin and me—"

"I'm Joshua's father. I know what he needs. You and the good pastor think you know what is best for my son? What credential gives you that right? Well I disagree. Now if you'll excuse me." Sam made another attempt to step around Miss James, but she quickly blocked his way again.

She held out her dainty, though shaking, white palm. Bold as the angel guarding the entrance into Eden, she raised her chin. "Please, Dr. Morgan, you and Joshua are very upset. I'm sure you want to do what is best for your son. What's one more day after all? He *did* just lose his mother."

Sam should have pushed her aside and headed up the stairs, but her words took the fight out of him . . . and he sensed Miss James wouldn't back down. For a little thing, she sure was filled with grit. Sam pulled his hand across the back of his neck. What difference would one more day make? After all, Joshua had become used to not having his father around for long periods of time.

"All right, Miss James. Joshua can stay the night, but . . . " Sam gave her a pointed look to make sure she knew he meant business. "I'll be back tomorrow afternoon. Please make sure Joshua is ready to leave by then."

Without another word, Sam stalked across the foyer but closed the door quietly behind him. Tomorrow he'd collect his son and then return with him to the surgical mission clinic in Guatemala. Obligations had to be met there before Joshua and he could move on to their new life. At least at the mission clinic, Sam knew he was doing something good. But here . . . in this town . . . his failures as a husband and father seemed to taunt him from every place Vicky and he used to walk.

What did he always pray in the Lord's Prayer? *Thy will be done.*

Cynical laughter stuck in Sam's throat. *This was God's will?* What kind of God would leave a disabled boy motherless?

He'd go back to the Guatemalan mission and do the surgical dentistry, but nothing more. He'd leave the preaching and teaching of God's word to the ministers, because deep down he finally knew the truth—God really didn't exist for him.

ABOUT THE AUTHOR

Olivia Rae is an award-winning author of historical and contemporary inspirational romance. She spent her school days dreaming of knights, princesses and far away kingdoms; it made those long, boring days in the classroom go by much faster. Nobody was more shocked than her when she decided to become a teacher. Besides getting her Master's degree, marrying her own prince, and raising a couple of kids, Olivia decided to breathe a little more life into her childhood stories by adding in what she's learned as an adult living in a small town on the edge of a big city. When not writing, she loves to travel, dragging her family to old castles and forts all across the world.

Olivia is the winner of the Angel Award, Book Buyers Best Award, Golden Quill Award, New England Readers' Choice Award, Southern Magic Contest, and the American Fiction Award. She is an Illumination Award Gold and Bronze medalist. She has also been a finalist in many other contests such as the National Readers' Choice Awards, and the National Romance Fiction Awards. She is currently hard at work on her next novel.

Contact Olivia at Oliviarae.books@gmail.com

For news and sneak peeks of upcoming novels visit:
www.oliviaraebooks.com